AF194410

# Business Organisation And Management

## (As per NEP Structure, Indian Universities)

*by*

Rahul Kumar Das
(Guest Faculty of Commerce, DODL
Dibrugarh University)
(Former Guest Faculty of Commerce,
Dibru College, Dibrugarh, Assam)

# Business Organisation And Management

**(As per NEP Structure, Indian Universities)**
**by Rahul Kumar Das**

ISBN: 978-93-64288-99-6

**Published by**

# DOUBLE 9 BOOKS

2/13-B, Ansari Road
Daryaganj, New Delhi – 110002
info@double9books.com
www.double9books.com
Tel. 011-40042856

# ABOUT THE AUTHOR

Rahul Kumar Das, born on 4th May 1992 in Tinsukia, Assam, is a distinguished scholar and author with a robust academic and professional background. He completed his schooling at Ganpat Rai Rasiwasia High School in Tinsukia, Assam, and went on to earn his Higher Secondary and Bachelor's degree in Commerce from Tinsukia College in 2013. Subsequently, Rahul pursued his Master's degree in Commerce (Accounting & Finance) from Dibrugarh University in 2015, followed by an M.Phil. in 2017. Currently, he is pursuing his PhD at Dibrugarh University. Rahul Kumar Das has authored several acclaimed books including 'Business Law', 'Business Organisation and Management (CBCS)', 'Corporate Accounting', 'Business Statistics (As Per CBCS)', 'Management Principles and Applications', 'Cost Accounting', 'Business Mathematics and Statistics', 'Multidisciplinary Course: Security Analysis and Portfolio Management', and 'Skill Enhancement Course'. Apart from this he has also written fiction book named "Mann Ki Gahraai". He has collaborated with esteemed publishers such as Kalyani Publisher, Banalata Publisher, Mahaveer Publisher, Notion Press, and Bluerose Publisher. With over 8 years of teaching experience, Rahul Kumar Das has demonstrated a commitment to education and academic excellence, making significant contributions to the field of commerce and management studies.

# CONTENTS

# PREFACE

It is a matter of great pleasure to release the **1st** edition of **BUSINESS ORGANISATION MANAGEMENT** for the students of B.Com 1st Semester of the New Education Policy (NEP) System under Dibrugarh University and other Indian Universities following the said pattern of examination. The present edition contains 5 chapters. All the chapters have been carefully presented to meet the requirements of the latest NEP syllabus of Human Resource Management.

## The present edition is characterised by the following features

- Adequate emphasis has been laid on conceptual clarity, working of human resource processes and application of basic concepts to satisfy the three learning.i.e. Knowledge, Understanding and Application.

- Diagrams, tables and boxes have been extensively used to make various topics self-explanatory

- Summary has been given at the end of each chapter for easy and quick recapitulation of the topics covered.

- To facilitate self-examination by the students, Short answer, Long answer type questions and Short Notes have been given in a logical sequence at the end of each chapter.

I am sure that the students, researchers and professors will find the book to their entire satisfaction. However it will be my pleasure to receive criticism and suggestions from all concerned.

I also like to thank to the publisher, " Double9 books " for bringing out this book in such a nice get up and also within a very short span. We express our hearty thanks to them.

*Author*
*Rahul Kumar Das*

# DIBRUGARH UNIVERSITY

**(Also suitable for all Indian Universities following NEP- 2020 Pattern of Syllabus)**

Course Title: **BUSINESS ORGANISATION AND MANAGEMENT**

Course Code: C-1

Nature of the Course: CORE

Course Credit: 04 Credits

Distribution of Marks: 80 (End Sem) + 20 (In-Sem)

**Course Objective:**

- To gain a basic understanding of the structure and forms of business organisations and the primary functions of management that are vital for the smooth operation of business organisations.

| UNIT | Contents | L | T | P |
|------|----------|---|---|---|
| I | Forms of Business Organisation – Sole Proprietorship; Joint Hindu Family Firm; Partnership Firm; Joint Stock Company; Cooperative Society; Limited Liability Partnership | 05 | — | — |
| | Forms of Public Enterprises; International Business – Types | 05 | 02 | — |
| II | Planning, Organising and Decision Making; Policy and Strategy Formulation | 06 | — | — |
| | Departmentation – Functional, Project, Matrix and Network | 04 | | |

| UNIT | Contents | L | T | P |
|---|---|---|---|---|
| III | Authority Relationships – Line and Staff; Delegation of Authority; Decentralisation; Groups and Teams; Reporting and Accountability | 06 | 02 | — |
| | Leadership – Nature, Types, Leadership Theories | 04 | — | — |
| IV | Motivation – Theories and Practices: Herzberg's Theory, Vroom's Expectancy Theory, Z-theory, Control – Concept and Process | 06 | — | — |
| | Communication and Coordination – Process of Communication; Formal and Informal Channels of Communication; Leakages in Organisational Communication; Interpersonal Communication. | 05 | 02 | — |
| V | Indian Ethos for Management: Value-Oriented Holistic Management; Business Process Reengineering (BPR), Learning Organisation, Outsourcing | 05 | — | — |
| | Subaltern Management Ideas from India; Diversity & inclusion; Work-life Balance; Freelancing; Flexitime and work from home; Co-sharing/co-working | 06 | 02 | — |

**Course Outcome**: The students should be able to understand the distinctive significance of each functional sphere of management and take meaningful decisions regarding the same for effective their application in different types of organisations.

# UNIT 1A
# FORMS OF BUSINESS ORGANISATION

**Chapter Outline**

Forms of Business Organisation

Sole Proprietorship

Joint Hindu Family Firm

Partnership Firm

Joint Stock Company

Cooperative Society

Limited Liability Partnership

Choice of Form of Organisation

## CONTENTS

1. Concept Of Business Organisation
2. Sole Proprietorship
   2.1 Concept of Sole Proprietorship
   2.2 Definitions of Sole Proprietorship
   2.3 Features/Characteristics of Sole Proprietorship
   2.4 Advantages/Merits of Sole Proprietorship
   2.5 Disadvantages/Demerits of Sole Proprietorship
   2.6 Formation of Sole Proprietorship form of Business Organisation
3. Joint Hindu Family Business
   3.1 Concept of Joint Hindu Family Business
   3.2 Characteristics of Joint Hindu Family Form of Business Organisation
   3.3 Advantages/ Merits of JHF Form of Business Organisation

# 1. CONCEPT OF BUSINESS ORGANISATION

Business organization encompasses all the essential arrangements necessary for operating a business. It involves the steps required to establish effective relationships among people, materials, and machinery to efficiently conduct business and generate profits. This is known as the process of organizing. The structure that results from this organizing process is referred to as a business undertaking or organization. Choosing the appropriate form of organization is crucial when starting a business because it influences the business's operations, control, capital acquisition, risk distribution, profit allocation, and legal requirements. The main types of business organization are as follows:

- Sole Proprietorship
- Joint Hindu Family Firm
- Partnership firm
- Joint Stock Company
- Cooperative society
- Limited Liability Partnership

Let us discuss these forms of business organisation in details.

# 2. SOLE PROPRIETORSHIP

## 2.1 Concept of Sole Proprietorship

A sole proprietorship is a type of private sector enterprise owned, managed, and controlled by a single individual. It is the most common and simplest form of business entity. A sole proprietorship is not a separate legal entity; rather, it designates a person who is solely responsible for providing the capital, bearing the risks, and managing the business. This type of business can operate under the owner's name or a trade name, which does not create a separate legal entity from the owner. Sole proprietorships are ideal for individuals who wish to run a business independently with minimal investment.

## 2.2 Definitions of Sole Proprietorship

*"A sole proprietor is a person who carries on business exclusively by and for himself. He is not only the owner of the capital of the undertaking, but is usually the organizer and manager and takes all the profits or responsibility for losses"*

**James Stephenson**

*"The sole proprietorship is the form of business organization at the head of which stands an individual as one who is responsible, who directs its operations and who alone runs the risk of failure"*

**L.H. Haney**

*"A sole proprietor is a person who carries on business exclusively by and for himself. He is not only the owner of the capital of the undertaking, but is usually the organizer and manager and takes all the profits or responsibility for losses"*

**James Stephenson**

*"The sole proprietorship is the form of business organization at the head of which stands an individual as one who is responsible, who directs its operations and who alone runs the risk of failure"*

**L.H. Haney**

*"Sole trader business is a type of business unit where one person is solely responsible for providing the capital, for bearing the risk of the enterprise and for the management of business"*

**J.L. Hansen**

*"The sole proprietor is the supreme judge of all matters pertaining to his business subject only to general laws of land and to such special legislations as may affect his particular line of business"*

**Kimball and Kimball**

*"The sole trader is a person who carries on business of his own, that is, without the assistance of a partner. He brings in his own capital and uses all his labour. He also gets himself assisted by others to whom he pays a salary by way of remuneration"*

**S.R. Darvar**

## 2.3 Features/Characteristics of Sole Proprietorship

The main features of sole proprietorship firm are mentioned below:

1. **Single Ownership**: A sole proprietorship is a business fully owned by a single individual, who provides all the capital either from personal funds or through borrowing.

2. **One-man Control**: The owner makes all business decisions independently without needing to consult anyone else. Ownership and management are combined in one person, although employees may be hired to assist, ultimate control remains with the owner.

3. **No Separate Legal Entity**: A sole proprietorship does not have a separate legal identity from its owner. Legally, the owner and the business are considered one and the same.

4. **Unlimited Liability**: The owner is personally liable for all business debts. If the business assets are insufficient to cover debts, the owner's personal property can be used to meet the obligations.

5. **No Profit-sharing**: The sole proprietor receives all the profits and bears all the losses of the business. There is no sharing of profits or losses with others.

6. **No Legal Formalities**: Starting, managing, and dissolving a sole proprietorship involves minimal government regulation. Generally, no legal formalities are required, except for obtaining necessary licenses for certain types of businesses.

7. **Small Size**: Sole proprietorships typically operate on a small scale, as all funding, management, and control are the responsibility of a single individual.

## 2.4 Advantages/Merits of Sole Proprietorship

Following are the advantages of Sole proprietorship form of business

1. **Easy to Form and Dissolve**: Establishing a sole proprietorship is straightforward and requires no legal formalities. Similarly, the business can be dissolved at any time at the owner's discretion.

2. **Quick Decision-Making and Prompt Action**: With no interference from others, the owner can swiftly make decisions and act on various business matters.

3. **Operational Flexibility**: Changes to the business can be easily implemented as needed, with minimal formalities compared to other business structures.

4. **Secrecy**: Sole proprietors can keep their business strategies and operations confidential, which can contribute to their success.

5. **Direct Incentive**: The direct relationship between effort and reward motivates the proprietor to work harder, as increased effort directly translates to higher income.

6. **Independent Control**: The owner independently makes all business decisions, maintaining full control over the operations. Employees may be hired to assist, but ultimate control remains with the owner.

7. **Sole Benefits**: The proprietor retains all profits earned by the business.

8. **Personal Touch**: Direct management by the owner allows for personalized customer service and strong relationships with employees, aiding in smooth business operations.

9. **Suitable for Small-Scale Operations**: Ideal for small businesses, a sole proprietorship suits enterprises with low capital requirements and the need for personal attention.

10. **Self-Employment**: This business structure provides an opportunity for individuals to be self-employed and operate independently, without working for others.

## 2.5 Disadvantages/Demerits of Sole Proprietorship

Sole proprietorship form of business suffers from the following limitations:

1. **Limited Resources:** In a sole proprietorship, the proprietor funds the business from personal wealth or borrowings. There is a limit to how much one person can invest, restricting the potential for business growth. The available funds are typically insufficient for medium or large-scale operations.

2. **Limited Managerial Ability:** All business activities are managed by a single individual, who cannot be an expert in every field. Limited resources also prevent the hiring of professional help.

3. **Unlimited Liability:** The proprietor is personally liable for all business debts. If business assets are insufficient to cover these

debts, the owner's personal property can be used to meet the obligations.

4. **Unsuitable for Large-Scale Operations:** Due to limited resources and managerial capacity, a sole proprietorship is not suitable for large-scale business ventures.

5. **Uncertain Continuity:** The continuity of a sole proprietorship is uncertain. The business exists only as long as the proprietor does. If the proprietor becomes incapacitated or dies, the business ceases to operate.

## 2.6 Formation of Sole Proprietorship form of Business Organisation

Establishing a sole proprietorship is very straightforward. Anyone with the desire and necessary resources can start this type of business. Generally, there are no legal formalities required to start and operate a sole proprietorship. However, certain businesses, such as restaurants or pharmacies, may require permission from the relevant authorities before commencing operations. Similarly, setting up a factory might require approval from local authorities. Despite these exceptions, forming a sole proprietorship is typically uncomplicated.

## 3. JOINT HINDU FAMILY BUSINESS

## 3.1 Concept of Joint Hindu Family Business

Having explored sole proprietorships, let's now examine a unique form of business organization specific to India, particularly among Hindus. The Joint Hindu Family (JHF) business is operated by a Hindu Undivided Family (HUF), where family members across three successive generations collectively own the business. The head of the family, known as the Karta, manages the business. The other members, called co-parceners, all have equal ownership rights over the business properties. Membership in the JHF is acquired by birth within the family, with no age restrictions, allowing minors to be members as well.

Under Hindu Law there are two systems of inheritance. These are:

1. **Dayabhaga System of Hindu Law:** Under the Dayabhaga system, both male and female family members are considered joint owners. This system is applicable in the state of West Bengal.

2. **Mitakshara System of Hindu Law:** The Mitakshara system stipulates that only male family members can be coparceners. This system applies to the rest of India.

## 3.2 Characteristics of Joint Hindu Family Form of Business Organisation

The main features or characteristics of Joint Hindu Family (JHF) business are mentioned below:

1. **Formation:** A JHF business requires at least two family members and some ancestral property. It is established by operation of law, not by agreement.

2. **Legal Status:** The JHF business is jointly owned and governed by the Hindu Succession Act of 1956.

3. **Membership:** Outsiders cannot become coparceners in a JHF business. Only members of the undivided family acquire coparcenary rights by birth.

4. **Profit Sharing:** All coparceners share equally in the business profits.

5. **Management:** The senior-most family member, known as the Karta, manages the business. Other members do not participate in management and cannot question the Karta's decisions. If dissatisfied, coparceners can dissolve the HUF status through mutual agreement.

6. **Liability:** Coparceners' liability is limited to their share in the business, but the Karta has unlimited liability, meaning his personal property can be used to meet business debts.

7. **Continuity:** The business continues despite the death of any coparcener. Upon the Karta's death, the eldest coparcener assumes the role. The JHF business can be dissolved through mutual agreement or a partition suit in court.

# 3.3 Advantages/ Merits of JHF Form of Business Organisation

Since the Joint Hindu Family business possesses unique features as discussed above, it offers the following advantages:

1. **Assured Shares in Profits:** Every coparcener is guaranteed an equal share in the profits, regardless of their involvement in the business operations. This safeguards the interests of minors, sick, physically, and mentally challenged coparceners.

2. **Quick Decision Making:** The Karta enjoys complete autonomy in managing the business, allowing for swift decision-making without interference.

3. **Sharing of Knowledge and Experience:** A JHF business provides an opportunity for younger family members to benefit from the knowledge and experience of elder members. It also fosters virtues such as discipline, self-sacrifice, and tolerance.

4. **Limited Liability of Members:** Coparceners (except the Karta) have limited liability, restricted to the extent of their share in the business. This allows them to operate the business freely by following the Karta's instructions or directions.

5. **Unlimited Liability of the Karta:** Due to the Karta's unlimited liability, their personal properties are at risk if the business fails to meet its obligations to creditors. This aspect of the JHF business encourages the Karta to manage the business with utmost care and efficiency.

6. **Continued Existence:** The death or insolvency of any member does not affect the continuity of the business, enabling it to operate over a long period.

7. **Tax Benefits:** An HUF is treated as a separate entity for tax purposes. The share of coparceners is not included in their individual income for tax purposes, providing tax benefits.

## 3.4 Disadvantages of JHF Form of Business Organisation

Following are the limitations or disadvantages of a Joint Hindu Family business:

1. **Limited Resources:** The JHF business typically has limited financial and managerial resources, which makes it less suitable for large-scale enterprises.

2. **Lack of Motivation:** Coparceners receive an equal share in the business profits regardless of their involvement, which often reduces their motivation to perform at their best.

3. **Scope for Misuse of Power:** The Karta has complete freedom to manage the business, which may lead to the potential misuse of authority for personal gain. Additionally, the Karta may have their own limitations.

4. **Instability:** The continuity of a JHF business is often precarious. Even minor disputes within the family can lead to demands for partition, affecting the business's stability.

## 3.5 Suitability of Joint Hindu Family form of Business Organisation

The Joint Hindu Family form of business organization is suitable when a family inherits a running business and wishes to continue operating it jointly. Additionally, this form of business is considered appropriate for enterprises requiring limited financial and managerial resources, and operating within a small geographic area. Typically, JHF businesses are involved in trading, indigenous banking, small-scale industry, crafts, and similar sectors.

## 3.6 Formation of Joint Hindu Family Form of Business Organisation

A Joint Hindu Family business is established according to Hindu law. It begins upon the death of the person who initiated the business, with their successors automatically becoming coparceners if they opt to continue it as a joint family enterprise. Children become members of the business by birth, and the eldest family member assumes the role of Karta. No legal formalities are necessary for its formation, but registration with the Income Tax Department is required to benefit from tax concessions.

# 4. PARTNERSHIP FIRM

## 4.1 Concept of Partnership

**"Partnership"** is an arrangement where two or more individuals combine their financial and managerial resources to conduct a business and share its profits. Each individual involved is called a partner, collectively they form a firm or partnership firm, and the name under which their business operates is known as the **"firm-name"**. Partnership form of business organisation in India is governed by the Indian Partnership Act, 1932 which defines partnership as "the relation between persons who have agreed to share the profits of the business carried on by all or any of them acting for all".

## 4.2 Definitions of Partnership

*"Partnership is the relation between persons who have agreed to share the profits of the business carried on by all or any of them acting for all"*

**The Indian Partnership Act 1932**

*"Partnership has two or more members, each of whom is responsible for the partnership. Each of the partners may bind the others for debts of the partnership"*

**William R. Spriegel**

*"A partnership firm is a group of men who have joined capital or services for the prosecuting of some enterprise"*

**Kimball**

*" Partnership is a contractual relationship, based upon a written, oral or implied agreement between two or more persons who combine their resources and activities in a joint enterprise and share in varying degrees and by specific agreement in the management and in the profits or losses"*

**Eric L. Kohler**

*"Partnership is the relation existing between persons, component to make contracts who have agreed to carry on a lawful business in common with a view to private gain"*

***Prof. L.H. Haney***

## 4.3 Characteristics/Nature of Partnership

Based on the definition of partnership as given above, the various characteristics of partnership form of business organisation can be summarised as follows:

1. **Number of Persons**: According to the Partnership Act, 1932, a partnership firm requires a minimum of two persons. The maximum number of partners is ten for banking businesses and 20 for other types of businesses. However, under the Companies Act, 2013 (Section 464), up to 100 members can form a partnership business. If the number exceeds these limits, the partnership is considered illegal, and the relationship cannot be recognized as a partnership.

2. **Contractual Relationship**: A partnership is formed through an agreement among individuals who are competent to contract. Minors, lunatics, and insolvent persons are not eligible to become partners, although a minor can be admitted to the benefits of a partnership firm, meaning they can share in the profits without being liable for losses.

3. **Sharing Profits and Losses**: Partners must agree to share the profits and losses of the partnership business. If two or more persons share the income of a jointly owned property, it does not constitute a partnership.

4. **Lawful Business**: The business in which the partners agree to share profits must be lawful. Agreements to engage in illegal activities such as smuggling or black marketing are not considered partnerships in the eyes of the law.

5. **Principal-Agent Relationship**: Every partner acts both as a principal and an agent of the firm. When a partner transacts with third parties, they act as an agent for the other partners, who are the principals.

6. **Unlimited Liability:** Partners in a firm have unlimited liability. They are jointly and individually liable for the debts and obligations of the firm. If the firm's assets are insufficient to cover its liabilities, the personal assets of the partners can be used to meet these obligations. However, the liability of a minor partner is limited to the extent of their share in the profits.

7. **Voluntary Registration:** Registration of a partnership firm is not mandatory, but an unregistered firm faces certain limitations that practically necessitate registration:

   - The firm cannot sue outsiders, although outsiders can sue the firm.

   - Disputes among partners cannot be settled in court.

   - The firm cannot claim adjustments for amounts payable to or receivable from other parties.

## 4.4 Merits/Advantages of Partnership Form of Business Organisation

Following are the merits or advantages of Partnership business:

1. **Simplified Formation Process:** A partnership can be formed easily without extensive legal formalities. Registration of the firm is not compulsory; a simple agreement, whether oral, written, or implied, is sufficient to establish a partnership firm.

2. **Pooling of Greater Resources:** In a partnership, two or more partners come together, which allows for pooling more resources compared to a sole proprietorship.

3. **Consensual Decision-Making:** In a partnership firm, each partner has the right to participate in the management. Major decisions are made collectively, with the consent of all partners. This fosters collective wisdom and reduces the likelihood of reckless or hasty decisions.

4. **Flexibility:** A partnership firm is flexible in its structure. Partners can decide to change the size, nature of business, or area of operation at any time, provided all partners agree.

5. **Shared Risks:** Losses incurred by the firm are shared equally among all partners or as per the agreed-upon ratio.

6. **Personal Investment:** Partners share profits and losses, which encourages them to take a keen interest in the business's operations.

7. **Utilization of Specialized Skills:** Each partner contributes according to their specialization and knowledge. For instance, in a partnership providing legal consultancy, one partner may handle civil cases, another criminal cases, and another labor cases. Similarly, doctors with different specialties can join together to start a clinic.

8. **Protection of Interests:** The rights and interests of each partner are fully protected in a partnership. If a partner is dissatisfied with a decision, they can request dissolution of the firm or withdraw from the partnership.

9. **Confidentiality:** Business secrets remain within the partnership, as there is no requirement to disclose information to outsiders. There is also no obligation to publish the firm's annual accounts.

## 4.5 Limitations/Disadvantages of Partnership Form of Business Organisation

A partnership firm also suffers from certain limitations. These are as follows:

1. **Unlimited Liability:** The primary drawback of a partnership firm is that partners have unlimited liability, meaning they are personally liable for the debts and obligations of the firm. This implies that their personal assets can be used to settle the firm's liabilities.

2. **Instability:** Every partnership firm has an uncertain lifespan. The death, insolvency, incapacity, or retirement of any partner can lead to the dissolution of the firm. Additionally, any partner can issue a notice at any time for the dissolution of the partnership.

3. **Limited Capital:** Since the total number of partners cannot exceed 20, the ability to raise funds remains limited compared to a joint-stock company where there is no restriction on the number of shareholders.

4. **Non-transferability of Interest:** The interest or share of any partner cannot be transferred to another partner or outsider. This limitation can inconvenience partners who wish to transfer their share partially or fully, as the only alternative is to dissolve the firm.

5. **Potential for Conflicts:** In a partnership firm, every partner has an equal right to participate in management and voice their opinions on any matter. This democratic setup can sometimes lead to friction and disputes among partners. Differences of opinion may escalate into conflicts that could ultimately result in the dissolution of the firm.

## 4.6 Types of Partners

We have learned that typically, every partner in a firm contributes to its capital, participates in the day-to-day management of the firm's activities, and shares its profits and losses according to the agreed-upon ratio. Essentially, all partners are expected to be active participants. However, there are cases where partners have a limited role. They may contribute capital but do not actively participate in the firm's management, and thus cannot be termed as active partners. Additionally, some individuals may merely lend their name to the firm without contributing any capital; these individuals are partners only in name.

Thus, partners can be classified into various categories depending on the extent of their participation, profit-sharing arrangements, liability, etc. These categories are summarized as follows:

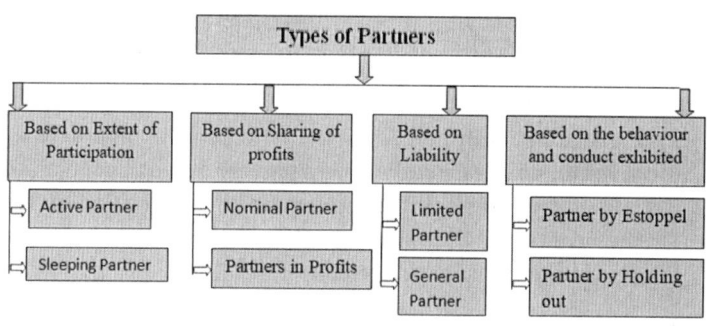

*Types of partners*

1. **Based on the extent of participation:**
   a. **Active Partners:** Partners who actively participate in the day-to-day operations of the business are known as active partners or working partners.
   b. **Sleeping or Dormant Partners:** Partners who do not participate in the day-to-day activities of the business are known as sleeping or dormant partners. These partners simply contribute capital and share the profits and losses.

2. **Based on sharing of profits:**
   a. **Nominal Partners:** Nominal partners allow the firm to use their name as a partner but do not invest any capital or participate in the day-to-day operations. They are not entitled to share the profits of the firm but are liable to third parties for all acts of the firm.
   b. **Partners in Profits:** Individuals who share the profits of the business without being liable for the losses are known as partners in profits. This status applies only to minors who are admitted to the benefits of the firm, and their liability is limited to their capital contribution.

3. **Based on Liability:**
   a. **Limited Partners:** The liability of limited partners is limited to the extent of their capital contribution. This type of partnership exists in Limited Partnership firms in some European countries and the USA, but it is not allowed in India currently. However, the Limited Liability Partnership Act is under consideration by Parliament.
   b. **General Partners:** Partners who have unlimited liability are called general partners or partners with unlimited liability. Every partner who is not a limited partner is treated as a general partner.

4. **Based on behavior and conduct:**
   a. **Partner by Estoppel:** A person who behaves in a way that gives the impression they are a partner of the firm is called a partner by estoppel. These partners are not entitled to share the profits of the firm but are fully liable if someone suffers due to their false representation.
   b. **Partner by Holding out:** If a partner or partnership firm declares that a particular person is a partner of their firm,

and that person does not disclaim it, then they are known as a partner by holding out. These partners are not entitled to profits but are fully liable for the firm's debts.

## 4.7 Rights and Duties of Partner

The partnership deed outlines the mutual rights, duties, and obligations of the partners. In cases where the partnership deed is absent or silent on any point, the Partnership Act mandates provisions regarding the rights and obligations of partners.

**Rights of a partner:** The rights of a partner are as follows:

1. Right of the partner to participate in the day-to-day management of the firm.

2. Right to be consulted and heard in decisions regarding the business.

3. Right of access to books of accounts and to request copies of the same.

4. Right to share the profits equally or as agreed upon by the partners.

5. Right to receive interest on capital contributed by the partners to the firm.

6. Right to receive interest on advances paid by the partners for business purposes.

7. Right to use partnership property exclusively for partnership business, not personal use.

8. Right to be indemnified for payments made, liabilities incurred, or losses sustained while protecting the firm.

9. Right as an agent of the firm with implied authority to bind the firm for any act carried out in the course of business.

10. Right to prevent the admission of new partners or the expulsion of existing partners.

11. Right to continue as a partner unless and until he himself ceases to be a partner.

**Duties of a partner:** The duties of a partner are as follows:

1. **To conduct the business for the greatest common advantage:** Every partner is obligated to conduct the firm's business to

achieve the greatest common benefit. This means using their knowledge and skills to ensure the firm's maximum benefit.

2.  **To be fair and faithful to each other**: Partners must treat each other with fairness and fidelity. They are required to uphold the highest standards of good faith and fairness in all business activities.

3.  **To maintain accurate accounts**: Each partner must maintain accurate and proper accounts and provide them to their co-partners. Every entry in the books must be supported by vouchers and explanations if requested by other partners.

4.  **To provide full information**: Partners must share complete information about any activities that affect the firm with their co-partners. No information should be kept secret among partners.

5.  **To diligently perform duties**: Each partner must diligently fulfill their duties in managing the firm's business.

6.  **To work without receiving remuneration**: Partners are not entitled to receive any form of remuneration for participating in the management of the business. However, in practice, working partners are often paid remuneration as per the partnership agreement.

7.  **To indemnify for losses caused by fraud or neglect**: If a partner causes a loss to the firm due to willful neglect or fraud in conducting the business, they must indemnify the firm for the loss.

8.  **To hold and use partnership property exclusively for the firm**: Partners must hold and use partnership property exclusively for the firm's business purposes, not for personal benefit.

9.  **To account for personal profits**: If a partner obtains any personal profit from a partnership transaction or by using the firm's property or business connections, they must account for the profit and pay it to the firm.

10. **Not to engage in competing business**: Partners are prohibited from engaging in any business that competes with the firm's business. If a partner does so and earns a profit, they must account for the profit and pay it to the firm.

11. **To share losses**: Partners are responsible for bearing the firm's losses. Unless otherwise agreed, partners share losses equally or as per their profit-sharing ratio.

12. **To act within authority**: Partners must act within the scope of their authority. If a partner exceeds their authority and causes a loss to the firm, they must compensate the firm for the loss.

13. **Duty to be jointly and severally liable**: Each partner is jointly and severally liable to third parties for all acts of the firm during their tenure as a partner.

14. **Duty not to assign interest**: A partner cannot assign or transfer their partnership interest to an outsider to make them a partner without the consent of the other partners. However, they can assign their share of profits and assets, with the assignee having no right to interfere in the firm's business operations.

## 4.8 Suitability of Partnership Form of Business Organisation

We have already understood that individuals with diverse abilities, skills, or expertise can come together to establish a partnership firm for conducting business. Activities such as construction, legal services, medical services, etc., can be effectively operated under the partnership form of business organization. It is also considered suitable where the capital requirement is of a medium size. Therefore, businesses such as wholesale trade, professional services, mercantile houses, and small manufacturing units can thrive successfully under the partnership structure.

## 4.9 Formation of Partnership Form of Business Organisation

The following steps are to be taken in order to form a partnership firm:

1. **Number of Members**: A partnership requires a minimum of two members. The maximum limit is ten for banking and 20 for other businesses.

2. **Partnership Deed**: An agreement among partners to conduct business and share profits and losses is essential. This document, known as the Partnership Deed, is written on a stamped paper and includes the rules, regulations, and terms of the partnership business. It also outlines the rights and duties of the partners. The Partnership Deed must include the following:

a. *Name of the Firm:* The firm's name must not be identical to that of existing firms.

b. *Nature of the Business:* Partners must decide on the type of business they will collectively undertake.

c. *Names and Addresses of Partners:* Names, addresses, and contact details of each partner must be provided.

d. *Location of Business:* The firm's address where business will be conducted must be specified.

e. *Duration of Partnership:* If applicable, the duration of the partnership must be stated.

f. *Capital Contribution by Each Partner:* The amount of capital each partner will contribute must be decided. Capital may be contributed based on the profit ratio or otherwise.

g. *Profit and Loss Sharing Ratio:* Partners must agree on the ratio for sharing profits and losses. In the absence of an agreement, profits and losses will be shared equally.

h. *Duties, Powers, and Obligations of Partners:* The Partnership Deed must specify the powers, duties, rights, and functions of each partner.

i. *Salaries and Withdrawals of Partners:* If partners will receive salaries, fees, commission, or bonuses from the firm for their work, these amounts must be specified in the agreement.

j. *Valuation of Goodwill:* The method for valuing goodwill on the admission, retirement, death of a partner, or dissolution of the firm must be determined.

k. *Valuation of Assets:* The procedure for valuing the firm's assets in case of reconstitution should be outlined.

l. *Preparation of Accounts and Auditing:* The agreement should state whether the firm's accounts will be kept on a cash basis, mercantile system, or hybrid system.

m. *Procedure for Dissolution of the Firm:* The Partnership Deed must include the procedure for the dissolution of the firm.

n. *Procedure for Settlement of Disputes*: In case of disputes among partners, the method for resolution, appointment of arbitrators, and arbitration process must be detailed.

3. **Registration of Firm:** Partners should register the firm with the Registrar of Firms of the concerned state. While registration is not compulsory, it is advisable to avoid the consequences of non-registration. The registration procedure is as follows:

   a. *Application to Registrar:* The firm must apply to the Registrar of Firms of the concerned state using the prescribed form.

   b. *Signature of Partners:* The application form must be signed by all partners.

   c. *Submission of Form:* The filled-in form, along with the prescribed registration fee, should be submitted to the Registrar of Firms.

   d. *Scrutiny and Registration*: The Registrar will scrutinize the application. If satisfied with all formalities, the Registrar will enter the firm's name in the register and issue a Certificate of Registration.

## 5. JOINT STOCK COMPANY

## 5.1 Concept of a Joint Stock Company

The Joint Stock Company form of business organization has gained immense popularity as it offers solutions to overcome the limitations of partnership and sole proprietorship businesses. A company is a registered association that acts as an artificial legal person. It has an independent legal existence with perpetual succession, a common seal for its signatures, a share capital comprised of transferable shares, and carries limited liability. Multinational corporations such as Coca-Cola and General Motors have investors and customers spread across the globe. Some of the prominent Indian companies include names like Reliance, Tata, Bajaj Auto, Infosys Technologies, Hindustan Unilever Ltd., Ranbaxy Laboratories Ltd., and Larsen & Toubro, among others.

## 5.2 Definitions of a Joint Stock Company

"A company incorporated under the Companies Act 2013 or any previous company law"

*Section 2 (20) of the Companies Act, 2013*

"A company is a person, artificial, invisible, intangible, and existing only in the contemplation of the law. Being a mere creature of law, it possesses only those properties which the character of its creation of its creation confers upon it either expressly or as incidental to its very existence"

*Chief Justice Marshall of USA*

"A company is meant an association of many persons who contribute money or money's worth to a common stock and employ it in some trade or business, and who share the profit and loss (as the case may be) arising there from. The common stock contributed is denoted in money and is the capital of the company. The persons who contribute it, or to whom it belongs, are members. The proportion of capital to which each member is entitled is his share. Shares are always transferable although the right to transfer them is often more or less restricted"

*Lord Justice Lindley*

"Joint Stock Company is a voluntary association of individuals for profit, having a capital divided into transferable shares. The ownership of which is the condition of membership".

*Prof. Haney*

## 5.3 Characteristics/Nature of a Joint Stock Company

The main characteristics of a Joint stock company are:

1. **Incorporated Association:** A company is established when it is registered under the Companies Act. Its existence begins from the date specified in the certificate of incorporation.

2. **Number of Members:** According to the Companies Act 2013, a public company requires a minimum of seven members with no upper limit, and a private company requires a minimum of two members and a maximum of two hundred members. These individuals must subscribe to the Memorandum of Association

and fulfill other legal requirements to form and incorporate a company, either with or without limited liability.

3. **Artificial Legal Person:** A company is an artificial person recognized by law. It cannot act on its own and operates through a board of directors elected by its shareholders.

4. **Separate Legal Entity:** A company possesses a distinct legal entity that is separate from its members. Creditors can only recover debts from the company and its assets, not from individual members. Similarly, the company is not liable for the personal debts of its members. The company's assets are used exclusively for its benefit, not for the personal benefit of shareholders.

5. **Perpetual Existence:** A company is a stable form of business organization. Its continuity is not affected by the death, insolvency, or retirement of its shareholders or directors. It is created by law and can only be dissolved by law. Members may come and go, but the company can continue indefinitely.

6. **Common Seal:** Since a company, being an artificial person, cannot sign documents on its own, it acts through natural persons known as directors. To legally bind the company, the law provides for the use of a common seal engraved with the company's name as a substitute for its signature. Any document bearing the company's common seal is legally binding.

7. **Limited Liability:** A company may be limited by shares or by guarantee. In a company limited by shares, the liability of members is limited to the unpaid amount on their shares. For example, if a share has a face value of Rs. 100 and a member has paid Rs. 80 per share, they may be required to pay up to Rs. 20 per share during the life of the company. In a company limited by guarantee, members' liability is limited to the amount they agree to contribute to the company's assets in the event of its winding up.

8. **Transferable Shares:** In a public company, shares are freely transferable. The right to transfer shares is statutory and cannot be taken away by provisions in the articles. However, the articles may specify the manner of transfer and include bona fide and reasonable restrictions on the right of members to transfer their shares. Absolute restrictions on this right are unlawful. In

the case of a private company, the articles restrict the right of members to transfer shares as defined by statute.

9. **Separate Property:** As a distinct legal entity, a company can own, enjoy, and dispose of property in its own name. Although shareholders contribute to its capital and assets, they do not jointly own the company's property. The company itself is the legal entity vested with all its property, and it manages, controls, and disposes of these assets.

10. **Delegated Management:** A joint-stock company is an autonomous, self-governing organization. Due to its large number of members, all cannot participate in managing its affairs. Therefore, shareholders delegate control and management to their elected representatives, known as directors.

## 5.4 Merits/Advantages of Joint Stock Company

1. **Large Financial Resources:** A joint-stock company can accumulate significant capital through small contributions from a large number of people. In a public limited company, shares can be offered to the general public to raise capital. Companies can also accept deposits and issue debentures to raise funds.

2. **Limited Liability:** In a company, the liability of its members is restricted to the value of shares held by them. The personal assets of members cannot be seized for the company's debts. This feature attracts many investors to invest their savings in the company and encourages owners to take more risks.

3. **Professional Management:** The management of a company is entrusted to directors who are democratically elected by the shareholders. These directors form the Board of Directors (or simply the Board) and manage the company's affairs, being accountable to all shareholders. Shareholders elect capable individuals with sound financial, legal, and business knowledge to the board to ensure efficient management.

4. **Growth and Expansion:** The company structure provides ample opportunities for growth and expansion. Companies have access to substantial financial resources and often enjoy high profit rates. They can utilize accumulated or retained profits for expansion and growth.

5. **Large-Scale Production:** Joint-stock companies can engage in large-scale production due to their substantial financial resources and technical expertise. This capability enables efficient production at a lower cost.

6. **Transfer of Shares:** Joint-stock companies facilitate easy transferability of shares. Shares can be easily bought and sold in the market. If a shareholder needs funds or is dissatisfied with the company's management, they can transfer their shares to another person.

## 5.5 Demerits/Disadvantages of Joint Stock Company

Despite the numerous advantages of the company form of business organization, it also faces several limitations. Let's discuss the drawbacks of Joint Stock Companies:

1. **Complex Formation Process:** The formation or registration of a joint stock company involves a complex procedure. It requires the completion of numerous legal documents and formalities before the company can commence its operations. Specialists such as Chartered Accountants, Company Secretaries, etc., are needed, making the formation costs very high.

2. **Government Regulation:** Joint stock companies are heavily regulated by the government through the Companies Act and other economic legislations. Public limited companies, in particular, must adhere to various legal formalities as stipulated in the Companies Act and other laws. Non-compliance can result in heavy penalties, affecting the smooth functioning of the companies.

3. **Delay in Decision-Making:** Policy decisions are generally made during board meetings of the company. Moreover, the company must fulfill certain procedural formalities, which are time-consuming and may delay the implementation of decisions.

4. **Conflicts of Interest:** In a company, various groups are involved such as shareholders, debenture holders, employees, and directors, each with different interests. This diversity can lead to conflicts between these groups.

5. **Concentration of Economic Power:** Joint stock companies are large-scale organizations with substantial resources, which concentrate economic and other powers in the hands of those

managing the company. Misuse of this power can lead to unhealthy conditions in society, such as monopolies in certain industries or products, and exploitation of workers, consumers, and investors.

6. **Oligarchic Management**: While company management may appear democratic, in practice, it often operates as an oligarchy—a small group of individuals controlling the company. Directors who are elected may use various means to maintain their positions, sometimes prioritizing personal interests over those of the shareholders.

7. **Speculation**: Joint stock companies provide opportunities for speculation in shares, where profits can be made by manipulating share prices without actually owning the shares. Directors, having access to all company information, may use this knowledge for personal gain. For instance, directors might buy or sell shares knowing that prices will rise or fall due to anticipated profits. As a result, innocent shareholders may suffer losses.

## 5.6 Suitability of Joint Stock Company

The joint stock company form of business organization is found to be appropriate in cases where the scale of operations is large and substantial financial resources are required. Due to the limited liability of its members, it becomes feasible to raise capital from the public without significant difficulty. This organizational structure is also suitable for ventures involving high risks. Moreover, for businesses requiring public trust and confidence, the joint stock form is preferred due to its distinct legal status. Certain types of businesses, such as pharmaceutical production, machine manufacturing, information technology, iron and steel, aluminum, fertilizers, cement, etc., are typically structured as joint stock companies.

## 5.7 Types of Company

### I. Classification of Companies by Mode of Incorporation

Joint stock companies can be classified into different types based on their mode of incorporation. These are:

[A] **Chartered Companies**: These companies are incorporated under a special charter granted by a monarch. For example, The

East India Company and The Bank of England were chartered companies in England. The powers and nature of business of a chartered company are defined by the charter that incorporates it. A chartered company has extensive powers, including the ability to deal with its property and enter into contracts like any ordinary person. The Sovereign has the authority to revoke the charter and dissolve the company if it deviates from its prescribed business. Chartered companies are not present in India.

[B] **Statutory Companies**: These companies are incorporated by a Special Act passed by the Central or State legislature. Examples include the Reserve Bank of India, State Bank of India, Industrial Finance Corporation, Unit Trust of India, State Trading Corporation, and Life Insurance Corporation. Statutory companies do not have a memorandum or articles of association. They derive their powers from the Acts that constitute them and enjoy certain privileges similar to those of companies incorporated under the Companies Act. Amendments in their powers can be made through legislative amendments. The provisions of the Companies Act apply to these companies, except where they are inconsistent with the provisions of their Special Acts. Statutory companies are generally established to meet social needs rather than for profit-making purposes.

[C] **Registered or Incorporated Companies**: These companies are formed under the Companies Act, 1956 or earlier Companies Acts. They come into existence only upon registration under the Act and the issuance of a certificate of incorporation by the Registrar of Companies. This is the most common mode of incorporating a company. Registered companies can be further divided into the following categories:

[a] *Companies Limited by Shares*: These companies have a share capital, and the liability of each member is limited to the extent of the face value of the shares subscribed by them. During the existence of the company or in the event of its winding up, a member can only be called upon to pay the remaining unpaid amount on the shares subscribed by them. Such companies may be either public or private. This is the most popular type of company.

[b] *Companies Limited by Guarantee:* These companies may or may not have a share capital. Each member undertakes

to pay a fixed sum specified in the Memorandum in the event of the company's liquidation to cover its debts and liabilities. This fixed sum is called a 'guarantee'. The Articles of Association state the number of members with which the company is to be registered. Such companies depend on entrance and subscription fees for their existence. The liability of each member is limited to the amount of their guarantee and, if the company has a share capital, to the face value of the shares subscribed by them. Non-trading or non-profit companies established for promoting culture, art, science, religion, commerce, charity, sports, etc., are generally formed as companies limited by guarantee.

[c]. *Unlimited Companies:* A company that does not have any limit on the liability of its members is called an 'unlimited company'. It may or may not have a share capital. If it has a share capital, it may be either public or private. The articles of an unlimited company state the amount of share capital with which the company is to be registered. The articles also state the number of members with which the company is to be registered.

### II. On the Basis of Number of Members

Based on the number of members, a company may be:

[A] *Private Company:* A private company can be formed by at least two individuals, and the total membership cannot exceed 200 (excluding employees who are members or ex-employees who were and continue to be members). Shares allotted to its members are not freely transferable. These companies are not allowed to raise money from the public through open invitations. They are required to use "Private Limited" after their names. Examples of such companies include Combined Marketing Services Private Limited, Indian Publishers and Distributors Private Limited, Oricom Systems Private Limited, etc.

[B] *Public Company:* A minimum of seven members is required to form a public limited company, and there is no restriction on the maximum number of members. Shares allotted to members are freely transferable. These companies can raise funds from the general public through open invitations by selling their shares or accepting fixed deposits. They are required to use either

"Public Limited" or "Limited" after their names. Examples of such companies include Hyundai Motors India Limited, Steel Authority of India Limited, Jhandu Pharmaceuticals Limited, etc.

*(No minimum paid-up capital requirement will now apply for incorporating private as well as public companies in India- Companies Act Amendment 2015)*

## 5.8 Differences between a Public Company and a Private company

Following are the main points of differences between a Public company and a Private company:

1. **Minimum Number of Members**: A public company requires a minimum of 7 persons to form, while a private company requires a minimum of 2 persons.

2. **Maximum Number of Members**: There is no restriction on the maximum number of members in a public company. In contrast, a private company cannot exceed 50 members.

3. **Number of Directors**: A public company must have at least 3 directors, whereas a private company must have at least 2 directors.

4. **Appointment of Directors**: Directors of a public company must file their consent to act as directors or sign an undertaking for their qualification shares with the Registrar. This requirement does not apply to directors of a private company.

5. **Invitation to Subscribe for Shares**: A public company invites the general public to subscribe for its shares or debentures. Conversely, a private company, by its Articles, prohibits the invitation to the public to subscribe for its shares.

6. **Name of the Company**: A private company must add the words "Private Limited" at the end of its name.

7. **Public Subscription**: A private company cannot invite the public to purchase its shares or debentures, whereas a public company may do so.

8. **Issue of Prospectus**: Unlike a public company, a private company is not required to issue a prospectus or file a statement in lieu of prospectus with the Registrar before allotting shares.

9. **Transferability of Shares**: Shares of a public company are freely transferable, while the right to transfer shares in a private company is restricted by its Articles.

10. **Special Privileges**: A private company enjoys certain special privileges, whereas a public company does not.

11. **Quorum**: Unless specified otherwise in the Articles, a quorum for a meeting of a public company requires 5 members personally present. For a private company, the quorum is 2 members personally present.

12. **Commencement of Business**: A private company may commence its business immediately after obtaining a certificate of incorporation. On the other hand, a public company cannot commence its business until it is granted a "Certificate of Commencement of Business.

These are the main differences between public and private companies based on their legal requirements and operational aspects.

## 5.9 Special privileges of a Private Company

The following Privileges are available to every of a Private Company:

1. Every private company, including a private company which is a subsidiary of a public company or deemed to be a public company, enjoys the following privileges:

2. A private company can be formed with only two members.

3. It can commence the allotment of shares even before the minimum subscription is subscribed or paid.

4. A private company is not required to issue a prospectus to the public or file a statement in lieu of a prospectus.

5. Restrictions imposed on public companies regarding the further issue of capital do not apply to private companies.

6. It is not required to keep an index of its members.

7. A private company can commence its business after obtaining a certificate of incorporation; a certificate of commencement of business is not required.

8. It need not hold a statutory meeting or file a statutory report.

9. Unless the articles provide for a larger number, a quorum in a private company requires only two persons personally present,

while in a public company, at least five members personally present form the quorum.

10. Directors of a private company are not required to file consent to act as such with the Registrar.

11. Similarly, the provisions of the Act regarding undertaking to take up qualification shares and pay for them are not applicable to directors of a private company.

12. In a private company, a poll can be demanded by one member if not more than seven members are present, and by two members if more than seven members are present. In contrast, in a public company, a poll can be demanded by persons having not less than one-tenth of the total voting power in respect of the resolution or holding shares on which an aggregate sum of not less than fifty thousand rupees has been paid-up.

13. A private company need not have more than two directors, while a public company must have at least three directors.

14. These are the specific privileges that a private company enjoys under the Companies Act, providing flexibility and reduced regulatory burden compared to public companies.

# 6. COOPERATIVE SOCIETY

## 6.1 Concept of Cooperative Society

The term "cooperation" originates from the Latin word 'co-operari', where 'Co' means 'with' and 'operari' means 'to work'. Therefore, cooperation means working together. Those individuals who wish to work together towards common economic objectives can establish a society known as a cooperative society. It is a voluntary association of persons who collaborate to promote their economic interests. Cooperative societies operate on the principles of self-help and mutual assistance. Their primary objective is to provide support to their members. Individuals come together as a group, pool their individual resources, use them effectively, and derive collective benefits from their efforts.

## 6.2 Definitions of Cooperative Society

*"Cooperative Society is a society, which has its objectives for the promotion of economic interests of its members in accordance with cooperative principles."*

**Section 4 of the Indian Cooperative Societies Act 1912**

*"A cooperative organisation is an association of persons usually of limited means, who have voluntarily joined together to achieve a common economic end, through the formation of democratically controlled business organisation, making equitable contribution to the capital required and accepting a fair share of risks and benefits of the undertakings"*

**International Labour Organisation (ILO)**

*"Cooperative is a form of organisation wherein persons voluntarily associates together as human beings on the basis of equality for the promotion of the economic interest of themselves"*

**H.C. Calvert**

*"Cooperative is self help as well as mutual help. It is a joint enterprise of those who are not financially strong and cannot stands on their legs and therefore come together not with a view to get profits but to overcome disability arising out of the want of adequate financial resources"*

**H.N. Kunzen**

## 6.3 Characteristics/Nature of Cooperative Society

Based on the above definition we can identify the following characteristics of cooperative society form of business organisation:

1. **Voluntary Association**: Members join the cooperative society voluntarily, by their own choice. Individuals with common economic objectives can join the society as they wish, continue for as long as they like, and leave whenever they want.

2. **Open Membership**: Membership is open to all individuals with a common economic interest. Any person can become a member regardless of their caste, creed, religion, color, sex, etc.

3. **Number of Members**: A minimum of 10 members is required to form a cooperative society. In the case of multi-state cooperative societies, the minimum number of members should be 50 from

each state if the members are individuals. The Cooperative Societies Act does not specify a maximum number of members for any cooperative society. However, after the formation of the society, members may decide on a maximum number of members.

4. **Equal Voting Rights**: Cooperative societies operate on the democratic principle of "one member, one vote". Each member has one voting right, regardless of the capital they have contributed.

5. **Registration of the Society**: In India, cooperative societies are registered under the Cooperative Societies Act of 1912 or under the State Cooperative Societies Act. Multi-state Cooperative Societies are registered under the Multi-state Cooperative Societies Act of 2002. Once registered, the society becomes a separate legal entity with certain characteristics:

   (i)   The society enjoys perpetual succession.

   (ii)  It has its own common seal.

   (iii) It can enter into agreements with others.

   (iv)  It can sue others in a court of law.

   (v)   It can own properties in its name.

6. **State Control**: Since the registration of cooperative societies is mandatory, every cooperative society comes under the control and supervision of the government. The cooperative department monitors the functioning of the societies, and every society must get its accounts audited by the cooperative department of the government.

7. **Capital**: The capital of a cooperative society is contributed by its members. Since members' contributions are often limited, societies may depend on loans from government and apex cooperative institutions, or receive grants and assistance from the state and central government.

8. **Democratic Setup**: Cooperative societies are managed democratically. Every member has the right to participate in the management of the society. However, the society elects a managing committee for effective management. Members of the managing committee are elected based on the "one member, one vote" principle, regardless of the number of shares held by any

member. The general body of the society lays down the broad framework within which the managing committee functions.

9. **Service Motive:** The primary objective of all cooperative societies is to provide services to their members.

10. **Return on Capital Investment:** Members receive returns on their capital investments in the form of dividends.

11. **Distribution of Surplus:** After providing a limited dividend to the members, surplus profits are distributed in the form of bonuses, with a certain percentage set aside as reserves and for the general welfare of the society.

## 6.4 Merits/Advantages of Cooperative Society

The cooperative society is a unique form of business organization that prioritizes its members over maximizing profits. After examining its characteristics and various types, we can now explore the advantages of this business form.

1. **Ease of Formation:** A group of ten adult members can voluntarily form an association and register it with the Registrar of Cooperative Societies. The registration process is straightforward and does not involve extensive legal formalities.

2. **Limited Liability:** Members of cooperative societies have limited liability up to their capital contribution. They are not personally liable for the debts of the society.

3. **Open Membership:** Any competent individual with similar economic objectives can join a cooperative society at any time. There are no restrictions based on caste, creed, gender, color, etc. Members can join or leave the society freely.

4. **State Assistance:** Cooperative societies receive support from the state and central governments in the form of loans, grants, subsidies, etc. This assistance is crucial for the economic development of weaker sections.

5. **Perpetual Existence:** Cooperative societies enjoy the benefit of perpetual succession. The society continues to exist independently of the death, resignation, or insolvency of its members due to its separate legal entity.

6. **Tax Concessions:** Governments often provide tax concessions and exemptions to encourage the formation of cooperative

societies. These concessions may vary and are updated periodically.

7. **Democratic Management**: Cooperative societies are managed by a Managing Committee elected by the members. The members establish their own rules and regulations within the framework provided by the law.

## 6.5 Limitations/Disadvantages of Cooperative Society

Although the basic aim of forming a cooperative society is to develop a system of mutual help and cooperation among its members, yet the feeling of cooperation does not remain for long. Cooperative societies usually suffer from the following limitations.

1. **Limited Capital**: Many cooperative societies struggle with insufficient capital. As members typically come from a confined area or socioeconomic class and have limited financial resources, it is challenging to gather substantial capital from them. Additionally, government assistance is often insufficient.

2. **Lack of Managerial Expertise**: The Managing Committee of a cooperative society often lacks the managerial expertise required for effective and efficient management. Furthermore, due to limited funds, they are unable to afford professional management services.

3. **Less Motivation**: The members are not always fully engaged in the society's activities because the return on their capital investment is relatively low.

4. **Lack of Interest**: After the initial enthusiasm for starting and running the cooperative fades, internal conflicts and factionalism often emerge among members, leading to a decline in activity and vitality within the cooperative.

5. **Corruption**: Despite government regulations and periodic audits of cooperative society accounts, corrupt practices in management can still persist.

## 6.6 Types of Cooperative Societies

Cooperative organizations are established across various sectors to enhance the economic well-being of different segments of society.

Consequently, based on the needs of the people, various types of cooperative societies exist in India. Some of the key types are listed below.

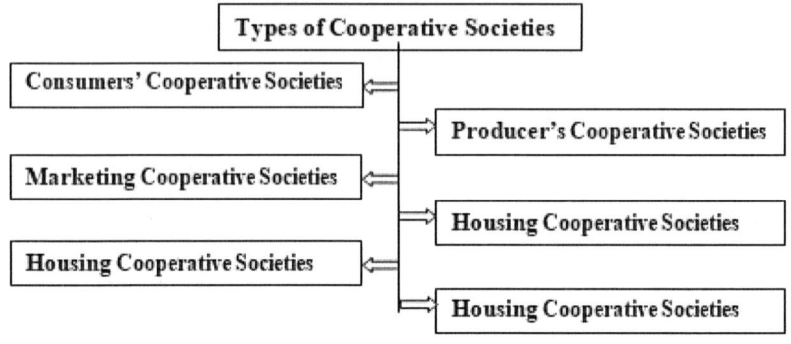

*Types of Cooperative Societies*

1. **Consumers' Cooperative Societies**: These societies are established to safeguard consumer interests by providing high-quality goods at reasonable prices.

2. **Producers' Cooperative Societies**: These societies aim to support small producers and artisans by supplying necessary production items such as raw materials, tools, and equipment.

3. **Marketing Cooperative Societies**: Small producers form these societies to address challenges in marketing their products.

4. **Housing Cooperative Societies**: These societies, typically found in urban areas, are created to provide residential housing for their members.

5. **Farming Cooperative Societies**: Small farmers establish these societies to benefit from large-scale farming practices.

6. **Credit Cooperative Societies**: These societies are initiated by individuals in need of credit. They collect deposits from members and offer loans at reasonable interest rates.

## 6.7 Suitability of Cooperative Society

We have already learned that a cooperative society is a voluntary association of individuals who lack strong financial resources and cannot independently start and run a business. This form of business organization is ideal for addressing common problems or meeting shared needs. By coming together, people can obtain consumer products, build residential houses, market their products, and provide loans and advances. This type of business organization is generally well-suited for small and medium-sized operations.

## 6.8 Formation of Cooperative Society

Cooperative societies are registered under the Societies Act of 1912 or the Cooperative Societies Acts of the respective states. The common requirements for registering a cooperative society include:

1. **Number of Members**: There must be at least ten individuals with a common economic interest who are capable of entering into a contract. For multi-state cooperative societies, at least 50 individual members from each state are required.

2. **A Suitable Name**: A suitable name must be proposed for the society.

3. **Draft Bye-laws**: The draft bye-laws of the society should be prepared.

4. **Registration**: After completing the above steps, the society should proceed with registration. An application in the prescribed form must be submitted to the Registrar of Cooperative Societies in the state where the society is to be established. The application must include four copies of the proposed bye-laws and be signed by every member of the society. After reviewing the application and bye-laws, the registrar issues the registration certificate, allowing the society to commence operations.

# 7. LIMITED LIABILITY PARTNERSHIP (LLP)

## 7.1 Concept of Limited Liability Partnership (LLP )

LLP, a globally recognized legal form, has been introduced in India under the Limited Liability Partnership Act of 2008, effective from April 1, 2009. An LLP merges the simplicity of running a partnership with the benefits of a separate legal entity and the limited liability of a company. It is a corporate business structure that allows the combination of professional expertise and entrepreneurial initiative to operate in a flexible, innovative, and efficient manner. This provides the advantages of limited liability while allowing members to organize their internal structure like a partnership.

*"Limited Liability Partnership is a corporate business vehicle that enables professional expertise and entrepreneurial initiative to combine and operate in flexible, innovative and efficient manner, providing benefits of limited liability while allowing its members the flexibility for organizing their internal structure as a partnership"*

**Limited Liability Partnership Act, 2008**

## 7.2 Characteristics/ features of a Limited Liability Partnership (LLP)

The main characteristics of a limited liability partnership are discussed below:

1. **Governed by:** The Limited Liability Partnership (LLP) is governed by the Limited Liability Partnership Act, 2008, which came into effect on April 1, 2009. The Indian Partnership Act, 1932 does not apply to LLPs.

2. **Number of Members:** A minimum of two members is required to form an LLP, with no restriction on the maximum number of partners. Any two or more persons who wish to conduct a lawful business for profit can form an LLP by subscribing their names to an incorporation document and filing it with the registrar.

3. **Separate Legal Entity:** An LLP is a separate legal entity distinct from its partners, meaning the LLP and its partners are separate entities.

4. **No Minimum Capital Requirement:** An LLP can be established with minimal capital. Capital can be in the form of tangible, movable assets like land and machinery or intangible assets. There is no mandatory capital requirement specified for LLPs.

5. **Limited Liability:** The liability of LLP members is limited to the extent of their capital contribution to the partnership.

6. **Perpetual Succession:** An LLP has perpetual succession, meaning changes in partners do not affect the LLP's existence, rights, or liabilities.

7. **Right to Manage:** Unlike corporate shareholders, partners in an LLP have the right to manage the business directly.

8. **Responsibility:** One partner is not responsible or liable for another partner's misconduct or negligence.

9. **Profit-Making Organization:** An LLP is a business entity formed with the motive of earning profit.

10. **Rights and Duties of Partners:** The rights and duties of partners in an LLP are governed by an agreement among the partners, allowing them flexibility in its design. The duties and obligations of Designated Partners are as provided by law.

## 7.3 Merits/Advantages of Limited Liability Partnership

Following are the merits of Limited Liability Partnership:

1. **Separate Legal Entity:** An LLP is a distinct legal entity, meaning it owns assets in its own name and can sue or be sued. Additionally, one partner is not liable for another partner's misconduct or negligence.

2. **No Owner/Manager Distinction:** In an LLP, partners both own and manage the business, unlike a private limited company where directors may be different from shareholders. This structure makes LLPs less attractive to venture capitalists.

3. **Flexible Agreement:** Partners have the freedom to draft their agreement, outlining their rights and duties as they see fit.

4. **Limited Liability:** Partners' liability is limited to their contribution to the LLP. Unless fraud is involved, partners' personal assets are protected from the LLP's liabilities.

5. **Fewer Compliance Requirements:** Running an LLP is simpler and more cost-effective than a private limited company, as it requires only three annual compliances, compared to the numerous compliances and mandatory audits required for private limited companies.

6. **Easy to Wind Up:** Starting and winding up an LLP is straightforward and uncomplicated.

## 7.4 Demerits/Limitations of Limited Liability Partnership

Following are the merits of Limited Liability Partnership:

1. **Limitation in the Formation of Partnership:** The basic structure of an LLP is similar to a partnership firm, requiring a minimum of two partners for formation. Therefore, an LLP cannot be formed by a single person. If an NRI or foreign national wants

to form an LLP in India, at least one partner must be a resident of India. Two foreign partners cannot form an LLP without including at least one resident Indian partner.

2. **Assets of LLP**: Partners contribute cash or assets to the LLP when executing the LLP agreement. Once these contributions are made, they cannot be returned to the partners unless explicitly provided for in the LLP agreement.

3. **Difficulty in Transfer of Ownership**: Transferring ownership in an LLP is challenging as it requires the consent of all partners. If a partner wishes to transfer their ownership, they must obtain approval from all other partners, necessitating a resolution passed by the majority.

4. **Lengthy Admission:** Admitting a new member to an LLP is a lengthy process. A supplementary agreement must be created with the new member's details and contribution. The existing partners must then adjust their contributions to accommodate the new member. Finally, this change must be registered with the Registrar of Companies.

## 7.5 Differences between LLP and Partnership Firm

The following are the main points of differences between a Limited Liability Partnership and a Partnership business:

| | Basis | LLP | Partnership firm |
|---|---|---|---|
| 1 | Governing law | Limited Liability Partnership is governed by the Limited Liability Partnership Act, 2008. | Partnership firm is governed by the Indian Partnership Act, 1932 |
| 2 | Registration | Registration of Limited Liability Partnership is compulsory. | It is not compulsory to register a partnership firm. |
| 3 | Creation | A Limited Liability Partnership is created by law. | A Partnership firm is created by partnership agreement among all the partners. |

| | Basis | LLP | Partnership firm |
|---|---|---|---|
| 4 | Legal status | A Limited Liability Partnership has separate legal status apart from partners. | Partners collectively known as firms; the firm has no separate legal status. |
| 5 | Succession | A Limited Liability Partnership is not affected on change in partnership (Perpetual succession). | A firm ceases to exist upon change in partnership, unless otherwise provided in agreement. |
| 6 | Ownership of assets | A Limited Liability Partnership can own assets in his own name. | A Partnership cannot own assets in its own name; assets must be in the name of partners. |
| 7 | Liability | Partners in a Limited Liability Partnership have limited liability | Partners in a Partnership firm have unlimited liability |
| 8 | Minor's position | The law is silent on the position of minors. | Minor can be admitted to the benefits of partnership. |

## 7.6 Differences between LLP and Company

The following are the main points of differences between a Limited Liability Partnership and a Company:

| S. No. | Basis | Limited Liability Partnership | Company |
|---|---|---|---|
| 1 | Incorporation Procedure | Incorporation procedure is relatively simple and expeditious. | Incorporation procedure is comparatively more complex than LLP |

| S. No. | Basis | Limited Liability Partnership | Company |
|---|---|---|---|
| 2 | Management Structure | LLP has a flexible management structure where Partners participate in management. | Companies have a complex management structure; shareholders do not ordinarily participate in day-to-day management. |
| 3 | Capital Structure | LLP has a Flexible capital structure. | Companies have relatively less flexible capital structure than LLP. |
| 4 | Redressal Provisions. | There are no specific provisions related to redressal in case of oppression and mismanagement | Companies have elaborate provisions related to redressal in case of oppression and mismanagement. |
| 5 | Statutory Compliance | LLP has limited statutory compliances as compared to Companies. | Companies have Complex statutory compliance requirements. |

## 7.7 Designated Partner

A designated partner is defined as 'a partner designated under section 7(23)'. The key distinction lies in that designated partners have limited liability solely as per the LLP Agreement and their acts under sections 27 to 29 of the LLP Act. Designated partners bear the responsibility of increased liability for all penalties imposed on the LLP for contravention of provisions that require compliance, as outlined in section 8(a) of the LLP Act. This includes the filing of documents, returns, statements, etc. In cases of contravention or non-compliance, designated partners may be personally and severally liable for punishments or penalties under the LLP Act.

## 7.8 Major duties of Designated Partners

Some major duties of designated partners include:

1. Inform Registrar of Companies about any changes in the LLP.

2. Notify Registrar of Companies of any alterations in partners' names and residential addresses from the Registered Office address.

3. File Annual Return, Statement of Accounts, and other documents as required under the LLP Act with the Registrar of Companies.

4. Designated partners of the LLP must sign Statements of Accounts and Solvency.

5. Secure and present to an inspector, or any other authorized person with prior approval from the Central Government, all books and papers relating to the LLP or any other entity that are in their custody or control.

## 7.9 Difference between a Partner and a Designated Partner in LLP

Both partners and designated partners in an LLP are responsible for all acts, matters, and obligations required to be carried out within the LLP. The duties of designated partners in an LLP are equivalent to those of partners, and they perform similar roles as directors in a company. They are governed by mutual rights and obligations as outlined in the LLP Agreement. However, there are specific differences in the definition and functions of partners and designated partners in an LLP, which are as follows:

| S. No | Basis | Partners | Designated Partners |
|---|---|---|---|
| 1. | Term | Partner is a generic term used in General Partnerships. | Designated Partner is a term used specifically in LLP's. |
| 2. | Duties and Rights | The duties, rights and liabilities of a partner are generally specified in a partnership deed. | Designated Partners duties, rights and liabilities are outlined in the LLP Agreement. |

| S. No | Basis | Partners | Designated Partners |
|-------|-------|----------|---------------------|
| 3. | Liability | A partner's liability to third parties is unlimited and extends to personal assets. | A designated partner's liability is limited to the capital they introduced or as per the LLP Agreement. |
| 4. | Responsibility | Partners are not responsible for managing the LLP and execute acts only as agreed. | Designated partners are responsible for managing the LLP and execute all necessary acts, including compliance with LLP Act requirement like filling documents/ returns/ statements. |
| 5. | Defined in | It is defined under the LLP Act 2(9). | It is defined under the LLP Act 7(23). |

**FROM HERE.**

## 7.10 Incorporation of Limited Liability Partnership

To incorporate a limited liability partnership (LLP), the following basic requirements must be met:

a. Two or more individuals must come together to engage in a lawful business with the intention of making a profit, and they must sign an incorporation document.

b. The incorporation document must be completed according to the prescribed manner and fees, and filed with the Registrar of the State where the LLP's registered office will be located.

c. The incorporation document must be filed along with a prescribed statement, which must be made by an advocate, a Company Secretary, a Chartered Accountant, or a Cost Accountant involved in the LLP's formation. Additionally, one of the individuals who signed the incorporation document must confirm that all the requirements of this Act and its rules regarding incorporation and related matters have been complied with.

## 7.11 Formation of the Incorporation Document

The Incorporation Document must:

(a)  Be in a prescribed form,

(b). State the name of the limited liability partnership,

(c)  Specify the proposed business of the LLP,

(d)  Provide the address of the LLP's registered office,

(e)  Include the name and address of each person who will be a partner in the LLP upon incorporation,

(f)  Include the name and address of those who will be designated partners in the LLP upon incorporation,

(g)  Contain any additional information regarding the proposed LLP as may be prescribed.

If a person makes a statement under clause (c) of sub-section (1) that they:

(a)  Know to be false, or

(b)  Do not believe to be true, shall be punishable with imprisonment for up to two years and a fine ranging from ten thousand rupees to five lakh rupees.

## Incorporation by Registration [sec. 7(2)]

Upon registration, the Registrar will issue a Certificate of Incorporation, certifying that the company is incorporated, and if applicable, that it is a limited company. Currently, the Registrar of Companies issues a registration with a Corporate Identity Number (CIN) consisting of 21 digits.

From the date of incorporation specified in the Certificate, the subscribers to the memorandum and any other individuals who become members of the company will form a corporate entity under the name specified in the memorandum. This entity will be capable of performing all functions of an incorporated company, with perpetual succession and a common seal. From this incorporation date, the company becomes a legal entity separate from its shareholders.

## 7.12 The legal effect of incorporation:

### The legal effect of incorporation is as under:

1.  A company becomes a distinct legal entity from its members:** The company's existence begins from the first moment of its

incorporation day, and it is considered to have been in existence for the entire day on which it was incorporated.

2. **A company has perpetual succession and a common seal:**\*\* The company is an immortal entity. The death, bankruptcy, or insanity of any member does not affect the company's existence. It remains in existence until it is dissolved through liquidation.

3. **A company has the right to own and transfer property:**\*\* The property belongs to the company itself, not to the individual members. Therefore, even the largest shareholder has no insurable interest in the company's property.

4. **The company's debts and obligations are its own liabilities:**\*\* These cannot be enforced against individual shareholders. Once the memorandum is signed and registered, the subscribers form a corporate body capable of exercising all functions of an incorporated company immediately. The company is mature at its inception, with no period of minority or incapacity. However, a public company cannot commence business until it meets specific requirements.

## 8. CHOICE OF FORM OF ORGANISATION

Selecting the right form of business organization based on ownership and management is a crucial task for an entrepreneur. Once a form is chosen, changing it is difficult because it requires winding up the existing organization, which wastes time, effort, and money. Therefore, careful thought and consideration must go into this decision. Several factors must be considered when choosing the appropriate form of business organization. These factors are interrelated and interdependent. Let's examine them one by one.

1. **Nature of Business:** The type of business is a key factor in determining the most suitable form of organization. Sole proprietorship or partnership is ideal for service-oriented activities, while partnership or company structures are better suited for manufacturing businesses.

2. **Volume of Business:** The scale of operations also influences the choice of business form. For small-scale operations, a sole proprietorship or partnership is ideal. For large-scale operations, a company structure is more appropriate.

3. **Area of Operation:** If the business operates over a wide geographic area, a company structure is preferable. For businesses confined to a specific locality or region, other forms of organization may be more suitable.

4. **Capital Consideration:** The required amount of finance is another crucial factor. Businesses needing less capital typically prefer sole proprietorship or partnership forms, while those requiring substantial financial resources tend to opt for a company structure.

5. **Independence:** Companies and cooperatives are subject to strict government regulations. Entrepreneurs seeking more freedom and less governmental interference might prefer sole proprietorship or partnership forms.

6. **Ownership and Control:** If direct control and ownership are important, sole proprietorship or partnership is best. For those comfortable with shared control, a company or cooperative structure may be appropriate.

7. **Liability:** Individuals willing to bear unlimited liability might choose sole proprietorship or partnership. Those who cannot shoulder this burden may opt for a company or cooperative structure, which limits personal liability.

## SUMMARY OF THE CHAPTER

1. **Business organisation** refers to all necessary arrangements required to conduct a business. It refers to all those steps that need to be undertaken for establishing relationship between men, material, and machinery to carry on business efficiently for earning profits.

2. The most important **forms of business organisation** are as follows:
   - Sole Proprietorship
   - Joint Hindu Family Firm
   - Partnership firm
   - Joint Stock Company
   - Cooperative society
   - Limited Liability Partnership

3. The **sole proprietorship** is a form of private sector enterprise which is owned, managed and controlled by a single individual.

4. The main **features of sole proprietorship** firm are mentioned below:
   - Single Ownership
   - One-man control
   - No legal entity
   - Unlimited Liability
   - No profit-sharing
   - No legal formalities
   - Small size

5. Following are **the advantages of Sole proprietorship** form of business
   - Easy to Form and Wind Up
   - Quick Decision and Prompt Action
   - Flexibility in Operation
   - Secrecy
   - Direct Incentive
   - Independent control
   - Sole benefits
   - Personal Touch
   - Suitable for small scale operation
   - Self-Employment

6. **Sole proprietorship** form of business suffers from the following **limitations**
   - Limited Resources
   - Limited Managerial Ability
   - Unlimited Liability
   - Not Suitable for Large Scale Operations
   - Uncertain Continuity

7. It is very simple to establish a sole proprietary concern. Any person who is willing to start a business and has the necessary resources can set up this form of business organization.

8. The Joint Hindu Family (JHF) business is a form of business organisation run by Hindu Undivided Family (HUF), where the family members of three successive generations own the business jointly. The head of the family known as Karta manages the business. The other members are called co-parceners and all of them have equal ownership right over the properties of the business.

9. Under Hindu Law there are two systems of inheritance. These are:

- **Dayabhag system of Hindu Law:**
- **Mitakashara system of Hindu Law**

10. The main **features or characteristics of Joint Hindu Family (JHF) business** are mentioned below:

- **Formation:** In JHF business there must be at least two members in the family, and family should have some ancestral property.
- **Legal Status:** It is governed by the Hindu Succession Act 1956.
- **Membership:** Only the members of undivided family acquire co-parcenership rights by birth.
- **Profit Sharing:** All coparceners have equal share in the profits of the business.
- **Management:** The business is managed by the senior most member of the family known as Karta.
- **Liability:** The liability of coparceners is limited to the extent of their share in the business. But the Karta has an unlimited liability.
- **Continuity:** Death of any coparceners does not affect the continuity of business.

11. The main **Advantages/Merits of Joint Hindu Family (JHF) business** are mentioned below

- **Assured Shares in Profits:** Every coparcener is assured of an equal share in the profits.
- **Quick Decision:** The Karta enjoys full freedom in managing the business. **Sharing of Knowledge and Experience:** A JHF business provides opportunity for the young members of

the family to get the benefits of knowledge and experience of the elder members.

- **Limited Liability of Members:** The liability of the coparceners except the Karta is limited to the extent of his share in the business.

- **Continued Existence:** The death or insolvency of any member does not affect the continuity of the business.

- **Tax Benefits:** HUF is regarded as an independent assessee for tax purposes.

12. Following are the **limitations or disadvantages of a Joint Hindu Family business:**

- Limited Resources

- Lack of Motivation

- Scope for Misuse of Power

- Instability

13. The Joint Hindu Family form of business organisation is suitable where the family inherits a running business and the members of the family want to continue that business jointly as a family business.

14. A Joint Hindu Family business is formed as per the provision of Hindu law. It comes into existence on the death of the person who established the business.

15. **Partnership** is an association of two or more persons who pool their financial and managerial resources and agree to carry on a business, and share its profit.

16. Characteristics of partnership form of business organization:

- Two or More Persons

- Contractual Relationship

- Sharing Profits and Business

- Existence of Lawful Business

- Principal Agent Relationship

- Unlimited Liability

- Voluntary Registration

17. Following are the merits or advantages of Partnership business:
    - Easy to Form
    - Availability of Larger Resources
    - Better Decisions
    - Flexibility.
    - Sharing of Risks
    - Keen Interest
    - Benefits of Specialisation
    - Protection of Interest
    - Secrecy
18. A partnership firm also suffers from certain **limitations**. These are as follows:
    - Unlimited Liability
    - Instability
    - Limited Capital
    - Non-transferability of share
    - Possibility of Conflicts
19. **Rights of a partner**:
    - Right of the partner to take part in the day to day management of the firm.
    - Right to be consulted and heard while taking any decision regarding the business.
    - Right of access to books of accounts and call for the copy of the same.
    - Right to share the profits equally or as agreed upon by the partners.
    - Right to get interest on capital contributed by the partners to the firm.   '
    - Right to avail interest on advances paid by the partners for business purposes.
    - Right to the use of partnership properly exclusively for partnership business only not himself.
    - Right to be indemnified in respect of payment made or liabilities incurred or for protecting the firm from losses.

- Right as agent of the firm and implied authority to bind the firm for any act done in carrying the business.
- Right to prevent admission of new partners/ expulsion of existing partner.
- Right to continue unless and otherwise be himself cease to become partner

20. Duties of a partner:
   - To carry on the business to the greatest common advantage
   - To be just and faithful to each other
   - To render true accounts
   - To provide full information
   - To attend diligently to his duties
   - To work without remuneration
   - To indemnify for loss caused by fraud or willful neglect
   - To hold and use partnership properly inclusively for the firm
   - To account for personal profits
   - Not to carry on any competing business
   - To share losses
   - To act within authority
   - Duty to be liable jointly and severally
   - Duty not to assign his interest

21. **Joint Stock Company** is a voluntary association of individuals for profit, having a capital divided into transferable shares. The ownership of which is the condition of membership.

22. The main **characteristics of a Joint stock company** are:
   - Incorporated association
   - Number of Members
   - Artificial legal person
   - Separate Legal Entity
   - Perpetual Existence
   - Common Seal
   - Limited Liability

- Transferable Shares
- Separate Property.
- Delegated Management

23. The following are the **advantages of Joint stock companies**:
    - Large financial resources
    - Limited Liability
    - Professional management
    - Growth and Expansion
    - Large-scale production
    - Transfer of shares

24. The **limitations of Joint Stock Companies**.
    - Difficult to form
    - Excessive government control
    - Delay in policy decisions
    - Conflicts in Interest
    - Concentration of economic power and wealth in few hands
    - Oligarchic management
    - Speculation

25. A joint stock company form of business organisation is found to be suitable where the volume of business is large and huge financial resources are needed.

26. Joint Stock Company can be of various types. The following are the important types of company:

# I. Classification of Companies by Mode of Incorporation

A. **Chartered companies.** These are incorporated under a special charter by a monarch. The East India Company and The Bank of England are examples of chartered incorporated in England.

B. **Statutory Companies.** These companies are incorporated by a Special Act passed by the Central or State legislature. Reserve Bank of India, State Bank of India, Industrial Finance Corporation, Unit Trust of India, State Trading Corporation and Life Insurance Corporation are some of the examples of statutory companies.

C. **Registered or incorporated companies:** These are formed under the Companies Act, 1956 or under the Companies Act passed earlier to this. Such companies come into existence only when they are registered under the Act and a certificate of incorporation has been issued by the Registrar of Companies. This is the most popular mode of incorporating a company. Registered companies may further be divided into three categories of the following:

- **Companies limited by Shares:** These types of companies have a share capital and the liability of each member or the company is limited by the Memorandum to the extent of face value of share subscribed by him.

- **Companies Limited by Guarantee:** These types of companies may or may not have a share capital. Each member promises to pay a fixed sum of money specified in the Memorandum in the event of liquidation of the company for payment of the debts and liabilities of the company.

- **Unlimited Companies:** A company not having any limit on the liability of its members is called an 'unlimited company'. An unlimited company may or may not have a share capital.

## II. On the Basis of Number of Members

A. **Private Company:** A private company can be formed by at least two individuals and the total membership of the company cannot exceed 200 (excluding employees who are members or ex-employees who were and continue to be members). The shares allotted to its members are also not freely transferable between them.

B. **Public company:** A minimum of seven members are required to form a public limited company and there is no restriction of maximum number of members. The shares allotted to the members are freely transferable.

27. **Co-operative society** is a voluntary association of persons who work together to promote their economic interest. It works on the principle of self-help and mutual help. The primary objective is to provide support to the members.

28. **Characteristics of co-operative society form of business organisation :**
    - Voluntary Association
    - Open Membership.
    - Number of Members
    - Equal Voting Rights
    - Registration of the Society
    - State Control
    - Capital
    - Democratic Set Up
    - Service Motive
    - Return on Capital Investment
    - Distribution of Surplus

29. Merits **of co-operative society form of business organisation.**
    - Easy to Form
    - Limited Liability
    - Open Membership
    - State Assistance
    - Stable Life
    - Tax Concession
    - Democratic Management

30. **Co-operative Societies** usually suffer from the following **limitations.**
    - Limited Capital
    - Lack of Managerial Expertise
    - Less Motivation
    - Lack of Interest
    - Corruption

31. Types of Co-operative Society:
    - Consumers' Cooperative Societies
    - Producer's Cooperative Societies
    - Marketing Cooperative Societies

- Housing Cooperative Societies
- Farming Cooperative Societies
- Credit Cooperative Societies

32. **Limited Liability Partnership** is a corporate business vehicle that enables professional expertise and entrepreneurial initiative to combine and operate in flexible, innovative and efficient manner, providing benefits of limited liability while allowing its members the flexibility for organizing their internal structure as a partnership"

33. Following are the **merits of Limited Liability Partnership**:
- Separate legal entity
- No owner/manager distinction
- Flexible agreement.
- Limited liability
- Fewer compliance requirements
- Easy to wind-up

34. A **designated Partner** has been defined as "a partner designated under section 7(23)". The difference lays about designated partners is that whose liability is limited solely to the LLP Agreement and their acts as per "section 27 to 29" of the LLP Act.

## QUESTIONS

1. What do you mean by business organisation?
2. What is Sole proprietorship business?
3. Define Sole proprietorship.
4. What are the characteristics of Sole proprietorship business?
5. What are the merits of Sole proprietorship business?
6. What are the demerits of Sole proprietorship business?
7. State the steps to form a Sole proprietorship business.
8. Write down the concept of Joint Hindu Family business.

9. What are the two systems of inheritance under JHF business?

10. What are the characteristics of JHF business?

11. State the advantages or merits of JHF business.

12. What are the demerits of JHF business?

13. What is Partnership?

14. Define Partnership.

15. What are the characteristics of Partnership business?

16. What are the merits of Partnership business?

17. What are the demerits of Partnership business?

18. What are different types of partners?

19. State the rights of a partner.

20. What are the duties of a partner?

21. What do you mean by Partnership deed? Mention its clauses.

22. What is Joint Stock Company?

23. Define a company.

24. What are the characteristics of a Joint Stock Company?

25. What are the merits of a Joint Stock Company?

26. What are the demerits of a Joint Stock Company?

27. Discuss the different types of company?

28. Differentiate between Public Company and Private Company.

29. State the special privileges available to a company.

30. What do you mean by Cooperative Society?

31. Define Cooperative Society.

32. What are the characteristics of a Cooperative society?

33. State the merits of a Cooperative Society.

34. What are the demerits of a Cooperative Society?

35. What are different types of Cooperative Society? Discuss.

36. Discuss the steps to form a Cooperative Society.

37. Write down the concept of Limited Liability Partnership.

38. Define LLP.

39. What are the features of LLP?

40. What are the merits of LLP?

41. What are the demerits of LLP?

42. Differentiate between LLP and Partnership.

43. Differentiate between LLP and Company.

44. What do you mean by Designated partner?

45. What are the duties of a Designated partner?

46. Differentiate between a Partner and a Designated partner.

47. Discuss the factors to be taken into consideration while forming a suitable form of business organisation.

# UNIT 1B
# FORMS OF PUBLIC ENTERPRISES

Forms of Public Enterprises

International Business – Types

## CONTENTS

# 1. CONCEPT OF PUBLIC ENTERPRISES

A public sector enterprise is an organization owned, managed, controlled, and operated by local, state, or central government to maximize social welfare and uphold public interest. The primary aim of a state enterprise is to provide goods and services to the public at reasonable rates, with profit earning being secondary to social service. Public enterprises include nationalized private sector entities, such as banks and the Life Insurance Corporation of India, as well as new enterprises established by the government, such as Hindustan Machine Tools (HMT), Gas Authority of India (GAIL), and the State Trading Corporation (STC).

# 2. DEFINITIONS OF PUBLIC ENTERPRISES

*"Public enterprises are autonomous or semi-autonomous corporations and companies established, owned and controlled by the state and engaged in industrial and commercial activities"*

**N.N. Mallya**

*" the industrial, commercial and economic activities, carried on by the central or by a state government, and in each case either soley or in association with private enterprise, so long it is managed by self-contained management."*

**S.S. Khera**

*"Public Enterprise means state ownership and operation of industrial, agricultural, financial and commercial undertakings."*

**A.H. Hansen**

# 3. CHARACTERISTICS OF PUBLIC SECTOR ENTERPRISES

The main features or characteristics of public enterprises, also known as state enterprises or public sector undertakings, are as follows:

1. **Government Ownership and Management**: Public sector enterprises are owned, managed, controlled, and operated by local, state, or central governments. The government may wholly own these enterprises or share ownership with private industrialists and the public.

2. **Motive**: Public enterprises are not driven by profit. Their primary focus is on providing services or commodities at reasonable prices.

3. **Financed by Government**: Public enterprises receive their capital from government funds, with the government allocating their capital through its budget.

4. **Financial Independence**: Despite initial government investment, public enterprises become financially independent. They manage their own finances and generate profits, which can be reinvested for expansion and growth, reducing reliance on the government for day-to-day needs.

5. **Public Utility Services**: Public sector enterprises focus on providing essential public utility services such as transport, electricity, and telecommunications.

6. **Public Accountability**: Governed by public policies set by the government, public enterprises are accountable to the legislature.

7. **Monopoly Enterprises**: Public enterprises can operate as monopolies in sectors where private entry is restricted, such as Indian railways, coal mining, and energy.

8. **Excessive Formalities**: Government rules and regulations require public enterprises to follow numerous formalities, making management tasks sensitive and cumbersome.

## 4. FORMS OF PUBLIC SECTOR ENTERPRISES

Public sector undertakings are formed in three different forms

1. Departmental undertaking
2. Public Corporation/ Statutory Corporation
3. Government Company

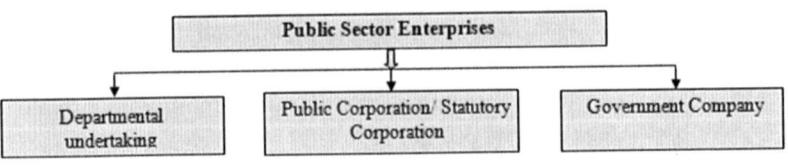

# 5. DEPARTMENTAL UNDERTAKING

Among the various forms of organization, the 'Departmental' form is the oldest and is equivalent to normal government departments in terms of appropriation, parliamentary control, and accountability. A departmental undertaking is organized, managed, and financed by the government, and it is overseen by a specific government department. Each department is led by a minister. This form is commonly used for administering national services such as posts and telegraphs, railways, and defense production units.

## 5.1 Features of Departmental Undertaking

The main features of the departmental form of organization are:

1. A departmental undertaking is established as a separate government department.

2. Each department is headed by a minister responsible for policy making and day-to-day administration.

3. These undertakings are part of the government and do not have a separate legal entity.

4. They are funded by the government through budgetary appropriations.

5. Departments lack financial autonomy, as the government exercises strict financial and budgetary control over them.

6. They follow routine administrative procedures, leaving no room for flexibility in decision-making and other matters.

7. Departments do not have autonomy in personnel matters. Personnel are recruited by the public service commission and are subject to strict government rules and regulations.

8. A department can be sued in the same manner as one would file a suit against the government.

## 5.2 Merits or Advantages of Departmental Undertakings

A departmental undertaking has the following advantages:

1. **Ease of Formation:** Departmental undertakings are easy to establish since no registration is required. They can be created through administrative decisions of the government without any additional legal formalities.

2. **Proper Utilization of Funds:** Financial matters in departmental undertakings are subject to ministerial sanction, budgetary control, accounting, and auditing, ensuring proper utilization of funds.

3. **Fulfillment of Social Objectives:** The government exercises total control over these undertakings, enabling it to fulfill its social and economic objectives effectively.

4. **Accountability:** Departmental undertakings are directly accountable to the parliament, where their performance can be discussed. This ensures public accountability.

5. **Revenue Source for Government:** The revenue generated by departmental undertakings is deposited into the government's treasury, thereby contributing to increased government revenue.

6. **Responsibility to Legislature:** These undertakings are responsible to the public through the parliament, ensuring transparency and accountability in their operations.

7. **Maintenance of Secrecy:** Departmental undertakings can maintain secrecy regarding their internal matters, which is crucial for departments dealing with sensitive areas like defense and atomic energy.

## 5.3 Limitations of Departmental Undertakings

Departmental undertakings have the following limitations:

1. **Influence of Bureaucracy:** Due to government control, departmental undertakings suffer from bureaucratic functioning, characterized by excessive red-tape and administrative complexities.

2. **Excessive Parliamentary Control:** Parliamentary oversight leads to challenges in day-to-day administration, as parliamentarians frequently inquire about the operations of the undertaking.

3. **Lack of Motivation:** Promotions are generally based on seniority rather than performance, resulting in a lack of motivation among employees to perform to their fullest potential.

4. **Lack of Professional Management:** Administrative officers managing departmental undertakings often lack business

experience and expertise, which can lead to inefficient management.

5. **Lack of Flexibility**: Departmental undertakings operate under strict parliamentary control and ministerial interference, limiting their flexibility and efficiency. They are treated similarly to government offices.

6. **Lack of Seriousness Towards Losses**: There is often a tendency to not address losses seriously, with little drastic action taken to improve the financial position of the undertaking. Efficiency standards for improvement are not effectively implemented.

7. **Inefficient Functioning**: These organizations suffer from inefficiencies due to incompetent staff and inadequate incentives to enhance employee efficiency.

# 6. STATUTORY CORPORATION (OR PUBLIC CORPORATION)

The term "Public Corporation" or "Statutory Corporation" refers to a type of public enterprise that is established under special Acts of Parliament or State Legislative Assemblies. It is an autonomous business entity created by law to carry out specific activities or businesses entrusted to it. The management structure, powers and functions, operational scope, rules and regulations for employees, and its relationship with government departments are all defined in the relevant Act. Examples of statutory corporations include the State Bank of India, Life Insurance Corporation of India, and the Industrial Finance Corporation of India. It should be noted that multiple corporations can be established under the same Act. State Electricity Boards and State Financial Corporations also fall into this category.

## 6.1 Features of Statutory Corporation (or Public Corporation)

The main features of the Statutory Corporations are:

1. It is established by a special statute enacted in the Parliament or the State Legislature.

2. It is a distinct legal entity with perpetual succession and a common seal.

3. It is owned by the government and is established for specific purposes.

4. The powers, objectives, and limitations of public corporations are defined exclusively in the Act.

5. The statutes establishing these corporations typically empower a body, often known as the 'Board of Directors,' to act on behalf of the 'Corporation,' subject to the government's authority to issue directives as necessary.

6. It operates as an autonomous body and is independent of government control in its internal management.

7. It is accountable to Parliament or the State legislature for its operations and must submit an annual report on its activities.

8. Employees of public corporations are not necessarily government employees. Their appointment, remuneration, and terms of service are determined by the corporation's rules.

9. The accounts of public corporations are generally audited by the Comptroller and Auditor General (CAG).

## 6.2 Advantages of Statutory Corporation (or Public Corporation)

Statutory Corporation as a form of organisation for public enterprises has certain advantages that can be summarised as follows:

1. **Expert Management**: Public corporations combine the advantages of both departmental and private undertakings. They operate on business principles under the guidance of expert and experienced directors.

2. **Improved Working Efficiency**: Public corporations can offer attractive terms of service and facilities to employees, resulting in greater working efficiency and fewer labor issues.

3. **Internal Autonomy**: These corporations enjoy autonomy in day-to-day management, free from direct government interference. This allows for prompt decision-making without obstacles.

4. **Service Orientation:** The activities of public corporations are scrutinized in parliament, ensuring they prioritize public interest and service.

5. **Accountability to Parliament:** Statutory organizations are accountable to Parliament, with their activities monitored by the press and the public. This ensures a high level of efficiency and accountability.

6. **Flexibility:** With independence in management and finances, public corporations operate with sufficient flexibility. This flexibility supports good performance and operational outcomes.

7. **Easy Access to Loans:** Government-owned public corporations can secure loan capital at relatively lower interest rates, given their advantageous position..

## 6.3 Limitations of Statutory Corporations (or Public Corporation)

The following limitations are observed in statutory corporations.

1. **Government Interference:** While statutory corporations are theoretically independent and flexible, in practice, there is often excessive government interference in most matters.

2. **Inefficiency in Management:** The efficiency of management in a public corporation is typically lower compared to that of a private enterprise. This is because the members of the Board of Directors are usually civil servants who may lack sufficient managerial skills and experience.

3. **Rigidity:** Amendments to the activities and rights of statutory corporations can only be made by Parliament, leading to significant obstacles in adapting to changing conditions and making bold decisions.

4. **Unfair Practices:** The government board of a public corporation may engage in unfair practices, such as charging unduly high prices to compensate for inefficiencies.

5. **Lack of Commercial Approach:** Statutory corporations often face little competition and may lack the motivation to perform well. As a result, they may neglect commercial principles in managing their operations.

# 7. GOVERNMENT COMPANY

The concept of a "Government Company" is a new organizational form widely adopted in India and several European countries for industrial and commercial undertakings. According to Section 2(45) of the Companies Act, 2013, a Government company is defined as "any company in which not less than 51% of the paid-up share capital is held by the Central Government, or by any State Government or Governments, or partly by the Central Government and partly by one or more State Governments, and includes a company which is a subsidiary of such a Government company." Therefore, the key characteristic of a government company is that at least 51% of its paid-up share capital is owned by the Central Government, State Government(s), or a combination thereof.

The popularity of the company form has increased due to its advantages such as easy formation, flexibility in administration, and freedom from governmental interference.

## 7.1 Features of Government Company

The main features of Government companies are as follows:

1. It is incorporated under the Companies Act, 2013.

2. A Government Company is wholly or partly owned by the government. The share capital of these companies is owned by the Government of India in the name of the President.

3. It has a distinct legal entity. It can initiate legal actions and can be sued, and has the ability to acquire property in its own name.

4. It is governed by a Board of Directors. All or a majority of the Directors are appointed by the government, depending on the extent of private participation.

5. Employees appointed by a government company are employees of the company itself and are not necessarily civil servants of the government.

6. Government companies are accountable to the concerned ministry or department.

7. The annual reports of government companies must be presented in parliament.

8. Their accounting and auditing practices are similar to those of private enterprises, and their auditors are Chartered Accountants appointed by the government.

9. Employees of government companies are not civil servants. Personnel policies are regulated according to their articles of association.

## 7.2 Advantages/Merits of Government Company

The merits of government company form of organising a public enterprise are as follows:

1. **Ease of Formation**: Forming a government company is straightforward, as it does not require passing a bill in parliament or the state legislature. It can be established by following the procedures outlined in the Companies Act.

2. **Effective Management**: Since the Annual Report of a government company is presented to both houses of Parliament for discussion, its management exercises caution in conducting activities and ensures efficiency in business operations.

3. **Increased Flexibility**: A government company is managed, financed, and audited like any other private sector company. This allows it to enjoy greater flexibility, operational freedom, and prompt decision-making.

4. **Efficient Business Operations**: Government companies can operate on business principles, being fully independent in financial and administrative matters. Their Board of Directors typically includes professionals and respected independent individuals.

5. **Collaboration**: These companies can benefit from the managerial skills, technical expertise, or know-how of private enterprises through effective collaboration.

6. **Promoting Healthy Competition**: Government companies often provide healthy competition to the private sector, thereby ensuring the availability of goods and services at reasonable prices without compromising quality.

## 7.3 Limitations/Demerits of Government Companies

The government companies suffer from the following limitations:

1. **Autonomy in Theory Only**: The freedom and flexibility theoretically offered to Government Companies exist only on paper. In reality, most functions are under the control of the government.

2. **Lack of Initiative**: Management of government companies often fears public accountability, leading to a lack of initiative in making timely decisions. Additionally, some directors may not actively participate in business decisions due to the fear of public criticism.

3. **Nullification of Separate Legal Existence**: The government's authority under the Indian Companies Act to exempt government companies from certain provisions has undermined their separate legal existence.

4. **Ministerial Interference**: Government companies experience frequent interference from ministers, limiting their independence in operations. Such interference often has detrimental effects.

5. **Lack of Business Experience**: Management of Government Companies typically comprises administrative service officers who may lack experience in managing businesses professionally. Consequently, they often fail to achieve the necessary efficiency levels.

6. **Policy and Management Changes**: The policies and management of these companies frequently change with changes in government. This constant alteration of rules, policies, and procedures creates an unstable business environment.

## 8. RATIONAL OF PUBLIC SECTOR

In a developing country such as India, industrial progress and overall economic growth cannot be accelerated without the active assistance and participation of the state. It is the responsibility of the state to create a favorable environment for industrial investment and employment. The state must provide opportunities for industrial growth, promote trade, and develop essential infrastructure for comprehensive development. The following considerations rationalize the establishment of public sector enterprises:

1. **Need for Planned Economy**: Economic growth needs to be accelerated through economic planning. Public sector enterprises

enable the government to ensure planned development of the economy according to priority areas. This responsibility is too significant to be left solely in the hands of the private sector.

2. **Building Industrial Infrastructure**: Infrastructure such as transportation, communication, power, irrigation, and construction of roads and bridges are fundamental for rapid industrialization and economic growth. Projects related to infrastructure have long gestation periods with lower returns on investment, which are generally unattractive to private sector investors. Hence, state enterprises must take on this responsibility.

3. **Public Utilities**: Essential services like water supply, electricity, gas, and public transportation are crucial for a decent standard of living. The government has the responsibility to provide these services to the public at reasonable prices in the interest of public welfare.

4. **Basic and Heavy Industries:** Industries such as iron and steel, coal, power, cement, fertilizers, and petroleum are essential for industrial development. These industries require massive capital investment, which often exceeds the capacity of private entrepreneurs.

5. **Defence Requirements**: Continuous supply of goods and services for the defence forces is critical for national security. Such strategic supplies cannot be entrusted solely to the private sector.

6. **Development of Backward Regions**: Private entrepreneurs are generally reluctant to establish industries in economically backward regions such as rural or hilly areas due to the lack of profitability in the initial stages. For balanced regional development, the government initiates industrial development in such areas.

7. **Economic Development and Full Employment**: Economic growth and full employment goals can only be achieved through substantial state investment. The government can mobilize resources and invest heavily in employment-generating development programs.

8. **Surplus for Economic Growth:** The surplus generated by public enterprises provides funds to the government for investment in economic growth programs. Taxation alone cannot provide sufficient funds for developmental purposes.

9. **Preventing Economic Power Concentration and Monopolies:** Public sector enterprises act as a counterbalance to the monopolistic tendencies of the private sector and help prevent concentration of income and wealth in the hands of a few individuals. They serve as significant competitors to the private sector.

10. **Socialistic Pattern of Society:** The Constitution of India mandates the achievement of a socialistic pattern of society. To fulfill this objective, the public sector needs to play a substantial role in the economy .

These considerations justify the establishment and active participation of public sector enterprises in the Indian economy.

## 9. INTERNATIONAL BUSINESS

## 9.1 Concept of International Business

International business, also known as foreign trade or international trade, refers to the exchange of goods and services between countries. It involves trade between two or more nations, where goods and services are bought and sold across national boundaries. This exchange occurs when citizens or entities of one nation engage in transactions with those of another nation. For example, India engages in trade with countries such as China, Japan, and France.

International business encompasses both private and government enterprises. These transactions include the transfer of goods, services, technology, managerial knowledge, and capital to other countries. It is also referred to as external trade.

International trade transactions are classified under three categories

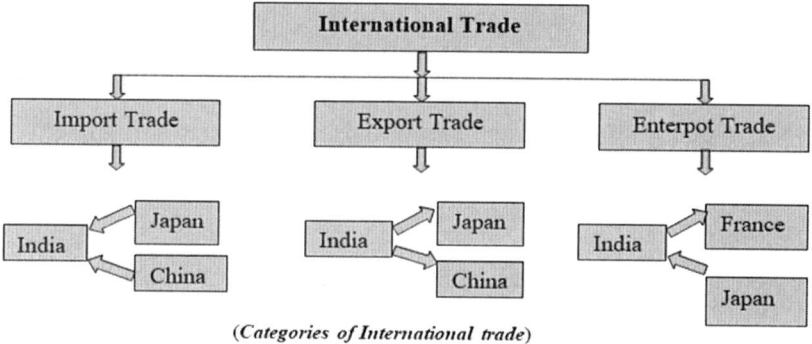

*(Categories of International trade)*

**Import Trade**: It refers to buying goods and services from foreign countries.

**Export Trade**: It refers to selling goods and services to foreign countries.

**Enterpot Trade**: It refers to import of goods and services not for consumption in home country but for exporting them to another country.

## 9.2 Characteristics/Nature of International trade

1. **Trade between two or more countries**: International trade involves the exchange of goods and services between two or more countries, where one country buys goods and services from another country.

2. **Payment in Foreign Currency**: In international trade, payment for imported goods and services is made in foreign currency, and payment for exports is also received in foreign currency.

3. **Legal Procedures**: International trade entails a lengthy and complex documentation procedure. Prior permission from the government is required before exporting or importing goods or services. This involves filling out numerous documents, obtaining customs clearance, converting currency into foreign currency, booking shipping, etc.

4. **Restrictions**: Unlike domestic trade, international trade is subject to restrictions on the movement of specific goods to specified countries.

5. **Risks:** International trade carries higher risks compared to domestic trade. Due to the long distances involved, there is a risk of goods being damaged in transit. There is also the risk of fluctuations in currency conversion rates.

6. **Language:** Language poses a barrier in international trade because different countries speak different languages. Traders must appoint someone who can understand, read, and write in the foreign language.

## 9.3 Differences between Internal trade and International trade/International business

The following are the main points of differences between internal trade and International trade

1. **Meaning:** Internal trade refers to the buying and selling of goods or services within the geographical boundary of a country. International trade, on the other hand, refers to the buying and selling of goods or services beyond the geographical limits of a country.

2. **Countries Involved:** Internal trade involves only one country because goods or services are bought and sold within the country itself. International trade involves at least two countries for the import and export of goods or services.

3. **Payment for Goods or Services:** In internal trade, payment for goods or services is made in domestic currency. In international trade, payment for goods or services is made in foreign currency.

4. **Degree of Risk:** Internal trade is less risky because buying and selling of goods and services is done within the country. In international trade, there is a higher degree of risk because goods are moved from one country to another.

5. **Mode of Payment:** In internal trade, payment is made either in cash or by cheque. In international trade, payment is made through a bill of exchange or through banks.

6. **Legal Rules and Regulations:** In internal trade, national laws, rules, and regulations apply. In international trade, international rules and regulations are applicable.

7. **Cost Involved**: The operating cost of internal trade is lower compared to international trade. The operating cost of international trade is higher due to the involvement of long distances.

8. **Mode of Transport**: Internal trade primarily uses road and railway modes of transport. International trade uses sea transport and air transport.

9. **Alternate Names**: Internal trade is also known as domestic trade. International trade is also known as foreign trade or international business.

## 9.4 Difficulties and Problems in Foreign Trade

Foreign trade is characterized by the following special problems or difficulties.

1. **Distance:** Due to the long distances between different countries, establishing quick and close trade contracts between traders is challenging. Buyers and sellers rarely meet each other, and personal contact is infrequent. There is a significant time lag between placing an order and receiving goods from foreign countries. Distance also increases transportation costs and risks.

2. **Language Differences:** Different languages are spoken and written in different countries. Price lists and catalogues are prepared in foreign languages, and advertisements and correspondence must also be conducted in these languages. Traders wishing to buy or sell goods abroad must either know the foreign language or employ someone who does.

3. **Transportation and Communication Difficulties**: Dispatching and receiving goods takes longer and involves considerable expenses in international trade. During wars and natural calamities, transportation of goods becomes even more difficult and costly. Similarly, the costs of sending or receiving information are very high.

4. **Risks in Transit:** Foreign trade involves much greater risk than domestic trade. Goods have to be transported over long distances and are exposed to perils such as those of the sea. Many of these risks can be covered through marine insurance, but this increases the cost of goods.

5. **Lack of Information about Foreign Businesspeople:** Due to the absence of direct and close relationships between buyers and sellers, special steps are necessary to verify the creditworthiness of foreign buyers. It is difficult to obtain reliable information concerning the financial position and business standing of foreign traders, thereby increasing credit risk.

6. **Import and Export Restrictions:** Every country imposes custom duties on imports to protect its domestic industries. Similarly, tariff rates are imposed on exports of raw materials. Importers and exporters have to navigate these tariff restrictions and fulfill several customs formalities and rules. Foreign trade policies, procedures, rules, and regulations differ from country to country and are subject to frequent changes.

7. **Payment Problems:** Every country has its own currency, and the exchange rate at which one currency can be exchanged for another fluctuates. Changes in exchange rates create additional risk. Remitting money for payments in foreign trade involves significant time and expense. Due to the wide time gap between dispatching goods and receiving payment, there is a greater risk of bad debts.

8. **Frequent Market Changes:** It is difficult to anticipate changes in demand and supply conditions abroad. Prices in international markets may change frequently due to the entry of new competitors, changes in buyers' preferences, and other factors.

## 10. IMPORT PROCEDURE

Following steps are involved in the process of importing goods from abroad:

1. **Import-Export Code Number:** The importer must first apply for an Import-Export Code (IEC) number to the Regional Import-Export Licensing Authority using the prescribed form. If the imported item does not belong to the negative list, the IEC number is sufficient for import.

2. **Obtaining Registration-Cum-Membership Certificate (RCMC):** An RCMC certificate is essential for availing benefits under the Export-Import Policy (EXIM Policy). To obtain this certificate, an application must be submitted to the concerned Commodity

Board or Export-Promotion Council in the prescribed form, along with the import-export code number.

3. **Obtaining Foreign Exchange:** An importer can obtain foreign exchange only from a bank approved by the Reserve Bank of India (RBI). The importer needs to submit the import license along with the prescribed form to secure the required foreign exchange for paying for goods ordered from another country. RBI sanctions foreign exchange to an importer based on the strength of the application, license, and the exchange policy of the Government of India.

4. **Placing an Order or Indent:** After obtaining the import license and arranging for foreign exchange, the importer places an import order or indent with the exporter for the supply of specified products. The import order includes information about the price, quantity, size, grade, and quality of the goods ordered, as well as instructions regarding packing, shipping, ports of shipment and destination, delivery schedule, insurance, and mode of payment. The import order should be carefully drafted to avoid ambiguity and potential conflicts between the importer and exporter.

5. **Sending a Letter of Credit:** Generally, the exporter wants assurance about the importer's creditworthiness. For this purpose, the importer sends a letter of credit as proof of their creditworthiness to the exporter. A letter of credit contains an undertaking by the bank to honor bills of exchange drawn by the exporter on the importer up to the amount specified in the letter of credit.

6. **Procuring Documents:** Upon receiving the letter of credit, the exporter ships the goods and informs the importer that the goods have been dispatched, along with the expected date of arrival in the importer's country.

7. **Receipt of Shipment Advice:** After loading the goods onto the vessel, the overseas supplier sends a shipment advice to the importer. The shipment advice includes details such as the invoice number, bill of lading/airway bill number and date, name of the vessel with date, port of export, description and quantity of goods, and the sailing date of the vessel.

8. **Appointment of Clearing Agent:** After receiving all the necessary papers, the importer appoints a clearing agent who

handles all the formalities regarding the import on behalf of the importer. The clearing agent charges a fee for the services provided.

9. **Clearing of Goods:** Upon arrival at the port, the ship's captain informs the customs authority about the goods. The importer or their agent must visit the shipping company's office to pay any remaining freight charges, if not paid by the exporter. The shipping company issues a delivery order or endorses the bill of lading for delivery. After receiving the delivery order, the importer or their agent obtains three forms of the bill of entry from the customs authorities and provides details of the imported goods, including quantity, weight, number of cases, marks, and price. Goods may be imported as duty-free goods, goods for home consumption, or goods to be kept in a bonded warehouse. Custom duty must be paid before taking delivery of the goods.

10. **Obtaining Delivery of Goods:** After completing the necessary formalities, the importer or their agent presents the delivery order to the dock officer who, if satisfied with the documents, issues a gate pass. The importer presents the bill of lading and takes delivery of the goods, making arrangements for transporting the goods.

11. **Making Payment:** If payment has not been made in advance, the importer will make payment upon presentation of the D/P (Documents against Payment) bill.

# 11. EXPORT PROCEDURE

Following steps are involved in the process of Exporting goods from one country to another country

1. **Receipt of Enquiry and Sending Quotations:** The first step in the export process involves receiving an enquiry from a prospective buyer and sending a quotation in response. The buyer sends an enquiry requesting information on price, quality, and terms for the export of goods. Exporters may also receive such enquiries through advertisements placed by the importer. The exporter responds with a quotation, typically in the form of a proforma

invoice. This document includes details about the price, quality, grade, size, weight, delivery mode, packing type, and payment terms.

2. **Receipt of Order or Indent:** If the prospective buyer agrees to the quotation, they will place an order for the goods, also known as an indent. The indent includes a description of the goods ordered, prices to be paid, delivery terms, packing and marking details, and delivery instructions.

3. **Assessing Importer's Creditworthiness:** Upon receiving the indent, the exporter requests a letter of credit to assess the buyer's creditworthiness. A letter of credit is a guarantee issued by the importer's bank to honour payment up to a specified amount of export bills to the exporter's bank. It is the most secure method of payment for settling international transactions.

4. **Obtaining Export Licence:** Once assured of payments, the exporting firm initiates compliance with export regulations. Export of goods in India is subject to customs laws, requiring exporters to have an export licence. Key prerequisites for obtaining an export licence include:

   - Opening a bank account in an RBI-authorized bank and obtaining an account number.
   - Obtaining an Import Export Code (IEC) number from the Directorate General of Foreign Trade (DGFT) or Regional Import-Export Licensing Authority.
   - Registering with the appropriate Export Promotion Council.
   - Registering with the Export Credit and Guarantee Corporation (ECGC) to protect against non-payment risks.

5. **Obtaining Registration Cum Membership Certificate (RCMC):** Exporters must become members of the appropriate Export Promotion Council and obtain a Registration Cum Membership Certificate (RCMC) to avail benefits from the government. Registration with the ECGC is necessary to safeguard overseas payments from political and commercial risks and to obtain financial assistance from banks and financial institutions.

6. **Obtaining Pre-Shipment Finance:** Once a confirmed order and letter of credit are received, the exporter approaches their bank for pre-shipment finance to begin export production. Pre-

shipment finance covers costs such as raw materials, processing, packing, and transportation to the port of shipment.

7. **Production or Procurement of Goods:** After obtaining pre-shipment finance, the exporter proceeds to produce or procure the goods according to the importer's specifications. This may involve manufacturing the goods or purchasing them from the market.

8. **Pre-Shipment Inspection:** Exporters must ensure that exported goods meet international standards. Quality control is maintained in accordance with export quality regulations and the buyer's specifications. In India, the Quality Control and Inspection Act mandates compulsory quality control and pre-shipment inspection. The Export Inspection Council and its agencies oversee quality assurance and provide inspection certificates.

9. **Obtaining Certificate of Origin:** Some importing countries offer tariff concessions or exemptions to goods originating from specific countries. To avail such benefits, the importer may request a certificate of origin from the exporter. This certificate verifies that the goods were manufactured in the exporting country. It can be obtained from the trade consulate in the exporter's country.

10. **Reservation of Shipping Space:** The exporter applies to a shipping company for, shipping space, specifying the goods types, expected shipment date, and destination port. Upon acceptance, the shipping company issues a shipping order, instructing the ship's captain to receive the specified goods after customs clearance at the designated port.

11. **Packing and Forwarding:** The goods are properly packed and marked with details such as importer's name and address, gross and net weight, port of shipment, destination, and country of origin. The exporter arranges transportation of goods to the port. Once loaded onto a railway wagon, the railway authorities issue a 'railway receipt', which serves as proof of goods title. The exporter endorses the railway receipt to their agent to enable goods delivery at the port of shipment.

12. **Insurance of Goods:** The exporter insures the goods with an insurance company against risks of loss or damage during transit by sea.

13. **Customs Clearance:** Goods cannot be exported without customs permission. Customs authorities ensure:

- Legitimate export or import
- Validation of export or import value
- Duty assessment
- Compliance with regulatory provisions
- Export and import date for compilation

Customs grants permission in a document called the Shipping Bill. After completing formalities, the Customs Preventive Officer at the dock grants shipment permission by endorsing the shipping bill with a 'Let Ship Order'. Once goods are received on the ship, the captain issues a Mate's Receipt to the exporter, confirming shipment.

14. **Excise Clearance:** As per the Central Excise Tariff Act, excise duty applies to materials used in manufacturing goods. The exporter applies to the regional Excise Commissioner with an invoice. If satisfied, the Commissioner may grant excise clearance. The government may exempt or later refund excise duty for export-bound goods to encourage exports and enhance competitiveness. Refunding excise duty is known as duty drawback, managed by the Directorate of Drawback.

15. **Submission of Documents to Customs Appraiser:** Five copies of the shipping bill, along with several documents, are submitted to the Customs Appraiser at the Customs House. Required documents include the export contract or order, letter of credit, commercial invoice, certificate of origin, certificate of inspection (if necessary), and marine insurance policy.

16. **Obtaining Carting Order:** After submitting documents, the exporter approaches the Superintendent of the Port Trust to obtain a carting order. This order instructs port gate staff to allow cargo entry into the dock. The cargo is physically moved into the port area and stored in the appropriate shed. Due to the exporter's inability to attend to these tasks at all times, a Clearing and Forwarding (C&F) agent handles these responsibilities.

17. **Obtaining Mate's Receipt:** Goods are loaded onto the ship, and the ship's captain issues a Mate's Receipt to the port superintendent. This receipt details the vessel's name, berth,

shipment date, package descriptions, marks and numbers, and cargo condition upon receipt aboard the ship. Upon receiving port dues, the port superintendent hands the Mate's Receipt to the C&F agent.

18. **Payment of Freight and Issuance of Bill of Lading:** The C&F agent presents the Mate's Receipt to the shipping company for freight calculation. Once freight is received, the shipping company issues a Bill of Lading, confirming acceptance of goods for carriage to the destination. If goods are sent by air, this document is called an Airway Bill.

19. **Preparation of Invoice:** After dispatching the goods, the exporter prepares an invoice detailing the quantity of goods sent and the amount payable by the importer. The C&F agent has this invoice attested by customs.

20. **Securing Payment: The exporter receives payment for goods in one of three ways:**

- **Documentary Bills of Exchange:** The exporter draws a bill of exchange on the importer and sends it, along with shipping documents, to a bank in the importer's country. The bill may be a D/P (Documents against Payment) or a D/A (Documents against Acceptance) bill. For D/P bills, documents are released upon payment or within a specified period. If the importer defaults, the bank may sell the goods on the exporter's behalf. For D/A bills, the bank hands shipping documents to the importer after bill acceptance.

- **Bank Advances under Hypothecation of Shipping Documents**: The exporter can obtain the shipment's full or partial value by pledging shipping documents with a bank having branches in the importer's and exporter's countries. This arrangement allows for advances against payment collected from the importer.

- **Direct Draft on Bankers:** The exporter's draft on the importer's bank is accepted by the banker. Upon acceptance, the exporter can easily discount the bill.

21. **Advice to the Importer:** After handing over documentary bills to the bank, the exporter writes to the importer, notifying them of goods and title document dispatch. An invoice copy is enclosed with this letter.

# 12. INTERNATIONAL TRADE INSTITUTIONS AND AGREEMENTS

## 12.1 International Monetary Fund (IMF)

The International Monetary Fund (IMF) is a global monetary organization that was established on December 27, 1945. The decision to create the IMF was made during the United Nations Monetary and Financial Conference, held in Bretton Woods, New Hampshire, involving representatives from 45 countries. The IMF's headquarters are located in Washington DC, and it operates under the governance and accountability framework of the governments of its nearly global membership.

The governments participating in the Bretton Woods Conference aimed to establish a framework for economic cooperation that would prevent a recurrence of the devastating economic policies that had contributed to the Great Depression of the 1930s. The IMF was founded with the mandate to promote global economic health, international monetary cooperation, exchange rate stability, and orderly exchange arrangements. Its objectives include fostering economic growth, achieving high levels of employment, and providing financial assistance to countries to facilitate balance of payments adjustments. Currently, the IMF has 189 member countries.

## 12.1.1 Objectives of IMF

Objectives of IMF according to 'Articles of Agreement' provide framework within which the fund function.

a. To promote international monetary cooperation.

b. To ensure exchange rate stability.

c. To ensure balanced international trade.

d. To eliminate or to minimise exchange restrictions by promoting the system of multilateral payments.

e. To grant economic assistance to member countries for eliminating the adverse imbalance in BoP.

f. To minimise imbalance in quantum and duration of international trade.

## 12.1.2 Functions of IMF

The IMF operates in accordance with the objectives outlined in the Bretton Woods Articles of Agreement. It is the IMF's responsibility to ensure that member countries adhere to these provisions.

1. The IMF is considered the guardian of good conduct in the sphere of Balance of Payments (BoP). It aims to reduce tariffs and other trade barriers among member countries.

2. The IMF monitors the policies adopted by member countries. It ensures that no member imposes restrictions on the making of payments, engages in discriminatory currency arrangements, or practices multiple currency practices without IMF approval.

3. The IMF aims to establish a system of stable exchange rates with orderly cross rates. Changes in exchange rates of more than ±1% require IMF permission. However, since 1971, the monetary system has shifted from fixed exchange rates to flexible exchange rates. Under the new system, member countries are not required to maintain and establish par values with gold and the dollar. The IMF does not control the adjustment policies of member countries but provides principles for guiding their exchange rate policies. Surveillance of adjustment policies occurs with all members about once a year.

4. In addition to its regulatory and consultative functions, the IMF acts as a significant financial institution. The majority of its financial resources come from quota subscriptions from member countries. Additionally, it increases its funds by selling gold to its members and borrows from governments, central banks, or private institutions in industrialized countries.

5. IMF lending helps member countries correct their Balance of Payments (BoP) disequilibrium. If a member has less currency with the IMF than its quota, the difference is called a reserve tranche. The member can draw on its reserve tranche automatically upon representation to the fund for its BoP needs. No interest is charged on such drawings, but repayment is required within a period of three to five years.

## 12.2 World Bank

The International Bank for Reconstruction and Development (IBRD), commonly known as the World Bank, was established alongside the IMF at the United Nations Monetary and Financial Conference held in Bretton Woods, New Hampshire in July 1944. It commenced operations in June 1946. The World Bank is an international agency owned by governments and operates through a Board of Governors that provides long-term loans to member countries. While the IMF was designed to provide temporary assistance in correcting Balance of Payments difficulties, there was a need for an institution to support long-term investment purposes. Therefore, the IBRD was created to promote long-term investment loans on reasonable terms.

The World Bank (IBRD) is an inter-governmental institution that operates as a corporate entity, with its capital stock entirely owned by its member governments. Initially, membership in the World Bank was restricted to nations that were members of the IMF; however, this restriction was later relaxed. Currently, the World Bank has 189 member countries. Generally, every member country of the IMF automatically becomes a member of the World Bank. Therefore, any country that withdraws from the IMF is automatically expelled from the World Bank's membership. However, under certain provisions, a country leaving the IMF can maintain its membership with the World Bank if 75% of the bank's members vote in favor of it."

## 12.2.1 Objectives of World Bank

The objectives of World Bank are given below:

1. To help in the reconstruction and development of member countries by facilitating the investment of capital for the productive purposes including the restoration and reconstruction of economies devastated by war.

2. To provide encouragement to the development of productive resources of less developed countries.

3. To promote private foreign investment by means such as participation in loans or guarantees for loans made by private investors.

4. To promote long-term balanced growth of international trade and the maintenance of equilibrium in the BoP of member countries by encouraging long term international investments.

5. To help in raising productivity, standard of living and conditions of labour in member countries.

6. To make arrangement for loans or guarantees in respect of international loans.

## 12.2.2 World Bank's Leading Operations

The World Bank advances loans to member countries in any of the following three ways:

1. **Loans Out of its Own Funds:** The World Bank raises funds through contributions from its member countries and also by issuing bonds to provide loans to countries in need. Loans are given in the member country's national currency or other designated currencies, subject to specific conditions that must be met before the loans are disbursed.

2. **Loans Out of Borrowed Capital:** Sometimes, the World Bank provides loans by borrowing from other member countries. The Bank pays interest to the member country from which it has borrowed funds for a specified period of time.

3. **Loans through Bank's Guarantee:** The World Bank sometimes encourages private investors in one country to lend their funds to another country by guaranteeing the repayment of loans and interest. However, before the Bank provides a guarantee, it must obtain consent from both the country of the private investors and the country to which the loans are proposed to be given.

## 12.3 International Finance Corporation (IFC)

The International Finance Corporation (IFC) is the private sector division of the World Bank group, established in July 1956. It is the primary multilateral organization dedicated to fostering productive private investment in developing countries. The IFC facilitates financing for private sector projects, mobilizing funds from international financial markets, and offers advisory services and technical assistance to businesses and governments.

## 12.3.1 Objectives of IFC

The objectives for which the IFC was set up have been laid down in Article 1 of its Articles of Agreement as under:

"The purpose of the Corporation is to further economic development by encouraging the growth of productive private enterprise in member countries, particularly in the less developed areas, thus supplementing the activities of the International Bank for Reconstruction and Development. In carrying out this purpose, the Corporation shall:

1. In association with private investors, assist in financing the establishment, improvement and expansion of productive private enterprise which would contribute to the development of its member countries by making investments, without guarantee of repayment by the member Government concerned, in cases where sufficient private investment is not available on reasonable terms;

2. Seek to bring together investment opportunities, domestic and foreign private capital, and experienced management; and

3. Seek to stimulate and to help create conditions conducive to the flow of private capital, domestic and foreign, into productive investment in member countries".

IFC is the largest multinational source of loan and equity financing for private sector projects in the developing world. It offers a full array of financial products and services to companies in its developing member countries:

a. Long-term loan in major currencies, at fixed or variable rates.

b. Equity investment.

c. Quasi-equity instruments (subordinated loans, preferred stock, income rates).

d. Guarantees and standby financing.

e. Risk management (intermediation of currency and interest rate, swaps, provision of hedging facilities).

## 12.4 World Trade Organisation (WTO)

The World Trade Organization (WTO) was founded on January 1st, 1995. It is an international organization that sets rules for global trade through consensus among its member states. The WTO also resolves disputes among its members, all of whom are signatories to its trade agreements.

The WTO aims to increase international trade by promoting the reduction of trade barriers and providing a platform for negotiating and resolving trade disputes. It represents the culmination of the Uruguay Round negotiations and is the successor to the General Agreement on Tariffs and Trade (GATT).

## 12.4.1 Objectives of WTO

Objectives of WTO are as follows:

1. To improve standard of living of people in the member countries.
2. To ensure full employment and broad increase in effective demand.
3. To enlarge production and trade of goods.
4. To ensure production and trade of services.
5. To ensure optimum utilisation of world resources.
6. To accept the concept of sustainable development.
7. To protect the environment.

## 12.4.2 Functions of WTO

1. To provide facilities for implementation administration, and operation of multilateral and bilateral agreements of the world trade.
2. To provide a platform to member countries to decide future strategies related to trade and tariff.
3. To administer the rules and processes related to dispute settlement.
4. To implement rules and provisions related to trade policy review mechanism.
5. To assist IMF and IBRD for establishing coherence in universal economic policy determination.
6. To ensure optimum use of world resource.

## 12.5 Multilateral Investment Guarantee Agency (MIGA)

The Multilateral Investment Guarantee Agency (MIGA), a subsidiary of the World Bank, was founded in 1988 with the objective of promoting foreign direct investment in developing countries. MIGA protects investors from non-commercial risks, particularly risks such as war or expropriation. It operates as a partnership between the International Bank for Reconstruction and Development (IBRD) and the International Finance Corporation (IFC). India became a member of MIGA in 1993.

## 12.5.1 Objectives of MIGA

1. To encourage the flow of direct foreign investment into the less developed member countries.

2. To provide insurance cover to investors against political risks.

3. To provide guarantee against non-commercial risks like danger involved in currency transfer, war and civil disturbances etc.

4. To insure new investments, expansion of existing investment, privatisation and financial restructuring.

5. To provide promotional and advisory services.

## SUMMARY OF THE CHAPTER

1. A public sector enterprise is one which is owned, managed, controlled and operated by local or state or central government with a view to maximise social welfare and uphold the public interest.

2. The following are the main features or characteristics of public enterprises or state enterprises or public sector undertakings:

3. The following are the main features or characteristics of public enterprises or state enterprises or public sector undertakings:

   - Government Ownership and Management
   - Motive
   - Financed by Government
   - Financial Independence
   - Public Utility Services
   - Public Accountability
   - Monopoly Enterprises
   - Excessive Formalities

4. Public sector undertakings are formed in three different forms

   - Departmental undertaking
   - Public Corporation/ Statutory Corporation
   - Government Company

5.  A **departmental undertaking** is organised, managed and financed by the Government. It is controlled by a specific department of the government. Each such department is headed by a minister.

6.  The main **features of the departmental form of organisation** are:

    - A departmental undertaking is established as a separate department of the government.
    - A department is headed by a minister who is responsible for policy making and day to day administration.
    - They are a part of government only, there is no separate entity.
    - These undertakings are funded by the government through budgetary appropriations.
    - Departments do not enjoy any financial autonomy, as the government exercises strict financial and budgetary control over them.
    - Department follows routine procedures of administration and this leaves no scope for any flexibility in taking decisions and other matters too.
    - A department can be sued in the same manner as one can file a suit against the government

7.  A **departmental undertaking** has the following **advantages**:

    - Easy to form
    - Proper utilisation of funds
    - Fulfillment of Social Objectives
    - Accountability
    - Provides a source of income to the government
    - Responsible to Legislature
    - Maintenance of secrecy

8.  Departmental undertakings suffer from the following limitations:

    - The Influence of Bureaucracy
    - Excessive Parliamentary Control
    - Lack of motivation

- Lack of Professional Management
- Lack of Flexibility.
- Losses never taken seriously
- Inefficient Functioning

9. The **Public Corporation or Statutory Corporation** refers to that form of public enterprise which is incorporated under the special Acts of the Parliament/State Legislative Assemblies.

10. The main **features of the Statutory Corporations** are:
    - It is created by a special statue passed in the Parliament or the State Legislature.
    - It is a separate legal entity with perpetual succession and a common seal.
    - It is owned by the government and it is established for some specific purpose.
    - The powers, objectives and limitations of public corporations are defined in the Act only.
    - The statutes creating the corporations also vest in a body, usually known as the 'Board of Directors' the powers to act in the name of the 'Corporation' subject to government's right to issue directions from time to time.
    - It is an autonomous body and is free from government control in respect of its internal management.
    - It is accountable to Parliament or State legislature for its operation. It has to submit its annual report on its working.
    - The employees of the public corporation are not necessarily the employees of the government. Their appointment, remuneration, and service conditions are determined by the rules of the corporation itself.
    - The accounts of Public Corporation are generally audited by the Controller of Auditor General.

11. **Advantages of Statutory Corporation**
    - Expert Management
    - Greater working efficiency
    - Internal Autonomy

- Service Motive
- Responsible to Parliament
- Flexibility
- Easy to Raise loans

12. The following limitations are observed in statutory corporations.
   - Government Interference
   - Inefficiency in management
   - Rigidity
   - Unfair Practices
   - Ignoring Commercial Approach

13. A "Government company" is defined under Section 2(45) of the Companies Act, 2013 as "any company in which not less than 51% of the paid-up share capital is held by the Central Government, or by any State Government or Governments, or partly by the Central Government and partly by one or more State Governments, and includes a company which is a subsidiary company of such a Government company".

14. The main features of Government companies are as follows:
   - It is registered under the Companies Act, 2013.
   - The Government Company is wholly or partly owned by the government.
   - It has a separate legal entity.
   - It is managed by the Board of Directors.
   - The employees appointed by the government company are the employees of the company only and they are not necessarily the civil servants of the government.
   - The government companies are accountable to the ministry or the department concerned.
   - The annual reports of the government companies are required to be presented in parliament.
   - Its accounting and audit practices are more like those of private enterprises and its auditors are Chartered Accountants appointed by the government.
   - Its employees are not civil servants.

15. The merits of government company form of organising a public enterprise are as follows:
    - Easy formation
    - Efficient Management
    - Greater Flexibility
    - Efficient Working on Business Lines
    - Collaboration
    - Healthy Competition

16. The government companies suffer from the following limitations:
    - Autonomy on Paper Only.
    - Lack of Initiative
    - Separate Legal existence nullified
    - Ministerial Interference
    - Lack of Business Experience
    - Change in Policies and Management

17. Trade between two or more nations or countries is called **International business or foreign trade** or international trade. It simply refers to the buying and selling of goods and services between two or more countries.

18. **Import Trade**: It refers to buying goods and services from foreign countries.

19. **Export Trade**: It refers to selling goods and services to foreign countries.

20. **Enterpot Trade**: It refers to import of goods and services not for consumption in home country but for exporting them to another country.

21. Characteristics of International Trade:
    - Trade between two or more countries
    - Payment in Foreign Currency
    - Legal Procedures
    - Restrictions
    - Risks
    - Different Language

22. **Differences between Internal trade and International trade/ International business**

- **Meaning:** Internal trade refers to buying and selling of goods or services within the geographical boundary of the country. International trade refers to buying and selling of goods or services beyond the geographical limit of the country.

- **Countries involved:** In case of internal trade only one country involves but International trade involves at least two countries for import and export of goods or services.

- **Payment for goods or services:** In case of internal trade payment for goods or services is made in domestic currency. In international trade payment for goods or services is made in foreign currency.

- **Degree of risk:** Internal trade is less risky as compared to international trade..

- **Mode of payment:** In internal trade payment is made either in cash or cheque. In international trade payment is made through bill of exchange or through banks.

- **Legal rules and regulations:** In internal trade national laws, rules and regulations are applicable. In international trade international rules and regulations are applicable.

- **Cost involved:** Operating cost of internal trade is lower in comparison to international trade. Operating cost of international trade is higher due to involvement of long distance.

- **Mode of transport:** Internal trade uses road, railway mode of transport. International trade uses sea transport and air transport.

- **Alternate names:** Internal trade is also known as domestic trade. International trade is also known as foreign trade or international business.

23. **Foreign trade** is characterized by the following special **problems or difficulties.**

- Distance
- Different languages

- Difficulty in Transportation and Communication
- Risk in Transit
- Lack of Information about Foreign Businessmen
- Import and Export Restrictions
- Problems in Payments
- Frequent Market Changes

24. Following **steps** are involved in the process of importing goods from abroad:
    - Import-Export Code Number
    - Obtaining Registration-Cum-Membership Certificate (RCMC)
    - Obtaining Foreign Exchange
    - Placing an order or Indent
    - Sending letter of credit
    - Procuring Documents
    - Receipt of shipment advice
    - Appointment of Clearing Agent
    - Clearing of goods
    - Obtaining delivery of Goods
    - Making payment

25. Following steps are involved in the process of Exporting goods from one country to another country
    - Receipt of enquiry and sending quotations
    - Receipt of order or indent
    - Assessing importer's creditworthiness
    - Obtaining export license
    - Obtaining Registration cum Membership Certificate (RCMC
    - Obtaining pre-shipment finance
    - Production or procurement of goods
    - Pre-shipment inspection
    - Obtaining certificate of origin

- Reservation of shipping space
- Packing and forwarding
- Insurance of goods
- Customs clearance
- Excise clearance
- Obtaining mates receipt
- Payment of freight and issuance of bill of lading
- Preparation of invoice
- Securing payment

26. The **IMF** is an international monetary organisation, which came into existence in 27th December, 1945. The IMF was established to promote the health of the world economy, international monetary corporation, exchange stability and orderly exchange arrangement to foster economic growth and high levels of employment and to provide financial assistance to countries to ease the Balance of Payment adjustments. Currently IMF has 189 members.

27. Objectives of IMF :
- To promote international monetary cooperation.
- To ensure exchange rate stability.
- To ensure balanced international trade.
- To eliminate or to minimise exchange restrictions by promoting the system of multilateral payments.
- To grant economic assistance to member countries for eliminating the adverse imbalance in BoP.
- To minimise imbalance in quantum and duration of international trade

28. The **International Bank for Reconstruction and Development** (IBRD) known popularly as the **World Bank** was set up at the same time as the IMF at the United Nations Monetary and Financial Conference held at Bretton Woods, New Hampshire

in July, 1944. It began its operation in June, 1946. It is an international agency owned by governments, which operated by Board of Governor making long-term loans to member countries.

29. **Objectives of World Bank**

   - To help in the reconstruction and development of member countries by facilitating the investment of capital for the productive purposes including the restoration and reconstruction of economies devastated by war.
   - To provide encouragement to the development of productive resources of less developed countries.
   - To promote private foreign investment by means such as participation in loans or guarantees for loans made by private investors.
   - To promote long-term balanced growth of international trade and the maintenance of equilibrium in the BoP of member countries by encouraging long term international investments.
   - To help in raising productivity, standard of living and conditions of labour in member countries.
   - To make arrangement for loans or guarantees in respect of international loans.

30. **World Bank's Leading Operations:** The World Bank advances loans to member countries in any of the following three ways:
   - Loans Out of its Own Funds
   - Loans Out of Borrowed Capital
   - Loans through Bank's Guarantee

31. The International Finance Corporation (IFC) is the private sector arm of the World Bank family which was established in July 1956. It is the major multilateral agency promoting productive private investment in developing private investment in developing countries.

32. The World Trade Organisation was established on 1st January, 1995. The World Trade Organisation is an international organisation that establishes rules for international trade through consensus among its member states. It also resolves disputes between the members, which are all signatories to its set of trade agreement.

33. Objectives of WTO are as follows:

- To improve standard of living of people in the member countries.
- To ensure full employment and broad increase in effective demand.
- To enlarge production and trade of goods.
- To ensure production and trade of services.
- To ensure optimum utilisation of world resources.
- To accept the concept of sustainable development.
- To protect the environment.

34. **Functions of WTO**

- To provide facilities for implementation administration, and operation of multilateral and bilateral agreements of the world trade.
- To provide a platform to member countries to decide future strategies related to trade and tariff.
- To administer the rules and processes related to dispute settlement.
- To implement rules and provisions related to trade policy review mechanism.
- To assist IMF and IBRD for establishing coherence in universal economic policy determination.
- To ensure optimum use of world resource

35. The Multilateral Investment Guarantee Agency (MIGA), also an affiliate of the World Bank, was established in 1988 to encourage foreign direct investment in developing countries by protecting investors from non-commercial risks, especially risks of war or repatriation. MIGA is a joint venture of IBRD and IFC. India joined MIGA in 1993.

36. **Objectives of MIGA**

- To encourage the flow of direct foreign investment into the less developed member countries.

- To provide insurance cover to investors against political risks.

- To provide guarantee against non-commercial risks like danger involved in currency transfer, war and civil disturbances etc.

- To insure new investments, expansion of existing investment, privatisation and financial restructuring.

- To provide promotional and advisory services

# QUESTIONS

1. Write down the concept of Public enterprises.

2. Define Public enterprise.

3. What are the characteristics of a public sector enterprise?

4. What are different forms of Public enterprise?

5. What do you mean by Departmental undertaking?

6. What are the characteristics of Departmental undertaking?

7. What are the merits of Departmental undertaking?

8. What are the demerits of Departmental undertaking?

9. What do you mean by Public Corporations?

10. What are the features of Public Corporations?

11. What are the merits of Public Corporations?

12. What are the demerits of Public Corporations?

13. Write down the meaning of Government Company.

14. What are the characteristics of a Government Company?

15. What are the merits of a Government Company?

16. What are the demerits of a Government Company?

17. Discuss the rational of Public sector enterprises.

18. What is International business?

19. What are the characteristics of International business?

20. Distinguish between Internal trade and External trade.

21. Discuss the difficulties faced in International trade.

22. Discuss the steps of Importing.

23. Discuss the procedures of exporting.

24. What are the objectives and functions of IMF?

25. State the objectives and functions of World Bank.

26. What is World Trade Organisation? What are its objectives and functions?

27. Write short notes on:

1. IMF          2. World Bank

3. IFC          4. WTO          5. MIGA

# UNIT II
# MANAGEMENT AND ORGANISATION

The Process of Management:

Planning

Organizing:

Decision-making;

Policy and Strategy Formulation

Departmentation – Functional, Project, Matrix and Network.

**CONTENTS**

1. Concept Of Management
2. Definitions Of Management
3. Characteristics Of Management
4. Significance Of Management
5. Management Functions /Process Of Management
6. Principles Of Management

# UNIT 2A
# BASICS OF MANAGEMENT

## 1. CONCEPT OF MANAGEMENT

Management can be broken down as 'manage-men-tactfully,' meaning it involves managing people tactfully to accomplish tasks. In essence, management is the art of achieving objectives through others. Modern definitions of management describe it as the process of creating an internal environment within an organization where individuals working in groups can perform efficiently and effectively toward collective goals. Management influences behavior by affecting how people perceive and execute their work, integrating human and non-human resources into a cohesive, effective unit.

Management can be understood in three distinct contexts: as a discipline, as a group of people, and as a process.

1. **Management as a Discipline**: This refers to a field of study with well-defined concepts and principles. As a discipline, management encompasses various relevant concepts and principles that aid in the effective administration of resources. Thus, management as a discipline can be defined as "the branch of knowledge concerned with the study of principles and practices of basic administration." It prescribes a code of conduct for managers and various methods for managing resources efficiently.

2. **Management as a Group of People**: This concept highlights the working relationship between management and labor within an organization. It divides people into two groups: those responsible for managerial functions and non-managerial

personnel. Therefore, management as a group of people can be defined as "the working relationship between managerial and non-managerial personnel in an organization."

3. **Management as a Process**: In this context, management involves various interrelated functions—planning, organizing, staffing, directing, coordinating, and controlling—that are performed to achieve the organization's goals. Hence, management as a process can be defined as "a series of interrelated functions that help achieve organizational goals efficiently."

## 2. DEFINITIONS OF MANAGEMENT

"Management is the art of knowing exactly, what you want your men to do and then seeing that they do it in the best and cheapest way"

*F.W.Taylor*

*"Management is the art of getting things done through and with people in formally organized groups"*

*Koontz*

"Management is a distinct process consisting of planning, organizing, actuating and controlling; utilizing in each both science and art, and followed in order to accomplish pre-determined objectives."

*George R. Terry*

"Management is a multipurpose organ that manage a business and manages managers and manages workers and work"

*Peter Fredinand Drucker*

"Management is the art of getting things done through people"

*Mary Parker Follett*

"Management is defined for conceptual, theoretical, and analytical purposes as that process by which managers create, direct, maintain, and operate purposive organizations through systematic, coordinated, cooperative human efforts."

*McFarland*

"Management is simply the process of decision making and control over the action of human beings for the expressed purpose of attaining pre-determined goals."

*Stanley Vance*

# 3. CHARACTERISTICS OF MANAGEMENT

An analysis of the definitions of management indicates that the management has the following characteristics:

1. **Management is an Activity:** Management involves the organized and efficient use of resources such as materials, money, and people within an organization.

2. **It is a Purposeful Activity:** Management focuses on achieving objectives through functions like planning, organizing, staffing, directing, and controlling. These objectives can be explicit or implicit.

3. **Group Efforts:** According to Appleby, management is about managing people, not just directing things. It inspires and motivates workers to maximize their efforts.

4. **Management is Getting Things Done:** Koontz and O'Donnell define management as the art of accomplishing tasks through and with people in formally organized groups. Managers delegate operating work to others rather than doing it themselves.

5. **Application of Economic Principles:** Dr. Kimball describes management as the art of applying economic principles to control men and materials within an enterprise.

6. **Involves Decision-Making:** Management is fundamentally about making decisions related to various aspects of an organization. Every management function involves decision-making.

7. **Coordination of All Activities:** Management coordinates all activities and resources through its functions to achieve the stated objectives.

8. **Universal Activity:** Management principles are applied universally, regardless of the enterprise or organizational

structure. Techniques and tools of management are widely applicable.

9. **Integrating Process:** Management integrates people, machines, and materials to carry out operations and achieve objectives. It is responsible for unifying men, methods, and machinery into a single working force.

10. **Direction and Control:** Management involves directing and controlling various activities to meet business objectives, particularly focusing on human effort.

11. **Intangible Nature:** Management is abstract and not visible, evidenced by organizational quality and outcomes like increased productivity and morale.

12. **Both a Science and an Art:** Management has established principles and laws (science) and involves applying knowledge to solve organizational problems (art).

13. **Management as a Profession:** Management is evolving into a profession with established principles being applied in practice.

14. **Interdisciplinary Approach:** Management draws on other social sciences like psychology, sociology, anthropology, engineering, economics, and mathematics.

15. **Economic Resource:** Management is one of the five factors of production (land, labor, capital, management, entrepreneur). It transforms resources into productive processes, acting as a catalyst for maximizing results.

16. **System of Authority:** Management involves directing tasks and wielding authority to get work done, inherent in the concept of management.

17. **Dynamic, Not Static:** Management adapts to social changes and introduces innovations in methodology.

## 4. SIGNIFICANCE OF MANAGEMENT

Management focuses on achieving maximum prosperity with minimal effort and is essential wherever group efforts are needed to achieve common goals. In today's management-conscious era, its significance cannot be overstated. As Koontz and O'Donnell observed, "There is no more important area of human activity than management since its task is getting things done through others." The importance of management in business activities is particularly pronounced. Labor, capital, and raw materials only become productive with the catalyst of management. It is widely recognized that management is crucial for the growth of any country. The following points further highlight its significance:

1. **Achievement of Group Goals**: Management enhances group efforts, creating teamwork and team spirit within an organization. It brings together human and material resources and motivates people to achieve organizational goals through a sound organizational structure.

2. **Optimal Utilization of Resources**: Management focuses on achieving the enterprise's objectives by utilizing resources efficiently, minimizing wastage and inefficiencies.

3. **Minimization of Costs**: In today's competitive environment, businesses must minimize production and distribution costs to survive. Management principles help in implementing techniques such as production control, budgetary control, cost control, financial control, and material control to reduce costs.

4. **Adaptation and Growth**: Businesses operate in ever-changing environments that present both risks and opportunities. Effective management helps enterprises adapt to changes and even influence their environment to ensure success. Many large corporations today started small and grew through effective management.

5. **Efficient and Smooth Operations**: Management ensures the efficient and smooth operation of businesses through better planning, sound organization, and effective control of production factors.

6. **Higher Profits**: Management increases profits by reducing costs, thus providing opportunities for future growth and development, as increasing sales revenue is often beyond the control of an enterprise.

7. **Innovation**: Management brings new ideas, imagination, and visions to an enterprise, fostering innovation.

8. **Social Benefits**: Management benefits society by improving the standard of living through higher production and efficient use of resources. It promotes peace and prosperity by fostering good relationships between different social groups.

9. **Importance for Developing Countries**: In developing countries, management plays a crucial role due to low productivity and limited resources. It is often said, "There are no under-developed countries, only under-managed ones."

10. **Sound Organizational Structure**: Management establishes a proper organizational structure, reducing conflicts between superiors and subordinates, fostering cooperation, mutual understanding, and a congenial working environment.

## 5. MANAGEMENT FUNCTIONS / PROCESS OF MANAGEMENT

There is enough disagreement among management writers on the classification of managerial functions. Newman and Summer recognize only four functions, namely, organizing, planning, leading and controlling. Henri Fayol identifies five functions of management, viz. planning, organizing, commanding, coordinating and controlling. Luther Gulick states seven such functions under the catch word "POSDCORB' which stands for planning, organizing, staffing, directing, coordinating, reporting and budgeting. Warren Haynes and Joseph Massie classify management functions into decision-making, organizing, staffing, planning, controlling, communicating and directing. Koontz and O'Donnell divide these functions into planning organizing, staffing, directing and controlling. For our purpose, we shall designate the following six as the functions of a manager: planning, organizing, staffing, directing, coordinating and controlling.

1. **Planning:** Planning is the most fundamental and the most pervasive of all management functions. If people working in groups have to perform effectively, they should know in advance what is to be done, what activities they have to perform in order to do what is to be done, and when it is to be done. Planning is concerned with 'what', 'how, and 'when' of performance. It is deciding in the present about the future objectives and the courses of action for their achievement.

It thus invo lves:

   (a) Determination of long and short-range objectives;

   (b) Development of strategies and courses of actions to be followed for the achievement of these objectives; and

(c) Formulation of policies, procedures, and rules, etc., for the implementation of strategies, and plans.

The organizational objectives are set by top management in the context of its basic purpose and mission, environmental factors, business forecasts, and available and potential resources. These objectives are both long-range as well as short-range. They are divided into divisional, departmental, sectional and individual objectives or goals. This is followed by the development of strategies and courses of action to be followed at various levels of management and in various segments of the organization. Policies, procedures and rules provide the framework of decision making, and the method and order for the making and implementation of these decisions. Every manager performs all these planning functions, or contributes to their performance. In some organizations, particularly those which are traditionally managed and the small ones, planning are often not done deliberately and systematically but it is still done. The plans may be in the minds of their managers rather than explicitly and precisely spelt out: they may be fuzzy rather than clear but they are always there. Planning is thus the most basic function of management. It is performed in all kinds of organizations by all managers at all levels of hierarchy.

2. **Organizing:** Organizing involves identification of activities required for the achievement of enterprise objectives and implementation of plans; grouping of activities into jobs; assignment of these jobs and activities to departments and individuals; delegation of responsibility and authority for performance, and provision for vertical and horizontal coordination of activities. Every manager has to decide what activities have to be undertaken in his department or section for the achievement of the goals entrusted to him. Having identified the activities, he has to group identical or similar activities in order to make jobs, assign these jobs or groups of activities to his subordinates, delegate authority to them so as to enable them to make decisions and initiate action for undertaking these activities, and provide for coordination between himself and his subordinates, and among his subordinates. Organizing thus involves the following sub-functions:

(a) Identification of activities required for the achievement of objectives and implementation of plans.

(b) Grouping the activities so as to create self-contained jobs.

(c) Assignment of jobs to employees.

(d) Delegation of authority so as to enable them to perform their jobs and to command the resources needed for their performance.

(e) Establishment of a network of coordinating relationships.

Organizing process results in a structure of the organization. It comprises organizational positions, accompanying tasks and responsibilities, and a network of roles and authority-responsibility relationships. Organizing is thus the basic process of combining and integrating human, physical and financial resources in productive interrelationships for the achievement of enterprise objectives. It aims at combining employees and interrelated tasks in an orderly manner so that organizational work is performed in a coordinated manner, and all efforts and activities pull together in the direction of organizational goals.

3. **Staffing:** Staffing is a continuous and vital function of management. After the objectives have been determined, strategies, policies, programmes, procedures and rules formulated for their achievement, activities for the implementation of strategies, policies, programmes, etc. identified and grouped into jobs, the next logical step in the management process is to procure suitable personnel for manning the jobs. Since the efficiency and effectiveness of an organization significantly depends on the quality of its personnel and since it is one of the primary functions of management to achieve qualified and trained people to fill various positions, staffing has been recognized as a distinct function of management. It comprises several sub functions:

(a) Manpower planning involving determination of the number and the kind of personnel required.

(b) Recruitment for attracting adequate number of potential employees to seek jobs in the enterprise.

(c) Selection of the most suitable persons for the jobs under consideration.

(d) Placement, induction and orientation.

(e) Transfers, promotions, termination and layoff.

(f) Training and development of employees.

As the importance of human factor in organizational effectiveness is being increasingly recognized, staffing is gaining acceptance as a distinct function of management. It need hardly any emphasize that no organization can ever be better than its people, and managers must perform the staffing function with as much concern as any other function.

4. **Directing:** Directing is the function of leading the employees to perform efficiently, and contribute their optimum to the achievement of organizational objectives. Jobs assigned to subordinates have to be explained and clarified, they have to be provided guidance in job performance and they are to be motivated to contribute their optimum performance with zeal and enthusiasm. The function of directing thus involves the following sub-functions:

(a) Communication

(b) Motivation

(c) Leadership

5. **Coordination:** Coordinating is the function of establishing such relationships among various parts of the organization that they altogether pull in the direction of organizational objectives. It is thus the process of tying together all the organizational decisions, operations, activities and efforts so as to achieve unity of action for the accomplishment of organizational objectives. The significance of the coordinating process has been aptly highlighted by Mary Parker Follet. The manager, in her view, should ensure that he has an organization "with all its parts coordinated, so moving together in their closely knit and adjusting activities, so linking, interlocking and interrelation, that they make a working unit, which is not a congeries of separate pieces, but what I have called a functional whole or

integrative unity". Coordination, as a management function, involves the following sub-functions:

(a) Clear definition of authority-responsibility relationships

(b) Unity of direction

(c) Unity of command

(d) Effective communication

(e) Effective leadership

6. **Controlling:** Controlling is the function of ensuring that the divisional, departmental, sectional and individual performances are consistent with the predetermined objectives and goals. Deviations from objectives and plans have to be identified and investigated, and correction action taken. Deviations from plans and objectives provide feedback to managers, and all other management processes including planning, organizing, staffing, directing and coordinating are continuously reviewed and modified, where necessary.

Controlling implies that objectives, goals and standards of performance exist and are known to employees and their superiors. It also implies a flexible and dynamic organization which will permit changes in objectives, plans, programmes, strategies, policies, organizational design, staffing policies and practices, leadership style, communication system, etc., for it is not uncommon that employees failure to achieve predetermined standards is due to defects or shortcomings in any one or more of the above dimensions of management. Thus, controlling involves the following process:

(a) Measurement of performance against predetermined goals.

(b) Identification of deviations from these goals.

(c) Corrective action to rectify deviations.

It may be pointed out that although management functions have been discussed in a particular sequence-planning, organizing, staffing, directing, coordinating and controlling – they are not performed in a sequential order. Management is an integral process and it is difficult to put its functions neatly in separate boxes. Management functions tend to coalesce, and it sometimes becomes difficult to separate one from the other. For example, when a production manager is discussing work problems with one of his subordinates, it is difficult to say whether he is guiding, developing or communicating, or doing all these things simultaneously. Moreover, managers often perform more than one function simultaneously.

## 7. PRINCIPLES OF MANAGEMENT

Henry Fayol, an industrialist and mining engineer, sought to identify sound management principles. Drawing from his extensive experience, Fayol authored the book "General and Industrial Administration" and is recognized as the father of general management. Based on his practical insights, he outlined and explained fourteen principles of management:

1. **Division of Work**: This principle applies to both managerial and technical work. It suggests that tasks should be divided into smaller sub-tasks and assigned to individuals based on their abilities and aptitudes. Specialization enhances efficiency, as repeated performance of the same job leads to proficiency. However, excessive specialization can result in monotony and loss of craftsmanship.

2. **Authority and Responsibility**: Authority refers to the right to give orders and expect obedience, while responsibility means the obligation to perform assigned tasks. Fayol emphasized a balance between the two. Authority without responsibility can lead to misuse, so sufficient authority should be delegated to enable effective duty discharge.

3. **Discipline**: In management, discipline means obedience, adherence to rules, respect for authority, and proper conduct. Discipline is essential for smooth operations and requires good leadership at all levels, clear agreements, and fair enforcement of penalties. It is necessary for both workers and management to ensure efficiency and harmonious relations.

4. **Unity of Command**: This principle states that a subordinate should receive orders from one boss only. Clear instructions from a single superior prevent confusion and enhance

performance. Violating this principle can undermine authority, disturb discipline, and create conflicts.

5. **Unity of Direction:** All activities aimed at the same objectives should be directed by one manager with one plan. This ensures better coordination and effective management. Unity of direction is necessary for organizational efficiency, while unity of command ensures clear accountability.

6. **Subordination of Individual Interest to General Interest:** The organization's interests should take precedence over individual interests in case of conflict. Both employees and management should align their interests with the organization's goals to ensure overall success.

7. **Remuneration of Employees:** Fayol advocated fair and reasonable remuneration to maximize satisfaction for both employees and employers. Wages should consider the work done, cost of living, the business's financial position, and industry standards. This principle fosters good relations between workers and management.

8. **Centralization and Decentralization:** Centralization involves concentrating authority in a few hands, while decentralization disperses it. Fayol suggested a balance between the two, with greater centralization in smaller organizations and more decentralization in larger ones.

9. **Scalar Chain:** Fayol defines the scalar chain as a hierarchy extending from top management to the lowest rank. It functions both as a chain of command and as a channel of communication. According to this principle, authority and communication flow in a straight line from the highest authority to the lowest subordinate. This chain is essential for issuing orders and instructions, which pass through intermediate managers before reaching the lower levels. Likewise, reports on achieved results are transmitted from lower levels up to higher management. As a communication chain, it mandates that all written and oral communication, whether moving upward or downward, must follow the established hierarchy. This principle ensures a smooth flow of communication within the organization, eliminating communication gaps and reinforcing unity of command.

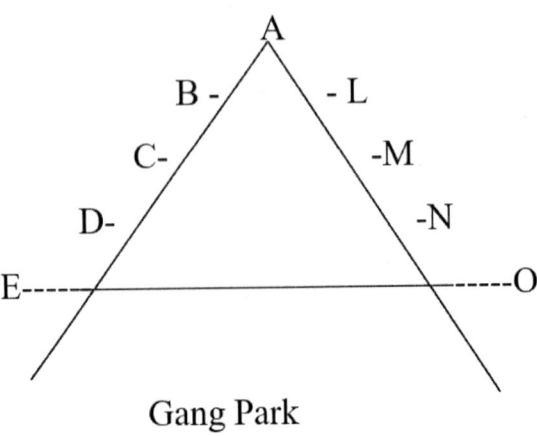

Gang Park

*Scalar Chain and Gang Plank*

Consider a situation where a head, 'A,' oversees two lines of authority. The first line includes B-C-D-E, and the second line includes L-M-N-O. If E needs to communicate with O, who is at the same level of authority, the standard route would be E-D-C-B-A-L-M-N-O. However, in an emergency, E can contact O directly through a Gang Plank, a shortcut designed to prevent communication delays. This concept of the Gang Plank illustrates that Fayol's management principles are not rigid rules but flexible guidelines that can be adapted to specific situations.

10. **Order:** The principle of order applies to both materials and personnel. The arrangement of things is known as material order, and the placement of personnel is called social or personnel order. Material order means "a right place for everything and everything in its right place."

11. **Equity:** According to this principle, managers should be fair and impartial when dealing with subordinates, avoiding favoritism and bias. The principle of equity implies that employees in similar positions should receive similar treatment without discrimination based on sex, religion, caste, creed, or color. Equity also requires kindness and justice in managers' behavior towards workers, though it does not exclude forcefulness or sternness when necessary.

12. **Stability of Tenure:** This principle suggests that employees should not be frequently removed from their positions.

Management should eliminate job insecurity among personnel by fixing reasonable periods of service in each position and allowing employees time to show results. Frequent transfers, shifts, or promotions can adversely affect performance. Minimizing employee turnover enhances organizational efficiency and job security, leading to higher employee efficiency and maximum contribution.

13. **Initiative:** Initiative means giving employees the freedom to propose and implement ideas, plans, or new techniques. Fayol advocated for encouraging employees to develop and carry out improvement plans. Managers should foster a sense of initiative within employees, allowing them to take action and make decisions within the limits of authority and discipline. This principle promotes a sense of belonging and satisfaction among employees.

14. **Esprit De Corps:** Esprit de corps means "Union is Strength." It refers to the spirit of loyalty and devotion that unites group members. The strength of a business enterprise lies in the cooperation and harmony of its workers. The principle suggests replacing "Divide and Rule" with "Union is Strength," emphasizing teamwork and collective effort.

## SUMMARY OF THE CHAPTER

1. **Management** is a distinct process consisting of planning, organizing, actuating and controlling; utilizing in each both science and art, and followed in order to accomplish pre-determined objectives.

2. **Management as a discipline** can be defined as "that branch of knowledge which is connected to study of principles and practices of basic administration."

3. **Management as a group** of people can be defined as "working relationship between managerial and non-managerial personnel in an organization."

4. **Management as a process** can be defined as "Series of inter-related functions of management that helps to achieve the goal efficiently."

5. **Characteristics of Management:**
   - Management is an activity
   - It is a purposeful activity
   - Group Efforts
   - Management is getting things done.
   - It applies economic principles
   - Involves decision-making
   - Coordination of all activities
   - Universal activity
   - Integrating process
   - Direction and Control.
   - It is intangible
   - Management is both a science and an art
   - Management is a profession
   - It is an interdisciplinary approach
   - Management is an economic resource
   - Management is a system of authority
   - Management is dynamic, not static

6. **Significance of management:**
   - Achievements of group goals
   - Optimum utilization of resources
   - Minimisation of cost
   - Change and growth
   - Efficient and smooth running of business
   - Higher profits
   - Provide innovation
   - Social benefits

- Useful for developing countries
- Sound organization structure

7. **Luther Gulick** states seven such functions under the catch word **"POSDCORB'** which stands for planning, organizing, staffing, directing, coordinating, reporting and budgeting.

8. **Planning** is concerned with 'what', 'how, and 'when' of performance.

9. **Organizing** involves identification of activities required for the achievement of enterprise objectives and implementation of plans; grouping of activities into jobs; assignment of these jobs and activities to departments and individuals; delegation of responsibility and authority for performance, and provision for vertical and horizontal coordination of activities.

10. **Staffing** has been recognized as a distinct function of management. It comprises several sub functions:

   - Manpower planning involving determination of the number and the kind of personnel required.

   - Recruitment for attracting adequate number of potential employees to seek jobs in the enterprise.

   - Selection of the most suitable persons for the jobs under consideration.

   - Placement, induction and orientation.

   - Transfers, promotions, termination and layoff.

   - Training and development of employees.

11. **Directing** is the function of leading the employees to perform efficiently, and contribute their optimum to the achievement of organizational objectives.

12. **Coordinating** is the function of establishing such relationships among various parts of the organization that they altogether pull in the direction of organizational objectives. It is thus the process of tying together all the organizational decisions, operations, activities and efforts so as to achieve unity of action for the accomplishment of organizational objectives.

13. **Controlling** is the function of ensuring that the divisional, departmental, sectional and individual performances are consistent with the predetermined objectives and goals. Deviations from objectives and plans have to be identified and investigated, and correction action taken.

14. **Henry Fayol** wrote a book entitled **General and Industrial Administration**. He is known as the **father of general management.**

15. **Henry Fayol** listed and explained fourteen principles of management which are as under:

- Division of work
- Authority and Responsibility
- Discipline
- Unity of Command
- Unity of Direction
- Subordination of Individual Interest to General Interest
- Remuneration of Employees
- Centralisation and Decentralisation
- Scalar Chain
- Order
- Equity
- Stability of Tenure
- Initiative
- Esprit De Corps

# QUESTIONS

1. Write down the meaning of management.
2. Define management.

3. Write a brief note on:
   a. Management as a discipline
   b. Management as a group of people.
   c. Management as a process.
4. What are the characteristics of management?
5. What is scalar chain?
6. Discuss the staffing function of management.
7. Write a brief note on Coordinating function of management.
8. Write short notes on Directing.
9. Discuss the significance of management.
10. Explain the different functions of management.
11. Discuss the 14 principles of management given by Henry Fayol.

# UNIT 2B
# PLANNING

## CONTENTS

# 1. CONCEPT OF PLANNING

Planning is the primary function of management. It involves determining a future course of action to achieve a desired outcome. Essentially, planning is the process of thinking before doing. It is an intellectual exercise involving the anticipation of future scenarios and the consideration of possible alternatives to decide the best course of action. In simple terms, planning entails deciding in advance what needs to be done, how it should be done, where it will take place, when it should occur, and who will be responsible for it. Planning bridges the gap between our current position and where we aim to be.

*Concept of Planning*

Planning as a process involves determining the future course of action, including what is to be done, how it is to be done, where it will take place, when it should occur, and who will be responsible for it. In planning, a manager utilizes facts, reasonable assumptions, and constraints to visualize and formulate the necessary activities. This includes determining how these activities will be conducted and assessing their contribution to achieving the desired results.

# 2. DEFINITIONS OF PLANNING

"Planning is the selection and relating of facts and making and using of assumptions regarding the future in the visualization and formalization of proposed activities believed necessary to achieve desired result."

*George R. Terry*

"Planning may be broadly defined as a concept of executive action that embodies the skills of anticipating, influencing, and controlling the nature and direction of change"

*McFarland*

"Planning is thinking process, the organized foresight, the vision based on facts and experience that is required for intelligent action."

*Alfred and Beatty*

"Planning is essentially decision-making since it involves choosing from among alternatives."

*Koontz and O'Donnell*

"Planning is deciding the best alternative to perform different managerial operations for achieving pre-determined goals."

*Henry Fayol*

"Planning is a continuous process of making present entrepreneurial decisions systematically."

*Peter Fredinand Drucker*

# 3. CHARACTERISTICS OF PLANNING

Following are the features of planning:

1.  **Thinking Process**: Planning involves thinking ahead. It is the process of considering and deciding on what, why, how, when, where, and by whom tasks will be performed before the actual work begins.

2. **Focus on Achieving Goals**: Planning specifies future objectives and outlines the necessary activities to achieve them. By setting these objectives, planning provides direction and purpose to activities.

3. **Primary Function**: Planning is the foundational function of management. It precedes other functions such as organizing, staffing, directing, and controlling. Without planning, none of these functions can be effectively performed.

4. **Selective in Nature**: Planning involves selecting the best course of action from various alternatives to achieve predetermined goals. It considers factors like time, money, and effort to choose the most efficient option.

5. **Continuous Process**: Planning is ongoing and never-ending. It begins with the establishment of an organization and continues as long as the organization exists.

6. **Pervasive Function**: Planning is required in every managerial function and at every level of the organization, making it a universal activity.

7. **Flexible**: Planning is adaptable, as it must respond to dynamic future conditions. This flexibility allows for adjustments based on changing circumstances.

## 4. OBJECTIVES OF PLANNING

Planning keeps the organization on the right path. Following are the main objectives of planning:

1. **Economic Operations:** Planning activities help to reduce inefficiencies and wastage, thereby promoting economy in operations. The primary objective of planning is to execute business activities in the most cost-effective and efficient manner possible. It prevents incorrect actions and reduces the frequency of failures.

2. **Providing Direction for Action:** By specifying in advance how work is to be done, planning provides clear direction for action. When goals are well-defined, employees understand what the organization needs to achieve and what they must

do to contribute to these goals. Without planning, employees might work in different directions, making it difficult for the organization to achieve its desired objectives.

3. **Reducing Overlapping and Wasteful Activities:** Planning ensures clarity in both thought and action, facilitating smooth and uninterrupted work. It minimizes or eliminates useless and wasteful activities. Through planning, inefficiencies can be more easily identified, allowing corrective measures to be taken to address them.

4. **Promoting Innovative Ideas:** Planning involves thinking ahead, creating opportunities to develop better ideas, methods, and procedures to achieve enterprise objectives and goals. This encourages managers to consider the future of the organization differently from the present, fostering innovation and creativity.

5. **Establishing Standards for Control:** Planning provides standards against which actual performance can be measured and evaluated. It helps to identify deviations from these standards and enables corrective actions to be taken promptly.

*'Controlling is blind without planning'*

Thus, planning is the basis or pre-requisite of controlling.

## 5. PROCESS OF PLANNING

Any logical and scientific planning must go through the following steps:

1. **Determination of Enterprise Objectives:** The first step in the planning process involves determining the objectives of the enterprise. Planning begins with setting objectives because all policies, procedures, and methods are designed to achieve these objectives. Objectives define the end results, where emphasis should be placed, and what needs to be accomplished. Therefore, objectives are fundamental to the planning process.

2. **Developing Planning Assumptions:** Planning premises are assumptions on which plans are based. These assumptions take the form of forecasts about factors such as demand for specific products, government policies, interest rates, tax rates, etc. Accurate forecasts are essential for the success of plans.

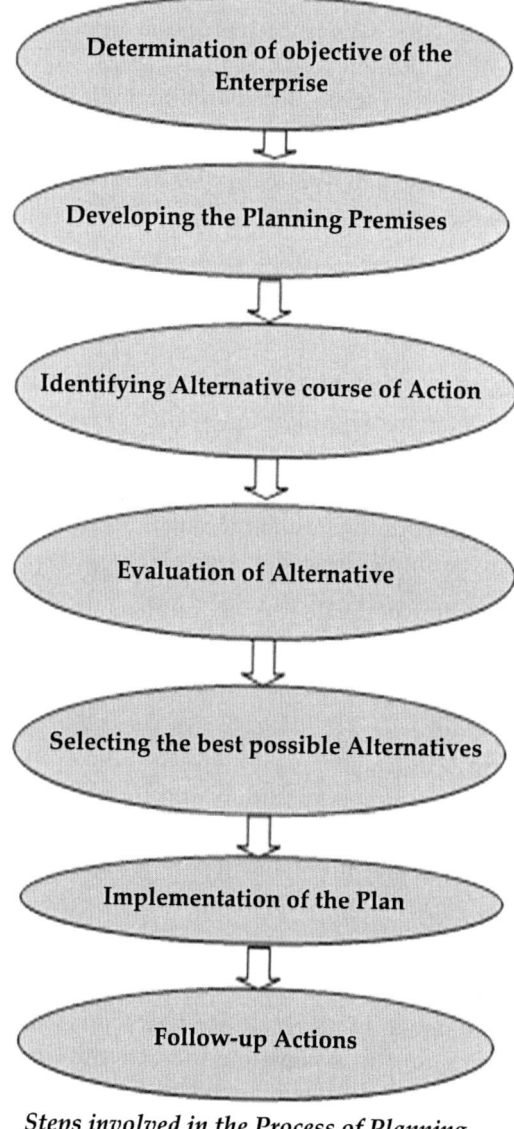

*Steps involved in the Process of Planning*

3. **Identifying Alternative Courses of Action:** There are usually multiple courses of action that can be taken to achieve an objective. Management should explore different ways and assess their effectiveness based on the planning premises. Without considering alternatives, planners may be limited by their own imaginations. Managers need to apply their creative and innovative skills to develop alternative courses of action.

4. **Evaluation of Alternatives:** Each proposal needs to be evaluated in terms of its positive and negative aspects, considering the objectives to be achieved, feasibility, and consequences. Each alternative should be examined against the following criteria:

   a. To what extent does it align with the basic objectives of the enterprise?

   b. To what extent does each alternative meet the requirements of cost, speed, quantity, and return on investment?

5. **Selection of the Best Alternative:** This is the decision-making stage. Decision-making techniques are applied to choose the most appropriate course of action or plan. Managers must analyze different permutations and combinations to select the best possible course of action. Sometimes, a combination of plans may be chosen instead of a single best plan.

6. **Implementation of the Plan:** After the plans are developed, they are put into action. Managers communicate the plans clearly to all employees and allocate the necessary resources (funds, machinery, etc.).

7. **Follow-up Action :** Planning outlines the future course of action. However, the future is uncertain, and there may be situations where the expected results are not achieved. Therefore, provisions are made for reviewing the plans in such situations.

## 6. LIMITATIONS OF PLANNING

Though planning is an essential step of management process but sometimes planning fails to achieve the pre-determined result. There are many causes of failure of planning in practice. Some of them are discussed below:

1. **Lack of reliable data:** Planning is based on the available facts and data. Sometimes, the data available may not be reliable. If the information used for planning is not dependable, the planning process loses its effectiveness.

2. **Time-consuming process:** Planning requires a significant amount of time. If insufficient time is allocated to the planning process, the resulting plan may not be fully realized.

3. **Expensive process:** Planning can also be costly. It involves expenses related to gathering and analyzing information, as well as evaluating various alternatives.

4. **Rigidity in organizational working:** Organizational inflexibility may force planners to create rigid plans. This can discourage managers from taking initiatives and engaging in innovative thinking.

5. **Resistance to change:** Planning may not be effective in a flexible business environment. Sometimes, planners themselves resist change, or they may not consider it desirable, which can hinder the planning process.

6. **External limitations:** The effectiveness of planning can be limited by external factors beyond the control of planners. External factors such as unexpected wars, government regulations, natural disasters, and other unpredictable events make plan execution challenging.

## 7. TYPES OF PLAN

Plans are broadly classified into two different categories i.e., Single use plan and Standing plans.

1. **Single Use Plan:** Single use plans are created to address unique or non-recurring problems. Also known as specific plans, they are tailored to fit particular situations and cannot be reused. These plans encompass budgets, programs, and projects, detailing the specific tasks and responsibilities of employees involved in their execution.

2. **Standing Plan:** A standing plan is employed for activities that regularly occur over a period of time. Its purpose is to ensure

the smooth internal operations of an organization, significantly enhancing efficiency in routine decision-making. Standing plans are typically established once but are adjusted periodically to meet evolving business requirements. They include policies, procedures, methods, and rules.

*The different types of plans prepared by managers are discussed below*

1.  **Objectives**: Objectives are the goals towards which an organization's activities are directed. They give direction to the various activities within the organization and guide the efforts of the company and its constituents. Objectives represent the endpoint of the planning process. Organizational objectives are established by the top management, while departmental objectives are set by departmental managers.

    Essential features of a good objective are as follows

    a.  Objectives should be framed for a single activity in mind.

    b.  It should relate to the desired outcome to be achieved.

    c.  Objectives should determine what is to be done.

    d.  They should be result oriented. The objective must not frame any actions

    e.  Objectives should not be vague.

    f.  Objectives should be quantitative and measurable.

    g.  They should not be unrealistic. Objectives must be achievable.

2.  **Strategy:** A strategy is a planned course of action by which an organization seeks to engage with its environment to gain specific advantages that facilitate the achievement of its objectives.

    **Chandler** defined Strategy as " *The determination of the basic long-term goals and objectives of an enterprise and the adoption of the course of action and the allocation of resources necessary for carrying out these goals* ".

    According to **Andrews** , " *Strategy is the pattern of objectives, purpose or goals, and major policies and plans for achieving these goals, stated in such a way, so as to define what business the company is in or to be and the kind of company it is or is to be* ".

Thus, we can say a strategy is a comprehensive plan for accomplishing organisational objectives. This comprehensive plan will include three dimensions:

(i) Determining long term objectives,

(ii) Adopting a particular course of action, and

(iii) Allocating resources necessary to achieve the objective. Whenever a strategy is formulated, the business environment needs to be taken into consideration. The changes in the economic, political, social, legal and technological environment will affect an organisation's strategy.

**Features of strategy:**

(i) Strategy relates the firm to its environment.

(ii) Strategy is the right combination of both internal and external factors.

(iii) It is relative combination of actions. The combination is to meet a particular condition, to solve certain problems, or to attain a desirable objective.

(iv) Strategy is expected to have a significant impact on the firm's future growth and prosperity.

3. **Policy:** A policy is a statement or general understanding that provides guidance to members of an organization regarding any course of action in decision-making.

According to **Kotler,** *"Policies define how the company will deal with stakeholders, employees, customers, suppliers, distributors, amd other important groups. Policies narrow the range of individual discretion so that employees act consistently on important issues".*

According to **Weihrich and Koontz,** *"Policies are general statements or understandings which guide or channel thinking in decision-making".*

On the basis of these definitions following features of policy can be identified:

(i) It provides guidelines to the members of the organisation for deciding a course of action.

(ii) It limits an area within which a decision is to be made.

(iii) Policies are generally expressed in qualitative, conditional, or general way.

(iv) Policy formulation is a function of all managers in the organisation.

4. **Procedures:** Procedures are plans that establish a method for handling future activities. They involve a planned sequence of operations for uniformly managing business activities. Simply put, procedures provide action guidelines by prescribing step-by-step instructions on how to perform an action.

According to **Terry and Franklin,** "A procedure is a series of related tasks that make up the chronological sequence and the established way of performing the work to be accomplished".

Procedures provide the guidelines for performing an action. They specify how each task in the organization will occur, when it will occur, and who will perform it.

Characteristics of a good procedure:

i. A procedure should be based on adequate facts of the particular situation and not on guesses or personal whims.

ii. A procedure should possess stability in that it provides a steadfastness of the established course.

iii. Flexibility of procedure is desirable in order to cope with a crisis or emergency.

iv. There should be a continuous review of the procedures so that their utility is ascertained.

5. **Methods:** A method is a step within a procedure. It can be defined as a prescribed manner for performing a specific task, taking into account the objectives, available resources, and the total expenditure of time, money, and effort. Therefore, a method specifies how a step of procedure is executed.

6. **Rules:** Rules are specific statements that dictate what must or must not be done. They do not allow for flexibility or discretion. Rules reflect a managerial decision that certain actions are mandatory or prohibited. They are typically the simplest type of plans because they do not allow for compromise or alteration unless a policy decision is made.

7. **Programmes:** A program is a detailed statement about a project that outlines the objectives, policies, procedures, rules, tasks, human and physical resources required, and the budget needed

to implement a specific course of action. Separate programs are prepared for accomplishing different tasks, as the same program may not be suitable for achieving other goals.

8. **Budget**: A budget is a type of single-use plan that expresses expected results in numerical terms. These results are anticipated to be achieved within a specified time period, typically one year. It quantifies future facts and figures, such as forecasting sales of different products in various areas for a specific month or predicting the number of workers required in the factory during peak production times. Because a budget represents all items in numerical terms, it facilitates the comparison of actual figures with expected figures, enabling corrective actions to be taken subsequently. Therefore, a budget also serves as a control device to manage deviations. However, creating a budget involves forecasting, clearly placing it within the realm of planning. It serves as a fundamental planning tool in many organizations.

## SUMMARY OF THE CHAPTER

1. **Planning** is the first and foremost function of management. Planning is the determination of future course of action to achieve any desired result. It is the process of thinking before doing.

2. **Following are the features of planning:**
   - Thinking process
   - Focus on achieving goals
   - Primary function
   - Selective in nature.
   - Continuous process
   - Pervasive function
   - Flexible

3. **Following are the main objectives of planning:**
   - Economic operations
   - Providing direction for action
   - Reducing overlapping and wasteful activities
   - Promoting innovative ideas
   - Establishing Standards for Controlling

4. **Steps involved in the process of planning :**
   - Determination of Objective of the Enterprise
   - Developing the Planning Premises
   - Identifying Alternative Course of Action
   - Evaluation of Alternatives
   - Selecting the best Possible Alternatives
   - Implementation of the Plan
   - Follow-up Action

5. There are many causes of **failure of planning** in practice. Some of them are discussed below:
   - Lack of reliable data
   - Time consuming process
   - Expensive Process
   - Rigidity in organizational working
   - Flexibility
   - External limitations

6. Plans are broadly classified into two different categories i.e., Single use plan and Standing plans.

7. **Single use plans** are made for handling unique or non-recurring problems. These plans are also known as specific plans as they are made to fit the specific situations.

8. **A standing plan** is used for activities that occur regularly over a period of time. It is designed to ensure that internal operations of an organisation run smoothly .

9. **Objectives** are the ends towards which the activities of an organisation are directed. They provide direction to various activities of the organisation.

10. Essential **features of a good objective** are as follows
    - Objectives should be framed for a single activity in mind.
    - It should relate to the desired outcome to be achieved.
    - Objectives should determine what is to be done.
    - They should be result oriented. The objective must not frame any actions

- Objectives should not be vague.
- Objectives should be quantitative and measurable.
- They should not be unrealistic. Objectives must be achievable .

11. **Strategy** is a course of action through which an organisation tries to relate with its environment to develop certain advantages which help in achieving its objectives.

12. **A policy** is the statement or general understanding which provides guidance in decision making to members of an organisation in respect to any course of action.

13. **Procedures** are plans that establish a method for handling future activities. It involves planned sequence of operations for handling business operations uniformly.

14. A **method** is one step of procedure. It can be defined as a prescribed manner for performing a given task with adequate consideration to the objective, facilities available, and total expenditure of time, money, and effort.

15. **Rules** are specific statements that inform what is to be done. They do not allow for any flexibility or discretion. It reflects a managerial decision that a certain action must or must not be taken.

16. A **programme** is a detailed statement about a project which outlines the objectives, policies, procedures, rules, tasks, human and physical resources required and the budget to implement any course of action.

17. **Budget** is a kind of single use plan of expected results expressed in numerical terms. These results are expected to be achieved within specified time period which is generally one year.

## QUESTIONS

1. Write down the meaning of planning.
2. Define planning.
3. Discuss the nature of planning.
4. Discuss the significance of planning.

5. What are the limitations of planning?

6. Discuss the process of planning.

7. What is single use plan?

8. What is standing plan?

9. What do you mean by objectives? What are its essential features?

10. Define strategy. What are its features?

11. Define policy. States its features.

12. What do you mean by procedures? What are the characteristics of a good procedure?

13. Write down the meaning of methods, rules, and programmes.

14. What is budget?

# UNIT 2C
# ORGANISING

## CONTENTS

# 1. CONCEPT OF ORGANISING

Organising is one of the fundamental functions of management. Broadly, organising pertains to the arrangement of various elements within an enterprise. The goal of organising is to establish relationships between people and tasks in order to achieve organisational objectives. It serves as the mechanism through which management guides, coordinates, and oversees business operations."

# 2. DEFINITIONS OF ORGANISING

"Organising is the process of defining and grouping the activities of the enterprise and establishing authority relationship among them"

*Theo Haimann*

"Organising is the establishment of authority relationship with the provision for coordination both vertically and horizontally between positions in the enterprise structure"

*Koontz and O'Donnell*

"Organising is the establishing of effective relationship among persons so, that they may work together efficiently for the purpose of achieving some definite goal"

*G.R. Terry*

"To organise a business is to provide it with everything useful to its functioning raw materials, machines and tools, capital and personnel"

*Henry Fayol*

"Organising is the process of identifying and grouping the work to be performed, defining authority and responsibility and establishing relationship for enabling people to work together most effectively in accomplishing objectives"

*Louis A. Allen*

Organizing entails identifying activities necessary to achieve enterprise objectives and implementing plans; grouping activities into jobs; assigning these jobs and activities to departments and individuals; delegating responsibility and authority for performance; and facilitating vertical and horizontal coordination of activities. Every manager must determine the activities required in their department or section to achieve assigned goals. Once activities are identified, similar or related activities are grouped to form jobs, which are then assigned to subordinates. Authority is delegated to empower subordinates to make decisions and take action, while provisions are made for coordination among subordinates and between the manager and subordinates. Organizing thus encompasses the following sub-functions:

a.  Identifying activities necessary to achieve objectives and implementing plans.

b.  Grouping activities to create self-contained jobs.

c.  Assigning jobs to employees.

d.  Delegating authority to enable them to perform their jobs and command the necessary resources.

e.  Establishing a network of coordinating relationships.

The organizing process leads to an organizational structure, encompassing positions, associated tasks and responsibilities, and a network of roles and authority-responsibility relationships. Organizing is, therefore, the fundamental process of aligning and integrating human, physical, and financial resources into productive relationships to achieve enterprise objectives. Its goal is to systematically combine employees and related tasks to ensure that organizational work is performed in a coordinated manner, with all efforts and activities aligned towards achieving organizational goals.

## 3. PROCESS OF ORGANISATION

Organising involves a series of steps aimed at achieving specific goals. The process of organising includes the following steps:

1.  **Identification and division of work**: The first step in organising is to identify various activities and divide the entire workload into manageable tasks or groups of similar activities according to predetermined plans. This helps in avoiding duplication and sharing the workload among employees.

2.  **Departmentalisation**: After dividing the work into different activities, the next step involves grouping similar activities together. This grouping process is known as departmentalisation

and facilitates specialisation. Departments can be created based on various criteria. For example, departments can be organised by geographical territory (e.g., north, south, west) or by product type (e.g., appliances, clothing, cosmetics).

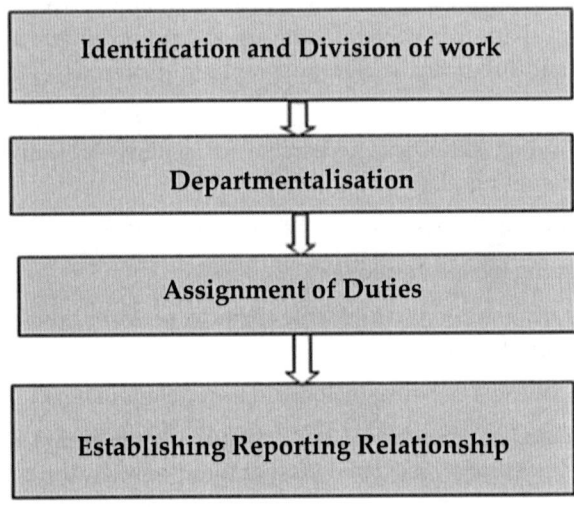

*Steps involved in the process of Organising*

3.  **Assignment of duties**: After grouping similar activities into different departments, the next step involves assigning duties to individuals or employees based on their skills and competencies. It is crucial for effective performance that duties are matched with the abilities of individuals. Work should be assigned to those who are best suited to perform it well.

4.  **Establishing reporting relationships**: Once duties are assigned to different employees based on their skills and competencies, it is essential to establish reporting relationships among them. Establishing reporting relationships involves allocating authority and responsibility among employees in a manner that clarifies who reports to whom and for what. There should be a balance between the responsibility assigned and the authority given. Establishing such clear relationships helps create a hierarchical structure and facilitates coordination among various departments.

# 4. SIGNIFICANCE OF ORGANISATION

The primary duty of management is to achieve the goals of the enterprise, which may be social, economic, political, or religious in nature. Proper organization of men, materials, money, and equipment is necessary for this purpose. Organization is the mechanism through which management directs, coordinates, and controls the business. A sound organization offers the following advantages, summarizing its importance:

1. **Enhancement of managerial efficiency**: A sound organization promotes proper coordination among various factors of production and ensures their optimum utilization. It eliminates confusion, duplication, and delays in work. By properly dividing work and labor, it motivates workers and reduces the workload of executives through delegation of authority.

2. **Growth, expansion, and diversification**: Organization provides the framework within which an enterprise can expand and grow. Through effective organization, management can leverage its resources. In a well-organized structure, resources and efforts are allocated in proportion to their contributions. Many firms have grown from humble beginnings to giant sizes due to effective organization.

3. **Specialization**: A well-structured organization facilitates specialization. Activities are allocated to individuals based on their qualifications, experience, and aptitude, thereby increasing efficiency. Systematic organization of activities helps achieve economies of scale and minimizes costs.

4. **Adoption of new technology**: A properly designed and balanced organization allows for prompt adoption and optimal use of technological advancements. It has the capability to absorb changes in the business environment and respond appropriately. A good organization fosters the development of new and improved methods of operation.

5. **Coordination**: Organization facilitates the coordination of diverse activities. Different functions are integrated to achieve desired objectives. Clear lines of authority and responsibility ensure mutual cooperation and harmony within the enterprise. A well-organized structure promotes teamwork and enables people to work with a spirit of cooperation.

6. **Training and Development**: By delegating authority to lower levels, a well-organized structure facilitates the training and development of future executives. It ensures that the right people are assigned to the right jobs and provides them with appropriate training and managerial development programs. By placing employees in different departments and assigning them various tasks, their training needs can be identified.

7. **Creativity, initiative, and innovation**: A good organization encourages initiative and creative thinking among employees. It motivates them to explore new ideas and adopt unconventional methods. A sound organization provides opportunities for recognizing and rewarding merit and creativity among personnel.

8. **Check on corrupt practices**: A weak and disorganized structure can be a source of corruption and inefficiency. A well-organized and disciplined organization boosts morale and motivation among workers. It fosters a sense of involvement, belongingness, dedication, honesty, and sincerity among employees. It prevents corruption, inefficiency, and wastage in an enterprise.

9. **Better human relations**: Human beings are the dynamic elements of an organization. A dedicated and satisfied group of individuals is an asset to any establishment. A well-organized structure, with clearly defined authority, responsibility, and accountability, enhances job satisfaction and promotes harmonious human relations. Organization involves human beings, and their satisfaction contributes to improved human relations.

Thus, organization forms the foundation of management. A sound organization is indispensable for efficient management and better business performance. It not only facilitates efficient administration but also encourages growth and diversification. It promotes the optimal use of new technology, stimulates innovation and creativity, and ensures harmonious human relations within the organization..

## 5. ORGANISATIONAL STRUCTURE

The organizational structure is the framework that defines the relationships among individuals operating at different levels within an enterprise. It consists of planned relationships between groups of related functions and between physical resources and personnel necessary to achieve organizational goals.

**Definitions**

"Organisational structure is that set of relationships, which exists among individuals and groups"

*A.W. Wickesburg*

"Organisational structure deals with the overall organisational arrangement in an enterprise"

*WH Newman*

"Organisational structures are patterns of relationships among the various positions in a firm and among the various people occupying the positions"

*Hurley*

# 5.1 FORMAL ORGANISATION

Formal organisation refers to a structured arrangement of clearly defined jobs, each with a specified level of authority, responsibility, and accountability. In simpler terms, formal organisation is the management-designed structure of an organisation aimed at achieving specific tasks. It clearly delineates the boundaries of authority and responsibility, ensuring systematic coordination among various activities to achieve organisational goals. The structure in a formal organisation can be either functional or divisional.

## 5.1.1 Definitions of Formal Organisation

"Formal organisation refers to the structure of well defined jobs, each bearing definite measure of authority, responsibility and accountability."

*JAC Brown*

"The formal organisation is a system of well-defined jobs, each bearing a definite measure of authority, responsibility and accountability."

*Louis Allen*

"Formal organisation is a system of consciously coordinated activities of two or more persons towards a common objectives"

*Chester Barnard*

## 5.1.2 Features of formal organisation

A formal organisation has the following essential features

1. Formal organization is founded on the division of labor and specialization.

2. It involves actions aimed at achieving the objectives specified in the plans, as it establishes the rules and procedures necessary for their attainment.

3. The organization does not consider emotional aspects.

4. It is intentionally designed by top management to facilitate the smooth operation of the organization.

5. It prioritizes the work to be performed over interpersonal relationships among employees.

## 5.1.3 Advantages of formal organisation

The following are the advantages of a formal organisation

1. Achievement of goals becomes easier in a formal organisation by providing a framework for the operations to be performed.

2. Fixing responsibility is simplified as mutual relationships are clearly defined.

3. Unity of command can be maintained due to the presence of a scalar chain of authority.

4. There is no overlap of work as tasks are clearly divided among departments and individuals.

5. Formal organisation provides stability to the organization, as the behavior of employees can be predicted fairly accurately due to specific rules guiding them.

## 5.1.4 Disadvantages of formal organisation

The formal organisation suffers from the following limitations/ disadvantages:

1. **Lack of initiative**: In a formal organization, rules and procedures are strictly followed, which can discourage employees from taking initiative.

2. **Excessive use of authority**: There is often excessive and undue use of authority in this type of organization. The autocratic attitude of managers can put employees under constant pressure, which adversely affects their efficiency.

3. **Delay in work**: Excessive rigidity in rules and regulations can lead to unnecessary delays in work.

4. **Lack of human feelings**: Formal organizations are impersonal, which means human feelings have no place within them.

## 5.2 INFORMAL ORGANISATION

Informal organisation refers to the network of social relationships between individuals within an organisation that are based on personal attitudes, sentiments, emotions, prejudices, likes, dislikes, and other informal aspects. These informal relationships are not governed by the procedures and regulations of the formal organisation. Typically, informal organisation arises spontaneously within the formal structure when individuals interact beyond their official roles and responsibilities. Informal relationships may form based on shared interests, language, culture, or other common factors.

## 5.2.1 Definitions of Informal Organisation

"Informal organisation is the network of personal and social relationships not established or required by formal organisation"

*Keith Davis*

"That organisation is informal, where the mutual relations are established unconsciously for common objectives"

*Chester Barnard*

## 5.2.2 Features of Informal Organisation

An informal organisation has the following features

1. It arises within the formal organisation due to personal interactions among employees.

2. The standards of behavior are shaped by group norms rather than official rules and regulations.

3. It lacks fixed lines of communication.

4. It emerges spontaneously and is not intentionally created by management.

5. It lacks a definite structure or form because it is a complex network of social relationships among members. .

### 5.2.3 Advantages of Informal Organisation

The informal organisation offers many benefits. Important among them are given below:

1. **Rapid communication**: In informal organisations, formal lines of communication are not strictly followed. Therefore, information spreads quickly and feedback is received promptly.

2. **Fulfillment of social needs**: Informal organisations help fulfill the social needs of their members. This enhances job satisfaction by providing a sense of belonging in the organization.

3. **Achievement of organisational objectives**: Due to camaraderie and mutual support, members of informal organisations assist each other in solving work-related problems. This collaborative approach makes it easier to achieve organisational objectives.

4. **Accurate feedback**: Through informal structures, top-level management can obtain genuine feedback from employees on various issues, policies, and plans.

### 5.2.4 Disadvantages of Informal Organisation

The informal organisation has certain disadvantages. Some of them are as follows:

1. **Disruptive influence:** Informal organisations can become disruptive when they spread rumors, which may undermine the interests of the formal organisation.

2. **Resistance to change:** Informal organisations may resist changes proposed by management, thereby impeding growth and causing delays in implementation.

3. **Preference for group interests:** Informal organisations can exert pressure on members to conform to group norms, which may be detrimental to the organisation if these norms conflict with organizational interests.

4. **Undermining the formal organization:** Overemphasis on informal organisation can potentially undermine the effectiveness of the formal organisation.

### 5.2.5 Comparison between Formal and Informal Organisation

| S. No. | Basis | Formal Organisation | Informal Organisation |
|---|---|---|---|
| 1 | Formation | Formal organization is intentionally established by management through a conscious efforts involving the delegation of authority. | Informal organization emerges spontaneously without deliberate efforts. It arises based on relationships, caste, culture, occupations and on personal interests etc. No delegation of authority is essential in informal organization |
| 2 | Basis | A formal organization is structured around rules and procedures. | An informal organization is shaped by attitudes and emotions of individuals. |
| 3 | Nature | A formal organization is characterised by stability and predictability, remaining unchanged by individual preferences. | An informal organization, is however, lacks stability and predictability |

| S. No. | Basis | Formal Organisation | Informal Organisation |
|--------|-------|---------------------|----------------------|
| 4 | Set up | A formal organization is a system of well defined relationships with a definite authority assigned to every individual. It follows predetermined lines of communication. | An informal organization has no definite form and there are no definite rules as to who is to report to. |
| 5 | Emphasis | Formal organisation priorities authority and functions. | Informal organization focuses on individuals and their relationships. |
| 6 | Authority | In formal organisation, authority is associated with a position and flows from top to bottom. | In informal organisation, authority is linked to individuals and may flows either downwards or horizontals. |
| 7 | Existence | A formal organisation exists independently of the informal groups that are formed within it. | An informal organization exists within the framework of a formal structure. |
| 8 | Rationality | A formal organization operates on logic rather than on sentiments or emotions. | In an informal organization, activities are influenced by emotions and sentiments of its members. |
| 9 | Depiction | Formal organization can be presented in an organization chart or a manual. | An informal organization cannot be depicted in the chart or manual of the enterprise. |

# 6. FUNCTIONAL ORGANISATION

When the entire workload is divided into different groups known as departments, each containing activities of a similar nature, and each department reports to a coordinating head, this type of organization is known as functional organization. For instance, in an industrial enterprise, major functions such as production, finance, marketing, and human resources may be grouped into different departments as illustrated below:

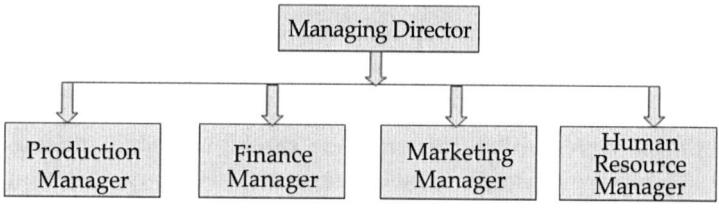

*Functional Organisation*

## 6.1 Advantages of Functional Organisation

The functional structure has many advantages to offer. Important among them are as follows:

1. **Specialization:** Functional organization ensures specialists are assigned to each area. Work is carried out by individuals who possess specialized knowledge in their respective fields.

2. **Efficiency:** This type of organization helps control waste of materials, money, and time because work is performed by specialists.

3. **Managerial effectiveness:** Functional organization enhances managerial and operational efficiency, thereby increasing profitability.

4. **Improved control and coordination:** It facilitates better control and coordination of activities within each department.

5. **Effective training:** It is easier to provide effective training to employees because they work within a defined area.

## 6.2 Disadvantages of Functional Organisation

1. **High degree of specialisation:** The functional structure requires specialists in each department, which can be challenging to establish.

2. **Monotonous work:** Work in this structure can be quite one-dimensional, leading employees to feel boredom or monotony over time. The lack of new challenges may decrease enthusiasm for the job.

3. **Complexity:** The operation of a functional organization can be overly complicated. Workers may have multiple supervisors, leading to overlapping authority and confusion within the organization.

4. **Potential for conflicts:** In this structure, managers must carefully manage the appraisal system. If not handled correctly, conflicts may arise among employees regarding promotions or performance evaluations.

5. **Lack of flexibility:** This structure can be inflexible, making it disruptive when personnel changes are necessary. It does not offer much scope for adaptation and can upset the balance of the entire system.

## 7. DIVISIONAL ORGANISATION

Divisional organisation, also known as Profit Decentralisation according to Newman and others, revolves around business units. In this structure, the organisation is segmented into several relatively autonomous units. Each unit is self-contained and has the resources to operate independently of other divisions. For instance, each division manages its own manufacturing, engineering, marketing, and other functions. Each unit is overseen by a manager who bears responsibility for the organisation's investments in facilities, capital, and personnel, as well as for the unit's development and performance.

### 7.1 Advantages of Divisional Organisation

Divisional structure provides the following advantages:

1. **Product specialization:** Divisional organization allows for focused attention on each product line, leading to efficiency and cost-effectiveness in operations. It ensures optimal utilization of specialized skills and capital equipment.

2. **Accountability:** Each divisional head is held accountable for costs, revenues, and profits, establishing a clear basis for performance evaluation.

3. **Flexibility and initiative:** It grants sufficient autonomy to each division, fostering flexibility in decision-making across different divisions.

4. **Profitability assessment:** It is easier to assess the profitability of each product based on the accounting information from the respective divisions.

5. **Expansion:** Divisional structure facilitates the expansion and growth of each product line.

## 7.2 Disadvantages of Divisional Organisation

There are certain disadvantages and challenges associated with divisional structure:

1. **Costly :** Divisional structure can be quite expensive because each division requires its own set of facilities and resources.

2. **Job dissatisfaction :** Due to the lack of emphasis on functional specialization, many professionals may not feel satisfied with this structure.

3. **Inter-divisional conflicts :** There may be conflicts among different divisions over the allocation of funds and other resources.

4. **Difficult to control :** Implementing a control system is a major challenge in divisionalisation. Although each unit is evaluated based on its contribution to the organization, this system may not function effectively if the information monitoring system is inadequate.

# 8. PROJECT ORGANISATION

A Project organisation is a temporary structure established to complete a specific project. It is a project-focused organisational framework where the project manager holds the ultimate authority over project decisions, priorities, and resource allocation. The project organisation specifically refers to an organisational setup in which the project manager leads the team and has the final authority to make all decisions related to the project. In a project structure, all work is treated as individual projects. Unlike in a functional structure, the project manager has complete control, and all team members report directly to the project manager. Once the project is completed, the project team is disbanded, and personnel return to their regular organisational units.

## 8.1 Advantages of Project Organisation

Project organisation offers the following advantages:

1. **Optimal Utilization of Specialized Knowledge:** Project departmentation facilitates the maximum utilization of specialized knowledge, ensuring that all projects have equal access to this expertise.

2. **Adaptability:** It enables the organization to be flexible and responsive to environmental demands, especially in fast-changing environments.

3. **Resource Allocation:** Project departmentation provides greater flexibility in resource allocation within the organization, directing resources to the projects where they are most needed.

## 8.2 Disadvantages of Project Organisation

Project organisation suffers from the following disadvantages:

1. **Insecurity:** Project organization fosters feelings of insecurity among employees due to its ad hoc nature and limited duration.

2. **Reduced Loyalty:** Employees struggle to identify with any specific department within the organization because they do not have permanent tenure with any project. This reduces loyalty to the organization.

3. **Role Ambiguity:** There is ambiguity among members about their roles in the organization.

4. **Challenges for Project Managers:** Project managers face numerous challenges because they often have to shoulder responsibilities without corresponding authority. As a result, they rely more on their personal qualities rather than formal authority.

## 9. MATRIX ORGANISATION

The matrix organization structure combines elements from both functional and pure project organization structures. It involves appointing a project manager to coordinate project activities, with personnel drawn from their respective functional departments. After completing the project, these individuals may return to their original departments for future assignments.

## 9.1 Advantages of Matrix Organisation

Matrix organisation offers the following advantages:

1. **Improved Planning and Control**: The matrix structure allows for better focus of attention, talent, and resources on individual projects, facilitating improved planning and control.

2. **Flexibility**: The matrix structure is more flexible compared to traditional functional structures.

3. **Maximum Contribution**: It provides an environment where professionals can test their competence and make maximum contributions.

4. **Motivation**: The matrix structure motivates project staff by allowing them to focus directly on completing specific projects.

## 9.2 Disadvantages of Matrix Organisation

Matrix organisation suffers from the following disadvantages:

1. **Violation of Unity of Command Principle**: The matrix structure violates the principle of unity of command, as each employee has two superiors—one functional superior and another project superior.

2. **Violation of Scalar Principle**: The scalar principle is also violated in the matrix structure, as there is no determinate hierarchy.

3. **Potential for Conflicts**: Conflicts may arise due to the heterogeneity of team members in the matrix structure.

4. **Complex Relationships**: The matrix structure leads to more complex organizational relationships. Apart from formal relationships, informal ones also arise, which can create coordination problems.

## SUMMARY OF THE CHAPTER

1. **Organising** refers to the relationship between various factors present in a given enterprise. The purpose of organising is to relate organisational people to each other and to work for the achievement of organisational goals.

2. The following steps are involved in the **process of organising:**
   - Identification and division of work
   - Departmentalisation
   - Assignment of duties
   - Establishing reporting relationships

3. A sound organization offers the following **advantages,** which summarizes its **importance :**
   - Enhancement of managerial efficiency
   - Growth, expansion and diversification
   - Specialization
   - Adoption of new technology
   - Coordination
   - Training and Development
   - Creativity, initiative and innovation
   - Check on corrupt practices
   - Better human relations

4. **Organisational structure** is the framework of relationship of persons operating at various levels in an enterprise. It is a set of planned relationship between groups of related functions and between physical factors and personnel required for the achievement of organisational goals.

5. **Formal organisation** refers to the structure of well defined jobs each bearing a definite measure of authority, responsibility and accountability.

6. A formal organisation has the following **essential features:**
   - Formal organisation is based on division of labour and specialisation.
   - It is actions to achieve the objectives specified in the plans, as it lays down the rules and procedures essential for their achievement.
   - The organisation does not take into consideration emotional aspects.
   - It is deliberately designed by the top management to facilitate the smooth functioning of the organisation.

- It places more emphasis on work to be performed than interpersonal relationships among the employees.

7. The following are the **advantages** of a **formal organization:**
   - Easy accomplishment of goals.
   - Fixation of responsibility
   - Unity of command is possible
   - No overlapping of work
   - Stability in the organisation

8. The **formal organisation** suffers from the following **limitations/ disadvantages:**
   - Lack of initiative
   - Excessive use of authority
   - Delay in work
   - No place for human feelings

9. **Informal organisation** refers to the network of social relationships between the people in the organisation based on personal attitudes, sentiments, emotions, prejudices, likes, dislikes etc. The informal relations are not bound by procedures and regulations laid down in the formal organisation.

10. **An informal organisation** has the following **features:**
    - It is originates from within the formal organisation as a result of personal interaction among employees of the organisation.
    - The standard of behaviour evolves from group norms rather than officially laid down rules and regulations.
    - It does not have fixed lines of communication.
    - It emerges spontaneously and is not deliberately created by the management.
    - It has no definite structure or form because it is a complex network of social relationships among members.

11. **Advantages of Informal Organisation:**
    - Faster communication
    - Fulfillment of social needs
    - Fulfills organisational objectives

12. **Disadvantages of Informal Organisation:**
    - Disruptive force.
    - Resistance to change
    - Priority to group interest
    - Danger to formal organisation

13. When the whole work is divided into different groups *called departments* where each department includes the activities of similar nature and where each department report to the coordinating head, then this type of organisation is called **functional organization.**

14. **Advantages of Functional Organisation:**
    - Specialisation
    - Economical
    - Managerial efficiency
    - Better control and coordination
    - Effective training

15. **Disadvantages of Functional Organisation:**
    - High degree of specialisation
    - One dimensional work.
    - Complicated
    - Chances of conflicts
    - Inflexible

16. **Divisional organisation** , also called Profit Decentralisation by Newman and others, is built around business units. In this form, the organisation is divided into several fairly autonomous units. Each unit is relatively self-contained in that it has the resources to operate independently of others divisions

17. **Advantages of Divisional Organisation:**
    - Product specialisation
    - Fixation of Accountability
    - Flexibility and Initiative
    - Assessment of Profitability.
    - Expansion

18. **Disadvantages of Divisional Organisation:**
    - Costly
    - Dissatisfaction
    - Conflict among divisions
    - Difficult to control

19. A **Project organisation** is a temporary organisation which is created to complete a project. Project organization is a project focused organizational structure where project manager has the final authority over the project to make project decisions, priorities, acquire and assign resources.

20. **Advantages of Project Organisation:**
    - Maximum use of specialized knowledge
    - Flexible
    - Utilisation of resources

21. **Disadvantages of Project Organisation:**
    - Insecurity
    - Less Loyalty
    - Lack of clarity
    - Numerous problems

22. **Matrix organisation** structure is the combination of functional and pure project organisation structures. These two organisation structures are merged together to create a matrix organisation structure. In matrix organisation structure a project manager is appointed to coordinate the activities of the project.

23. **Advantages of Matrix Organisation:**
    - Better planning and control
    - Flexible
    - Maximum contribution
    - Provides motivation

24. **Disadvantages of Matrix Organisation:**
    - Violates principle of unity of command
    - Violates scalar principle
    - Conflicts
    - Complex relationships

# QUESTIONS

1. Write down the concept of organising.
2. Define Organisation.
3. What are the characteristics of organising?
4. Discuss the process of organisation.
5. Explain the significance of organising.
6. What is organisational structure?
7. Define organisational structure.
8. What is formal organisation?
9. Define formal organisation.
10. What are the features of formal organisation?
11. Discuss the advantages of formal organisation.
12. Discuss the disadvantages of formal organisation.
13. What do you mean by informal organisation?
14. Define informal organisation.
15. What are the features of informal organisation?
16. Discuss the advantages of informal organisation.
17. What are the disadvantages of informal organisation?
18. Distinguish between formal and informal organisation.
19. What do you mean by functional organisation?
20. What are the advantages of functional organisation?
21. What are the disadvantages of functional organisation?
22. Write down the meaning of divisional organisation.
23. What are the merits of divisional organisation/
24. What are the demerits of divisional organisation?
25. What is project organisation?
26. What are the advantages of project organisation?
27. What are the disadvantages of project organisation?

28. What do you understand by matrix organisation?
29. What are the advantages of matrix organisation?
30. Discuss the demerits of matrix organisation.
31. Write short notes on:

    a. Formal Organisationa      b. Informal Organisation

    c. Functional Organisation      d. Matrix Organisation

    e. Project Organisation      f. Divisional Organisation

# UNIT 2D
# DECISION MAKING

## CONTENTS

# 1. CONCEPT OF DECISION MAKING

Decision-making is an essential aspect of modern management and a primary function thereof. A manager's principal responsibility is to make sound and rational decisions. Decision-making constitutes a crucial part of a manager's activities. A decision can be defined as a selected course of action consciously chosen from among a set of alternatives to achieve a desired outcome. It represents a well-balanced judgment and a commitment to action. It is often stated that one of the most important functions of management is to make decisions on various problems and situations. Decision-making pervades all managerial actions, linking means and ends together.

The word 'decision' is derived from the Latin words "desciso," which means a cutting away or a cutting off, or in a practical sense, to come to a conclusion. Decisions are made to achieve goals through appropriate follow-up actions. A manager must make decisions before preparing a plan for execution or taking action. Moreover, a manager's ability is frequently judged by the quality of the decisions they make. Therefore, management is inherently a decision-making process. The effectiveness of management hinges on the quality of decision-making. In this sense, management is aptly described as a decision-making process.

## 2. DEFINITIONS OF DECISION MAKING

"Decision-making involves the selection of a course of action from among two or more possible alternatives in order to arrive at a solution for a given problem."

*Trewatha and Newport*

"Management is a decision-making process.'. Decision-making will be followed by second function of management called planning. Decision making has priority over planning function.

*R.C. Davis*

"Decision making is the process of identifying and selecting a course of action to solve a specific problem".

*James Stoner*

"Whatever a manager does, he does through decision-making."

*Peter Drucker*

## 3. CHARACTERISTICS OF DECISION MAKING

The following are the essential characteristics of decision making:

1. **Decision-making involves making a choice:** It entails choosing from among multiple alternative courses of action. It is the process of selecting one solution from several available options. In any business problem, there are various alternative solutions. Managers must consider these alternatives and choose the best one for execution. Planners and decision-makers need to assess the available business environment and select the most promising alternative plan to effectively address the business problem.

2. **Continuous process:** Decision-making is a dynamic and ongoing process. It permeates all organizational activities. Managers continuously make decisions on various policy and administrative matters. It is an activity that never ends in business management.

3. **Mental and intellectual activity:** Decision-making is both a mental and intellectual process that requires knowledge, skills, experience, and maturity on the part of the decision-maker. It is fundamentally a human activity.

4. **Goal-oriented process:** Decision-making aims to provide a solution to a given problem or challenge faced by a business enterprise. It is a process oriented towards achieving specific goals and objectives and providing solutions to the problems encountered by a business unit.

5. **Time-consuming activity:** Decision-making is time-consuming because various aspects need careful consideration before a final decision can be made. Decision-makers must complete several steps, making decision-making a time-intensive activity.

6. **Means and not the end:** Decision-making is a means of solving a problem or achieving a target or objective, rather than being a plan in itself.

7. **Based on reliable information:** Good decision-making is always based on reliable information. The quality of decision-making at all levels of the organization can be enhanced with the support of an effective and efficient Management Information System (MIS).

## 4. PROCESS OF DECISION MAKING

The following procedure should be followed in arriving at a correct decision:

1. **Establishing objectives**: Rational decision-making begins with clearly defined objectives. Therefore, the initial step in decision-making is to establish objectives. An objective is the anticipated outcome of future actions. Before determining the future course of action, it is crucial to understand in advance what is being sought to achieve. Having precise knowledge of goals and objectives provides purpose in planning and coherence in efforts. Furthermore, objectives serve as the criteria against which the final outcome will be evaluated.

2. **Defining the problem**: It is widely acknowledged that a well-defined problem is halfway to being solved. Many poor decisions are made because the decision-maker lacks a clear understanding of the problem. It is essential for the decision-maker to identify and define the problem before making any decisions.

3. **Analyzing the problem**: After defining the problem, the next step in decision-making is its analysis. The problem should be thoroughly examined to gather sufficient background information and data related to the situation. The problem should be broken down into several sub-problems, and each component of the problem must be thoroughly and systematically investigated. Many factors can be involved in any problem, some of which are relevant and others are less so. These pertinent factors should be thoroughly discussed. This approach not only saves time but also reduces costs and effort.

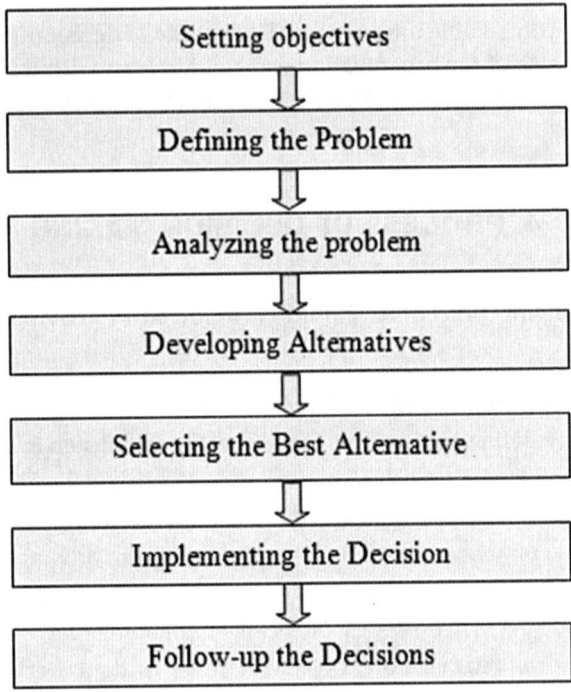

| Setting objectives |
| Defining the Problem |
| Analyzing the problem |
| Developing Alternatives |
| Selecting the Best Alternative |
| Implementing the Decision |
| Follow-up the Decisions |

*Steps involved in the process of decision making*

4. **Generating Alternatives**: After defining and analyzing the problem, the next step in the decision-making process is to generate alternative courses of action. Without engaging in the process of generating alternatives, a manager may be limited by their own imagination. Alternatives are rarely lacking for any course of action, but sometimes a manager may assume that there is only one way to accomplish something. In such cases, the manager likely hasn't forced themselves to consider other options. Without doing so, they cannot arrive at the best possible decision. This underscores a key planning principle, often termed the principle of alternatives: alternatives exist for every decision problem. Effective planning involves exploring alternatives toward achieving the desired goal.

5. **Selecting the Best Alternative**: After developing alternatives, one must evaluate all the possible options in order to select the best alternative. There are various methods for evaluating alternatives. The most common method is through intuition,

where a solution that seems good at the time is chosen. However, there is inherent risk in relying solely on intuition, as a manager's intuition may be wrong on multiple occasions.

6. **Implementing the Decision**: Choosing an alternative serves no purpose if it is not put into practice. The manager is not only concerned with making a decision but also with its implementation. They should ensure that systematic steps are taken to implement the decision. A primary challenge the manager may face during implementation is resistance from subordinates affected by the decision. If the manager cannot overcome this resistance, the energy and effort expended in decision-making will be wasted. To make the decision acceptable, it is necessary for the manager to help people understand the decision's implications, what is expected of them, and what they should expect from management.

7. **Monitoring and Evaluating Decisions**: Kenneth H. Blanchard has emphasized in his book that it is always better to check the results after putting the decision into practice. He has given reasons for following up on decisions, including:

(i) If the decision is a good one, one will know what to do if faced with the same problem again.

(ii) If the decision is a bad one, one will know what not to do the next time.

(iii) If the decision is bad and one follows-up soon enough, corrective action may still be possible.

In order to achieve proper follow-up, the management should devise an efficient system of feedback information. This information will be very useful in taking the corrective measures and in taking right decisions in the future.

## 5. TYPES OF DECISION

Decision-making is a fundamental element of the managerial process. When considering types of decision-making, managers must examine two aspects: the five types of decisions a manager might face or produce, and the four processes or styles employed in making those decisions.

1. **Non-reversible**: The first type of decision a manager might face is a non-reversible one. Such a decision cannot be undone or changed once implemented. For example, once NASA initiates a launch, there is no turning back.

2. **Reversible:** In contrast to irreversible decisions, reversible decisions can be changed or completely revoked at any time if deemed necessary. For instance, Coca-Cola discontinued 'New Coke' with a new formula and reintroduced Classic Coke to the market.

3. **Experimental**: Experimental decisions cannot be finalized until preliminary data results are in. For example, NASA will not proceed with its plan to build a station on the Moon until early missions reveal whether water can be found or made there.

4. **Trial and Error**: Through trial and error, knowledge gained from mistakes is used to fine-tune the correct course of action. Early choices might be blind guesses, but eventually, clarity is achieved.

5. **Conditional**: A conditional decision remains effective as long as external factors support it; however, it becomes unwise or no longer useful if these factors change. For example, Bank A may decide to close on Saturdays to save money, hoping Bank B will follow suit. If Bank B does not, Bank A reopens on Saturdays.

6. **Authoritative**: This style of decision-making comes from the top down. The decision is made by a leader who has all the facts and is the undisputed expert on the topic or situation. For instance, when the CEO or President makes a decision based on their expertise.

7. **Facilitative**: The facilitative process involves joint collaboration between the leader and subordinates. Department heads and employees with firsthand knowledge, experience, and expertise enhance the decision-making process. Information is presented, deliberated upon, and a group consensus forms the final decision.

8. **Consultative**: Similar to the facilitative style's first phase, consultative style also involves gathering advice from subordinates or outside sources. However, the leader makes the final decision. For instance, a leader may seek advice but ultimately decides alone.

9. **Delegative**: In the delegative style, a leader may pass the responsibility for a decision to a subordinate or subordinates, especially when they have greater expertise. This approach is often used for lesser decisions in the everyday management of large organizations.

## SUMMARY OF THE CHAPTER

1. Decision-making involves the selection of a course of action from among two or more possible alternatives in order to arrive at a solution for a given problem.

2. The following are the essential characteristics of decision making:

   - Decision-making implies choice
   - Continuous process
   - Mental activity
   - Goal oriented process
   - Time consuming activity
   - Means and not the end
   - Based on reliable information

3. The following procedure should be followed in arriving at a correct decision:

   - Setting objectives
   - Defining the Problem
   - Analyzing the problem
   - Developing Alternatives
   - Selecting the Best Alternative
   - Implementing the Decision
   - Follow-up the Decisions

4. **Types of Decision**:

   - **Irreversible**: The first kind of decision a manager might face is an irreversible one. Such decision cannot be undone or changed. Once NASA pushes the launch button, there is no turning back.

- **Reversible:** Unlike irreversible decision a reversible decision can be changed or totally revoked at any time, if it is deemed to be a mistake. e.g., Coca Cola discontinued 'New Coke' with a new formula was reintroduced classic coke to the market.

- **Experimental:** Experimental decision cannot be finalized until the results of the preliminary date are in. NASA will not proceed with its plan to build a station on the Moon until early mission reveal, if scientist can find or make water there.

- **Trial and Error:** Through trial and error, the knowledge gained from mistakes is used to fine tune the proper course. Early choices might be blind or wild guesses, but eventually things become more clear.

- **Conditional:** A conditional decision remains effective as long as external factors develop that make it unwise or no longer useful, at which point managers change the decision. e.g., Bank A may decide to close on Saturdays to save money, hoping Bank B will follow, if it doesn't Bank A opens on Saturdays again.

- **Authoritative:** This style of decision-making comes from the top. In this, the decision comes from the top in a defective way. e.g., when the CEO, the President or other leader has all the facts and is the undisputed expert on the topic or situation, he can arrive at a decision effectively.

- **Facilitative:** The facilitative process is a joint collaboration of the leader and his subordinates. Often the department heads and employees may have firsthand knowledge, experience and expertise that can enhance the decision-making process. The first phase involves a presentation of information, followed by a deliberative phase. Finally, a group arrives at a consensus jointly in the form of final decision.

- **Consultative:** It is similar to the first phase of the facilitative style, with the authoritative style coming in at the end. A leader may ask for advice from his subordinates or outside sources or however, in the end, he is the sole decision maker.

- **Delegative:** Sometimes a leader may use the Delegative style of decision-making to pass off the responsibility for the decision to a subordinate or subordinates.

# QUESTIONS

1. What do you mean by decision making?
2. Define decision making.
3. What are the characteristics of decision making? Discuss
4. Discuss the steps involved in the process of decision making.
5. What are different types of decision? Explain.

# UNIT 2E
# DEPARTMENTATION

## CONTENTS

# 1. CONCEPT OF DEPARTMENTATION

Departmentation involves grouping various activities, processes, and resources into logical units to accomplish organizational tasks. It can be considered the initial and fundamental step in designing an organizational structure. Departmentation is the first phase in organizing, which includes identifying activities and grouping them effectively. This process of grouping activities is commonly referred to as departmentation.

# 2. DEFINITIONS OF DEPARTMENTATION

"A department is a distinct area, division or branch of an enterprise over which a manager has authority for the performance of specified activities."

*Koontz and O'Donnell*

"Divisionalisation is a means of dividing the large and monolithic functional organisation into smaller flexible administrative units."

*Louis Allen*

"Departmentalisation is the grouping of jobs, processes and resources into logical units to perform some organisational task."

*Pearce and Robinson*

"Departmentalisation is the clustering of individuals into units and of units into departments and larger units in order to facilitate achieving organisational goals."

*Terry and Franklin*

# 3. NEED AND IMPORTANCE OF DEPARTMENTATION

The need for departmentation arises from the management's desire to achieve organizational goals through coordinated efforts of individuals working in the organization. Specifically, departmentation is essential for the following reasons:

1. **Specialisation Benefits**: Departmentation allows an enterprise to benefit from specialisation. When each department is responsible for a major function, the enterprise can develop and improve operational efficiency.

2. **Autonomy**: Departments typically operate with a degree of autonomy. The managers in charge can make independent decisions within the organization's overall framework. This autonomy enhances job satisfaction, motivation, and operational efficiency.

3. **Scalability**: A single manager can effectively supervise only a limited number of subordinates. Grouping activities and personnel into departments enables the enterprise to scale and expand.

4. **Clarity of Responsibility**: Departmentation helps clarify each person's role within the organization. Responsibilities and accountability for results can be defined precisely, enabling individuals to be held accountable for their performance.

5. **Managerial Skill Development**: Departmentation fosters the development of managerial skills in two ways. Managers can focus on specific problems, providing effective on-the-job training. It also identifies the need for further training, enabling managers to work more effectively in their specialized areas.

6. **Performance Appraisal**: Assigning specific tasks to departmental personnel makes it easier to appraise managerial performance. Clear divisions of activities and fixed performance standards facilitate effective performance evaluation.

7. **Administrative Control**: Departmentation divides large and complex organizations into manageable administrative units. This division of activities and personnel into smaller units facilitates administrative control, allowing precise determination of performance standards for each department.

In summary, departmentation is crucial for achieving organizational goals through coordinated efforts, enhancing operational efficiency, providing autonomy and managerial development, clarifying responsibilities, and facilitating effective performance appraisal and administrative control.

## 4. BASES OF DEPARTMENTATION

Departmentalization involves grouping jobs, processes, and resources into logical units to accomplish organizational tasks. There are various bases of departmentation commonly used, such as function, product, territory, process, and customer. Let's briefly discuss these:

### 4.1 FUNCTIONAL DEPARTMENTATION

Functional departmentation refers to the grouping of homogeneous or similar activities to form an organizational unit. It is the most widespread method of organizing activities found in nearly every enterprise. In a manufacturing organization, key functions include production, sales, finance, and personnel. Functional departmentation can also occur at lower levels of the organization. For instance, within the marketing department, activities might be categorized into marketing research, sales, and advertising. Essentially, functional differentiation can occur at successive levels within the organizational hierarchy.

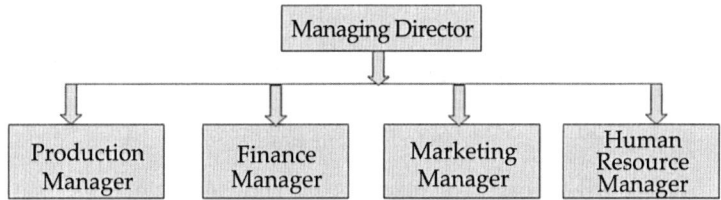

*Functional Departmentation*

### 4.1.1 Advantages of Functional Departmentation:

Functional departmentation offers several advantages, which include:

1. **Specialization**: It promotes specialization, ensuring optimal utilization of manpower and other resources.

2. **Managerial Efficiency**: It enhances managerial and operational efficiency, leading to increased profitability.

3. **Emphasis on Each Activity**: It emphasizes every activity, ensuring that each department contributes to the organization's objectives.

4. **Facilitates Delegation**: It facilitates the delegation of authority, thereby reducing the burden on the chief executive.

5. **Economical**: This organizational structure helps control waste of materials, money, and time because tasks are performed by specialists in their respective fields.

## 4.1.2 Disadvantages of Functional Departmentation

Functional departmentation has several disadvantages that organizations should consider before adopting it. Some of these drawbacks include:

1. **High Degree of Specialization**: This type of departmentation requires specialists in each department, which can be challenging to establish.

2. **One-dimensional Work**: The work can become monotonous over time, leading to boredom among employees. Lack of new challenges may reduce enthusiasm for the job.

3. **Complicated Operations**: Functional departmentation can be overly complicated. Employees may report to multiple supervisors, leading to overlapping authority and organizational confusion.

4. **Potential for Conflicts**: Managers must handle the appraisal system carefully. Incorrect approaches can lead to conflicts among employees, especially regarding promotions or appraisals.

5. **Inflexibility**: The structure can be rigid and may not easily accommodate necessary personnel changes or adapt to new circumstances.

In summary, while functional departmentation offers advantages, such as specialization and emphasis on activities, organizations should weigh these benefits against potential drawbacks, including complexity, monotony in work, and the potential for conflicts and inflexibility..

## 4.2. PRODUCT DEPARTMENTATION

Product departmentation involves creating departments based on products or product lines. It entails grouping all activities necessary for manufacturing a product or product line together. Each department is referred to as a division. Product departmentation is particularly useful when product expansion, diversification, and the specific engineering, manufacturing, and marketing characteristics of the product are primary considerations.

Under product departmentation, all activities related to a product line are grouped under the supervision of semi-autonomous divisional managers. These managers have the authority to develop the product according to market demand. This structure is particularly suitable for complex products requiring significant capital investment, such as those found in the automobile and electronics industries.

## 4.2.1 Advantages of Product Departmentation:

1. **Reduces Coordination Problems**: Product departmentation reduces the coordination issues that can arise in functional departmentation.

2. **Focus on Each Product Line**: It directs attention to each product line individually.

3. **Specialization**: Product departmentation leads to specialization of physical facilities based on products, resulting in economies of scale.

4. **Ease of Evaluation and Comparison**: It is easier to evaluate and compare the performance of different product divisions.

5. **Isolation**: It keeps production problems isolated from those of other product lines.

In summary, product departmentation organizes departments around products or product lines, allowing for focused attention, specialization, and easier evaluation of performance. It is particularly beneficial in industries where product complexity and significant capital investments are involved.

## 4.2.2 Disadvantages of product departmentation

The disadvantages of product departmentation are given below:

1. **Duplication**: There is duplication of physical facilities and functions. Each product division maintains separate facilities and functional personnel.

2. **Advantages of Centralization Lost:** The advantages of centralizing certain activities like accounting, finance, and marketing cannot be realized.

3. **Underutilization of Capacity:** There may be underutilization of plant capacity if the demand for the product is insufficient.

4. **Inflexibility:** It may be challenging for a company to adapt to changes in demand, technology, etc.

## 4.3 TERRITORY DEPARTMENTATION

Territorial departmentation, also known as geographical departmentation, is particularly beneficial for large organizations with activities that are geographically dispersed. This structure is commonly utilized in industries such as banking, insurance, and transportation. Organizations can divide their operations into zones, divisions, and branches based on geographical regions. For example, the Life Insurance Corporation of India has implemented territorial departmentation to organize its activities.

### 4.3.1 Advantages of territorial departmentation

The advantages of Territorial Departmentation can be summarized as follows:

1. **Local Operations Benefits :** It enables organizations to benefit from local operations. Local managers are familiar with the needs of their customers and can quickly and accurately adapt to local situations.

2. **Meeting Local Demand :** A marketing division can effectively meet local demands.

3. **Improved Coordination :** There is improved coordination of activities within a locality through the establishment of regional divisions.

4. **Facilitates Business Expansion :** It facilitates business expansion into different regions.

5. **Promotes Economic Development :** It contributes to the economic development of the country.

In essence, territorial departmentation enhances local operations, improves coordination, facilitates business growth in various regions, and contributes to economic development at the national level.

## 4.3.2 Disdvantages of territorial departmentation

The drawbacks of territorial departmentation can be outlined as follows:

1. **Challenges in Finding Efficient Managers** : It is difficult to find managers who are proficient in all functional areas.

2. **Duplication of Physical Facilities** : There is duplication of physical facilities, leading to higher operating costs.

3. **Reduced Administrative Control and Coordination** : Top managers may find it less effective to administratively control and coordinate different regional divisions.

4. **Integration Issues Among Regions** : There may be difficulties in integrating various regions into a cohesive whole.

In summary, Territorial Departmentation posses challenges in terms of managerial expertise, operational costs, administrative control, coordination, and regional integration.

## 4.4 CUSTOMER DEPARTMENTATION

Under customer-based departmentation, distinct departments are established to cater to the specific needs of different customer segments. This organizational approach enables managers to meet customer requirements more conveniently and effectively. A marketing organization, for example, might organize its activities based on customer classes, considering factors such as demand volume, language preferences, and specific customer preferences.

The primary advantage of customer departmentation is its focus on customers, who are the ultimate source of revenue for the organization. This approach ensures that the organization is structured to prioritize and meet the needs of its customer base efficiently.

### 4.4.1 Advantages of customer departmentation

Here are the advantages of Customer Departmentation:

1. **Enhanced Customer Satisfaction**: This type of departmentation emphasizes customer satisfaction by delivering better products and services.

2. **Focus on Potential Customers**: Such organizations can focus on clearly identified and potential customers.

3. **Easier Rapport Development**: It is easier to develop rapport with attractive and resourceful customers.

4. **Suitability for Customer-Oriented Organizations**: Customer departmentation is highly beneficial in customer-oriented organizations.

## 4.4.2 Disadvantages of Customer departmentation

Following are the disadvantages of Customer Departmentation

Here are the rephrased disadvantages of Customer Departmentation:

1. **Challenges in Considering All Customers**: It is nearly impossible to consider all customers, their interests, habits, and customs comprehensively.

2. **Coordination Issues**: Departmentation by customer can lead to coordination problems between sales personnel and production teams.

3. **Potential for Discrimination**: There is a risk that the organization may discriminate between affluent and less affluent customers.

## 4.5 PROCESS DEPARTMENTATION

In this type of departmentation, the processes involved in producing various types of equipment are used as the basis for organizing departments. This approach brings together similar types of labor and equipment. For example, a manufacturing enterprise may organize its activities based on the production processes of the equipment involved. The primary objective of this departmentation is to achieve economic efficiencies. The processes are structured in a way that allows for a series of operations to be performed economically.

## 4.5.1 Advantages of Process Departmentation

Following are the advantages of Process Departmentation:

1. **Effective Division of Work**: Process Departmentation ensures a proper division of work, making it an effective form of organizational structure.

2. **Efficient Operations:** Top-level management is focused on achieving the best results, ensuring efficient operations.

3. **Specialization Principles:** Departmentation by process adheres to the principles of specialization.

4. **Clear Authority and Responsibility:** Each department has clear authority and responsibility.

5. **Optimal Resource Utilization:** This type of departmentation facilitates proper and optimal use of resources.

6. **Effective Production Processes:** Due to specialization and division of work, production processes are effective in process departmentation.

### 4.5.2 Disadvantages of Process Departmentation

Followings are the major drawbacks of process Departmentation:

1. **Potential for Conflict:** There is a high potential for conflict in process Departmentation.

2. **Suitability for Large Manufacturing Units:** This type of Departmentation is primarily suitable for large manufacturing firms.

3. **Challenges in Coordination and Unity of Command:** It is difficult to maintain effective coordination and unity of command.

4. **High Costs:** Departmentation by process can be very costly.

## 4.6 PROJECT ORGANISATION

The project organization strategy consists of a set of horizontal departments focused on completing long-duration projects. Each project varies in size and is crucial for the organization. A team of specialists from different functional areas is assembled for each project, coordinated by a project manager.

This structure is temporary and created for a specific project with a defined time limit. Once the project is finished, the structure is dismantled, and the functional specialists return to their original departments. The project's objectives, start and end times, and required resources are clearly defined. The project department operates separately and independently from the functional departments. Project managers form their own teams in addition to the existing functional departments.

Project organization is employed in organizations where projects require high performance standards, such as aerospace, aircraft manufacturing, construction, and professional fields like management consulting. A project team is a temporary arrangement; once the project is completed, the team is disbanded, and functional specialists may return to their previous roles or be assigned to new projects.

## 4.6.1 Advantages of Project Organisation :

**Following are the Advantages of Project Organisation**

1. **Focus on Complex Projects :** Project organization directs attention to complex projects by integrating diverse actions toward their completion.

2. **Timely Project Completion :** It enables projects to be completed on time without disrupting the normal routine work of the entire organization.

3. **Utilization of Specialized Knowledge :** Project organization maximizes the use of specialized knowledge. Specialists are highly motivated when working on complex projects.

4. **Flexibility and Initiative :** It offers flexibility in completing work, encouraging initiative and creativity among project staff.

5. **Versatility through Experience :** Project members become versatile through their experience in different types of projects.

## 4.6.2 Disadvantages of Project Organisation:

**Following are the disadvantages of Project Organisation:**

1. **Challenges with Responsibility and Communication :** There is a lack of clearly defined responsibilities, communication lines, and performance standards for functional specialists. This makes the job of the project manager very challenging.

2. **Risk of Over-Specialization :** Due to specialists from various fields, there is a risk of over-specialization.

3. **Stressful Work Environment :** Each project has a deadline, which creates a stressful work environment.

4. **Job Insecurity :** It causes a sense of insecurity among team members, as they fear they might lose their jobs once the project is completed.

5. **Complex Decision Making :** Decision-making becomes complex due to the pressure from specialists in diverse fields.

## 4.7 MATRIX ORGANISATION

The matrix organization has been developed to meet the needs of large and complex organizations that require a structure more flexible and technically oriented than the functional organization structure. The primary objective is to successfully complete a series of projects. The matrix organization combines two organizational structures: functional and project-based. The organization is divided into various functional areas such as purchasing, production, marketing, human resources, etc., each headed by a functional manager. Additionally, the organization is structured around projects, with each project having its own project manager. Employees typically report to both a functional manager and a project manager. The authority of the project managers flows horizontally (across) the organization, while the authority of the functional managers flows vertically (downward), hence the name "Matrix Organization."

Project teams are formed from the functional departments and are placed under the authority of the project manager for the duration of the project. After completion of the assignment, team members return to their respective functional departments. The matrix organization structure challenges the principle of unity of command, as each individual reports to two bosses—the functional manager and the project manager. This can lead to issues such as indiscipline and confusion, which may adversely affect the organization's productivity and profitability. Therefore, it is crucial to clearly define the authority and responsibilities of each manager to ensure the smooth functioning of the organization.

The matrix organization structure is commonly used in industries with highly complex products, such as the aerospace industry, where project teams are formed for specific space and weapon systems. It is also suitable for multi-project organizations, such as construction companies engaged in simultaneous construction projects.

## 4.7.1 Advantages of Matrix Organisation

Matrix organisation offers the following benefits:

1. **Enhanced Coordination and Control :** It enhances proper coordination and control by assigning specialists from various functional areas to each project.

2. **Increased Flexibility :** The matrix structure is more flexible compared to traditional functional structures.

3. **Opportunity for Skill Enhancement :** In a matrix structure, individuals have the opportunity to enhance their skills and knowledge by interacting with specialists from diverse fields.

4. **Motivation through Competence :** It provides motivation to project staff as they utilize their competencies for the completion of specific projects.

5. **Efficient Resource Allocation :** Resources are not wasted in matrix organizations; each project is allocated the necessary physical, financial, and other resources. Personnel return to their functional departments upon project completion.

6. **Expertise and Quality Performance :** In matrix organizations, since each employee is an expert in their area, quality performance becomes achievable.

## 4.7.2 Disadvantages of Matrix Organisation

Matrix organisation suffers from the following limitations:

1. **Unity of Command Violation :** It violates the principle of unity of command as employees receive instructions from both their functional manager and the project manager. This creates confusion and can lead to jurisdictional conflicts within the organization.

2. **Lack of Line Authority :** In a matrix organization, people are temporarily assigned from different functional departments to project teams. The project manager does not have direct line authority over these personnel, which can hinder the coordination of efforts toward project objectives.

3. **Complex Organizational Relationships :** Organizational relationships become highly complex in a matrix structure. In addition to formal relationships, informal groups also operate within the organization, posing coordination challenges.

4. **Heterogeneous Group Structure :** Matrix organizations are not homogenous and compact groups. The multitude of vertical and horizontal relationships may reduce organizational efficiency.

5. **Unclear Working Relationships :** Working relationships in matrix organizations are often unclear. Balancing the authority of the project manager and functional manager can be difficult.

6. **Performance Appraisal Challenges :** Employees are temporarily assigned from functional departments and work on multiple projects over time. This makes it challenging for functional managers to appraise the performance of these employees.

## 4.8 NETWORK ORGANISATION

The network organization is formed by outsourcing major functions of a firm to separate enterprises and coordinating their activities under the principal firm. Data and information are shared electronically among participating firms, typically via the internet. The core firm, or hub organization, maintains control over the work performed by various subcontractors. The primary objective of the network structure is to eliminate traditional departments and conduct specialized functions through outsourcing, such as manufacturing, accounting, technical support, assembly, packaging, etc. Collaborating firms engage in strategic alliances, joint ventures, and outsourcing agreements.

The network organization differs from traditional hierarchical structures in that there is no superior-subordinate relationship; all members have equal status. Therefore, the network organization functions as a temporary network of autonomous organizations that collaborate based on complementary competencies. They are interconnected via networks to develop, manufacture, and distribute products cooperatively.

The network organization has the potential to respond to global opportunities and challenges. Large industrial houses in India are transitioning from traditional hierarchical structures to horizontal structures, reducing excessive formalization in organizational structures.

## 4.8.1 Advantages of Network Organisation

The main advantages of network structure are as follows:

1. **Elimination of Departmentalization:** Management identifies its core competencies and outsources non-core functions to other organizations. The management's responsibility is to maintain coordination among the contracting firms.

2. **Cost Minimization:** Workers are employed on a temporary basis for administrative work, and support services are outsourced to meet specific requirements. This helps minimize administrative costs.

3. **Emphasis on Specialization:** In a network organization, there is a focus on core competencies in specific areas. The collaboration of specialized companies helps acquire competitive advantages.

4. **Flexibility:** The network organization can adapt to meet the changing business environment. Management can hire employees with skills required for specialized tasks.

5. **Skill Development:** Participating firms learn new skills and acquire knowledge through the transfer of information.

## 4.8.2 Disadvantages of Network Organisation

Network organisation suffers from the following limitations:

1. **Potential for Conflict :** There is a potential for conflict between the principal firm and other firms, which may arise from non-completion of assigned tasks on time, deterioration in work quality, lack of coordination, etc.

2. **Challenges with Secrecy :** Maintaining secrecy regarding internal business matters is difficult. Sometimes, exchanging information becomes necessary to maintain coordination with core business operations, which can result in potential loss of business confidentiality.

3. **Coordination Challenges :** Network organizations rely heavily on coordination. Close and effective communication among all firms is essential to integrate activities and achieve common goals.

4. **Increased Dependency :** Network organizations increase the principal organization's dependency on other firms to meet various customer needs.

5. **Loss of Control :** Ensuring the quality of products or services is crucial for the long-term survival of the business. In a network organization structure, maintaining control over quality and performance is challenging, which may negatively impact organizational performance.

# 5. CHOICE OF BASES OF DEPARTMENTATION

The following factors should be considered when selecting an appropriate basis for departmentalization:

1. **Specialization**: Specialization leads to internal economies in business operations. Therefore, it is a critical consideration when choosing a departmentalization basis. Management should group activities into units that promote specialization of work. However, excessive specialization should be avoided as it may lead to reduced motivation among personnel.

2. **Economy**: The relevance of this factor increases with the number of departments to be created. Establishing a new department increases various costs such as personnel, space, and equipment. Therefore, management should ensure that the departments created make optimal use of these resources to achieve maximum economy.

3. **Emphasis on Key Areas**: All critical areas of the business that are crucial for its success must be given proper consideration. This is why functions such as production, finance, and marketing are typically positioned at the top of the organizational structure with separate departments. Local conditions may also be important, so management should pay attention to them when determining the basis for departmentalization.

4. **Conflict Minimization**: Clear jurisdiction of departments should be established to avoid conflicts among them. The authority of managers in different departments should be clearly specified.

5. **Coordination**: The primary purpose of departmentalization is to achieve organizational goals. Therefore, coordination among the operations of different departments is essential. Departmentalization should facilitate this coordination within the organization.

6. **Control**: Control is crucial for guiding and monitoring the activities of different departments and personnel. The chosen

basis of departmentalization should ensure effective control to achieve organizational goals more economically and efficiently. It should make it easier for top management to ensure performance and hold individuals accountable for results.

7. **Human Considerations**: Departmentalization should not only consider the technical aspects of the organization but also give due attention to the human factor. Informal groups, cultural patterns, and value systems should be considered when grouping personnel.

In summary, departmentalization, regardless of the basis chosen, should be aimed at promoting the economic and efficient attainment of organizational objectives. Managers making such decisions will naturally weigh the relative advantages and disadvantages of various types of departmentalization.

## SUMMARY OF THE CHAPTER

1. Departmentation is the process of grouping of various activities, processes and resources into logical units to perform some organisational task.

2. Departmentation is necessary on account of the following reasons:
   - Advantages of Specialisation
   - Feeling of Autonomy
   - ExpansionFixation of Responsibility
   - Facility in Appraisal
   - Administrative Control:

3. The grouping of homogeneous or similar activities to form an organisational unit is known as functional departmentation. Functional departmentation is the most common form of grouping activities prevalent almost in every enterprise.

4. **Advantages of Functional Departmentation:**
   - Specialisation
   - Managerial efficiency
   - Emphasis on each activity
   - Facilitates delegation
   - Economical

5. **Disadvantages of Functional Departmentation**
   - High degree of specialisation
   - One dimensional work
   - Complicated
   - Chances of conflicts
   - Inflexible

6. In the case of **product departmentation**, departments are created on the basis of products. It involves grouping together of all activities necessary to manufacture a product or product line.

7. **Advantages of product departmentation**
   - Reduces coordination problems.
   - Focus on each product line
   - Specialisation
   - Easy to evaluate and compare
   - Isolation

8. **Disadvantages of product departmentation**
   - Duplication:
   - Centralisation Advantages
   - Underutilization of capacity
   - Inflexible

9. **Territorial departmentation** also known as geographical departmentation is especially useful to large-sized organisations having activities which are physically or geographically spread such as banking, insurance, transportation etc.

10. **Advantages of territorial departmentation**
    - Benefit of local operations
    - Meet local demand
    - Better coordination
    - Facilitates Expansion
    - Economic development

11. **Disdvantages of territorial departmentation**
    - It is difficult to find efficient managers having knowledge of all the functional areas.

- There is duplication of physical facilities resulting in high operating costs.

- Administrative control and co-ordination of different regional divisions by the top managers becomes less effective.

- There may be a problem of integration of various regions

12. Under **customer basis of departmentation,** separate departments are created to serve the different needs of particular customers. Such an organisation helps managers to satisfy the customer's requirement more conveniently and successfully.

13. **Advantages of Customer departmentation**

- **Customer satisfaction**: This type of departmentation emphasis on customer satisfaction by providing better products and services.

- **Concentration on potential customers**: Such organisation can concentrate on clearly identified and potential customers.

- **Easy to develop rapport**: It is easier to develop rapport with attractive and resourceful customers.

- **Useful**: It is highly useful in customer-oriented organisation

14. **Disadvantages of Customer departmentation**

- **Difficult to consider all customers**: It is almost impossible to consider all the customers, their interests, habits and customs.

- **Coordination problems**: Departmentation by customer leaves coordination problems between sales personnel and production people.

- **Discrimination**: Organisation may discriminate between kith and poor customers.

15. Under process departmentation, processes involved in the production of various types of equipments used are taken as basis for departmentation.

16. **Advantages of Process Departmentation**
    - Proper division of work
    - Proper operation
    - Principles of specialisation
    - Clear authority and responsibility
    - Optimum use of resources
    - Effective process

17. **Disadvantages of Process Departmentation**
    - Chances of conflict
    - Suitable for large manufacturing unit
    - Difficult to maintain
    - Costly

18. The **project organisation** strategy consists of a new number of horizontal departments oriented towards the completion of projects of long duration. The size of project varies from one project to another.

19. **Matrix organisation** is a combination of two organisation structures- Functional and project. The organisation is divided into different functional areas, e.g., purchase, production, marketing, human resource, etc. Each function is headed by a functional manager.

20. The **network organisation** is created by subcontracting firm's major functions to separate enterprises and co-ordinating their activities by the principal firm. The data and information is shared by the participant firms electronically.

21. The following factors should be kept in mind while selecting a suitable basis of departmentation:
    - Specialisation
    - Economy
    - Appreciation of key areas
    - Minimum conflicts
    - Coordination
    - Control
    - Human Consideration

# QUESTIONS

1. Write down the concept of Departmentation.
2. Define a Department.
3. Discuss the need and importance of Departmentation.
4. What is functional departmentation?
5. What are the advantages of functional departmentation?
6. What are the disadvantages of functional departmentation?
7. What do you understand by product departmentation?
8. What are the advantages of product departmentation?
9. What are the disadvantages of product departmentation?
10. What do you mean by territory departmentation?
11. What are the advantages of territory departmentation?
12. What do you mean by customer departmentation?
13. What are the advantages of customer departmentation?
14. What are the disadvantages of customer departmentation?
15. What do you mean by process departmentation?
16. What are the advantages of process departmentation?
17. What are the disadvantages of process departmentation?
18. Discuss the bases of departmentation.
19. What do you understand by functional departmentation?
20. State the advantages and disadvantages of functional departmentation.
21. What do you mean by product departmentation?
22. Mention the merits and demerits of product departmentation.
23. Give the convept of territorial departmentation.
24. What are the advantages of territorial departmentation?
25. What are the disadvantages of territorial departmentation?
26. What do you understand by the term customer departmentation?
27. What are the merits and demerits of customer departmentation?
28. What do you understand by process departmentation?

29. State the merits and demerits of process departmentation.
30. What is matrix department?
31. Mention the merits and demerits of matrix departmentation.
32. What do you understand by the term network departmentation?
33. State the merits of network departmentation.
34. State the demerits of network departmentation.
35. Discuss the factors should be kept in mind while selecting a suitable basis of departmentation.
36. Write short notes on:

    a. Functional Departmentation  b. Product Departmentation

    c. Territory Departmentation   d. Process Departmentation

# UNIT 3A
# AUTHORITY RELATIONSHIP

Authority Relationships

Line and Staff

Delegation of Authority

Decentralisation

## CONTENTS

1.  Delegation of Authority

    1.1 Definition of Delegation Of Authority

    1.2 Features of Delegation Of Authority

    1.3 Elements of Delegation Of Authority

    1.4 Comparison of Authority, Responsibility And Accountability

    1.5 Principles of Delegation

    1.6 Advantages of Effective Delegation

    1.7 Barriers To Effective Delegation

2.  Decentralisation

    2.1 Comparison Between Centralisation and Decentralisation

    2.2 Comparison Between Delegation and Decentralisation

    2.3 Advantages of Decentralization

    2.4 Disadvantages of Decentralization

    2.5 Factors Determining The Degree of Decentralisation

# 1. DELEGATION OF AUTHORITY

Delegation involves transferring authority from one manager or organizational unit to another to complete specific tasks. A manager doesn't just delegate authority; they delegate it to ensure certain tasks are completed. Through delegation, a manager expands their area of operations. Delegation of authority is crucial in the organizing process and is fundamental to the existence of a formal organization. Organizational units created through departmentalization require that managers be granted appropriate authority. Assigning tasks to various managers creates responsibilities, and to fulfill these responsibilities, managers need matching authority. In essence, authority should align with responsibility.

## 1.1 DEFINITION OF DELEGATION OF AUTHORITY

"The delegation of authority is the delivery by one individual to another of the right to act, to make decisions, to acquire resources and to other tasks in order to fulfill job responsibilities".

*O. Jeff. Harris*

"Delegation of authority is the granting of authority by a superior to a subordinate to operate within the prescribed limits".

*Theo Haimman*

"Delegation is the dynamics of management, it is the process of a manager follows in dividing the work assigned to him so that he performs that part which only, he, because of his unique organisational placement, can perform effectively and so that he can get others to help him with what remains."

*Louise A. Allen*

"Delegation takes place when one person gives another the right to perform work on his behalf and in his name, and the second person accepts a corresponding duty or obligation to do what is required of him.

*O.S.Hiner*

## 1.2 FEATURES OF DELEGATION OF AUTHORITY

Delegation of authority has the following characteristics:

1. Delegation grants a manager the authorization to act within certain limits, defining the scope within which decisions can be made.

2. Delegation has a dual nature: the subordinate gains authority from the superior, but the superior retains their original authority.

3. Delegated authority can be increased, decreased, or revoked based on the situation and needs.

4. Authority is delegated to the position within the organization, not the individual. The authority is tied to the position and is reclaimed when the individual leaves that position.

5. A manager can only delegate authority that they themselves possess; they cannot delegate more authority than they have.

6. Delegation can be specific, with clearly defined actions for particular objectives, or general, with specified objectives but without detailed actions.

## 1.3 ELEMENTS OF DELEGATION OF AUTHORITY

Delegation of authority involves three essential elements:

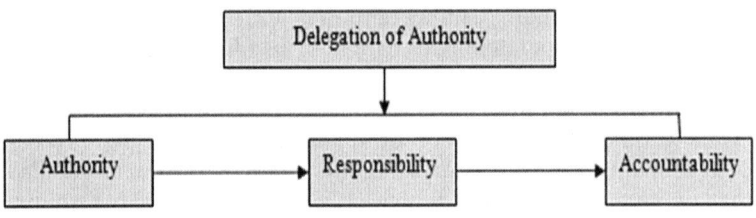

*Elements of delegation of authority*

1. **Authority**: Authority refers to a manager's right to command subordinates and take action within the scope of their position. It empowers the manager to make decisions, issue instructions to subordinates to accomplish tasks, and take corrective action if those instructions are not fully followed. Authority is inherently linked to a position; without a position, there is no authority. As an individual's position within the organization rises, their authority increases, and it decreases as their position lowers. Authority is derived from the position within the organization, being greatest at the top level and diminishing as it flows

downward. This establishes a relationship where superiors have authority over their subordinates and expect them to execute decisions according to the issued guidelines.

According to **Henri Fayol**, "Authority is the right to give order and the power to exact obedience".

According to **Mooney and Reily**, "Authority is the principle at the root of organisation and so important that it is impossible to conceive of an organisation at all unless some person or persons are in a position to require action of others".

2. **Responsibility**: Responsibility refers to the tasks or duties assigned to an individual based on their position within the organization. To ensure subordinates can effectively fulfill their responsibilities, the superior must clearly define the tasks or duties assigned to them.

   Responsibility is the obligation of a subordinate to perform the assigned tasks efficiently. It stems from the superior-subordinate relationship and obligates the subordinate to carry out the duties assigned by their superior. Responsibility flows upwards, meaning a subordinate is always accountable to their superior. Additionally, subordinates must be granted the appropriate level of authority necessary to carry out their assigned tasks, ensuring that the authority matches the responsibility given.

   According to **Davis**, "Responsibility is an obligation of individual to perform assigned duties to the best of his ability under the direction of his executive leader".

   In the words of **Theo Haimann**, "Responsibility is the obligation of a subordinate to perform the duty as required by his superior".

   **McFarland** defines responsibility as, "The duties and activities assigned to a person or an executive".

3. **Accountability**: Accountability is the obligation to fulfill responsibilities and be answerable for the final outcomes. It involves holding an individual responsible for the results of their actions. A subordinate is accountable to their superior for the outcomes of their assigned tasks. The delegation of authority

process is incomplete without establishing accountability.

**According to McFarland,** "Accountability is the obligation of an individual to report formally to his superior about the work he has done to discharge the responsibility".

When authority is delegated to a subordinate, the subordinate becomes accountable to their superior for their performance on the assigned duties. If the subordinate performs poorly, the superior cannot avoid responsibility by blaming the subordinate. Typically, a superior is responsible for the actions of all groups under their supervision, even if multiple layers exist within the hierarchy. Simply put, accountability means the subordinate must explain the reasons for any non-performance or inadequate performance.

Accountability is characterised by the following features:

1. Accountability is the obligation to carry out the responsibility or duties by the use of delegated authority.

2. Accountability always flows upward.

3. Accountability cannot be delegated.

4. Accountability is always limited to the range of duties assigned to a subordinate.

**Authority can be delegated but responsibility can't be delegated :** Here, the term 'responsibility' is used in the sense of accountability for the use of authority. Accountability arises because of delegation of authority. The person who has been granted authority should use such authority properly and be responsible to the superior. He can't avoid responsibility.

## 1.4 COMPARISON OF AUTHORITY, RESPONSIBILITY AND ACCOUNTABILITY

| Basis | Authority | Responsibility | Accountability |
|-------|-----------|----------------|----------------|
| Meaning | It is the right of a manager to command his/her subordinates | It is the duty of a subordinate to perform the jobs assigned to him/her by his/her boss. | It means answerability for the results. |

| Basis | Authority | Responsibility | Accountability |
|---|---|---|---|
| Delegation | Authority can be delegated to the subordinates | Duty or job assignment can be given by a superior to a subordinate, but responsibility to perform it cannot be further delegated by the subordinate. | It cannot be delegated. It is absolute. |
| Origin | It arises because of a formal position in the organisation. Whosoever occupies the position has the right to command the subordinate. | It arises from a superior-subordinate relationship. The subordinate is accountable since he/she owes an explanation to his/her superior for the performance of duties assigned. | It arises from responsibility or duties assigned. |
| Flow of direction | It always flows downwards from the superior to the subordinate. | It is assigned by the superior to the subordinate. This means it flows in the downward direction. | It moves upward from subordinate to superior as subordinate is responsible to his/her superior. |

## 1.5 PRINCIPLES OF DELEGATION

The following principles are guides to delegation of authority:

1. **Delegation by Results Expected**: Before delegating authority, a manager should first consider the goals to be achieved and then delegate enough authority to achieve the expected results.

2. **Principle of Functional Definition**: There should be clear definitions of the expected results and the activities to be undertaken. The clearer these definitions, the better individuals can contribute to accomplishing the enterprise's objectives.

3. **Scalar Principle:** This principle involves a clear chain of direct authority relationships from superior to subordinate throughout the organization. Subordinates should clearly understand who delegates authority to them and to whom they must refer matters beyond their authority.

4. **Authority-level Principle:** Decisions that fall within an individual's authority should be made by that individual and not referred upward in the organizational structure. Managers at each level should make decisions within their delegated authority, referring only those matters they cannot decide due to authority limitations to their superiors.

5. **Unity of Command:** An individual should report to only one superior to avoid conflicts.

6. **Absoluteness of Responsibility:** A manager who has delegated authority and assigned duties cannot escape responsibility for the activities of their subordinates. This responsibility is absolute and cannot be delegated.

7. **Parity of Authority and Responsibility:** The amount of authority given should match the amount of responsibility assigned. Managers should not hold subordinates responsible for duties without providing the necessary authority.

## 1.6 ADVANTAGES OF EFFECTIVE DELEGATION

Delegation has several important advantages.

1. **More Delegation, More Opportunities:** The more tasks managers can delegate, the more opportunities they have to seek and accept increased responsibilities from higher-level managers.

2. **Better Decisions:** Delegation often results in better decisions, as subordinates who are closer to the actual operating level typically have a clearer understanding of the facts.

3. **Time Saving:** Effective delegation speeds up decision-making. When subordinates are authorized to make decisions on the spot, valuable time is saved as they no longer need to check with their superiors before deciding.

4. **Enhance Self-Confidence:** Delegation encourages subordinates to accept responsibility and exercise judgment. This not only helps to train them but also boosts their self-confidence and willingness to take initiative.

## 1.7 BARRIERS TO EFFECTIVE DELEGATION

Apart from the advantages discussed, many managers are reluctant to delegate authority, and many subordinates are hesitant to accept it. These barriers hinder effective delegation. The reasons for these barriers are outlined below:

**A. Reluctance to Delegate:** Managers often have various reasons for not delegating:

1. **Insecurity:** Managers may feel insecure about delegating because they are accountable for their subordinates' actions. They may be reluctant to take risks or fear losing power if the subordinate performs too well.

2. **Lack of Ability:** Some managers might lack the ability to delegate effectively. They may be too disorganized or inflexible to plan ahead, decide which tasks to delegate, or set up a system to monitor subordinates' actions.

3. **Lack of Confidence in Subordinates:** Managers may avoid delegation due to a lack of confidence in their subordinates. While this may be justified in the short term if subordinates lack skills or knowledge, it is the manager's responsibility to train them. Managers with an inflated sense of their own worth may limit their subordinates' freedom to act.

**B. Reluctance to Accept Delegation:** Subordinates can also be hesitant to accept delegated tasks due to:

1. **Avoidance:** Some subordinates prefer to avoid responsibility and risks, preferring their bosses to make all decisions.

2. **Fear of Criticism:** Subordinates who fear criticism or dismissal for mistakes may be reluctant to accept delegation.

3. **No Incentive for Extra Responsibility:** Subordinates may lack sufficient incentive to take on additional responsibilities.

Accepting delegation often means more work and greater pressure, and without adequate compensation, they may be unwilling to accept these tasks.

The delegation of authority by individual managers is closely related to an organization's decentralization of authority. Delegation involves assigning authority from one management level down to the next. Decentralization refers to systematic efforts to delegate all authority, except that which must be exercised centrally, to the lowest levels. Decentralization means dispersing decision-making authority to lower levels where problems arise, while reserving some authority, such as planning, organizing, directing, and controlling, with top management. This allows executives at the lowest levels to make decisions regarding the problems they face without seeking approval from higher levels.

The concepts of decentralization and centralization refer to the extent to which authority is passed down to lower levels (decentralization) or retained at the top (centralization). The more authority delegated throughout the organization, the more decentralized the organization is.

## 2.1 COMPARISON BETWEEN CENTRALISATION AND DECENTRALISATION

| S. No. | Basis | Centralisaation | Decentralisation |
|---|---|---|---|
| 1 | Meaning | The retention of planning and decision making powers with top management. | The distribution of authority, responsibility and accountability across various management levels. |
| 2 | Authority | Centralisation involves systematic and consistent reservation of authority. | Decentralisation involves systematic dispersal of authority |
| 3 | Decisions | Here all important decisions are taken at the top level. | Here all important decisions are taken at various levels of management. |

| S. No. | Basis | Centralisaation | Decentralisation |
|--------|-------|-----------------|------------------|
| 4 | Responsibility | In case of Centralisation, responsibility lies at the top level. | In case of Decentralisation, responsibility lies at different levels. |
| 5 | Flow of Information | There is a presence of vertical flow of information. | There is vertical and horizontal flow of information. |
| 6 | Suitability | Centralised organizations are best fit for companies of a smaller size. The central figure of authority is then able to make better and more well informed decisions. This is also fit for boutique consulting firms etc. | A decentralised model is best suited for huge multinationals that operate in many countries and have diversified employees to manage and varied rules and regulations to adhere to. |

## 2.2 COMPARISON BETWEEN DELEGATION AND DECENTRALISATION

| S. No. | Basis | Delegation | Decentralisation |
|--------|-------|------------|------------------|
| 1 | Meaning | Delegation means handling over an authority from one person of high level to the person of lower level. | Decentralisation is the final outcome achieved, when the delegation of authority is performed systematically and repeatedly to the lowest level. |

| S. No. | Basis | Delegation | Decentralisation |
|--------|-------|------------|------------------|
| 2 | Freedom of action | The person who delegates authority keeps the power to control with himself. The subordinate does not have much freedom of action. | Control is exercised by the top management in a general manner. The divisional managers enjoy sufficient autonomy or freedom of action. |
| 3 | Need | Delegation is essential to get things done by others. Unless otherwise authority is delegated it will difficult to assign responsibility. | Decentralisation is optional because it is the philosophy of management. Top management may or may not disperse authority. |
| 4 | Responsibility | In delegation, responsibility remains with the delegator. He/she can delegate authority and not responsibility. | In Decentralisation, head of the department is responsible for all activities under him/her. He/she is required to show better performance of the whole department. |
| 5 | Control | In delegation the final control over the activities of organisation lies with the top executive | In decentralisation the power of control is exercised by the unit head to which the authority has been delegated. |

| S. No. | Basis | Delegation | Decentralisation |
|--------|-------|------------|------------------|
| 6 | Nature | Delegation is the result of human limitation to the span of management. | Decentralisation is the other hand, is the result of the big size and multi-furious functions of the enterprise. |

## 2.3 ADVANTAGES OF DECENTRALIZATION

Decentralization of authority has certain advantages, such as:

1. **Diversification of Activities :** Decentralization diversifies business activities by reducing the burden on chief executives for routine decisions. This allows them to focus on crucial tasks such as product diversification, securing finance, obtaining licenses, launching new production lines, and solving significant business problems, while routine matters are handled by middle and supervisory levels.

2. **Development of Managerial Personnel :** Decentralization offers many individuals the opportunity to act as managers within the organization. These managers learn through hands-on experience, enhancing their skills and capabilities.

3. **Effective Control and Supervision :** With decentralization, managers have full authority to make decisions and implement changes, enabling them to effectively supervise and control their subordinates' activities.

4. **Improvement of Morale :** By enhancing managerial abilities, decentralization boosts morale, leading to increased productivity.

5. **Satisfaction of Human Needs:** Decentralization satisfies human needs for power, independence, status, and prestige. This satisfaction fosters a cadre of contented managers who are committed to the company's work.

6. **Quick and Wise Decision-Making :** Decision-making authority is closer to the action, allowing those with authority to make timely, accurate, and wise decisions due to their awareness of the situation's realities. This also reduces delays in communication.

7. **Better Utilization of Management** : Decentralization ensures better utilization of lower and middle management, providing greater incentives, improved training opportunities, and a balanced focus on all products.

8. **Enhanced Employee Management:** Decentralization enables closer and more effective employee management and community relations within smaller administrative units. It leads to a broader distribution of roles and responsibilities, which can mitigate the negative impact of sales declines.

9. **Increase in Social Net Product** : Decentralization can increase the managerial social net product, benefiting the community. This includes more individual freedom of action, greater opportunities for constructive participation, and reduced social stratification within the business.

10. **Reduction of Top Executives' Burden :** Decentralization relieves top managers from handling too many operational decisions, allowing them to specialize and focus on future planning and strategic thinking.

## 2.4 DISADVANTAGES OF DECENTRALIZATION

Despite the advantages of decentralization, there are certain challenges in applying it universally. The major limitations of decentralization include:

1. **Lack of Uniform Policies**: Under decentralization, it is difficult to maintain uniform policies and standardized procedures. Each manager may develop policies based on their own expertise.

2. **Coordination Issues**: Decentralization can lead to coordination problems because authority is widely dispersed throughout the organization.

3. **Increased Financial Burden**: Decentralization requires hiring trained personnel to handle authority, which can be financially burdensome. Small enterprises may struggle to afford experts in various fields.

4. **Higher Costs**: It raises administrative expenses due to the need to hire highly-paid managers. Creating various departments and employing specialists in each department results in higher operational costs.

5. **Unsuitability for Small Firms**: Decentralization is generally unsuitable for small firms due to its high operating costs.

6. **Reliance on Managers**: Decentralized organizations heavily depend on the competence of divisional managers. If these managers lack the necessary skills or competence, the enterprise risks significant losses due to poor decisions.

## 2.5 FACTORS DETERMINING THE DEGREE OF DECENTRALISATION

The appropriate degree of decentralization for an organization will vary with time, circumstances, and across different subunits. For instance, production and sales departments might be highly decentralized, while financial departments may need to be more centralized. When determining the appropriate level of decentralization, the following factors are usually considered:

1. **Costliness of the Decision**: Generally, the more costly the decision, the more likely it is to be made at higher management levels. For example, quality control in drug manufacturing, where mistakes can endanger lives and the company's reputation, would be managed at a high level, whereas quality inspection in toy manufacturing might be managed at a lower level.

2. **Desire for Uniformity of Policy**: A desire for consistent policies favors centralization, as it ensures uniform treatment of customers regarding quality, price, credit, delivery, and service, and standardizes public relations and supplier dealings. High uniformity requirements limit the degree of decentralization.

3. **Size of the Organization**: Larger organizations have more decisions to make in various locations, complicating coordination. As the size of an organization increases, so does the need for a higher degree of decentralization.

4. **History of the Enterprise**: The degree of decentralization often depends on the organization's history. Enterprises expanding internally under the guidance of their owner-founders tend to remain centralized, while those resulting from mergers and consolidations are more likely to retain decentralized authority, allowing merged units to maintain some independence.

5. **Management Philosophy**: The philosophy and character of top executives significantly influence the extent of decentralization.

Authoritarian managers who do not tolerate interference tend to favor centralized structures, while more democratic managers support decentralized structures.

6. **Availability of Managers**: A shortage of qualified managers can limit decentralization, as delegation requires capable individuals to whom authority can be given. However, the scarcity of managers is sometimes used as an excuse for centralization, with executives exaggerating their own value to the firm.

7. **Control Techniques**: The availability and willingness to use control techniques also influence decentralization. Managers who lack knowledge of control methods may be reluctant to delegate authority, fearing it takes more time to correct mistakes than to do the job themselves.

8. **Decentralized Performance**: When an organization's operations are geographically dispersed, authority tends to be decentralized. Decentralized performance limits the ability to centralize authority, though centralization of performance does not necessarily mean authority will be centralized.

9. **Environmental Influences**: External factors such as government controls, labor unionism, and policies affect decentralization. Government regulations can restrict decentralization by limiting the freedom of sales and purchase managers. National labor unions centralize negotiations, reducing the scope for decentralization. In contrast, local union negotiations allow more decentralized authority.

## SUMMARY OF THE CHAPTER

1. **Delegation** refers to transfer of authority from one manager or organisational unit to another in order to accomplish particular assignments.

2. Delegation of authority has the following **features**:

   • Delegation is authorization to a manager to act in a certain manner

   • Delegation has dual characteristics.

   • Authority once delegated can be enhanced, reduced, or withdrawn depending on the situation and requirement.

   • Delegation of authority is always to the position created

through the process of organizing.

- A manager delegates authority out of the authority vesting in him/her.
- Delegation of authority may be specific or general.

3. Delegation of authority involves three essential elements i.e. *Authority, Responsibility and Accountability.*

4. *Authority* refers to the right of a manager to command his/her subordinates and to take action within the scope of his/her position.

5. *Responsibility* means the works or duties assigned to a person by virtue of his/her position in the organisation.

6. *Accountability* is the obligation to carry out responsibility, i.e., being answerable for the final outcome.

7. Authority can be delegated but responsibility can't be delegated.

8. The following **principles are guides to delegation of authority**:
- Delegation by Results Expected
- Principle of Functional Definition
- Scalar Principle
- Authority-level Principle
- Unity of Command
- Absoluteness of Responsibility
- Parity of Authority and Responsibility

9. **Delegation has several important advantages .**
- More delegation more opportunities
- Better decisions
- Time saving
- Enhance self confidence

10. **Barriers to effective delegation**
   A. *Reluctance to Delegate.*
   - Insecurity
   - Lack of ability
   - Lack of confidence in subordinates

B   *Reluctance to Accept Delegation*

- Avoidance
- Fear of criticism
- No incentive for extra responsibility

11. **Decentralisation** refers to the systematic efforts to delegate to the lowest levels all authority except that which can only be exercised at the central points.

12. **Decentralization of authority** has certain **advantages**, such as:

- Diversification of activities
- Development of the Managerial Personnel
- Effective Control and Supervision
- Improvement of morale
- Satisfaction of human needs
- Quick and wise decision possible
- Better utilization of Management
- Employee Management
- Increase Social Net Product
- Reduces the Burden of Top Executives

13. The serious **limitations of decentralization** are as follows:

- Uniform policies not Followed
- Problem of Co-Ordination.
- More Financial Burden
- Costly
- Unsuitable for Small Firms
- Reliance on the Manager:

14. **Factors determining the degree of decentralization:**

- Costliness of the Decision
- Desire for Uniformity of policy
- Size of the Organisation
- History of the Enterprise

- Management Philosophy
- Availability of Managers
- Control Techniques
- Decentralised Performance
- Environmental Influences

# QUESTIONS

1. What is Delegation of Authority?

2. Define Delegation of Authority.

3. Why is Delegation considered essential for effective organising?

4. What are the features of Delegation of Authority?

5. What are the elements of Delegation of Authority?

6. What is Authority?

7. Define Authority.

8. What is Responsibility?

9. Define Responsibility.

10. What is Accountability?

11. Define Accountability.

12. Differentiate between Authority and Responsibility.

13. Differentiate between Authority and Accountability.

14. Differentiate between Responsibility and Accountability.

15. Discuss the Principles of Delegation.

16. What are the advantages of Delegation?

17. What are the disadvantages of Delegation?

18. What do you mean by Decentralisation?

19. What do you mean by Centralisation?

20. What are the main points of differences between Centralisation

and Decentralisation?

21. What are the differences between Delegation and Decentralisation of Authority?

22. Discuss the advantages of Decentralisation.

23. What are the disadvantages of Decentralisation?

24. Discuss the factors determining degree of Decentralisation.

25. Write short notes on:

    a.  Delegation             b.  Decentralisation

    c.  Centralisation          d.  Authority

    e.  Responsibility          f.  Accountability

# UNIT 3B
# GROUP AND TEAM

**CONTENTS**

# 1. CONCEPT OF GROUP

In the previous chapter, we explored the concepts of delegation of authority and decentralization. Now, we will delve into the concept of a group. A group consists of two or more individuals who interact in a way that each person influences and is influenced by the others. Essentially, when two or more individuals work together towards a specific objective or goal and impact each other's behavior and actions, they are collectively known as a group. Therefore, a group is an integration of two or more individuals who collaborate to achieve a common objective or goal, interact with each other, are aware of each other's actions, and each considers themselves part of the group.

## 1.1 DEFINITIONS OF GROUP

*"Two or more persons who are interacting with one another in such a manner that each person influences and is influenced by each other"*

**Marvin E. Shaw**

*"When two or more persons work under one another to attain a specific objective or goal and influence each other's behaviour and actions, then they are called a Group collectively"*

**Robbins**

*"A group may be defined as a social phenomenon in which two or more persons decide to interact with one another, share common ideology and perceive themselves as a group."*

**Edgar H.Schien**

## 1.2 DIFFERENT KINDS OF GROUPS

Groups can be classified in various ways. Some important types of groups are discussed below:

1.  **Formal Group**: A formal group is formed by an organization to perform specific activities and achieve particular goals, following established rules and disciplines. These groups are deliberately created to ensure desired results and have predefined authorities, responsibilities, and accountabilities. The relationships within these groups are clearly defined

in advance and are established by a competent authority. Examples include the board of directors, purchase committees, and grievance management committees. Formal groups can be further classified into:

i. *Command Group:* Consisting of a manager and the employees who report to them, command groups are defined by the organization's hierarchy. Membership is determined by each employee's position in the organizational chart.

ii. *Task Group:* Task groups are composed of employees who collaborate to complete a specific task or project. These groups can cross command relationships and are not limited to their immediate hierarchical superior. Membership arises from the responsibilities assigned to the employees. Task groups can be temporary or open-ended.

iii. *Committee:* A committee is a group of individuals officially delegated to perform a specific function, such as investigating, considering, reporting, or acting on a matter. Committees analyze, debate, and make recommendations on issues, and typically have their own members, including advisory authorities and secretaries. Their recommendations are sent to the responsible authority for implementation.

2. **Informal Groups**: Informal groups form naturally among members of an organization to meet personal goals. These groups do not have predefined authorities and responsibilities, but their members share common objectives. They arise in response to the need for social contact and are influenced by factors such as proximity, shared attitudes, personalities, or economic status. Informal groups include:

i. Friendship Groups: Formed based on common characteristics, such as age, political views, or educational background, friendship groups often extend beyond the workplace.

ii. Interest Groups: Comprised of individuals who may not be part of the same command or task group but come together to achieve a specific objective of mutual concern.

iii. Reference Groups: Used as a basis for comparison in decision-making or opinion formation. These groups can be internal or external to the organization, such as family, coworkers, friends, or religious groups. Reference groups can also serve as negative reference points.

iv. Membership Groups: Groups to which individuals actually belong, both formal and informal. Members have responsibilities and benefits, contributing to the group's wellbeing and enjoying the friendship within the group.

v. Cliques: Relatively permanent informal groups centered around friendships. Cliques often include individuals from various professions and develop their own norms, beliefs, and social control mechanisms, influencing members to conform to group expectations. They serve as a system for making sense of organizational events.

## 1.3 COMPARISON BETWEEN FORMAL GROUP AND INFORMAL GROUP

| S.No | Basis | Formal Group | Informal Group |
|------|-------|--------------|----------------|
| 1 | *Formation* | Legally constituted, rationally designed, and consciously planned. | Emerges naturally and spontaneously. |
| 2 | *Existence* | Normally formal group does not arise because of informal group. | Informal group emerges while working in a formal group. |
| 3 | *Purpose* | Well-defined and centers around survival, growth. Profit, service to society. | Ill-defined and centers around friendship, goodwill, unity and so on. |
| 4 | *Relationship* | Superior-subordinate relationship | Personal and social relationship |

| S.No | Basis | Formal Group | Informal Group |
|------|-------|--------------|----------------|
| 5 | *Influenced by* | Rationality and leaves no scope for personal, social and emotional factors | Personal, social and emotional factors present. |
| 6 | *Communication* | Unity of command and line of authority followed. | Pattern is grapevine, which is natural, haphazard and intricate. |
| 7 | *Leadership* | Based on formal authority and position. | Based on individual competence and group acceptance. |
| 8 | *Boundaries* | Operates within set boundaries | No bounds, operates in different directions. |
| 9 | *Nature and emphasis* | Normative and idealistic, emphasis on efficiency, discipline, conformity, consistency and control bring in rigidity and bureaucracy in processes and practices. | Reflects actual functioning, characterised by relative freedom, spontaneity, homeliness and warmth. |

## 1.4 REASONS OR DYNAMICS OF GROUP FORMATION

Understanding why people form groups is essential for comprehending group dynamics. There are several theories regarding the reasons behind group formation:

1. **Propinquity**: This theory emphasizes that group relationships are established due to geographical proximity. Employees in the same organization, workers in the same office, or individuals on a mission often form groups due to their physical closeness.

2. **Activity, Interaction, and Sentiments**: Group formation depends on three elements: activities, interactions, and sentiments. The more people engage in activities together, the more they interact and develop emotional bonds, leading to the formation of a group.

3. **Group Activities**: Individuals may be motivated to join a group because they enjoy the activities the group engages in, such as jogging, playing games, or flying model airplanes. These activities are often more enjoyable or require multiple participants. However, if the level of interpersonal attraction within the group is very low, a person might choose not to join despite the appealing activities.

4. **Need Satisfaction**: People join groups to satisfy various needs, such as physical, social, security, status, respect, and self-development needs. Since individuals cannot fulfill all these needs on their own, they either join existing groups or form new ones.

5. **Group Goals**: The goals of a group can also motivate individuals to join. For example, people join organizations like the Sierra Club for environmental conservation because they support its mission, even if they do not personally connect with all the members or enjoy every group activity. Similarly, workers join unions like the United Auto Workers because they align with the union's goals.

6. **Exchange**: According to *Thaibaut and Kelly*, people form groups to achieve certain results. If an individual believes that associating with others will help them attain their goals or fulfill their desires, they are likely to join the group.

7. **Similarity**: *Newcomb's Balanced Theory* suggests that people are attracted to those with similar thoughts, habits, interests,

and goals. This similarity encourages them to come together and form groups.

## 1.5 PROCESS OR STAGES OF FORMATION OF GROUP

When interpreting the behavior of a specific group, it's crucial to acknowledge not just the overall developmental patterns but also the distinctive characteristics of that particular group and the circumstances that either foster or hinder its development. The development of a specific group is influenced by factors such as how often its members interact and the personal traits of its members. However, it's commonly accepted that groups typically progress through a standard sequence of five stages:

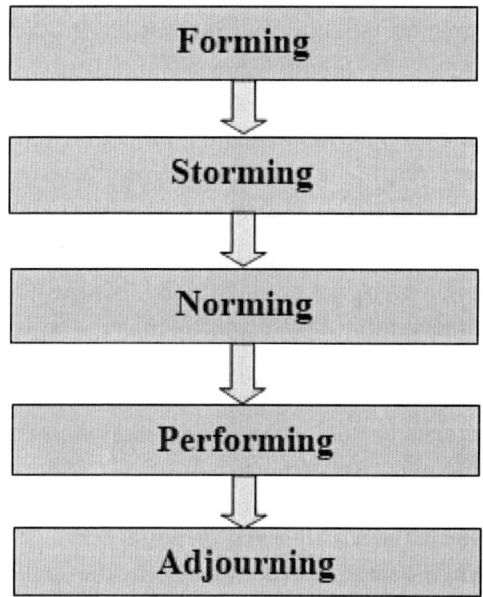

*Stages in the formation of a group*

1. **Forming**: When a group is first established, its members cannot accomplish much until they agree on their purpose, how they will work together, and similar issues. Addressing these questions brings members face-to-face with initial challenges: uncertainty, anxiety, and disagreements over power and

authority. During this stage, the focus is on interpersonal relationships among members. They evaluate each other in terms of trustworthiness, emotional comfort, and acceptance of ideas. Therefore, the forming stage is marked by uncertainty about the group's purpose, structure, and leadership. Members are testing boundaries to understand acceptable behavior. This stage concludes when members begin to identify themselves as part of the group.

2. **Storming:** The storming stage involves intergroup conflict. Members acknowledge the group's existence but resist the constraints it imposes on individuality. Additionally, there is conflict over who will control the group. Once a group leader emerges, the remaining members must establish their roles. Even if all members accept the leader, the group faces challenges and disagreements. Followers may challenge the leader, and the group may divide into factions supporting or opposing the leader. If the group becomes stuck in this phase, members may engage in power struggles and political tactics. Completion of this stage results in a clear leadership hierarchy within the group.

3. **Norming:** During this stage, close relationships form and the group demonstrates cohesion. Moving into the cohesion phase requires intervention by a group member who is emotionally detached from power and authority issues. Typically, this person encourages open discussion of these issues. When the group engages in this process, the cohesion phase progresses quickly. Members understand their roles, and the group agrees on its operational procedures. A new leader may emerge, or the existing leader may better recognize members' contributions. The norming stage concludes when the group structure stabilizes and members share common expectations regarding appropriate behavior.

4. **Performing:** The performing stage is when the group is fully functional and accepted. Group energy shifts from getting acquainted to performing the task at hand. Members focus on self-motivation and motivating others to achieve the task. Some members initiate activities to drive progress, while others maintain motivation and commitment through support,

encouragement, and recognition of contributions. They also establish standards for evaluating performance.

5. **Adjourning**: Performing is the final stage for permanent work groups. Temporary groups, however, proceed to the adjourning stage. Here, the group prepares for disbandment. High task performance is no longer the top priority. Instead, attention turns toward wrapping up activities .

## 1.6 GROUP BEHAVIOUR

Group behavior refers to the organized and collective actions of a group. It encompasses the ways people act in both large and small group settings. Individuals join groups for various reasons, primarily because membership fulfills certain needs. Group behavior can be categorized into intra-group and inter-group behavior. Intra-group behavior examines the interactions among members within the same group, while inter-group behavior analyzes how one group interacts with other groups.

Several factors influence group behavior, including group activities, goals, size, structure, and the characteristics of its members. Group behavior often differs from individual behavior, so these factors must be understood to fully grasp group dynamics. Key elements affecting group effectiveness include group roles, decision-making processes, leadership, norms, and cohesiveness.

## 1.7 FACTORS AFFECTING EFFECTIVENESS OF GROUP BEHAVIOUR

The factors that affect the effectiveness of group behavior are as follows:

1. **Group Decision-making**: In contemporary settings, decisions are often made collectively by committees, boards of directors, etc., rather than individually. Group decisions are often more effective and technically accurate than those made by individuals. Group decision-making offers several benefits, such as stability and practicality, since a group can gather more facts and data than an individual. A group can consider multiple alternatives and solutions within a broader context, enhancing coordination among members and increasing their satisfaction. Additionally, group involvement in the decision-making process fosters a sense of participation, which facilitates the implementation of decisions, especially those involving significant changes.

2. **Group Roles**: Roles refer to the behaviors expected from group members. Each member, like a team player, fulfills roles assigned by leadership. Roles can be formally defined through job descriptions and titles or can be informal, shaped by individual approaches, expectations, and activities. There can be a difference between expected and actual behavior. Roles can be classified as 'on the job' (e.g., manager, accountant, supervisor) and 'off the job' (e.g., father, husband, son, player, singer). Understanding group roles is crucial for assessing group effectiveness.

3. **Group Norms**: According to J. Jackson, "Group norms are the informal rules of behavior that provide some order to group activities." Norms are standards for evaluating the performance and behavior of group members, defining what members should or should not do. Over time, groups establish norms to achieve desired goals or objectives. These norms guide members on what is expected of them and how they should behave. Group norms can be set by members or based on traditions and values. Types of group norms include:

   - Behavior Norms
   - Performance Norms
   - Formal Norms
   - Informal Norms
   - Norms applicable to all or some members

4. **Group Cohesiveness**: Cohesiveness refers to the harmony between group members. It establishes the framework within which members work in an organized manner, recognizing their goals and culture and wanting to remain part of the group. Committed and loyal members contribute to the group's survival and growth, functioning like an individual entity. Cohesiveness creates a sense of closeness, where members see themselves as inseparable from the group. Factors influencing group cohesiveness include group size, composition, proximity, external pressures, and the satisfaction of members' needs.

5. **Group Leadership**: Leadership is the ability to influence others' behavior, involving the leader, followers, and their positions.

A leader serves as an ideal for followers, directing, controlling, and meeting their needs. A group seeking to achieve its goals, social satisfaction, development, and growth, looks for effective leadership to help them succeed.

## 2. CONCEPT OF TEAM

A team is a group of individuals working together towards a common purpose. Ideally, team members should share similar interests and objectives, thinking along the same lines. In essence, a team is a relatively permanent work group where members must coordinate their activities to achieve one or more shared goals. These objectives might include advising others within the organization, producing goods or services, or completing a project. The need for coordination means that team members rely on each other and must interact regularly. A work team generates positive synergy through coordinated effort, resulting in performance that exceeds the sum of individual contributions. Teams play a crucial role in today's workplace, becoming essential to business operations. People with vastly different tastes cannot form an effective team; their goals must align. Each team is established to achieve a specific goal, and every member is responsible for contributing their best to accomplish the task within the given timeframe. Team members should complement and support each other whenever necessary.

## 2.1 COMMON CHARACTERISTICS OF AN EFFECTIVE TEAM

An effective team should possess the following essential characteristics:

1. All team members should know and understand the purpose, mission, or main objective.

2. Communication within the team should be open, direct, and honest.

3. Adequate leadership should be present in the team.

4. The team's performance toward achieving its purpose should be regularly reviewed.

5. There should be an agreed-upon organizational structure for the team.

6. Adequate resources, including skills, tools, facilities, and budgets, should be available to enable the team to perform its functions.

7. Synergy should be present, allowing the team to achieve performance levels greater than the sum of its individual parts.

## 2.2 TYPES OF TEAMS

There are various types of teams, including permanent teams, temporary teams, task forces, committees, cross-functional teams, self-managed teams, and virtual teams. Let's briefly discuss each type:

1. **Permanent Teams**: These teams operate on a continuous basis and are not disbanded after completing a task. They are formed for long-term projects and responsibilities.

2. **Temporary Teams**: These teams are assembled for a specific short-term task or project and disband once the task is completed. They often assist permanent teams or handle overflow work.

3. **Task Force**: Formed to address a specific project or critical issue, task forces are temporary and focus on finding solutions to problems. For instance, governments may create task forces to investigate significant incidents like terrorist attacks.

4. **Committee**: Committees can be either permanent or temporary and are created to work on specific assignments. Members share common interests and work together to achieve a particular goal. For example, organizing a cultural event might involve forming a committee to handle various tasks.

5. **Work Force**: These teams operate within organizations under the guidance of a leader or supervisor. The leader directs the team to achieve common goals, fostering cooperation and minimizing conflicts.

6. **Self-Managed Teams**: These teams consist of individuals working together without a designated leader. Each member is accountable for their performance, and the team collectively manages their tasks and responsibilities.

7. **Cross-Functional Teams**: Comprising employees from different functional areas (such as marketing, finance, and engineering), these teams collaborate to achieve a specific objective, improving coordination and innovation across the organization.

8. **Virtual Teams**: Virtual teams are composed of members who are geographically dispersed and connected via the internet. They communicate online and work together towards a common goal. Examples include groups on social networking sites supporting a particular community.

## 2.3 DIFFERENCES BETWEEN GROUP AND TEAM

| S. No. | Group | Team |
|--------|-------|------|
| 1 | Everyone thinks about his/her own interest | All of them think as one unit, the goal of the team |
| 2 | People join only for administration. | People understand interdependence. |
| 3 | Members work independently, sometimes against each other also. | Goals are accomplished by mutual support. |
| 4 | Members are told what to do. | Members contribute knowledge and talents to team objectives. |
| 5 | Members distrust each other and do not understand each other's role. | There is a climate of trust, where people are encouraged to express their ideas. |
| 6 | Members are seen like employees | They have sense of ownership and commitment of goals |
| 7 | Members may or may not be involved in decision making. | Members are involved in decision making. |
| 8 | Conformity is more important than result. | Positive results are the goals. |

## SUMMARY OF THE CHAPTER

1. Group refers to two or more persons who are interacting with each other in such a manner that each person influences and is influenced by each other.

2. Groups can be classified on different bases:

- **Formal Group**: Formal group refers to the group formed by the enterprise, which follows certain fixed rules and disciplines to perform certain activities in order to accomplish a particular goal. Formal groups may be Command Group, Task Group or Committee etc.

- **Informal Group**: Informal group refers to the group formed by the members of the organisation in order to meet their personal goals. Inormal groups may be Friendship Groups, Interest Groups, Membership Groups, Cliques etc.

3. **Reasons of group formation** are as follows:
   - Propinquity
   - Activity, Interaction and Sentiments
   - Group Activities
   - Need Satisfaction
   - Group Goals
   - Exchange
   - Similarity

4. **Process or Stages of Formation of Group**:
   - Forming
   - Storming
   - Norming
   - Performing
   - Adjourning

5. **Group behaviour** means the organised and collective behaviour of a group. It can be defined as the ways people behave in large- or small-group situations.

6. **Factors affecting effectiveness of Group**:
   - Group Decision-making
   - Group Roles
   - Group Norms
   - Group Cohesiveness
   - Group Leadership

7. **A team** is a group of individuals, all working together for a common purpose. The individuals forming a team should ideally think more or less on the same lines and should have similar interests and objective.

8. An **effective team** should have the following **essential characteristics**.

   - The purpose, mission, or main objective should be known and understood by all team members.
   - Communication in the team should be open, direct and honest.
   - Sufficient leadership should be available in the team.
   - There should be regular review of how well the team is performing toward achieving its purpose.
   - There should be an agreed organizational structure to the team.
   - Adequate resources should be available to permit the team to perform its function, including skills, tools, facilities, and budgets.
   - Synergy should exist, so that the team can perform in a way that is greater than the sum of its parts.

9. **Types of Teams:**

   - Permanent teams
   - Temporary teams
   - Task Force
   - Committee
   - Organization/Work Force
   - Self Managed Teams
   - Cross Functional Team
   - Virtual Teams

## 10. Differences between Group and Team

| S. No. | Group | Team |
|---|---|---|
| 1 | Everyone thinks about his/her own interest | All of them think as one unit, the goal of the team |
| 2 | People join only for administration. | People understand interdependence. |
| 3 | Members work independently, sometimes against each other also. | Goals are accomplished by mutual support. |
| 4 | Members are told what to do. | Members contribute knowledge and talents to team objectives. |
| 5 | Members distrust each other and do not understand each other's role. | There is a climate of trust, where people are encouraged to express their ideas. |
| 6 | Members are seen like employees | They have sense of ownership and commitment of goals |
| 7 | Members may or may not be involved in decision making. | Members are involved in decision making. |
| 8 | Conformity is more important than result. | Positive results are the goals. |

# QUESTIONS

1. What do you mean by Group?

2. Define Group.

3. What is formal group?

4. What is informal group?

5. What are the various types of formal group?

6. What are various types of informal group?

7.  Compare and contrast between formal group and informal group.

8.  Give some reasons for forming a group.

9.  Discuss the process of formation of a group.

10. What is forming?

11. What is storming?

12. What is Norming?

13. What do you understand by performing?

14. What is adjourning?

15. What do you mean by group behaviour?

16. Discuss the factors affecting effectiveness of group behaviour

17. Write short notes on:

|     |                   |     |                          |
|-----|-------------------|-----|--------------------------|
| a.  | Group Behaviour   | b.  | Group Roles              |
| c.  | Group Leadership  | d.  | Group Cohesiveness       |
| e.  | Group Norms       | f.  | Storming                 |
| g.  | Group Roles       | h.  | Formal and Informal Group |

18. What do you mean by team?

19. Mention the characteristics of a team.

20. What is permanent team?

21. What is temporary team?

22. What is task force?

23. What is committee?

24. What do you mean by work force?

25. What do you mean by self managed team?

26. What do you understand by cross functional team?

27. What do you mean by virtual team?

28. Discuss the various types of team.

29. Differentiate between team and group.

# UNIT 3C
# LEADERSHIP

Leadership – Nature, Types, Leadership Theories

**CONTENTS**

1.  Concept Of Leadership
    1.1 Definitions Of Leadership
    1.2 Characteristics Or Nature Of Leadership
    1.3 Significance/Importance Of Leadership
2.  Leadership Styles
    2.1 Autocratic Or Dictatorial Or Monothetic Leadership
        2.1.1 Nature Or Characteristics Of Autocratic Leadership
        2.1.2 Advantages Of Autocratic Technique
        2.1.3 Disadvantages Of Autocratic Technique
    2.2 Participative Leadership
        2.2.1 Nature or Characteristics Of Participative Leadership
        2.2.2 Advantages of Participative Leadership
        2.2.3 Disadvantages of Participative Leadership
    2.3 Laissez-Faire or Free Rein Leadership
        2.3.1 Nature or Characteristics Of Free Rein Leadership
        2.3.2 Advantages of Laissez-Faire Leadership
        2.3.4 Disadvantages of Laissez-Faire Leadership
3.  Qualities Of A Leader
4.  Trait Theory Of Leadership
5.  Situational Theory Of Leadership
6.  Blake And Mouton's Managerial Grid Theory
7.  House Path-Goal Theory
8.  Transformational Leadership

# 1. CONCEPT OF LEADERSHIP

Leadership is a quality that enables an individual to guide a group towards specific goals, typically without using force. This involves securing the willing cooperation of others by influencing their behavior. When we hear about the success of an organization, its leaders often come to mind. It is the leader's responsibility to motivate the organization's workers to complete their assigned tasks within the specified time frame, encouraging them to give their best efforts.

A leader is someone who influences and directs the efforts of a group of individuals, known as followers. Leadership reflects an individual's ability to maintain good interpersonal relationships with followers and inspire them to contribute towards achieving the organization's goals or objectives.

## 1.1 DEFINITIONS OF LEADERSHIP

"Leadership is the ability to persuade others to seek defined objectives enthusiastically. It is the human factor, which binds a group together and motivates it towards goals"

*Keith Davis*

"Leadership is the art or process of influencing people, so that they will strive willingly and enthusiastically towards the achievement of group goals"

*Harold Koontz and Heinz Weihrich*

"Leadership is the ability to secure desirable actions from a group of followers voluntarily, without the use of coercion"

*Allford and Beaty*

"Leadership is the activity of influencing people to strive willingly for group objectives"

*George R. Terry*

"Leadership is the initiation of acts which result in a consistent pattern of group interaction directed towards the solution of mutual problem"

*Hemphill J.K.*

## 1.2 CHARACTERISTICS OR NATURE OF LEADERSHIP

The key characteristics of leadership are as follows:

1. **Personal Quality of the Leader**: Leadership relies on the personal abilities, tact, and competence of the leader to direct, coordinate, and channelize group efforts toward the business's desired goals. While some aspects of leadership are inherent, it can also be developed.

2. **Influencing Process**: Leadership involves influencing the behavior and actions of people in a specific direction.

3. **Behavioral Change**: Leadership has the power to alter the behavior of followers, creating a desire for higher performance among them.

4. **Situation-Specific**: Leadership is always tied to a particular situation, at a given time, and under specific circumstances.

5. **Achieving Common Goals**: The purpose of leadership is to persuade and motivate followers to willingly strive towards the common goals or objectives of the organization.

6. **Continuous Process**: Leadership is an ongoing process, where the leader continuously influences and directs the behavior of the followers.

## 1.3 SIGNIFICANCE/IMPORTANCE OF LEADERSHIP

Leadership is considered a vital quality for managers. Its importance can be outlined as follows:

1. **Achieving Organizational Goals**: Leadership motivates individuals to channel their energies positively toward achieving organizational goals. Effective leaders consistently produce good results through their followers.

2. **Building Employee Confidence**: Leaders maintain personal relationships with their followers, helping them fulfill their needs and instilling confidence in their abilities. They provide psychological support and inspire enthusiasm through their conduct and expressions.

3.  **Securing Cooperation**: Effective leadership secures the voluntary cooperation of subordinates. Leaders influence employees to willingly work toward organizational objectives by demonstrating that achieving these goals leads to rewards, fostering a sense of teamwork.

4.  **Creating a Conducive Environment:** Performance efficiency relies on the work environment. Leadership aims to create and maintain a satisfactory environment where employees can maximize their contributions toward achieving goals.

5.  **Facilitating Change**: In today's dynamic environment, rapid changes occur within organizations. Leaders play a crucial role in introducing necessary changes, persuading and inspiring people to accept these changes, thus minimizing resistance and discontent.

6.  **Managing Conflicts Effectively**: Good leaders prevent conflicts between employers and employees. When conflicts arise, they handle them effectively, allowing followers to express their feelings and disagreements while providing suitable clarifications to resolve issues.

7.  **Building Higher Morale**: Effective leadership is essential for high employee morale. Leaders shape the group's thinking and attitudes, maintain discipline, foster good human relations, and facilitate interactions, ensuring voluntary cooperation and discipline.

8.  **Fulfilling Followers' Needs**: Leaders act as liaisons between management and employees, fostering mutual trust and confidence. They create a congenial work environment and help employees fulfill their needs, providing job satisfaction through monetary compensation and favorable working conditions.

9.  **Training and Developing Subordinates**: Leaders act as friends, philosophers, and guides to their followers. They provide training, share their superior knowledge, and build confidence in their subordinates, preparing them to become future leaders.

# 2. LEADERSHIP STYLES

Leadership style refers to the approach a leader takes to guide the group towards achieving organizational goals. It encompasses the pattern of behavior a leader uses to influence the actions of their followers. The leadership style adopted can vary based on the leader's personality, the situation at hand, the organizational culture, and the objectives, as well as the working behavior of the followers. Let's delve into the various styles of leadership in detail.

## 2.1 Autocratic or Dictatorial or Monothetic Leadership :

The autocratic leadership style is characterized by centralizing decision-making power under the leader's control. The leader structures the entire situation for their employees, who are expected to follow instructions without question. This type of leader may not be well-liked by followers or subordinates because they do not seek suggestions or opinions when making decisions, and they do not grant complete freedom for subordinates to perform tasks in their preferred manner.

## 2.1.1 Nature or characteristics of Autocratic leadership:

Following are the features of Autocratic leadership technique:

1. **Decision-making power:** In autocratic leadership, the leader centralizes decision-making power and does not seek advice or suggestions from subordinates.

2. **Limited freedom:** This leadership style restricts the freedom of subordinates or followers, who are expected to follow directions given by the leader.

3. **One-way communication:** Autocratic leaders use one-way communication, where they do not consult with subordinates or allow them to express their opinions.

4. **Quick decisions:** Decisions are made swiftly in autocratic leadership, often by a single person.

5. **Strict adherence:** Autocratic leaders strictly adhere to their style of leadership.

6. **Influence methods:** Their method of influencing subordinate behavior often involves negative motivation, such as criticism and imposing penalties.

7. **Covering incompetence:** Some superiors adopt autocratic leadership to mask their own incompetence, as other leadership styles might expose their shortcomings to subordinates.

## 2.1.2 Advantages of Autocratic technique

Following are the advantages of Autocratic leadership technique:

1. Many employees within organizations prefer working under a centralized authority structure and strict discipline, finding satisfaction in this style.

2. This style provides strong motivation and rewards for managers who exercise it.

3. It allows for very quick decision-making since most decisions are made by a single person.

4. Less competent subordinates also have the opportunity to work within the organization under this leadership style, as they are not required to engage in significant planning, organizing, or decision-making.

5. Autocratic leadership can be beneficial in certain instances, such as when decisions need to be made rapidly without consulting a large group of people.

## 2.1.3 Disadvantages of Autocratic technique

Autocratic leadership technique suffers from the following limitations:

1. The autocratic leadership style is generally disliked by people in the organization, especially when it is strict and uses negative motivational tactics.

2. Employees under this leadership style often lack motivation, leading to frustration, low morale, and conflicts that can jeopardize organizational efficiency.

3. Autocratic leadership fosters more dependence and less individuality within the organization, hindering the development of future leaders.

4. Autocratic rule places a significant burden on the leader. Since they take full responsibility for team decisions and oversee their work closely, autocratic leaders tend to remain extremely busy, which can lead to high stress and health problems.

## 2.2 Participative Leadership

Unlike autocratic leadership, participative leadership involves the leader actively participating in activities with subordinates. The leader also seeks advice or suggestions from subordinates when making decisions. This style of leadership is also referred to as democratic, consultative, or ideographic leadership. In participative leadership, subordinates are thoroughly informed about the conditions affecting them and their jobs.

Participation is defined as the mental and emotional involvement of a person in a group situation, which encourages them to contribute to group goals and share responsibility for them.

### 2.2.1 Nature or characteristics of Participative Leadership:

Following are the features or Participative leadership technique:

1. **Decision-making:** A participative leader always considers the opinions of his/her subordinates or followers when making decisions.

2. **Freedom:** Under this leadership style, employees are given the freedom to do their work in the manner they prefer.

3. **Two-way communication:** The participative leader adopts two-way communication. They consult with subordinates and give them a chance to provide their opinions when making important decisions.

4. **Slow decisions:** Under this leadership style, decisions are made more slowly compared to autocratic leadership, as the leader consults with subordinates before making decisions.

5. **Method of influencing:** The participative leader influences subordinates' behavior through positive motivation, such as appreciating and rewarding them.

### 2.2.2 Advantages of Participative leadership

Following are the advantages or merits of Participative leadership technique:

1. It is a highly motivating technique for employees, as they feel valued when their ideas and suggestions are considered in decision-making.

2. Employee productivity is high because they are involved in the decision-making process, and as a result, they implement decisions whole-heartedly.

3. Employees share responsibility with their superiors and support them as well.

4. This leadership style provides organizational stability by boosting morale and fostering favorable attitudes among employees. Additionally, it prepares leaders to take on higher organizational positions.

### 2.2.3 Disadvantages of Participative leadership

Participative leadership technique suffers from the following limitations:

1. The complex nature of organizations requires a deep understanding of their issues, which lower-level employees may not possess. Therefore, participation may not always be meaningful.

2. Some individuals in the organization prefer minimal interaction with their superiors or colleagues. For them, participatory techniques can be discouraging rather than encouraging.

3. Participation can sometimes be used covertly to manipulate employees. As a result, some employees may prefer the open control of an autocrat compared to the hidden manipulation of a group.

4. Decisions are made, but not as swiftly as in autocratic leadership. This leadership style involves consulting with and obtaining input from subordinates, which slows down the decision-making process.

## 2.3 Laissez-faire or Free Rein Leadership

The free rein or laissez-faire technique involves giving complete freedom to subordinates. In this style, the manager sets policies, programs, and boundaries for action, and then delegates the entire process to the subordinates. Group members handle all tasks, while the manager typically maintains contacts with external parties to provide the information and materials needed by the group. This leadership approach is suitable in organizations where subordinates are capable of fulfilling their responsibilities without significant support from their superiors. It helps subordinates develop an independent personality. Under this leadership style, the leader establishes objectives, and employees (subordinates) are granted full autonomy to determine the best way to achieve those objectives.

## 2.3.1 Nature or characteristics of Free rein Leadership

Following are the essential features of Free Rein Leadership technique:

1. **No direct supervision:** In this leadership style, followers or subordinates operate independently and must demonstrate their capabilities through accomplishments without direct supervision by the leader.

2. **Decision-making:** The entire decision-making authority is delegated to the followers or subordinates.

3. **Complete freedom:** Under this leadership technique, subordinates or followers are granted complete freedom to choose the methods they deem appropriate to achieve the goals or objectives.

4. **Role of leader:** The leader's involvement is minimal. He or she typically maintains contacts with external parties to provide information and materials to group members needed for the accomplishment of the given task.

5. **Suitability:** This leadership technique is suitable in organizations where subordinates are competent enough to fulfill their responsibilities with minimal support from their superiors.

## 2.3.2 Advantages of Laissez-faire leadership

Following are the advantages of Laissez-faire leadership technique:

1. **Job satisfaction:** This leadership style enhances job satisfaction and morale among employees because they have the freedom to choose how they complete assigned tasks.

2. **Scope for development:** There is ample opportunity for employee development under this leadership style since they are empowered to make their own decisions.

3. **Full utilization of potential:** Employees have the freedom to work in their preferred manner, enabling them to fully utilize their potential under this leadership style.

### 2.3.3 Disadvantages of Laissez-faire leadership

Apart from the advantages, Laissez faire leadership suffers from the following demerits:

1. **Guidance and support:** In this leadership style, subordinates do not receive as much guidance and support from their leader.

2. **Ignores the contribution of the leader:** This leadership style tends to overlook the leader's contribution since the leader does not actively participate in activities, but only provides the necessary information and resources to their subordinates.

3. **Chances of chaos:** Giving subordinates the freedom to work in their own style or direction can lead to chaos.

4. **Chances of wrong decision:** If subordinates lack sufficient knowledge and experience, they may make incorrect decisions.

## 3. QUALITIES OF A LEADER

Qualities of a leader in management refer to the characteristics and attributes that enable an individual to effectively lead and manage a team or organization. Here are some qualities of a leader in management:

1. **Visionary:** A leader in management should have a clear vision of where the organization is headed and the ability to communicate that vision to their team.

2. **Decisive:** Leaders need to make timely and effective decisions, even in difficult or ambiguous situations.

3. **Communicative:** Effective communication skills are crucial for a leader to articulate goals, provide feedback, and inspire their team.

4. **Integrity:** Leaders must demonstrate honesty, transparency, and ethical behavior in all their actions.

5. **Empathetic:** Understanding and empathizing with team members' concerns and challenges builds trust and morale.

6. **Resilient:** Leaders should be able to bounce back from setbacks and maintain a positive attitude, even in challenging times.

7. **Adaptable:** The ability to adapt to changing circumstances and embrace innovation is essential for a leader in a dynamic environment.

8. **Motivational:** Inspiring and motivating team members to achieve their best and reach organizational goals.

9. **Accountable:** Leaders take responsibility for their decisions and actions, as well as those of their team.

10. **Collaborative:** Encouraging collaboration and teamwork among team members to achieve common goals.

11. **Strategic:** Thinking strategically to develop long-term plans and solutions for the organization.

12. **Assertive:** Being assertive in making decisions and leading the team, while also respecting the opinions and ideas of others.

13. **Credible:** Building credibility through consistent actions and demonstrating competence in their field.

14. **Innovative:** Encouraging creativity and innovation to solve problems and improve processes within the organization.

15. **Patient:** Patience is important for a leader, especially when dealing with challenges or when results take time to achieve.

16. **Supportive:** Providing support and development opportunities for team members to help them grow and succeed.

17. **Confident:** A leader needs to be confident in their abilities and decisions, which inspires confidence in their team.

18. **Proactive:** Taking initiative to address issues and seize opportunities before they become problems.

19. **Accountable:** Holding themselves and others accountable for their actions and performance.

20. **Goal-oriented:** Focused on achieving organizational goals and aligning team efforts to those goals.

These qualities collectively contribute to effective leadership in management, fostering a positive and productive work environment and driving organizational success.

## 4. TRAIT THEORY OF LEADERSHIP

The trait approach to leadership focuses on identifying enduring qualities that contribute to an individual's effectiveness as a leader. Since the early days, it has been emphasized that certain individuals are successful leaders due to specific qualities or characteristics they possess.

Various research studies have identified intelligence, attitudes, personality, and biological factors as key ingredients for effective leadership. Stodill's review of these studies suggests several traits that contribute to successful leadership, including: (i) Physical and constitutional factors (such as height, weight, physique, energy, health, appearance); (ii) Intelligence; (iii) Self-confidence; (iv) Sociability; (v) Will; (vi) Dominance; and (vii) Surgency.

Anderson Consulting conducted a study to identify the qualities required for an ideal chief executive, highlighting 14 key qualities. According to this study, an ideal chief executive thinks globally, anticipates opportunities, creates a shared vision, develops and empowers people, appreciates cultural diversity, builds teamwork and partnerships, embraces change, demonstrates technological savvy, encourages constructive challenge, ensures customer satisfaction, achieves competitive advantage, demonstrates personal mastery, shares leadership, and lives the values.

These various studies indicate wide variations in leadership traits. Leadership traits can be broadly classified into two categories: innate qualities and acquirable qualities.

A. **Innate Qualities:** These are qualities that individuals possess from birth and are considered natural or God-gifted. The following are innate qualities seen in successful leaders:

1. **Physical features:** Leadership success is influenced by physical characteristics and the rate of maturation, which contribute to personality formation. Height, weight, physique, health, and appearance to some extent affect leadership.

2. **Intelligence:** Higher levels of intelligence are required for effective leadership. Mental ability and intelligence are natural qualities directly linked to brain function.

B. **Acquirable Qualities:** These are qualities acquired through various processes such as training programs. The following are major qualities essential for leadership:

1. **Human relations:** Successful leaders should possess adequate knowledge of human relations, understanding how to effectively interact with others and their relationships.

2. **Emotional stability:** A leader must exhibit a high level of emotional stability, remaining unbiased, consistent in action, and avoiding anger.

3. **Empathy:** Empathy involves understanding situations from others' perspectives. Leaders should possess the ability to empathize, understanding what others are thinking in particular situations.

4. **Motivational skills:** Besides being self-motivated, leaders should be able to motivate their subordinates. They must understand their team well enough to know how to inspire them.

5. **Objectivity:** Leaders should base their actions on relevant facts and information, assessing situations without bias or prejudice, thus maintaining objectivity in their decision-making and relationships.

6. **Technical skills:** Leaders need technical skills to plan, organize, delegate, analyze, seek advice, make decisions, and control operations. Technical competence can win support from followers.

7. **Communication skills:** Effective leaders must communicate skillfully, using communication for persuasive, informative, and motivational purposes.

8. **Social skills:** Successful leaders possess social skills, understanding people, their strengths, and weaknesses. They have the ability to work with others, conduct themselves to gain confidence and loyalty, and elicit willing cooperation.

### Implications of the theory

This theory has two significant implications:

1. Firstly, the theory underscores that a leader needs specific traits and qualities to be effective.

2. Secondly, many of these qualities can be cultivated in individuals through training and development programs.

### Limitations or Criticisms of the theory

1. Generalizing traits for a successful leader is not feasible, as evidenced by various research studies on leadership traits.

2. There is no evidence about the extent to which various traits impact leadership, as individuals possess traits to varying degrees.

3. Measuring traits poses challenges. While there are several tests available to measure personality traits, definitive conclusions are difficult to draw.

4. Many individuals possess traits specified for a leader but fail to become effective leaders. This is because there is no direct cause-effect relationship between a person's traits and their behavior.

## 5. SITUATIONAL THEORY OF LEADERSHIP

The situational leadership theory, initially developed in the late 1960s by Paul Hersey and Ken Blanchard, was originally known as the "Life Cycle Theory of Leadership." By the mid-1970s, it was renamed "Situational Leadership Theory."

Situational Leadership requires the leader or manager to adapt their style to match the development level of the followers they are leading. This model views leaders as adjusting their emphasis on task and relationship behaviors to effectively deal with varying levels of follower maturity.

Hersey and Blanchard categorized leadership styles based on the amount of task behavior and relationship behavior that the leader provides to their subordinates. They identified four behavior types, labeled S1 to S4. The first two styles (Telling and Selling) focus on achieving the task, while the latter two (Participating and Delegating) are more concerned with the personal development of team members.

Hersey –Blanchard Situational Leadership Model

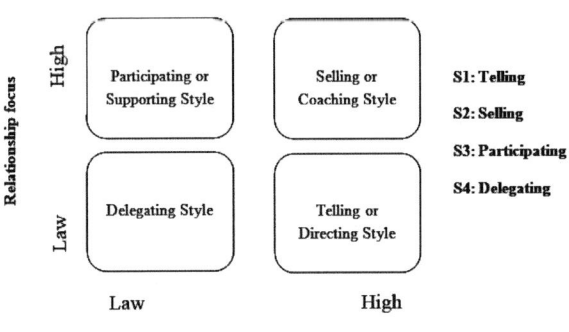

**S1 Style (Telling or Directing):** Under this style, the leader provides specific instructions to subordinates on "what to do" and "how to do it." The leader makes final decisions and ensures clear, composed tasks for the employees. This approach is commonly used in law enforcement, military, and manufacturing assembly lines, where tasks are clearly defined and employees span various experience levels.

**S2 Style (Selling or Coaching):** At this level, employees have a desire to work independently but lack the capability to do so. They need guidance and coaching from the leader. This style involves explaining decisions, listening to employees, and providing undivided attention. The leader "sells" tasks to the employee, ensuring specific instructions and maintaining open communication. It's important for the leader to answer questions and clarify the purpose of tasks. When the employee shows progress, they should be complimented to boost confidence.

**S3 Style (Participating or Supporting):** At this level, employees are capable but may be temporarily unwilling due to workload or insecurity. The leader supports employees by involving them in decision-making and boosting their confidence. This style requires the leader to confer with employees, provide support, and encourage them to regain confidence in their abilities. Employees benefit from calm, face-to-face discussions and brainstorming sessions to increase their confidence.

**S4 Style (Delegating):** At this level, employees are capable and motivated to work independently. They have a high level of task maturity and require minimal support from the leader. Employees inform the leader of their progress and any issues they encounter. The leader delegates tasks and responsibilities, provides the final goal and deadlines, and plans evaluation moments. Delegating requires the leader to maintain distance and let employees take responsibility for their decisions. Compliments are given when things go well to boost confidence and encourage autonomy.

Finding the appropriate leadership style depends on the individual or group being led. The Hersey-Blanchard Situational Leadership Theory identifies four Levels of Maturity (M1 to M4), which help leaders determine the most effective approach for the current situation.

**M1 (Maturity level 1):** Followers lack the specific skills required for the task and are unable to take responsibility for it.

**M2 (Maturity level 2):** They are willing to work on the task but lack the ability to take responsibility. They are novices but enthusiastic.

**M3 (Maturity level 3):** They have the skills to perform the task but lack the confidence or willingness to take responsibility.

**M4 (Maturity level 4):** They are experienced with the task and confident in their ability to perform it. They are both able and willing to take responsibility.

Maturity levels are task-specific. A person may be generally skilled, confident, and motivated in their job, but could still be at maturity level M1 when asked to perform a task that requires skills they do not possess.

Hersey-Blanchard model maps each leadership style to each maturity level, as shown below.

| Maturity Level | Most Appropriate Leadership Style |
|---|---|
| M1 : Low Maturity | S1 : Telling/ Directing |
| M2 : Medium Maturity, Limited Skills | S2 : Selling/Coaching |
| M3 : Medium Maturity, Higher Skills but Lacking Confidence | S3 : Participating/ Supporting |
| M4 : High Maturity | S4 : Delegating |

**M1 = S1:** If the employee has a low level of skills, knowledge, and competence, it is advantageous to use the leadership style S1. This could be the case when a new and untrained employee joins the organization or when trained personnel's tasks change radically.

**M2 = S2:** At this stage, the follower is more familiar with their tasks but may be starting to lose motivation. In this situation, S2 might be the appropriate leadership style, where leaders should try to persuade followers about the importance of the tasks and why they should strive to develop the necessary skills.

**M3 = S3:** At this stage, where the follower's competence is high, leaders could act as consultants, advising the followers on how to accomplish the tasks. Similarly, followers at this high level of maturity may be motivated by being involved in decision-making and having the opportunity to shape the content of their tasks.

**M4 = S4:** In this final stage of maturity, the employee can perform their duties independently and is highly committed to achieving tasks. In this situation, leaders could effectively adopt the S4 leadership style, where followers are allowed to carry out and complete tasks independently, with minimal supervision from leaders.

By applying the Situational Leadership Model, leaders can flexibly adjust their leadership approach to support followers with varying capabilities and job-related needs. By addressing individual needs, leaders can enhance the learning curve of followers, resulting in a more skilled and motivated workforce.

Maturity levels are also specific to tasks. A person may be generally skilled, confident, and motivated in their job, but may still exhibit M1 maturity level when asked to perform a task that requires skills they do not possess.

## 6. BLAKE AND MOUTON'S MANAGERIAL GRID THEORY

The Managerial Grid theory was introduced by Robert R. Blake and Jane S. Mouton. This theory illustrates two dimensions of leader behavior: concern for people (prioritizing their needs) on the y-axis and concern for production (maintaining tight schedules) on the x-axis. Each dimension ranges from low (1) to high (9), resulting in 81 possible positions where a leader's style may fall. The primary goal of this model is to identify and classify the leadership style of a leader.

Figure 1: Managerial Grid

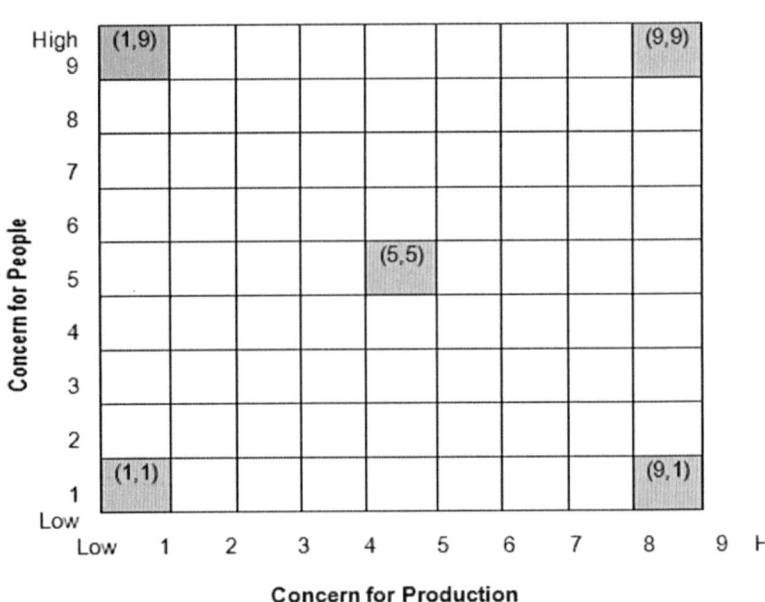

Out of these 81 styles, the five styles the most famous five styles are:

1.  **Impoverished Management (1, 1):** Managers adopting this approach are low on both dimensions and exert minimal effort to get the work done from subordinates. The leader shows low concern for employee satisfaction and meeting work deadlines, leading to disharmony and disorganization within the organization. Such leaders are considered ineffective, focusing primarily on job preservation and seniority.

2.  **Task Management (9, 1):** Also known as dictatorial or autocratic style, leaders in this category prioritize production over people's needs. This style is based on Theory X of McGregor, where employees' needs are not considered significant, viewing them merely as a means to achieve results. The leader believes that efficiency can only be achieved through well-organized work systems and may resort to eliminating people wherever possible. While this style can increase organizational output in the short term, its strict policies often lead to high turnover.

3.  **Middle-of-the-Road (5, 5):** This is a compromising style where the leader attempts to balance company goals with the needs of people. The leader avoids pushing the boundaries of achievement, resulting in average organizational performance. In this style, neither employee nor production needs are fully met, aiming for a moderate approach overall.

4.  **Country Club (1, 9):** This is a collegial style characterized by low task and high people orientation. The leader gives thoughtful attention to the needs of people, providing a friendly and comfortable environment. The leader believes that such treatment will motivate employees to work hard on their own. However, the low focus on tasks can hamper production and lead to questionable results.

5.  **Team Management (9, 9):** Characterized by high people and task focus, this style is based on Theory Y of McGregor and is considered the most effective style according to Blake and Mouton. The leader emphasizes empowerment, commitment, trust, and respect to create a team atmosphere that enhances both employee satisfaction and production.

# 7. HOUSE PATH-GOAL THEORY

Robert House's Path-Goal theory is one of the most respected approaches to leadership. The core idea of the theory is that it is the leader's responsibility to assist followers in achieving their goals and to provide the necessary direction and support to ensure these goals are aligned with the overall objectives of the group or organization. According to this theory, leaders influence their subordinates' perceptions of the rewards of achieving their goals and demonstrate ways to achieve them. Therefore, a leader's behavior is considered motivational to the extent that it:

(a) Makes subordinate satisfaction contingent on effective performance,

(b) Provides coaching, guidance, support, and rewards necessary for effective performance.

To test these statements, House identified four leadership behaviors or styles:

(a) **Directive Style**: The leader informs subordinates about expectations, provides guidance on what needs to be done, and shows them how to accomplish tasks.

(b) **Supportive Style**: The leader demonstrates concern for the well-being and needs of subordinates by being friendly and approachable.

(c) **Participative Style**: The leader involves subordinates in decision-making, consults them about the situation, seeks their suggestions, considers those suggestions in decision-making, and sometimes allows subordinates to make decisions independently.

(d) **Achievement-Oriented Style**: The leader assists subordinates in setting goals, rewards goal accomplishment, and encourages subordinates to take responsibility for achieving their goals.

House assumes that leaders are flexible and suggests that the same leader can exhibit any or all of these behaviors depending on the situation.

**Applying Path-Goal Theory**:

The leader will start by selecting a leadership style that matches the situation. To do so, the leader needs to evaluate five aspects of the situation and the people involved:

(a) **Assess the task:** Structured tasks with clear goals require less direction compared to unstructured tasks with unclear goals.

(b) **Assess the leader's formal authority:** Leaders with formal authority typically should avoid using a directive style, as it duplicates their authority. Instead, they may use supportive, achievement-oriented, or participative styles.

(c) **Assess the nature of the work group:** The leader should evaluate the group's cohesiveness and its experience working together. A highly cohesive group requires less supportive leadership, as the group's unity already provides support.

(d) **Assess the organization's culture:** A culture that supports participation also supports a participative leadership style. A culture that values goal accomplishment or a results orientation reinforces an achievement-oriented style.

(e) **Assess the subordinate's skills and needs:** Subordinates who are skilled in their tasks require less direction compared to those who are less skilled. Subordinates with high achievement needs require a leadership style that helps meet these needs, while those with social needs require a style that addresses these needs.

## 8. TRANSFORMATIONAL LEADERSHIP

Transformational leadership is a leadership approach that aims to bring about change in individuals and social systems. In its ideal form, it generates valuable and positive changes in followers, ultimately developing them into leaders themselves. When practiced authentically, transformational leadership enhances the motivation, morale, and performance of followers through various mechanisms. These include linking the follower's sense of identity and self to the mission and collective identity of the organization, serving as a role model that inspires followers, challenging followers to take greater ownership of their work, and understanding the strengths and weaknesses of followers to align them with tasks that optimize their performance.

The term "Transformational Leadership" was coined by James V. Downton and further developed by leadership expert James MacGregor Burns. According to Burns, transformational leadership is a process in which "leaders and followers help each other to advance to a higher level of moral and motivation.

**Characteristics of Transformational Leaders:**

1. **Inspirational Motivation:** Transformational leaders establish a compelling vision, mission, and set of values, inspiring members with consistent purpose and direction. Their vision is so compelling that they know what they want from every interaction. These leaders guide followers by providing them with a sense of meaning and challenge, fostering teamwork and commitment through enthusiasm and optimism.

2. **Intellectual Stimulation:** Such leaders encourage creativity and innovation among their followers. They welcome new ideas and avoid publicly criticizing mistakes. They focus on problem-solving rather than assigning blame, and are willing to discard ineffective practices.

3. **Idealized Influence:** Transformational leaders believe that leaders can influence followers only when they practice what they preach. They act as role models that followers seek to emulate, earning trust and respect through their actions. These leaders typically prioritize followers' needs over their own, sacrificing personal gain for the benefit of their team, and demonstrate high standards of ethical conduct. Their use of power is aimed at influencing followers to strive for the organization's common goals.

4. **Individualized Consideration:** Leaders act as mentors to their followers, rewarding creativity and innovation. They treat followers differently based on their talents and knowledge, empowering them to make decisions and providing necessary support for implementation.

**Advantages of the Theory:**

1. **Emphasis on Task and Organizational Integrity:** This theory focuses attention on defining tasks appropriately and maintaining organizational integrity.

2. **Increased Workforce Productivity:** Transformational leaders inspire their workforce to be more productive and perform at their best to achieve organizational goals.

3. **Employee Growth:** Transformational leaders ensure that employees grow together with the organization, fostering personal and professional development.

4. **Enhanced Leader-Employee Bond:** Transformational leaders create a strong bond between themselves and their employees, which reduces employee turnover.

**Disadvantages of the Theory:**

1. **Confusion with Transactional Leadership:** Leaders may confuse transformational and transactional leadership styles, mixing rewards for performance (transactional) with motivation strategies.

2. **Applicability Limited to Participative Employees:** Transformational leadership may only apply effectively to employees who are willing to be part of the process; team dynamics vary across different companies.

3. **Unrealistic Vision:** Sometimes, transformational leaders' visions may not be realistic, leading followers to blindly follow their passion without practical consideration.

4. **Employee Favouritism:** There may be issues of employee favouritism if leaders focus only on employees who contribute more, neglecting others and causing demotivation.

## SUMMARY OF THE CHAPTER

1. **Leadership** is a quality whereby an individual is able to move a group towards specified goals normally without exerting force.

2. The major **characteristics of leadership** are:
   - Personal Quality of Manager
   - Influencing process
   - Behaviour changing process
   - Related to a situation
   - Achieving common goal
   - Continuous process

3. The **importance or significance of leadership** can be discussed as follows:
   - Helps in achieving organizational goal
   - Creates confidence among the employees
   - Securing cooperation
   - Providing conductive environment

- Helps in introducing required changes
- Management of conflicts effectively
- Building higher morale
- Helps followers in fulfilling their needs
- Helps in training and development of subordinates

4. **Leadership style** is the way that a leader adopts to lead the group in order to achieve the goals of the organization. It is a pattern of behaviour which a leader adopts in influencing the behaviour of his/her followers (subordinates).

5. The **various styles of leadership** are:
   - Autocratic or Dictatorial or Monothetic Leadership
   - Participative Leadership
   - Laissez-faire or Free Rein Leadership

6. **Autocratic leadership** style is one, where a leader centralizes the decision-making power under his/her control.

7. **A participative leadership** is one, where, the leader participates in all activities with his/her subordinates. He/she also takes advices or suggestions from the subordinates while taking decisions. This style of leadership is also called democratic, consultative, or ideographic leadership.

8. **Free rein or laissez-faire** technique means giving complete freedom to subordinates. In this style, manager once determines policies, programmes, and limitations for action and the entire process is left to subordinates.

9. **A successful leader should posses the following essential qualities.**
   - Physical features
   - Knowledge
   - Integrity.
   - Initiative
   - Communication skill
   - Motivational skill
   - Self confidence:

# QUESTIONS

1. What do you mean by leadership?
2. Who is a leader?
3. Define leadership.
4. What are the characteristics of leadership?
5. Discuss the significance of leadership.
6. What are the different types of leadership styles?
7. What is Autocratic leadership? What are its features?
8. What are the advantages of Autocratic leadership style?
9. What are the disadvantages of Autocratic leadership style?
10. What do you mean by Participative leadership technique? What are its features?
11. What are the advantages of Participative leadership technique/
12. What are the disadvantages of Participative leadership technique?
13. What is Free Rein leadership? What are its characteristics?
14. What are the advantages of Free Rein leadership?
15. What are the disadvantages of Free Rein leadership?
16. Discuss the qualities of a successful leader.
17. Discuss the Trait theory of leadership.
18. Discuss the Situational theory of leadership.
19. Write short notes on:
1. Autocratic Leadership
2. Participative Leadership
3. Free Rein Leadership

# UNIT 4A
# MOTIVATION

Motivation – Theories and Practices:

Herzberg's Theory

Vroom's Expectancy Theory

Z-theory

## CONTENTS

1. Concept Of Motivation

    1.1 Definitions Of Motivation

    1.2 Features/Characteristics Of Motivation

    1.3 Importance/Significance Of Motivation

2. Maslow's Need Hierarchy Theory Of Motivation

3. Alderfer's Erg Theory

4. Herzberg's Two Factors Theory Of Motivation

5. Comparison Between Maslow And Herzberg Theory Of Motivation

6. Vroom Expectancy Theory Of Motivation

7. William's Ouchi's Z Theory

# 1. CONCEPT OF MOTIVATION

Motivation involves stimulating, encouraging, and inciting employees to perform to their best capacity. In simpler terms, motivation combines various forces that inspire a person to intensify their willingness to use their maximum capabilities to achieve predetermined objectives. It entails arousing needs and desires in people to initiate and direct their behavior in a purposeful manner. When discussing motivation, it's important to understand three related terms:

1. **Motive**: A motive is an inner state that energizes, activates, and directs behavior towards goals. Motives arise from individual needs, such as the need for food. Examples of such motives include hunger and thirst.

2. **Motivating**: Motivating refers to one person (typically a manager in an organizational context) inducing another person (an employee) to engage in action (work behavior) by ensuring that a means to satisfy the motive becomes available and accessible to the individual.

3. **Motivator**: A motivator is a technique used to motivate people within an organization. Managers use diverse motivators such as pay, bonuses, and promotions to influence people to contribute their best.

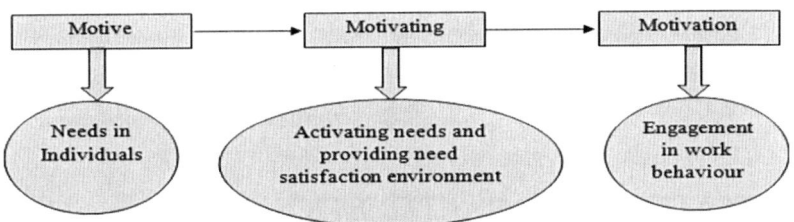

*Relationship between motive, motivating and motivation*

## 1.1 DEFINITIONS OF MOTIVATION

"Motivation is the art of stimulating someone or oneself to take desired course of action"

*M.J.Jucius*

"To motivate is to induce people to act in a desired manner"

*Koontz and O'Donnell*

"Motivation refers to the way in which urges, drives, desires, aspirations, strivings, or needs direct, control, or explain the behaviour of human beings"

*McFarland*

"Motivation is the complex set of forces starting and keeping a person at work in an organization. Motivation is something that moves the person to action, and continues him in the course of action already initiated."

*Robert Dubin*

"Motivation is a willingness to expand energy to achieve a goal or reward. It is a force that activates dormant energies and sets in motion the action of the people. It is the function that kindles a burning passion for action among the human beings of an organization."

*C.B.Mamoria*

"Motivation is the psychological process that gives behaviour purpose and direction."

*Kreitner*

"Motivation is a predisposition to behave in a purposive manner to achieve specific, unmet needs."

*Buford, Bedeian and Lindner*

# 1.2 FEATURES/CHARACTERISTICS OF MOTIVATION

The analysis of various definitions of motivation reveals the following characteristics of motivation:

1.  **Internal Instinct**: Motivation is a psychological phenomenon that originates from within an individual. It is a personal and internal feeling that arises from the needs and desires of a person. For example, individuals may have urges or aspirations for possessions like a motorcycle, a comfortable house, or a good reputation in society. These urges are internal to an individual.

2.  **Produces Goal-Directed Behavior**: Motivation is directed towards the achievement of specific goals, which determine the behavior of individuals. A motivated person requires minimal

supervision and will work in a desired manner. For instance, if a person is motivated to receive a promotion, they will work efficiently towards achieving that goal.

3. **Positive or Negative Motivation**: Motivation can be either positive or negative. Positive motivation aims to create a conducive environment for employees to work more effectively by providing rewards such as increments, bonuses, and promotions. On the other hand, negative motivation seeks to instill a sense of fear and an unfavorable atmosphere through means such as warnings, salary cuts, or demotions.

4. **Complex Process**: Motivation is a complex and challenging task because needs are psychologically interconnected and cannot be accurately measured. Additionally, human needs change over time, and individuals satisfy their needs in various ways. Not all types of motivation have a uniform effect on all people.

5. **Dynamic and Continuous Process**: Motivation is a dynamic and continuous process. Human needs are unlimited and continually evolve. The satisfaction of one need leads to the emergence of another, requiring managers to continuously engage in the function of motivation.

6. **Person Motivated as a Whole**: Motivation affects a person as a whole and not in parts. Each individual in an organization is a self-contained unit, and their needs are interconnected, influencing their behavior in diverse ways. Furthermore, the feelings of needs and their satisfaction are ongoing processes, contributing to the continuity in behavior.

7. **Universal Management Function**: Motivation is a universal managerial function utilized at every level of the organization's operation.

## 1.3 IMPORTANCE/SIGNIFICANCE OF MOTIVATION

"Motivation is the core of management. It is through motivation that managers can inspire their subordinates to give their best to the organization. It should be noted that a worker may possess immense capability, but achieving anything is impossible if they are not willing to work.

The following points underscore the importance of motivation in an organization:

1. **Improves Performance Level**: Motivation enhances the performance level of employees. It instills the will to work among employees and enables management to achieve the best possible utilization of all resources. Motivation bridges the gap between the ability to work and the willingness to work. By encouraging people to work more effectively, motivation helps increase productivity, reduce operational costs, and enhance overall efficiency.

2. **Development of Positive Attitude**: Motivation helps transform negative or indifferent attitudes of employees into positive ones to achieve organizational goals. Management offers various monetary and non-monetary rewards such as promotional opportunities, recognition of efficient work, fringe benefits, and involvement in decision-making. These satisfy the needs of employees, leading to a change in their attitude from negative or indifferent to positive.

3. **Reduction in Employee Turnover**: Motivation helps reduce employee turnover and thereby saves costs related to new recruitment and training. By identifying the motivational needs of employees and providing suitable financial and non-financial incentives, managers can discourage employees from leaving the organization. Motivated workers have fewer grievances against management. They are content with their working conditions and exhibit loyalty and commitment to the organization.

4. **Introducing Changes Smoothly**: Normally, organizational changes face resistance. Motivation helps managers introduce changes smoothly with minimal resistance from employees. Motivated employees support all changes that are in the organization's interests because they link their own advancement with the enterprise's prosperity.

5. **Reduction in Absenteeism**: Motivation helps reduce absenteeism in the organization. A sound motivational system, including increments, bonuses, rewards, respect, recognition, and good working conditions, brings job satisfaction to employees. Motivated employees take pleasure in their work, attend to their duties regularly, and do not willingly stay absent from the organization.

These points illustrate the critical role of motivation in fostering a productive and committed workforce within an organization."

# 2. MASLOW'S NEED HIERARCHY THEORY OF MOTIVATION

Needs serve as the foundation of motivation. Abraham Maslow, a prominent American psychologist, developed a comprehensive theory of motivation known as the Need Hierarchy Theory. He posited that individuals are driven by a variety of needs that motivate them to strive for their fulfillment. Maslow emphasized two significant characteristics of human needs. Firstly, an individual's needs are entirely dependent on what they currently possess. Therefore, once needs are satisfied, they no longer drive behavior. It can be argued that managers must continually identify the unsatisfied needs of individuals within the organization so that they can take appropriate steps to motivate them by providing opportunities for need satisfaction. Secondly, human needs are arranged in a hierarchy of importance, based on a sequential chain of needs. As lower-level needs are fulfilled or satisfied, higher-level needs emerge and demand satisfaction.

Maslow classified human needs into five categories in order to priority

1. **Physiological Needs:** Physiological needs are positioned at the base of the hierarchy due to their potent strength until they are adequately satisfied. These needs are essential for sustaining human life and include food, clothing, shelter, air, water, and other basic necessities. They are directly related to the survival and maintenance of human life, often referred to as survival needs.

2. **Safety or Security Needs:** Once physiological needs are reasonably fulfilled, safety needs become paramount. This level of needs encompasses the desire to be free from physical danger and to secure oneself. It includes protection against risks such as fire, accidents, diseases, crime, and other physical hazards. Economic security, such as job security and planning for retirement, is also part of this level. Social security includes protection during illness, disability, or old age.

3. **Social Needs:** After physiological and safety needs are met, social needs take precedence in the hierarchy. As humans are social beings, they desire interaction, companionship, affection, and a sense of belonging. Social needs involve the desire for love, friendship, and acceptance within family, friends, and community. They encompass the natural inclination to socialize and connect with others.

4.  **Esteem or Status Needs:** Esteem needs, also known as ego needs, come next in the hierarchy. These needs include self-confidence, independence, achievement, competence, knowledge, initiative, and recognition. Esteem needs are related to the desire for respect, recognition, and appreciation from others, as well as self-respect and confidence in one's abilities.

5.  **Self-Actualization Needs:** These needs represent the highest level in the hierarchy. They emerge once the lower needs (physiological, safety, social, and esteem) are sufficiently fulfilled. Self-actualization needs are about fulfilling one's potential and achieving personal growth. They involve striving to become the best one can be and fulfilling one's purpose in life. For example, Mahatma Gandhi's mission to achieve independence for India exemplifies self-actualization needs.

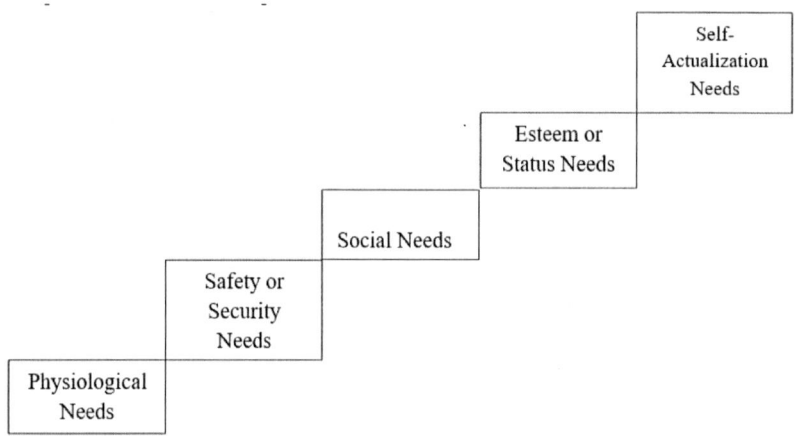

**Figure:** Maslow's need hierarchy

**Assumptions of Maslow's Theory**

Maslow's theory is grounded on the following assumptions:

1.  Human behavior is driven by their needs. When these needs are satisfied, they influence behavior.

2.  Needs are arranged in a hierarchy, beginning with basic needs and progressing to higher-level needs.

3.  Once a need is satisfied, it ceases to motivate the individual. Only the next higher need in the hierarchy can motivate them.

4.  An individual moves to the next higher level of the hierarchy only after the lower need is sufficiently satisfied.

**Applicability of Maslow's Theory**

a.  It is the most popular and widely cited theory of motivation, with wide applicability.

b.  Maslow's theory is particularly applicable to poor and developing countries where money remains a motivating factor.

**Criticisms**

1.  Researchers have demonstrated that there is a lack of a strict hierarchical structure of needs as suggested by Maslow, although every individual prioritizes their need satisfaction in some manner. Some individuals may lack lower-level needs but still strive for self-actualization needs. Mahatma Gandhi's example is particularly noteworthy in this context.

2.  There is a lack of a direct cause-and-effect relationship between needs and behavior. A specific need may lead to different types of behavior in different people. Conversely, a particular behavior may result from different needs. Therefore, the need hierarchy is not as straightforward as it initially appears.

3.  There is considerable disordering among physiological needs, safety needs, social needs, and esteem needs, particularly in an organizational context. For instance, many people may prioritize social needs over job security. Similarly, some individuals may not prioritize social needs but focus on self-esteem needs.

4.  Another issue in applying the theory into practice is that individuals pursue their higher-level needs only when their lower-level needs are reasonably satisfied. Defining what constitutes a "reasonable level" is subjective and varies from person to person.

5.  Another challenge with Maslow's theory of motivation is the operationalization of some of his concepts, making it difficult for researchers to test the theory empirically. For example, how does one measure self-actualization?

Despite its drawbacks, Maslow's theory offers managers a good handle on understanding the motives or needs of individuals and how to motivate organizational members.

## 3. ALDERFER'S ERG THEORY

The ERG need theory, developed by Clayton Alderfer, refines Maslow's hierarchy of needs by condensing the five needs into three categories: Existence, Relatedness, and Growth, represented by the initials E, R, and G.

1. **Existence needs**: These needs are akin to Maslow's physiological and safety needs. They are primarily satisfied by material incentives and include basic physiological needs like sustenance and shelter, as well as safety needs related to physical and psychological well-being.

2. **Relatedness needs**: These needs are similar to Maslow's social and esteem needs. They are fulfilled through personal relationships and social interactions within the organization. Relatedness needs involve open communication, honest exchange of thoughts, and emotional connections with other members.

3. **Growth needs**: These needs are about personal development, growth, and reaching one's full potential, similar to Maslow's self-actualization needs. They are satisfied through active involvement in the organizational environment and embracing new opportunities and challenges.

ERG theory differs from Maslow's in suggesting that individuals can be motivated by more than one type of need simultaneously. While Maslow proposed a strict hierarchy where lower-level needs must be satisfied before higher-level needs can motivate, ERG theory allows for movement between levels. If a person is frustrated in attempting to satisfy needs at a higher level, they may regress to lower-level needs. For example, a manager whose existence needs are fulfilled may seek challenging tasks to satisfy their self-esteem needs. If they face obstacles or frustration in meeting these challenges, they might revert to seeking more material benefits to fulfill their existence needs.

# 4. HERZBERG'S TWO FACTORS THEORY OF MOTIVATION

In 1959, Frederick Herzberg, a behavioral scientist, introduced a two-factor theory known as the motivator-hygiene theory. Herzberg proposed that there are certain job factors that lead to satisfaction, while there are other job factors that prevent dissatisfaction. He categorized these factors into two distinct groups.

According to Herzberg, the opposite of " **Satisfaction** " is " **No satisfaction** ," and the opposite of " **Dissatisfaction** " is " **No Dissatisfaction** ."

**Hygiene Factors:** According to Herzberg, there are certain factors that are not an intrinsic part of the job itself but are related to the conditions under which the job is performed. He referred to these factors as "Hygiene" or "Maintenance" factors. According to him, there are ten maintenance or hygiene factors.

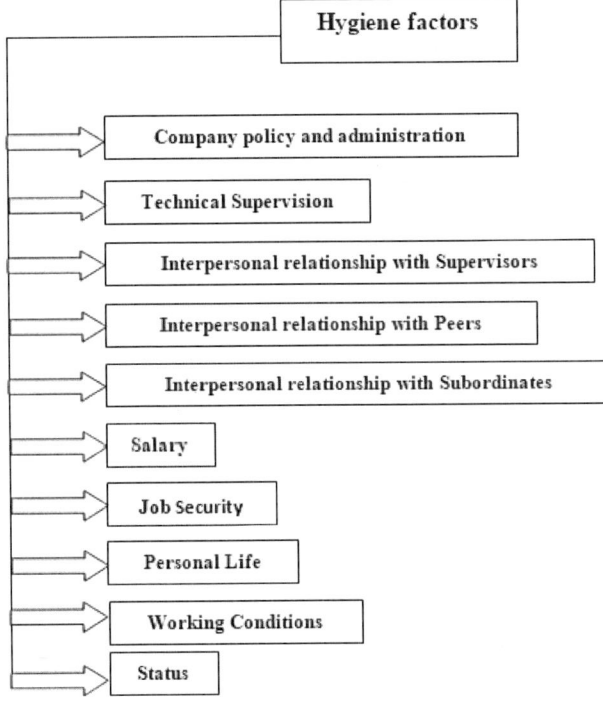

*Hygiene Factors of Herzberg theory*

They do not contribute to increased worker output; instead, they prevent decreases in worker performance due to work constraints. These maintenance factors are necessary to maintain a reasonable level of satisfaction in employees. Increasing them beyond this level will not provide additional satisfaction to the employees; however, reducing them below this level will cause dissatisfaction. Therefore, they are also referred to as dissatisfiers. Since an increase in these factors does not affect employees' satisfaction level, they are not useful for motivating them.

**Motivational Factors:** These factors pertain to the nature of the work itself (job content) and are inherent to the job. They have a positive impact on morale, satisfaction, efficiency, and increased productivity. Herzberg identifies six factors that serve to motivate employees. These factors include::

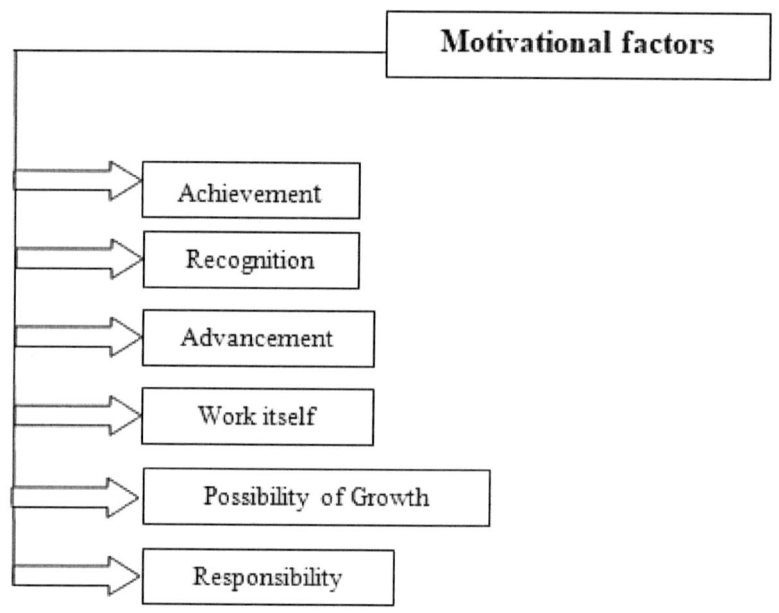

*Motivational Factors of Herzberg theory*

Most of these factors are related to job content. An increase in these factors will satisfy the employees; however, any decrease will not affect their level of satisfaction.

## Applicability

a. Hertzberg theory is an extension of Maslow's theory of motivation. Its applicability is also narrow.

b. Hertzberg's theory is applicable to rich countries where money is less important motivating factor.

## Limitations of Two-Factor Theory

The two factor theory is not free from limitations:

1. The two-factor theory does not account for situational variables.

2. Herzberg assumed a correlation between satisfaction and productivity, but the research conducted by Herzberg focused on satisfaction and overlooked productivity.

3. The theory's reliability is uncertain. Analysis needs to be conducted by raters, who may bias the findings by interpreting the same responses differently.

4. No comprehensive measure of satisfaction was used. An employee may find his job acceptable despite hating or objecting to certain parts of it.

5. The two-factor theory is not free from bias, as it relies on employees' natural reactions when asked about the sources of satisfaction and dissatisfaction at work. Employees tend to attribute dissatisfaction to external factors such as salary structure, company policies, and peer relationships, while attributing satisfaction to themselves.

6. The theory ignores blue-collar workers. Despite these limitations, Herzberg's Two-Factor theory is broadly accepted.

## 5. COMPARISON BETWEEN MASLOW AND HERZBERG THEORY OF MOTIVATION

| S. No | Basis | Maslow Theory of Motivation | Herzberg Theory of Motivation |
|-------|-------|-----------------------------|-------------------------------|
| 1 | Meaning | Maslow's theory is based on the concept of human needs and their satisfaction | Hertzberg's theory is based on the use of motivators which include achievement, recognition and opportunity for growth. |

| S. No | Basis | Maslow Theory of Motivation | Herzberg Theory of Motivation |
|---|---|---|---|
| 2 | Basis of theory | Maslow's theory is based on the hierarchy of human needs. He identified five sets of needs (on priority basis) and their satisfaction in motivating employees) | Hertzberg refers to hygiene factors and motivating factors in his theory. Hygiene factors are dissatisfies while motivating factors motivate subordinates. Hierarchical arrangement of needs is not given. |
| 3 | Nature of theory | Maslow's theory is rather simple and descriptive. The theory is based long experience about human needs. | Hertzberg's theory is more prescriptive. It suggests the motivating factors which can be used effectively. This theory is based on actual information collected by Hertzberg by interviewing 200 engineers and accountants |
| 4 | Applicability | It is most popular and widely cited theory of motivation and has wide applicability.

Maslow's theory is mostly applicable to poor and developing countries where money is still a motivating factor | Hertzberg theory is an extension of Maslow's theory of motivation. Its applicability is also narrow.

Hertzberg's theory is applicable to rich countries where money is less important motivating factor |

| S. No | Basis | Maslow Theory of Motivation | Herzberg Theory of Motivation |
|-------|-------|----------------------------|-------------------------------|
| 5 | Descriptive/ Perspective | Maslow's theory (model) is descriptive in nature. | Hertzberg's theory (model) is perspective in nature |
| 6 | Motivators | According to Maslow's model, any need can act as motivator provided it is not satisfied or relatively less satisfied. | In the dual factor model of Hertzberg, hygiene factors (lower level needs) do not act as motivators. Only the higher order needs (Achievement, recognition, challenging work) act as motivators. |

## 6. VROOM EXPECTANCY THEORY OF MOTIVATION

Several motivation theories, including those proposed by Maslow and Herzberg, attempt to elucidate the relationship between internal needs and the efforts expended to satisfy them.

Vroom's expectancy theory, on the other hand, distinguishes between effort (arising from motivation), performance, and outcomes. This cognitive model is grounded in conscious thoughts about situations, detailing not only how individuals feel and behave but also why they react in particular ways. Vroom's theory assumes that an individual's behavior stems from conscious choices made to maximize pleasure and minimize pain. He acknowledged that an employee's performance is influenced by individual factors such as personality, skills, knowledge, experience, and abilities. Vroom posited that effort, performance, and motivation are interlinked in an individual's motivation. To explain this, he introduced the variables of Expectancy, Instrumentality, and Valence. His theory is considered predictive in terms of motivation.

The motivational relationship may be expressed in the form of formula:

$$\text{Motivation} = V \times E \times I$$

Where,

V = Valence, E = Expectancy, I = Instrumentality

The theory suggests that although individuals may have different sets of goals, they can be motivated if they believe that:

- There is a positive correlation between efforts and performance
- Favorable performance will result in a desirable reward
- The reward will satisfy an important need
- The desire to satisfy the need is strong enough to make the effort worthwhile.

The different variables of the theory are explained as follows:

**Expectancy** is the belief that increased effort will lead to increased performance i.e. 'if I work harder then this will be better". This is affected by things such as:

- Having the right resources available (e.g. raw materials, time)
- Having the right skills to do the job
- Having the necessary support to get the job done (e.g. supervisor support, or correct information on the job)

People typically hold certain expectations regarding the likelihood of their actions succeeding. If individuals perceive their chances of success as zero, they are unlikely to even attempt the task. Expectancy is subjective and varies from person to person. Different people attach different expectations to the outcomes they desire. Competent and confident individuals tend to view expectancy more positively compared to those who are less competent and more pessimistic. Educational managers can positively influence employees' expectancies by aligning individuals with jobs or tasks that match their abilities.

Employees have varying expectations and levels of confidence in their capabilities. Institutions must identify the resources, training, or supervision that employees need.

**Instrumentality** refers to the belief that if you perform well, you will receive a valued outcome. It measures the degree to which a first-level outcome (like good performance) will lead to a second-level outcome (like a reward). In simpler terms, it's the belief that "if I do a good job, there is something in it for me." Instrumentality can be influenced by factors such as:

- Clear understanding of the relationship between performance and outcomes - e.g. the rules of the reward 'game'
- Trust in the people who will take the decisions on who gets what outcome

- Transparency of the process that decides who gets what outcome

Perceived instrumentality is also a subjective perception. When people believe that their performance is adequately rewarded, they perceive instrumentality positively. Conversely, if they believe that their performance does not affect their rewards, the instrumentality perception will be low. Employees' perception plays a crucial role in whether they believe they will receive the rewards they desire, even if promised by management. Therefore, management must ensure that promises of rewards are fulfilled and that employees are aware of this.

**Valence** is the importance that an individual places on an expected outcome. For valence to be positive, the person must prefer achieving the outcome over not achieving it. For instance, if someone is primarily motivated by money, they might not value offers of additional time off. Valence can be defined as the strength of a person's preference for one outcome compared to others. It represents the subjective value attached to an incentive or reward. Valence refers to the emotional orientation people have towards outcomes (rewards). It is the degree of desire an employee has for extrinsic rewards (such as money, promotion, time-off, benefits) or intrinsic rewards (such as job satisfaction). Management must identify what employees value.

The three elements crucial for choosing one over another are clearly defined: effort-performance expectancy (E>P expectancy) and performance-outcome expectancy (P>O expectancy).

**E>P expectancy**: This involves an individual's assessment that one's efforts will lead to the required performance.

**P>O expectancy**: This involves an individual's assessment that one's successful performance will lead to certain outcomes.

Vroom's expectancy theory operates based on perceptions. Therefore, even if an employer believes they have provided everything necessary for motivation and even if this works for most people in the organization, it does not guarantee that someone won't perceive it differently. Initially, expectancy theory appears most relevant to traditional work situations where an employee's motivation depends on whether they desire the reward offered for doing a good job and whether they believe increased effort will lead to that reward.

However, this theory can equally apply to any situation where someone takes action because they anticipate a specific outcome. For instance, "I recycle paper because I value conserving resources and taking a stand on environmental issues (valence); I believe that the more effort I put into recycling, the more paper I will recycle (expectancy); and I think that recycling more paper will reduce resource consumption (instrumentality)." Thus, Vroom's expectancy theory of motivation does not focus solely on self-interest in rewards, but on the connections people make with expected outcomes and the contribution they believe they can make toward those outcomes. Vroom suggests that an employee's beliefs about expectancy, instrumentality, and valence interact psychologically to create a motivational force, prompting the employee to act in ways that bring pleasure and avoid pain.

## 7. WILLIAM'S OUCHI'S Z THEORY:

Professor William G. Ouchi developed this theory of motivation based on his comparative study of American and Japanese management practices. He highlighted the key aspects of Japanese management that make it superior to American management. The central premise of his theory is to engage employees with the organization, which he believes is crucial for the productivity of the Japanese economy.

According to Prof. Ouchi, motivation is a gift from employees' trust in the organization, subtlety, and intimacy. Subtlety refers to a deep recognition of employees' personalities, enabling a supervisor to understand how employees work best with each other. This subtlety helps in forming effective work teams. He asserts that the essence of Japanese management can be summed up in three words: trust, subtlety, and intimacy.

The distinguishing features of Theory Z are as follows:

1. **Mutual Trust** : According to Ouchi, trust, integrity, and openness are fundamental elements of an effective organization. When trust and openness exist between employees, work groups, unions, and management, conflicts are minimized, and employees cooperate fully to achieve the organization's objectives.

2. **Strong Bond between Organization and Employees** : Various methods can be employed to establish a strong bond between the enterprise and its employees. For instance, employees may be offered lifetime employment, which fosters loyalty towards the enterprise. During adverse business conditions, shareholders may forgo dividends to prevent worker layoffs. There should be a focus on slowing down promotions and emphasizing

horizontal movement of employees, which reduces stagnation. Career planning for employees ensures proper placement, resulting in a more stable and conducive work environment.

3. **Employee Involvement** : Theory Z suggests that involving employees in relevant matters enhances their commitment and performance. This involvement entails meaningful participation of employees in the decision-making process, particularly in matters directly affecting them. Such participation fosters a sense of responsibility and increases enthusiasm in implementing decisions. Top managers act as facilitators rather than decision-makers.

4. **Integrated Organization** : Under Theory Z, the emphasis is on sharing information and resources rather than on charts, divisions, or formal structures. An integrated organization promotes job rotation, which enhances understanding of the interdependence of tasks and fosters a sense of teamwork.

5. **Coordination** : The leader's role should be to coordinate human efforts. To develop a common culture and a sense of unity in the organization, leaders must use communication processes, debates, and analysis.

6. **Informal Control System** : Organizational control systems should be informal. Emphasis should be placed on mutual trust and cooperation rather than on superior-subordinate relationships.

7. **Human Resource Development** : Managers should cultivate new skills among employees. Under Theory Z, the potential of every person is recognized, and efforts are made to develop and utilize it through job enlargement, career planning, training, etc.

Thus, Theory Z is a hybrid system that incorporates the strengths of American management (individual freedom, risk-taking, quick decision-making, etc.) and Japanese management (job security, group decision-making, social cohesion, holistic concern for employees, etc.) systems.

Japanese companies operating in the United States have successfully implemented Theory Z. After collaboration between Japanese and Indian companies, some experts have suggested applying this theory in India. For instance, Maruti Udyog, which collaborates with Suzuki Motors of Japan, has attempted to apply Theory Z.

The workplace has been designed based on the Japanese pattern, which includes open offices. A uniform dress code has been introduced for all employees, regardless of their designation. Similarly, there is a common canteen for everyone. These practices are expected to minimize status differentials and foster teamwork among employees in the company.

**Limitations of Theory Z:**

Theory Z suffers from the following limitations:

1. Providing lifetime employment to employees in order to build a strong bond between the organization and its employees may not effectively motivate employees with higher-level needs. It primarily offers job security and may fail to foster loyalty among employees. An employee may choose to leave the organization if better opportunities are offered elsewhere. Additionally, complete job security may lead to complacency among employees. Employers may also be reluctant to retain inefficient employees permanently.

2. Employee participation in the decision-making process can be challenging. Managers may resist participation as it could challenge their authority and decision-making freedom. Employees may also be hesitant to participate due to fear of criticism and lack of motivation. Even if they participate in management discussions, their contributions may be limited unless they fully understand the issues and take initiative. Involving all employees in decision-making may also slow down the decision-making process.

3. Theory Z proposes an organization without a formal structure. However, without structure, there may be chaos in the organization as it may not be clear who is responsible to whom.

4. Developing a common organizational culture may be difficult because people differ in their attitudes, habits, languages, religions, customs, etc.

5. Theory Z is based on Japanese management practices, which have evolved from Japan's unique culture. Therefore, the theory may not be universally applicable across different cultures.

Thus, Theory Z does not provide complete solution to motivational problems of all organisations operating under different types of environment. However, it is not merely a theory of motivation but a philosophy of managing.

# SUMMARY OF THE CHAPTER

1. **Motivation** means stimulating, inducing, inciting the employees to perform to their best capacity.

2. **Motive** is an inner state that energises, activates and directs behaviour towards goals.

3. **Motivating** is a term which implies that one person (in the organizational context, a manager) induces another, (say, employee) to engage in action (work behaviour) by ensuring that a channel to satisfy the motive becomes available and accessible to the individual

4. **Features of motivation:**
   - Internal instinct
   - Produces goal directed behavior
   - Positive or Negative Motivation
   - Complex Process
   - Dynamic and Continuous Process
   - Person motivated in totally
   - Universal Management function

5. **Importance/Significance of Motivation:**
   - Improves Performance Level
   - Development of Positive Attitude
   - Reduction in Employees Turnover
   - Introduce Changes Smoothly
   - Reduce Absenteeism

6. **Maslow** classified human needs into **five categories** in order to priority.
   - Physiological Needs
   - Safety or Security Needs
   - Social Needs
   - Esteem or Status Needs
   - Self Actualisation Needs

7. The ERG need theory, developed by Clayton Alerter is a refinement of Maslow's needs hierarchy. Instead of Maslow's five needs, ERG theory condenses these five needs into three needs. These three needs are those of Existence, Relatedness and- Growth. The E, Rand G is the initials for these needs.

8. According to Herzberg, there are some factors which are not intrinsic part of a job, but are related to conditions under which a job is performed. He called these factors as "Hygiene or Maintenance factors'.

9. Motivational factors are related to the nature of work (job content) and are intrinsic to the job itself. These factors have a positive influence on morale, satisfaction, efficiency and higher productivity. Herzberg includes six factors that motivate employees.

## QUESTIONS

1. Write down the concept of motivation.
2. Define motivation.
3. What are the characteristics of motivation?
4. Discuss the significance of motivation.
5. Discuss the Maslow's Need Hierarchy Theory of Motivation.
6. What are the assumptions of Maslow's Need Hierarchy Theory of Motivation?
7. Criticise the Maslow's Need Hierarchy Theory of Motivation
8. Discuss the Herzberg Two Factor theory of Motivation.
9. Distinguish between Maslow's and Herzberg theory of Motivation

# UNIT 4B
# CONTROLLING

Control –

Concept and Process

## CONTENTS

# 1. CONCEPT OF CONTROLLING

Managerial control involves the function of limiting and directing actions in alignment with plans to achieve specific objectives. It encompasses checking, measuring, and regulating ongoing organizational activities to ensure they adhere to predetermined plans and yield desired outcomes. In essence, controlling is the process of verifying whether work is being executed according to schedule or established plans, and taking corrective action if needed. This process involves comparing and verifying actual performance against planned performance, identifying any discrepancies, determining the causes of these deviations, and implementing corrective measures as necessary.

# 2. DEFINITIONS OF CONTROLLING

"Controlling consists of verifying whether everything occurs in conformity with the plans adopted, the instructions issued and the principles established. It has for its object to point out weakness and errors in order to rectify them and prevent recurrence."

*Henri Fayol*

"Control is the process of taking steps to bring actual results and desired results closer together."

*Phillip Kotler*

"Controlling is determining what is being accomplished that is evaluating the performance, and if necessary, applying correct measures so that the performance takes place according to plans."

*George R. Terry*

"Management Control is the process by which managers assures that resources are obtained and used effectively in the accomplishment of an organization's objectives." Robert N. Anthony

"The measurement and correction of the performance of activities of subordinates in order to make sure that enterprise objectives and plans devised to attain them are being accomplished."

*Koontz and O'Donnel*

## 3. CHARACTERISTICS OF CONTROLLING

The characteristics of control can be easily understood from the following facts :

1.  **Controlling is a Fundamental Management Function**: Controlling is the most crucial function performed by management. Through this function, management assesses whether activities are being executed according to plans. Every managerial activity aims to achieve desired goals, necessitating effective control.

2.  **Controlling is a Continuous Activity**: Control is an ongoing, perpetual activity throughout the lifespan of an organization. The cycle involves appraising work against established standards, identifying deviations, and taking corrective actions. Corrective action is based on a review of actual performance and results, potentially leading to changes in planning, organizing, staffing, etc.

3.  **Controlling is an Essential Function of Management**: Controlling is practiced at all levels of management, from top to bottom, although its nature and scope may vary. For example, top management focuses on administrative control, middle-level management on policy control, and lower-level management on the execution of activities.

4.  **Controlling is a Pervasive Function**: It is a primary function of every manager. Managers at all levels — top, middle, and lower — must perform controlling functions to maintain control over activities in their respective areas. Controlling is just as essential in educational institutions, the military, hospitals, clubs, and any business organization.

5.  **Controlling is Forward Looking as well as Backward Looking**: Effective control is forward-looking because the past cannot be controlled. When deviations from standards are identified, they serve as a guide for future improvements. Measures can

be devised to control the future based on past performance. Controlling also involves looking backward to appraise past activities, identifying control points to prevent the recurrence of mistakes.

6. **Controlling has both Positive and Negative Approaches**: The positive approach to control aims at effectively using all available resources in the enterprise, while the negative approach aims at preventing misuse of resources. Controlling encourages approved programs and policies and discourages non-plan actions.

7. **Controlling is Action-Oriented**: Control involves taking corrective actions whenever necessary. Various control systems provide feedback to managers, and the control process is completed when managers take appropriate actions based on the reports received. A good control system facilitates timely action to minimize wastage of resources, time, and energy.

8. **Controlling is Related to Planning**: Controlling is closely tied to planning. Planning without control is futile, and control without planning is meaningless. The control process uses performance standards determined during the planning stage. Additionally, the control process identifies deficiencies in planning and initiates the revision of various plans.

## 4. SIGNIFICANCE OF CONTROLLING

Controlling is an essential function of management, serving as the soul of effective organizational management. A robust control system assists an organization in the following ways:

1. **Helps in Achieving Organizational Goals**: Management begins with setting organizational goals and establishing procedures to achieve them. Control monitors performance closely, ensuring that plans are executed and objectives are accomplished by regulating actual performance and taking corrective action in case of deviations. This guidance keeps the organization on the right track towards achieving its goals.

2. **Aid to Delegation**: Effective control relies on proper assignment of duties and delegation of authority. It encourages delegation

of authority to lower-level workers, fostering their involvement in the enterprise's operations.

3. **Helps in Evaluating Accuracy of Standards**: The control process establishes standards for appraising and measuring actual performance. These performance standards are set during managerial planning, considering the desired outcomes of efforts. Through controlling, managers can assess the accuracy of these standards and revise them as necessary to align with environmental changes.

4. **Helps in Achieving Better Coordination**: Control facilitates efficient coordination of individual operations, providing direction to activities and efforts aimed at achieving organizational goals in accordance with plans and programs. All departments and individuals adhere to performance standards and goals laid out in the plans, ensuring efficient and orderly work performance.

5. **Helps in Making Efficient Use of Resources**: Controlling ensures optimal utilization of human, physical, and financial resources, aiming to reduce wastage and misuse. It guarantees that work is performed according to established standards in terms of quality, quantity, time, and cost, thus promoting effective and efficient resource utilization.

6. **Helps in Improving Employee Motivation**: An effective control system communicates goals and performance appraisal standards to employees in advance. This clarity motivates employees to perform their best, knowing what is expected of them and how their performance will be evaluated.

7. **Ensuring Order and Discipline**: Controlling fosters an atmosphere of order and discipline within the organization. It minimizes dishonest behavior by monitoring employee activities closely. Regular performance evaluation encourages employees to improve their work and maximize their contributions.

8. **Facilitating Coordination in Action**: Managerial control across various organizational levels promotes harmony in work. It keeps activities and efforts within their boundaries and schedules, directing them towards a common direction. This prevents overlap and duplication of activities and ensures prompt correction of any deviations, thereby ensuring the accomplishment of organizational objectives.

In summary, controlling plays a crucial role in guiding and directing organizational activities towards achieving set goals, ensuring efficient use of resources, improving employee motivation, and maintaining discipline and order within the organization.

## 5. PROCESS OF CONTROLLING

Controlling is an ongoing process that begins with establishing standards of work before the commencement of activities. It involves monitoring actual performance to ensure it aligns with expected performance. This process includes comparing and verifying actual performance against planned performance, identifying any deviations, and determining the reasons for these discrepancies. Therefore, the control process consists of a series of four steps, which are explained below.

1.  **Establishing Performance Standards:** According to Koontz and O'Donnel, "Standards are predetermined criteria against which actual results are measured." Therefore, the initial step in the control process is to establish standards of measurement, which should be clearly defined in quantitative terms. Without performance standards, measuring actual performance serves no purpose.

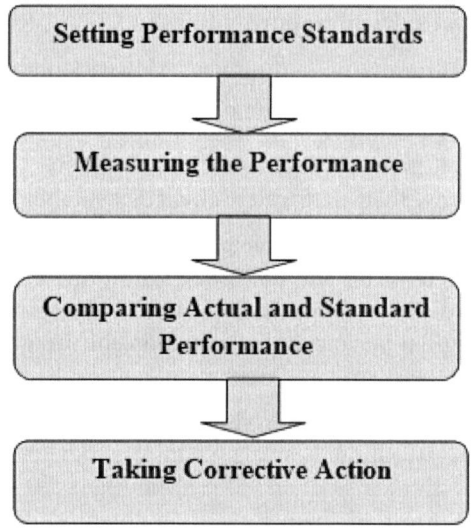

*Process of Controlling*

The prescribed standards should posses the following conditions:

    a. Standards should be pre-determined.

    b. It should be attainable.

    c. It should lay emphasis on key factor.

    d. It should be concerned with results rather than procedures.

    e. it should be definite and reasonable.

    f. It should be measurable and verifiable.

    g. It should be fixed in quantitative terms and not qualitative terms.

2. **Measuring Performance**: The second step in the control process involves measuring the actual performance of individuals, groups, or units against the predetermined standards. This allows management to assess whether work is being conducted in accordance with the plans.

3. **Comparing Actual and Standard Performance**: The subsequent step in the control process is to compare the actual performance with the established standards. This comparison enables managers to determine if performance is in line with the planned objectives. If actual performance aligns with the standards, the controlling function concludes; however, if deviations exist, further steps are taken. The main objectives of this comparison are:

    a. To identify any deviations.

    b. To determine the reasons for these deviations.

While comparing actual performance with standards, permissible limits are set. Minor deviations within these limits do not raise concern. However, significant deviations beyond the prescribed limits require immediate action. This approach is often referred to as "Management by exception".

4. **Taking Corrective Action:** Upon comparing actual performance with planned performance, managers identify deviations between the plan and actual execution. The next step involves understanding the reasons for these deviations and taking corrective measures to realign performance with the plan. Corrective actions may include:

a. Maintaining the status quo if deviations are minor.

b. Adjusting or revising plans or strategies that are outdated or not aligned with the current business environment.

c. Implementing corrective measures to enhance performance so that future results conform to the plan.

## 6. RELATIONSHIP BETWEEN PLANNING AND CONTROLLING

Controlling is closely interconnected with planning. Planning serves as the foundation for control, as it lays out the entire framework upon which the control function relies. Planning becomes meaningless without controlling, and controlling without planning is directionless or unfocused. In practice, these two terms are often used together in departmental designations, such as production planning, scheduling, and routing, highlighting the presence of a plan that guides organizational behavior and activities.

Control assesses and evaluates these behaviors and activities, suggesting corrective actions to address any deviations. Furthermore, control implies the existence of specific goals and standards, which are established through the planning process. Control is the outcome of specific plans, goals, or policies. Therefore, planning both provides and influences control.

Moreover, planning is also influenced by control, as many of the insights provided by control mechanisms are used for planning and replanning. Thus, there exists a reciprocal relationship between planning and controlling, as illustrated in the figure.

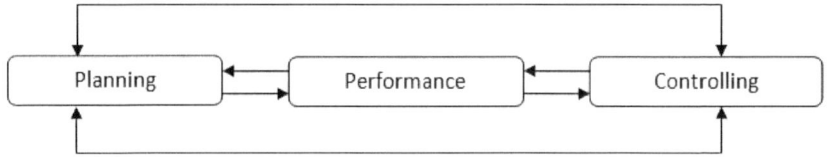

*Planning and Controlling Relationship*

It is often stated that planning looks ahead, while controlling looks back. Plans are formulated for the future and are based on forecasts of future conditions, making planning a forward-looking function. Conversely, controlling is seen as a backward-looking function because it measures and compares actual performance against standards established in the past. It involves a review of past activities to identify any deviations from those standards, similar to conducting a postmortem analysis.

Therefore, various elements of planning define what is intended and expected, as well as the means by which goals are to be achieved. They provide a mechanism for reporting progress made towards these goals and establish a general framework for making new decisions and taking actions in a coherent manner. Well-conceived plans thus become a crucial component in implementing effective control.

## 7. LIMITATIONS OF CONTROLLING

Controlling function of management suffers from the following limitations:

1. **Difficulty in Establishing Quantitative Standards**: The effectiveness of a control system diminishes when standards of performance cannot be clearly defined in quantitative terms. This challenge is particularly evident in areas related to job satisfaction, human behavior, and employee morale.

2. **Lack of Control over External Factors**: An organization cannot influence external factors such as government policies, competition, technological changes, and shifts in fashion that impact the business environment.

3. **Cost Considerations**: Implementing and maintaining a control system can be expensive, requiring significant expenditure, time, and effort. Managers must ensure that the costs associated with setting up and operating the control system do not exceed the anticipated benefits.

4. **Resistance from Employees**: Employees often resist control systems because they perceive them as constraints on their freedom. For instance, surveillance through closed-circuit television (CCTV) is typically met with resistance.

# 8. PRINCIPLES OF EFFECTIVE CONTROL

A control system involves a multi-step process used for different types of control activities. Managers encounter several challenges when designing a control system that delivers accurate feedback promptly and cost-effectively, and is acceptable to organizational members. Many of these challenges arise from decisions about what should be controlled and the frequency of progress measurement. To address these challenges effectively, managers should design their control systems based on the following principles:

1. **Integrating Strategic Planning and Control Systems:** Strategic planning and management control are vital processes that contribute significantly to the effectiveness of business organizations. Therefore, there should be a seamless integration of these two systems. This integration can be achieved by ensuring consistency between strategic objectives and performance measures.

2. **Identifying Strategic Control Points:** To establish an effective control system, managers need to identify strategic control points within the system where monitoring or data collection should occur. The method for selecting strategic control points involves focusing on the most critical elements in a given operation.

3. **Organizational Communication:** The organization must establish a communication network for transmitting control information both downward and upward. Downward communication involves superiors informing subordinates about their expected tasks, while upward communication gathers control information from subordinates regarding what has been accomplished.

4. **Motivational Dynamics:** Control is influenced by the motivational dynamics of individuals and how the organization intends to satisfy various needs. Motivational dynamics play a dual role in control.

a. First, how the various attempts at control are in tune with the needs of the people.

b. Second, the organisation itself provides motivation or demotivation to the people to work.

Thus, organisational phenomenon of how people are motivated is a crucial factor in control of behaviour of people in the organisation.

## 9. TECHNIQUES OF CONTROL

We have learned that managers need to perform the function of controlling to ensure that the organization is achieving its set goals. Various control techniques provide managers with the necessary information to measure and monitor employee performance in pursuit of organizational objectives. These control techniques can be broadly classified into two categories:

1. Traditional control techniques; and

2. Advance control techniques

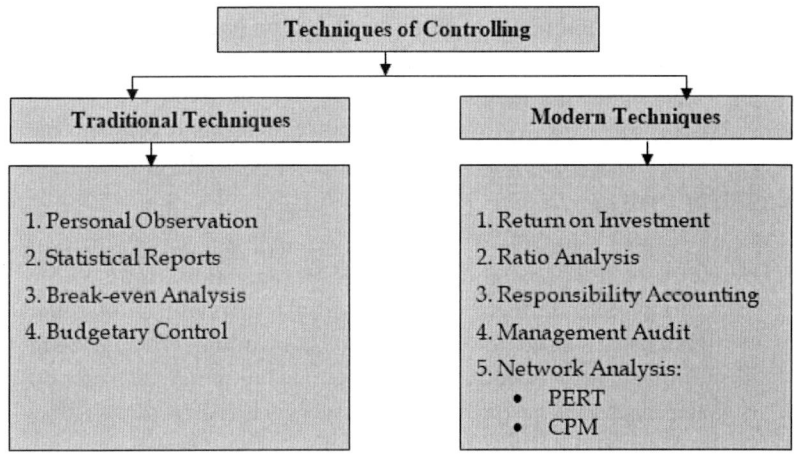

*Techniques of Controlling*

# 9.1 TRADITIONAL TECHNIQUES OF CONTROL

Traditional control techniques are methods that have been used by managers over the long term. These techniques include:

a. **Personal Observation:** Personal observation is the most traditional method of control. This method allows a manager to observe operations in the workplace. Through this technique, a manager can correct operations on the spot and provide direction to a worker if their work does not meet the standards.

   Employees feel psychological pressure and tend to perform well knowing that they are being personally observed. However, this technique is very time-consuming and may not be suitable for all types of jobs.

b. **Statistical Reports:** A manager may utilize statistical analysis in the form of averages, percentages, ratios, correlations, etc., to gather valuable information regarding the performance of an organization across different areas. This information, presented in tables, graphs, etc., allows a manager to compare the organization's current period performance with that of previous periods.

c. **Break-even Analysis:** The break-even point is the point at which the total revenue of an organization equals its total cost, resulting in neither profit nor loss. A manager may utilize break-even analysis to examine the connection between production costs, production volume, output price levels, and profits. This technique allows a manager to estimate profits at various levels of activity.

d. **Budgetary Control:** A budget is a numerical statement that expresses the plans and goals of an organization for a specific future period. Budgetary control is a system in which budgeted activities are used for purposes of controlling and planning within an organization. This technique allows a manager to compare actual performance with budgeted performance after the completion of a particular activity. If there is any negative deviation, the manager needs to take necessary action to achieve organizational goals. The most common types of budgets used by organizations include sales budgets, production budgets, material budgets, cash budgets, capital budgets, and research and development budgets.

## 9.2 MODERN CONTROL TECHNIQUES

Modern control techniques are those which are of recent origin and are comparatively new in management literature. Advance control techniques include:

a. **Return on Investment**: Return on investment (ROI) is considered a valuable control technique. It measures the rate of profitability on the capital employed, and is therefore also referred to as return on capital employed. ROI can be calculated as follows:

$$\text{Return on Investment (ROI)} = \frac{\text{Net Income (Profit)}}{\text{(Total Investment)}}$$

A manager can use ROI to measure overall performance of an organisation or of its individual departments or divisions.

b. **Ratio Analysis**: A manager may calculate ratios to analyze financial statements. The most commonly used ratios can be categorized into the following groups:

   i. **Liquidity Ratio**: A manager needs to calculate liquidity ratios to assess the short-term solvency of a business. By analyzing the current availability of liquid funds, they can determine the organization's ability to meet its obligations to stakeholders. Examples of some commonly used liquidity ratios include the Current Ratio and Quick Ratio.

   ii. **Solvency Ratio**: A manager needs to calculate solvency ratios to assess the financial soundness of an organization and its ability to meet both short-term and long-term obligations. Examples of some commonly used ratios include Debt-Equity Ratio, Proprietary Ratio, and Interest Coverage Ratio.

   iii. **Profitability Ratio**: A manager must calculate profitability ratios to analyze the business's profitability position. These ratios assess profits in relation to sales, funds, or capital employed. Examples of some profitability ratios used by managers include: Gross Profit Ratio, Net Profit Ratio, and Return on Capital Employed, among others.

   iv. **Turnover Ratio**: A manager can calculate turnover ratios to assess the efficiency of operations based on the effective utilization of resources. A higher turnover indicates better utilization of resources. Examples of some common turnover ratios frequently used by managers include: inventory turnover ratio, stock turnover ratio, debtor turnover ratio, and so on.

c. **Responsibility Accounting**: Responsibility accounting is an accounting system where various sections, divisions, and departments within an organization are established as 'Responsibility Centers'. The manager or head of each center is accountable for achieving the targets set for their respective center. Responsibility centers can be categorized into the following types:

   i. **Cost Centre**: In a cost or expense center, the manager is accountable for the costs incurred within the center. For instance, in a manufacturing organization, the production department is categorized as a cost center.

   ii. **Revenue Centre**: In a revenue center, the manager is primarily responsible for generating revenue. For example, the marketing department of an organization may be classified as a revenue center.

   iii. **Profit Centre**: In a profit center, the manager is responsible for both revenues and costs. For example, the repairs and maintenance department of an organization may be treated as a profit center if it also provides services to other production departments.

   iv. **Investment Centre**: In an investment center, the manager is responsible not only for profits but also for the investments made in the center in the form of assets.

d. **Management Audit**: Traditional control methods have proven inadequate in evaluating the quality of managerial personnel, which is crucial for an organization's success. A step in the right direction is management audit, which involves the systematic assessment of the overall performance of an organization's management. This audit can be conducted by external consultants or an organization's internal audit staff. Management audit identifies deficiencies in the performance of management functions such as planning, organizing, staffing, directing, and controlling, and proposes potential improvements.

e. **Network Analysis**: Network analysis involves the use of network techniques to solve large, complex problems that consist of many interrelated activities performed in a specific sequence. For instance, in projects such as metro construction or bridge construction, network analysis is crucial for ensuring successful completion within the scheduled time.

A network is a graphical representation of these interconnected activities, arranged in the order of their occurrence and connected by arrows, which are represented by nodes. Network analysis aims to create such a network and subsequently plan, schedule, and control the performance of activities in a large and complex project.

**There are primarily two network techniques which are widely applied. These are:**

1.  **Programme Evaluation Review Technique (PERT):** PERT, short for Program (Project) Evaluation and Review Technique, involves the planning, organizing, coordinating, and controlling of uncertain activities. The technique analyzes and outlines the tasks necessary to complete a project, aiming to identify the minimum time required for each task and the overall project completion time. It was originally developed in the late 1950s to manage the Polaris weapon system. The PERT network analysis consists of the following steps:

    a.  Clearly defining the goal of the project.

    b.  Obtaining a work-break structure to a set of individual jobs, and arranging them in a logical fashion.

    c.  Estimating the job duration, making provisions for optimistic and pessimistic schedules.

    d.  Identifying the resource requirement constraints.

    e.  Locating the schedule of dates for each activity by planning a detailed control structure.

    f.  Preparing project control system and identifying the requirements of progress reports for different levels of management.

    g.  Developing the critical path or slack times.

    h.  Crashing the time-optimum cost levels on the basis of costs.

i. Updating the network continuously by systematized methods

j. Monitoring, evaluating and reviewing the network constantly

In simple words it can be said that PERT is a technique applicable for projects with non-repetitive activities. PERT is a probabilistic approach where time of completion of each activity is not certainly known.

2. **Critical Path Method (CPM)**: CPM is a project evaluation technique aimed at determining the total duration for project completion and identifying the shortest path to achieve it. It is a deterministic networking technique where the time required for activity completion is known with certainty. CPM was initially utilized in 1957 by E.I. du Pont de Nemours & Co. to enhance the planning, scheduling, and coordination of its new plant construction efforts. Subsequently, the method spread to large construction companies, research projects, technology development, building construction, plant maintenance, and industrial projects. The technique was introduced in response to escalating costs and the time needed to transition new products from research to production. Similar to PERT, CPM is based on the network principle where events are represented by circles, and activities are represented by arrows that connect events. An event signifies a specific program milestone at a particular point in time, while an activity represents the time and resources required to progress from one event to another. Once the network arrow diagram is established, time and cost estimates—both normal and crash—are assigned to each activity. The normal estimate focuses on minimizing costs associated with the associated time, as attempts will later be made to reduce it, with the normal time considered the maximum time. The costs associated with normal times are assumed to be minimum costs. The crash estimate represents the absolute minimum time and its associated maximum cost. It is assumed that there is a linear cost relationship

between normal and crash estimates for each activity. Managers may use PERT and CPM to manage time scheduling and resource allocation for a variety of complex, interconnected activities. These techniques aim to execute projects effectively within given time schedules and cost structures. Under these techniques, a manager must divide a project into clearly identifiable activities or tasks, prepare a network diagram to illustrate the sequence of activities from the start to the project's completion, and assign time and cost estimates to each activity. Subsequently, the longest time path through the network is computed, which is known as the critical path. Finally, the manager may adjust the plan to control project execution and ensure timely completion. PERT and CPM are extensively used in industries such as shipbuilding, construction projects, aircraft manufacturing, and others where complex projects with interconnected activities require careful management of time and resources.

3. **Management Information System (MIS):** The management information system (MIS) is primarily focused on converting data into actionable information, which is then distributed to all levels of personnel and departments within an organization to support effective decision-making. It ensures that top management receives timely and relevant data and information, allowing them to develop suitable control techniques in response to deviations from standards. In a nutshell, managerial control techniques help in measuring the overall efficiency of management from different perspectives to suit various conditions and requirements. Control technique provide managers with the type and amount of information they need to measure and monitor performance. The information from various controls must be tailored to a specific management level, department, unit or operation.

# SUMMARY OF THE CHAPTER

1. **Controlling** is the process of checking, measuring and regulating the on-going activities of the organization to ensure that they are in conformity with the pre-determined plans and produce the desired result.

2. **Characteristics of Controlling**
   - Controlling is a Fundamental Management Function
   - Controlling is a Continuous Activity
   - Controlling is Essential Function of Management
   - Controlling is a Pervasive Function
   - Controlling is Forward Looking as well as Backward Looking
   - Controlling has both Positive and Negative Approach
   - Controlling is Action Oriented
   - Controlling is Related with Planning

3. **Significance of Controlling**
   - Helps in Accomplishing Organisational Goal
   - Aid to delegation
   - Helps on Judging Accuracy of Standards
   - Helps in Achieving Better Coordination
   - Helps in Making Efficient Use of Resources
   - Helps in Improving Employees Motivation
   - Ensuring Order and Discipline
   - Facilitating Coordination in Action

4. The **process of control** comprises a series of four steps which are listed below:
   - Setting Performance Standards
   - Measuring the Performance
   - Comparing Actual and Standard performance
   - Taking Corrective Action

5. Controlling is closely related with planning. Planning is the basis for control in the sense that it provides the entire spectrum on which control function is based. Planning is an empty exercise

without controlling and controlling without planning is aimless or blind.

6. **Limitations of Controlling**:
   - Difficulty in Setting Quantitative Standards
   - No Control on External Factors
   - Costly affair
   - Resistance from Employees

7. **Principles of Effective Control:**
   - Integrating Strategic Planning and Control System
   - Identifying Strategic Control Points
   - Organisational Communication
   - Motivational Dynamics

8. **Major Techniques of Control:**
   A. Traditional Techniques:
      - Personal Observation
      - Statistical Reports
      - Break-even Analysis
      - Budgetary Control
   B. Modern Techniques:
      - Return on Investment
      - Ratio Analysis
      - Responsibility Accounting
      - Management Audit
      - Network Analysis:
        o PERT
        o CPM

9. **Responsibility accounting** is a system of accounting in which different sections, divisions and departments of an organisation are set up as 'Responsibility Centres'.

10 **Network analysis** refers to use of network techniques for solving large, complex problems comprising of many interrelated activities to be performed in a particular order.

11. **PERT** is an acronym form Program (Project) Evaluation and Review Technique, in which planning, organising, co-ordinating and controlling uncertain activities take place.

12. **CPM** is a project evaluation technique which aims at identification of total duration for the project completion time along with the shortest path for its completion. CPM is a deterministic networking technique where activity completion time is known with certainty.

13. **Management information system (MIS)** is basically concerned with processing data into information, which is then communicated to all levels of personnel and departments in an organisation for appropriate decision-making.

# QUESTIONS

**SHORT ANSWER QUESTIONS**

1. What do you mean by controlling?

2. Define controlling.

3. State any three features of controlling.

4. Discuss any three significance of controlling.

5. What are the steps in the process of controlling?

6. What do you understand by actual and standard performances?

7. How would you determine the deviations between actual and standard performances?

8. State any three limitations of controlling.

9. Mention the relationship between planning and controlling.

10. Discuss any three principles of effective controlling.

11. What are the traditional techniques of controlling?

12. Mention any three traditional techniques of controlling.

13. Discuss personal observation as a useful tool for controlling.

14. What do you mean by break-even analysis?
15. What is statistical report?
16. Give the meaning of budgetary control.
17. Give the concept of ratio analysis.
18. What is liquidity ratio?
19. What is solvency ratio?
20. What is profitability ratio?
21. What is turnover ratio?
22. What is meant by responsibility accounting?
23. What are different responsibility centres?
24. Give the meaning of cost, revenue, profit and investment centres.
25. How management audit is a useful tool for controlling?
26. What do you understand by network analysis?
27. What do you mean by PERT?
28. What do you understand by CPM?
29. What do you mean by management information system?
30. Give the meaning of budget .

## SHORT NOTES
1. Controlling
2. Significance of Controlling
3. Process of Controlling.
4. Relationship between Planning and Controlling.
5. Limitations of Controlling.
6. Traditional Techniques of Control.
7. Modern Techniques of Control.
8. Responsibility Centres.
9. PERT
10. CPM.
11. Budgetary Control.

## LONG ANSWER QUESTIONS

1. What do you mean by controlling? Discuss its essential features.
2. Explain the significance of controlling in management.
3. Define controlling. Discuss the process of controlling.
4. Discuss how planning and controlling are inter-related. Also state the limitations of controlling.
5. Discuss the traditional techniques of controlling.
6. Discuss the modern techniques of controlling.
7. Explain the concept of PERT and CPM. Discuss how these terms are useful in project management.

# UNIT 4C
# COMMUNICATION

Communication and Coordination – Process of Communication
Formal and Informal Channels of Communication
Leakages in Organisational Communication
Interpersonal Communication .

## CONTENTS

1. Concept of Communication
2. Definitions of Communication
3. Characteristics/Nature of Communication
4. Process of Communication
5. Types of Communication
6. Communication Network

    6.1 Formal Channel of Communication

    6.2 Informal Channel of Communication
7. Barriers in Effective Communication
8. Measures to Overcome Communication Barriers
9. Essentials of Good Communication System

# 1. CONCEPT OF COMMUNICATION

The term 'communication' originates from the Latin word 'communis,' meaning 'common.' Therefore, communication involves sharing information, ideas, or attitudes among two or more people. Communication requires at least two individuals because one cannot communicate alone. The person who shares information is known as the 'sender,' while the individual or group receiving the information is the 'receiver.'

Communication is the process where two or more individuals exchange ideas and feelings through various means. It is not just about sending and receiving messages but also about understanding them. For communication to be effective, the receiver must comprehend the message as the sender intended. The content of communication is conveyed through specific forms or methods, which can include words (spoken or written), pictures, diagrams, actions, or gestures, such as lip movements, winking, hand waves, or signals.

# 2. DEFINITIONS OF COMMUNICATION

"Communication is the sum of all things one person does, when he wants to create understanding in the mind of another. It involves systematic and continuous process of telling, listening and understanding"

*Louis Allen*

"Communication is the transfer of information from one person to another person. It is a way of reaching others by transmitting ideas, facts, thoughts, feelings, and values"

*Newstrom and Davis*

"Communication is transfer of information from one person to another, whether or not it elicits confidence. But the information transferred must be understandable to the receiver"

*G.G. Brown*

"Communication is the intercourse by words, letters or message"

*Fred G. Meyer*

"Communication is the process of passing information and understanding-from one person to another"

*Keith Davis*

"Communication is the process by which information is transmitted between individuals or organizations so that an understanding response results"

*Peter Little*

"Communication is an exchange of facts, ideas, opinions or emotions by two or more people"

*Koontz and O'Donnell*

"Communication is transmission of ideas, information, emotions and skills using words, symbols, pictures, body and graphs etc."

*Berelson and Steiner*

"Communication is the process of establishing commonness or oneness of thought between a sender and a receiver"

*Wilbur Schramn*

"Communication is the transmission/interchange of facts, ideas, feelings or course of action"

*Leland Brown*

## 3. CHARACTERISTICS/NATURE OF COMMUNICATION

The following are the important features of communication:

1. **Communication is a process:** It involves transmitting information, ideas, emotions, and understanding from one person to another.

2. **Communication involves at least two people:** It requires at least two individuals, as one cannot communicate alone. The individual sharing information is called the 'sender,' and the individual or group receiving it is the 'receiver.'

3. **Communication contains a message:** The message is the core element of communication. Without it, communication is incomplete. Messages can be conveyed through words (spoken

or written), pictures, diagrams, actions, or gestures like lip movements, winking, hand waves, or signals.

4. **Communication channel:** This refers to the medium through which the sender transmits information to the receivers. Common channels in business communication include telephones, emails, letters, reports, and memos.

5. **Purpose of communication:** The main goal is to create understanding in the receiver's mind. The receiver should comprehend the message and respond accordingly.

6. **Forms of communication:** Communication can take various forms depending on feedback availability and the use of verbal or non-verbal signs. Popular forms include intrapersonal and interpersonal communication, verbal and non-verbal communication, and formal and informal communication.

7. **Communication is a goal-oriented process:** It is effective only when the goals of the sender and receiver align.

8. **Communication is unavoidable:** Communication is a constant and unavoidable phenomenon. Even silence, along with facial expressions, gestures, and other behaviors, conveys a lot about a person's attitude.

## 4. PROCESS OF COMMUNICATION

As a process, communication must include certain elements to be complete. According to the Shannon-Weaver Model, the elements are Source, Transmitter, Channel, Receiver, and Destination. In the Berlo Model, the elements are Sender, Encoder, Message, Channel, Decoder, and Receiver. Different models of communication highlight various elements, such as sender, message, encoding, channel, receiver, decoding, and feedback. Let's briefly examine these elements.

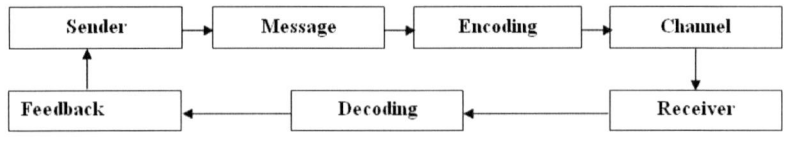

*Process of Communication*

1. **Sender:** The sender is the individual or group that initiates the message to the receiver(s). This person develops and conceptualizes the idea to be communicated, then encodes it and sends it through an appropriate communication channel.

2. **Message:** The message is the core content of the communication, often referred to as the heart of the process. Without a message, communication cannot occur. It represents the information or idea that the sender intends to convey to the receiver. Messages can be verbal (written or spoken) or non-verbal (pictorial or symbolic).

3. **Encoding:** Encoding is a crucial step where the sender translates the idea into a perceivable form, which can be verbal or non-verbal depending on the context, timing, and nature of the message. The sender uses symbols, pictures, or words to ensure the receiver can clearly understand the message. Proper encoding is vital, as incorrect encoding can misrepresent the intended message.

4. **Channel:** Once the message is encoded, the next step is to choose the appropriate channel or medium to transmit it to the receiver(s). The message can be delivered orally or in writing through various means such as memoranda, telephone calls, apps, television, postal mail, fax, or email. Selecting the most effective channel is essential for efficient communication.

5. **Receiver:** The receiver is as critical in the communication process as the sender. This individual or group receives the sender's message, acting as the listener, reader, or viewer. The receiver must be in a suitable state to receive the message, with an active communication channel and minimal distractions to ensure adequate attention to the message.

6. **Decoding:** Decoding is the process where the receiver interprets the sender's message, aiming to understand it as intended. Effective communication occurs when the receiver accurately grasps the message's meaning as the sender intended.

7. **Feedback:** Feedback is the final step that confirms the receiver has received and correctly interpreted the message. It enhances communication effectiveness by allowing the sender to gauge how well the message was understood. Feedback can be either verbal or non-verbal.

# 5. TYPES OF COMMUNICATION

Communication, as a means of conveying and exchanging ideas, opinions, and emotions, can occur in numerous forms. Below are some forms of communication categorized by relationship elements, channels, purpose, and style.

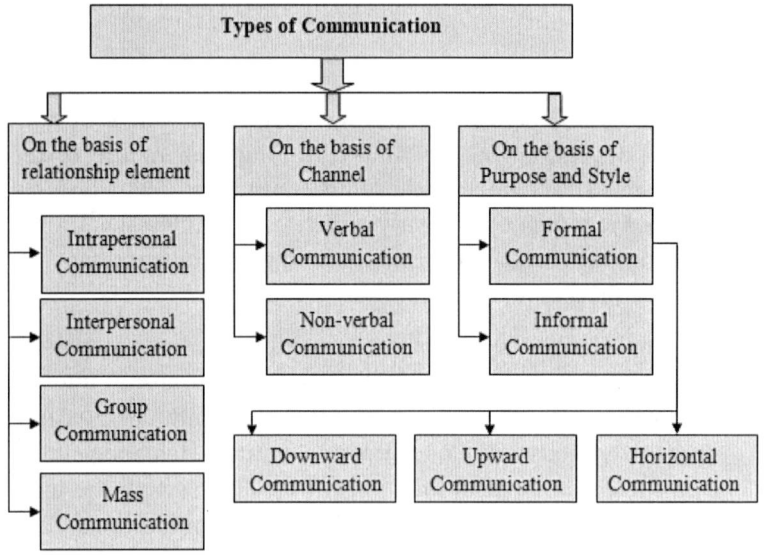

1. **Based on Relationship Element:**

   a. **Intrapersonal Communication:** This is the internal dialogue that occurs within an individual's mind. It can be clear or confused, depending on the individual's mental state. A troubled mind may produce unclear and vague messages, while a calm mind leads to clearer internal dialogue and broader perception.

   b. **Interpersonal Communication:** This involves communication between two or more people and is crucial in organizations. Executives and employees often spend a significant amount of time in interpersonal communication.

   c. **Group Communication:** This refers to the exchange of ideas, thoughts, and information among individuals using interpersonal skills. A group, consisting of two or more people, interacts in a way that each member influences the other. Groups can be formal, like committees or teams, formed to achieve specific goals, or informal, which spontaneously emerge to meet social needs.

d. **Mass Communication:** This involves communicating with the public through mass media such as television, the internet, films, and publications. It is essential for enhancing the image of a business and attracting customers.

2. **Based on Channels:**

a. **Verbal Communication:** This involves the use of spoken or written words. It includes two types:

   i. **Oral Communication:** Face-to-face conversations, telephone calls, video conferencing, etc.

   ii. **Written Communication:** Letters, memos, reports, etc.

b. **Non-verbal Communication:** This occurs without using spoken or written words. It involves facial expressions, hand movements, body language, postures, and gestures.

3. **Based on Purpose and Style:**

a. **Formal Communication:** Structured communication based on hierarchy, authority, and accountability. It follows pre-determined channels set by organizations, such as departmental meetings, conferences, circulars, company news, and interviews. It ensures uniformity and accountability and is further classified into:

   i. **Downward Communication:** Flows from the top to the bottom of the organizational hierarchy, from superiors to subordinates.

   ii. **Upward Communication:** Flows from the bottom to the top, from subordinates to superiors, using either oral or written media.

   iii. **Horizontal Communication:** Occurs between individuals at the same hierarchical level, allowing consultation and collaboration.

b. **Informal Communication:** This arises from channels outside the formal structure and does not follow lines of authority. It is built around social relationships within the organization, arising from personal needs, and is commonly known as the 'grapevine.'

# 6. COMMUNICATION NETWORK

A communication network is a system of interconnected lines through which messages flow in one or multiple directions. This network influences the speed, accuracy, and smoothness of message transmission within an organization.

In an organizational context, a network is a structured system composed of interconnected channels through which information is passed from one person to another. Essentially, organizational communication is the flow of information through this network of human relationships. Since people within an organization are connected both formally and informally, communication maintains these relationships.

Thus, an organizational communication network comprises two interrelated and interdependent types of channels: formal and informal. These channels are essential for communication within an organization, and they significantly affect the smoothness, speed, and accuracy of message flow. If a channel is too narrow for the volume of messages, delays or blockages can occur. Similarly, if the channel is too long or circuitous, it can cause the same issues. Moreover, the presence of multiple filtering points can alter the accuracy of messages, as content might be added or removed at each point.

Before discussing formal and informal channels in detail, it's important to understand the differences between formal and informal communication. Messages transmitted through formal channels are considered formal communication, while those through informal channels are informal communication. The differences between these two types are summarized in the table below:

| S. No. | Formal Communication | Informal Communication |
|--------|---------------------|------------------------|
| 1 | It follows the official chain of command | It is based on personal relationships and does not follow fixed pattern. |
| 2 | It is slow as it has to follow the path laid down by the management. | It is very fast as it is not supposed to follow a particular path |

| S. No. | Formal Communication | Informal Communication |
|--------|---------------------|------------------------|
| 3 | It is rigid as deviations are not allowed. | It is flexible as it moves freely. |
| 4 | Formal communication is generally accurate | Informal message may not be authentic. |
| 5 | Chances of wrong information are very few. | Chances of distribution of information are very high. |
| 6 | In case of formal communication, status or position of the parties is very important. | In case of informal communication, status or position of the parties has no relevance. |
| 7 | It serves needs of the organization. | It serves social needs of the members and also of the organization. |

## 6.1 FORMAL CHANNEL OF COMMUNICATION

The formal channel, as its name suggests, is the intentionally created and officially designated path for communication flow between various positions within an organization. It is a deliberate effort to regulate the flow of organizational communication to ensure it is orderly, smooth, accurate, and timely, reaching the required points efficiently. Additionally, it aims to filter information at various stages to prevent unnecessary flow and avoid information overload. The officially prescribed communication network can be designed with either a single channel or multiple channels, as illustrated in the accompanying figure.

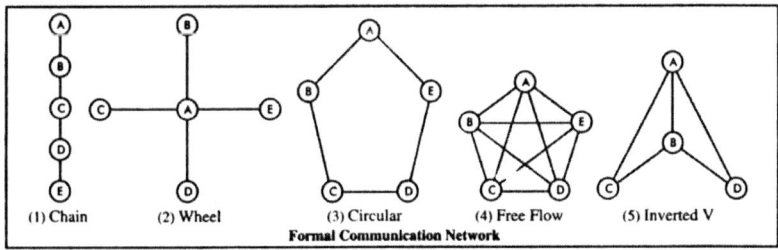

(1) Chain    (2) Wheel    (3) Circular    (4) Free Flow    (5) Inverted V

**Formal Communication Network**

1. **Chain Network:** In this network, messages flow in a direct vertical line along the chain of command. Subordinates receive

orders and instructions from a single superior. There is no horizontal or inter-functional communication at lower levels, making the chain network centralized.

2. **Wheel Network:** This network features one central member with four or more members at the ends of spokes. It is highly centralized, as the spoke members can only communicate with the individual at the center and not with each other.

3. **Circle Network:** In a circular network, messages move in a circle, with each person able to communicate only with their two neighboring colleagues. This network is somewhat decentralized since each individual can communicate with the two next to them. However, a significant drawback is that communication is very slow.

4. **Free-flow Network:** This network is highly decentralized, with no restrictions on communication flow. Every individual in the group can communicate directly with every other individual. This informal and unstructured network allows for a free flow of communication and is highly flexible.

5. **Inverted V Network:** In this network, an individual can communicate with their immediate superior and their superior's superior, with the subject matter of the communication being prescribed. This network allows for faster communication.

## 6.2 INFORMAL CHANNEL OF COMMUNICATION

The informal channel of communication, known as the grapevine, emerges from social interactions at the workplace rather than official actions. The term "grapevine" originated during the U.S. Civil War when intelligence telephone lines, loosely strung from tree to tree like grapevines, often carried distorted messages. Consequently, any rumor was said to come from the grapevine. Today, the term encompasses all informal communication. While formal communication addresses the functional needs of an organization, informal communication facilitates social, unplanned activities within the formal system's boundaries. It operates outside the official network but continuously interacts with it. The grapevine tends to be more active when. :

1. There is high organisational excitement, such as policy changes like automation, computerisation, etc., or personnel changes:

2. The Information is new rather stale;

3. People are physically located close enough to communicate with one another; and

4. People cluster or in groups check along the grapevine, that is, they have trust among themselves

The grapevine follows various types of networks. Typically, there are four patterns through which the grapevine travels: single strand, gossip, probability, and cluster. In each pattern, communication among individuals differs, as illustrated in the figure.

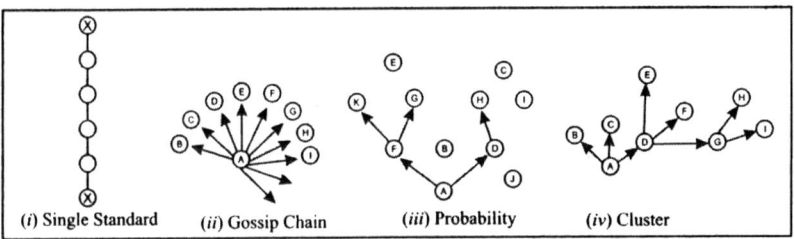

(*i*) Single Standard     (*ii*) Gossip Chain     (*iii*) Probability     (*iv*) Cluster

1. **Single Strand Network:** In this network, each person communicates sequentially with others, as depicted in Figure (i).

2. **Gossip Chain Network**: In a gossip chain network, one person communicates non-selectively with everyone else. For example, in Figure (ii), A communicates with all the members.

3. **Probability Network:** In a probability network, one person communicates randomly with others, as shown in Figure (iii).

4. **Cluster Network:** In a cluster network, a person communicates only with those individuals whom they trust, as illustrated in Figure (iv). In other words, information is passed on to a selected few people. Cluster networks are quite common in organizations.

## 7. BARRIERS IN EFFECTIVE COMMUNICATION

Communication barriers are obstacles or problems that hinder effective communication. These barriers can be categorized as follows:

1. **Organizational Barriers:** Complex organizational structures with layers of supervision and long communication lines

increase the distance between workers and top management, leading to breakdowns in communication.

2. **Status Barriers**: Status, which denotes a person's relative ranking in an organization, is a significant obstacle in organizational communication. Individuals with higher status may not communicate freely with those of lower status. Subordinates at lower levels may withhold unpleasant facts and only relay what superiors want to hear, leading to selective communication.

3. **Semantic Barriers**: In the communication process, the recipient is expected to understand the message in the same way as the sender intended. However, words and symbols used in communication may have different meanings for different people. For example, "profits" may mean one thing to a manager and something different to a worker. People interpret messages differently based on their social and cultural backgrounds, education, and experiences.

4. **Lack of Attention**: If the recipient does not pay full attention to the message, the sender's purpose in communicating is defeated.

5. **Perceptual Barriers**: Perception refers to the way individuals notice things and interpret messages based on their own thinking and biases. This leads to unconscious filtering of the message.

6. **Information Overload**: Managers often receive a flood of information from various sources, making it difficult to manage the flow of information effectively. This can lead to ignoring or misinterpreting important messages. Time constraints can also create communication problems, resulting in incomplete information being conveyed.

7. **Premature Evaluation**: Communication is hindered when the recipient forms judgments about the message's worth before receiving the entire communication. Such judgments may be based on the recipient's past experiences.

8. **Mechanical Barriers**: The flow of communication is affected by mechanical barriers such as inadequate provisions for transmitting messages, poor organizational layout, defective communication networks and media, etc.

In summary, these barriers can significantly impact the effectiveness of communication within an organization, making it essential to identify and address them to ensure clear and efficient communication.

## 8. MEASURES TO OVERCOME COMMUNICATION BARRIERS

Effective communication is crucial for successful management. Barriers to communication can be overcome by implementing the following measures:

1. **Clarity of Ideas**: The communicator must be clear about the information or idea they want to communicate.

2. **Simplicity of Language**: To ensure effective communication, the language used should be easily understandable by the recipients.

3. **Completeness**: The message must be comprehensive and adequate to avoid ineffective communication due to incomplete information.

4. **Careful Selection of Media and Channels**: Choosing the right communication channel is essential for effective communication. A balanced approach combining formal and informal communication channels can help achieve this.

5. **Empathy in Communication**: Empathy involves understanding the recipient's point of view. Communicators should be sensitive to the needs, feelings, and perceptions of the recipient to enhance effective communication.

6. **Active Listening**: Active listening, as opposed to passive hearing, is an intellectual process that helps in removing communication barriers.

7. **Regulation of Information Flow**: Regulating the flow of information ensures optimal communication. Following the principle of 'Management by Exception' can prevent information overload and allow managers to focus on high-priority messages.

8. **Feedback**: Establishing a two-way communication system is crucial for ensuring the full understanding of messages. Management should encourage feedback to facilitate effective communication.

9.  **Communication Training**: Providing communication training to employees enhances their speaking, listening, and writing skills, thereby promoting effective communication within the organization.

In summary, adopting these measures can help overcome barriers to communication and promote effective communication practices in management.

## 9. ESSENTIALS OF GOOD COMMUNICATION SYSTEM

A good communication system should meet the following requirements:

1.  **Clarity of Communication**: Effective communication starts with a clear and unambiguous message. The communicator must be clear about what they want to convey. The words and language used should be simple and familiar to the receiver. Each message should have a specific purpose and be directed to a particular person.

2.  **Adequacy of Communication**: Messages must be complete in terms of content and information flow. Incomplete messages lead to misunderstandings and inefficient actions. Every subordinate should receive the necessary information for effective job performance.

3.  **Consistency of Communication**: Messages should always align with the objectives and policies of the organization. They should support the chain of command and not contradict earlier messages. If a new message amends an old one, this should be clearly stated to avoid confusion. The communication system should reflect the needs and character of the organization.

4.  **Proper Timing**: All messages should be sent at the right time. Delayed communication creates doubt and gives rise to rumors. The desired response to a message can only be obtained when it is conveyed at the right time. Communication should be continuous, and each executive should consider it an integral part of their job.

5.  **Feedback**: Communication is a two-way process. The communicator should seek the reaction or response of the

receiver. In direct personal communication, feedback is immediate, but in other types of communication, the sender needs to use signals to obtain feedback. Communication should flow freely in both directions.

6. **Economy**: The cost of communication should be reasonable without sacrificing efficiency. Unnecessary transmission should be avoided. Communication lines should be direct and short wherever possible.

7. **Human Factor**: When sending messages, human relationships should be considered. The sender must understand the receiver's perspective and communicate in a way that respects their feelings. Management should create an environment of mutual trust and confidence.

In summary, a well-functioning communication system incorporates these elements to ensure clarity, completeness, consistency, timeliness, feedback, cost-efficiency, and consideration for human relationships.

## SUMMARY OF THE CHAPTER

saver Model- Source, Transmitter, Channel, Receiver and Destination are the elements of a communication process. According to Berlo Model- Sender, Encoder, Message, Channel, Decoder and Sender are the elements of a communication process. Thus various elements of communication have been presented in different models of communication. These are sender, message, encoding, channel, receiver, decoding, and feedback.

4. **Types of Communication**:

   **A. On the basis of relationship element**

   - Intrapersonal Communication
   - Interpersonal Communication
   - Group Communication
   - Mass Communication:

   **B. On the basis of Channels**

   - Verbal Communication
   - Non-verbal Communication:

C. **On the basis of Purpose and Style**

- Formal Communication

  o Downward Communication

  o Upward Communication

  o Horizontal Communication

- Informal Communication

5. **Communication network** is a pattern of inter-connected lines. It is a system where the message may flow in one direction or in several directions. A network determines the speed, accuracy and smoothness with which the message flows throughout the organization.

6. The **formal channel of communication** , as the very name implies, is the deliberately created, officially prescribed path for flow of communication between the various positions in the organisation. Formal channels of communication are:

- Chain Network

- Wheel NetworkCircle Network

- Free-flow Network

- Inverted V:

7. Difference between the two are presented in the table given below:

| S. No. | Formal Communication | Informal Communication |
|--------|----------------------|------------------------|
| 1 | It follows the official chain of command | It is based on personal relationships and does not follow fixed pattern. |
| 2 | It is slow as it has to follow the path laid down by the management. | It is very fast as it is not supposed to follow a particular path |
| 3 | It is rigid as deviations are not allowed. | It is flexible as it moves freely. |
| 4 | Formal communication is generally accurate | Informal message may not be authentic. |

| S. No. | Formal Communication | Informal Communication |
|--------|---------------------|------------------------|
| 5 | Chances of wrong information are very few. | Chances of distribution of information are very high. |
| 6 | In case of formal communication, status or position of the parties is very important. | In case of informal communication, status or position of the parties has no relevance. |
| 7 | It serves needs of the organization. | It serves social needs of the members and also of the organization. |

8   The **informal channel of communication**, also known as grapevine, is the result not of any official action, but of the operation of social forces at workplace. Informal channels of communication are:

- Single Strand Network
- Gossip Chain Network
- Probability Network
- Cluster Network

9.   These communication barriers are as follows:

- Organisational Barriers
- Status Barriers
- Semantic Barriers
- Lack of attentiveness
- Perceptual Barriers
- Overload
- Premature Evaluation
- Mechanical Barriers:

10. Barriers to communication can be overcome by adopting the following measures:

- Clarity of Idea
- Simplicity of the Language.
- Completeness

- Careful selection of Media and Channel
- Empathy in Communication
- Good Listening
- Regulating the Flow of Information
- Feedback
- Providing Communication Trading

11. A **good communication system** must satisfy the following **requirements**:
    - Clarity of Communication
    - Adequacy of Communication
    - Consistency of Communication
    - Proper Timing
    - Feedback
    - Economy
    - Human Factor

# QUESTIONS

1. Write down the meaning of Communication.
2. Define Communication.
3. What are the characteristics of Communication?
4. What are the elements of Communication?
5. Discuss the process of Communication.
6. What are different types of Communication? Discuss.
7. What do you mean by Formal and Informal Communication?
8. What do you mean by Interpersonal and Intrapersonal Communication?
9. What do you mean by Verbal and Non-verbal Communication?
10. What do you mean by Communication Network? What are different types of Communication Network?

11. What are the barriers in effective communication? Discuss.

12. The barriers to effective communication exist in all organisations. Explain the measures to overcome these barriers.

13. Write short notes on:

    a.  Interpersonal Communication

    b.  Intrapersonal Communication

    c.  Group Communication

    d.  Mass Communication

    e.  Verbal Communication

    f.  Non-verbal Communication

    g.  Formal Communication

    h.  Informal Communication

    i.  Downward Communication

    j.  Upward Communication

    k.  Horizontal Communication.

    l.  Communication Barriers

# UNIT 5A
# INDIAN ETHOS FOR MANAGEMENT

Indian Ethos for Management

Value-Oriented Holistic Management

Business Process Reengineering (BPR)

Learning Organisation

Outsourcing

## CONTENTS

# 1. INDIAN ETHOS

Ethos refers to "the moral ideas and attitudes that belong to a particular group or society." Indian ethos represents what can be described as "national ethos," stemming from the Hindu way of life. Indian life is guided by four fundamental goals (Purusharthas): Dharma (duty), Artha (wealth), Kama (desire), and Moksha (liberation). To achieve these goals, human life is divided into four stages: Brahmacharya (student life), Grahasthasrama (householder life), Vanaprastha (hermit life), and Sanyasrama (renunciate life). Indian philosophy outlines three fundamental paths to achieve these goals: Karma (action), Bhakti (devotion), and Jnana (knowledge). An individual can choose a particular path based on their psychological and spiritual development, as well as their Pravritti (inclination), Samskara (cultural conditioning), Vasana (desire), and Gunas. A person's Gunas include Sattva (the enlightening force), Rajas (the active force), and Tamas (the inertial force).

## 1.1 ELEMENTS OF INDIAN ETHOS

The Indian ethos consists of:

1. **Spirit and Matter:** Indian ethos emphasizes both the spiritual and material aspects of life, considering them interlinked in a holistic approach. This allows individuals to enjoy both the internal and external quality of life.

2. **Relationship between Man and Universe:** Indian ethos highlights the interconnectedness between humans and the cosmos. It stresses the intimate relationship between humans and nature, viewing all human beings and nature as interdependent and interconnected.

3. **Cooperation:** Indian ethos promotes cooperation in both professional and personal settings. Excessive competition within and between organizations can harm individuals and family life. Cooperation, mutual trust, respect, joint efforts, and team spirit can lead to overall prosperity and success for everyone.

4. **Self-Management:** Indian ethos asserts that individuals must manage themselves before they can manage others. Managers should understand their own strengths, weaknesses, dreams, goals, and ambitions before attempting to control their subordinates.

5. **Meditation:** Indian ethos advocates for achieving excellence in work through yoga and meditation. Meditation helps improve concentration and solve complex organizational problems, leading to a calm mind that enables clearer focus on issues.

6. **Dharma:** In Indian philosophy, Dharma means duty. It encompasses the ideals, philosophies, purposes, influences, teachings, and experiences that shape one's character. Every organization should follow its own dharma.

7. **The Spirit of Sacrifice:** Indian ethos values renunciation for its ability to bring mental peace, inner growth, and spiritual development, leading to a higher level of consciousness.

## 1.2 INDIAN ETHOS FOR MANAGEMENT

Indian ethos for management refers to the principles and values traditionally practiced in India for effective management. These values, derived from ancient Indian scriptures and teachings, have been passed down through generations.

## 1.3 PRINCIPLES OF INDIAN ETHOS FOR MANAGEMENT

Here are some key principles of Indian ethos for management:

1. **Karma Yoga:** The principle of Karma Yoga emphasizes performing one's duties without attachment to the outcome. It advocates focusing on effort and process rather than the result, underscoring the importance of hard work and dedication in achieving success.

2. **Seva:** The principle of Seva, or selfless service, emphasizes serving others by prioritizing their needs over one's own and working for the greater good of the community. This principle highlights the importance of ethical and socially responsible behavior in management.

3. **Dharma:** The principle of Dharma stresses the importance of doing what is right, just, and ethical. It involves adhering to moral principles and values in decision-making and acting in the best interests of all stakeholders. This principle underscores the importance of integrity and honesty in management.

4. **Ahimsa**: The principle of Ahimsa, or non-violence, emphasizes treating others with compassion and respect. It advocates avoiding harm to others and resolving conflicts peacefully. This principle highlights the importance of building positive relationships with employees, customers, and other stakeholders.

5. **Atithi Devo Bhava**: The principle of Atithi Devo Bhava, or "guest is god," emphasizes hospitality and respect towards others. It advocates treating others with warmth and kindness and providing excellent service to customers and stakeholders. This principle underscores the importance of customer satisfaction and relationship building in management.

In summary, Indian ethos for management emphasizes ethical, socially responsible, and compassionate behavior. These principles, rooted in ancient Indian teachings, have been integral to Indian business and society for centuries.

## 1.4 SALIENT FEATURES OF INDIAN ETHOS

Indian ethos is a set of principles and values deeply ingrained in Indian culture and tradition, influencing management practices over the years. Here are some key features of Indian ethos with examples:

1. **Holistic Approach**: Indian ethos emphasizes a holistic approach to life and work, advocating for balance and harmony in all aspects of life, including work, family, and spirituality. For instance, the widespread practice of yoga and meditation aims to achieve holistic well-being.

2. **Respect for Authority**: Indian ethos stresses the importance of respecting authority figures such as parents, elders, and leaders. This includes following the rules and guidelines set by authority figures and treating them with reverence. A traditional example is the practice of touching the feet of elders as a sign of respect.

3. **Social Responsibility**: Indian ethos highlights the importance of social responsibility and giving back to the community. Individuals are encouraged to use their skills and resources for the benefit of others and the greater good. An example is the corporate social responsibility initiatives by many Indian companies, such as providing education and healthcare to underprivileged communities.

4. **Non-Violence**: Indian ethos values non-violence and peaceful coexistence, promoting harmony in all relationships and avoiding conflict. A notable example is Mahatma Gandhi's non-violent movement, which was instrumental in India's struggle for independence from British rule.

5. **Spiritualism**: Indian ethos emphasizes spirituality and inner peace, encouraging individuals to seek a deeper understanding of the self and the universe and strive for spiritual growth. The growing popularity of mindfulness practices such as Vipassana meditation, based on ancient Indian teachings, exemplifies this principle.

In summary, Indian ethos encompasses principles that promote a balanced, respectful, socially responsible, peaceful, and spiritual approach to life and management.

## 2. VALUE-ORIENTED HOLISTIC MANAGEMENT

The most valuable human possessions are health, harmony, happiness, wisdom, and, above all, character that reflects ethical and human values. When these values are evident in our thoughts, speech, and actions, we are considered noble and enlightened individuals. Our sincere and constant thoughts shape who we become, and our actions and behavior reflect our ideas and feelings.

We work not for name, fame, money, power, or status, but for greater purposes: cultivating values, building strong character, and gaining wisdom to enhance our intrinsic worth. True greatness is not measured by tangible or extrinsic factors like name or fame, but by being pure, kind, true, and selfless. Health is more important than wealth, and character is more important than money..

**VALUES:** Human and ethical values constitute the wealth of character. They express dharma or divine nature as understood in the East, particularly in Indian ethos, and align with the ideas of integrity as understood in the West.

- **Integrity:** Integrity embodies wholeness, goodness, courage, and self-discipline to live by one's inner truth. Wholeness implies totality, soundness, perfection, and completeness. In the West, spirit in wholeness is often overlooked. Within all of us resides the unworshipped divine presence, but our ego, a false notion born from ignorance, pretends to be the ruler.

- **Goodness:** Goodness encompasses essential values such as honesty, morality, kindness, fairness, charity, truthfulness, and generosity. We need goodness in our thoughts, speech, and actions. The mantra "Be Good. Do Good" leads to the purification of thoughts, words, and deeds, aligning them with goodness. Good things do not happen easily; we must actively make them happen.

- **Courage:** In management, courage involves acts of bravery, such as speaking the truth despite risks. Courage means having the guts to take action, even when it is risky.

- **Self-discipline:** Self-discipline and self-control mean that the soul governs the mind, guiding it and the senses toward the goal known to the master. When the individual consciousness awakens, self-discipline and self-control enhance the quality of life, bringing greater harmony, happiness, and moderation.

- **Living by Inner Truth:** Living by inner truth means being guided by the inner mind, which is the right instrument within us, though often unrecognized. The voice of the inner mind can be heard only in silence. Living by inner truth at work means remaining incorruptible, clean, and inviolable in a world currently facing a crisis in human and ethical values.

- **Dharma:** Dharma is the law of right living, ensuring happiness for oneself and others. It encompasses all ideals, purposes, influences, institutions, and ways of life that shape character and evolution. Dharma, almost synonymous with integrity, has a broader scope, including spirituality, righteousness (godliness), and fearlessness.

  o **Spirit:** Man is essentially divine, and dharma evolves directly from this spirit. Unlike integrity, which often shies away from spirituality, dharma openly embraces it, combining spiritual and material aspects of life.

  o **Righteousness:** Dharma demands right action, emphasizing not just action but the righteousness of actions.

  o **Fearlessness:** Integrity implies courage, while dharma stresses fearlessness. When the divine presence is within, there is nothing to fear. A touch of divine awareness can transform difficulties into opportunities.

○ **Moral and Ethical Values:** The qualities of a good person are termed moral and ethical values, also known as Daivi sampati or divine qualities. Values are also called gunas, reflecting the inherent qualities within individuals. Some of the values are:

- Fearlessness
- Calmness Loyalty
- Charity
- Integrity
- Humility
- Modesty
- Non-violence
- Generosity
- Integration of thought, action and behaviour
- Purity of mind and heart
- Courage

In summary, Indian ethos encompasses principles that emphasize wholeness, goodness, courage, self-discipline, inner truth, and dharma. These values integrate spirituality and materialism, promoting a balanced and ethical approach to life and management:

## 2.1 WHY DO WE NEED VALUE-BASED HOLISTIC MANAGEMENT?

Let us consider two examples that demonstrate the necessity of value-based holistic management:

1. **Man-Machine Equation:** In the past, employees were treated like machines, hired and fired at the owners' discretion, with no regard for their feelings or emotions. Behavioral scientists have significantly improved this situation. Concepts like performance appraisal, motivation, job satisfaction, and job rotation now highlight the distinction between a human and a machine. Value-oriented management recognizes the divine aspect of humanity, helping to eliminate the man-machine equation. Human values for managers honor the essence of humanness, fostering harmony and balance between values as

ends. This approach ensures a judicious combination of values and skills.

2. **Prevention of Exploitation of Nature**: Science and technology have driven significant industrialization, often at the expense of indiscriminate and ruthless exploitation of nature. It is a misconception that humans have a birthright to exploit nature's resources at will. A holistic approach acknowledges the deep interconnection and interdependence between humans and nature, asserting that exploiting nature for selfish motives is as wrong as exploiting other humans. Many organizations, knowingly or unknowingly, pollute the environment. Value-based holistic management is essential to prevent this exploitation of nature.

## 2.2 RELEVANCE OF VALUES IN MANAGEMENT

In the increasingly complex corporate world, it is crucial for companies to prioritize customer values, shareholder values, employee values, societal values, and leadership values. According to Dr. Athreya, "value-based management is essential for the long-term success of a corporation. Living by principles and values is imperative for every corporate manager." Values and ethics are key elements for business success. An organization is merely a composite of individuals, and the organization's values are derived from the collective values of these individuals. Human values rooted in spiritual reality form the foundation for building the ethical and moral structure of management. Management must continuously work to develop and shape organizational values that are service-oriented and ethical.

Values serve as essential reminders that individuals adhere to, bringing order and meaning to their personal values. Without values, there is no guideline for direction. The core of any culture is its values, which are often misunderstood as mere preferences and priorities. In reality, values reflect what is most important.

In all organizations, values influence daily actions and behaviors. If an organization values profit, productivity, and quality, it will operate in a way that prioritizes actions reflecting those values. Similarly, an organization that values innovation, research, and learning will prioritize actions that reflect those values. If the values influencing daily behavior and actions are not aligned with the strategies, the organization's performance and results will suffer.

# 3. BUSINESS PROCESS REENGINEERING

The concept of Business Process Re-engineering (BPR) was introduced by Michael Hammer, Thomas Davenport, and James in 1990. They observed that in the dynamic business environment, nothing remains constant or predictable, including market growth, customer demand, product life cycles, technological advancements, and competitive landscape. Consequently, customers, competition, and change have acquired entirely new dynamics in the business world. Customers now have more choices and expect products tailored to their specific needs. In today's business landscape, competition is determined not only by price but also by factors such as quality, selection, service, and responsiveness.

Recognizing this volatile business environment, the pioneers argued for a shift from a task-oriented to a process-oriented approach. Business Process Reengineering focuses on fundamental business processes rather than individual departments or organizational units. It aims for significant improvements in operational effectiveness by redesigning critical business processes and supporting systems. BPR scrutinizes the minutiae of processes, including the reasons for the work, who performs it, where and when it occurs.

BPR entails analyzing and redesigning workflows and processes both within the organization and across external entities like suppliers, distributors, and service providers. The orientation of BPR efforts is essentially radical, involving a total deconstruction and reevaluation of business processes, free from existing structures and patterns. Its objective is to achieve a quantum leap in process performance regarding time, cost, output, quality, and responsiveness to customers.

Business Process Re-engineering is also referred to as business process redesign, business transformation, or business process change management. It addresses the following questions:

- How business processes currently operates?

- How to redesign these processes to eliminate wastage or redundant effort and improve efficiency?

- How to implement the process changes in order to gain competitiveness?

# 3.1 BENEFITS OF BUSINESS PROCESS REENGINEERING

There is no single set of benefits that reengineering a process will bring to an organization, as this will depend on factors such as the efficiency of the current process, the maturity of the organization, expected benefits, and the reengineering team. However, based on successful cases of organizations worldwide that have reengineered their business processes, we can summarize some typical benefits as follows:

1. **Adoption of New Technology**: Technology evolves rapidly, and with it, the way businesses operate changes. It is crucial for organizations to adopt new technologies to keep pace with the changing environment. However, adopting new technology can be costly. For instance, Amazon recently introduced robots in its warehouses to automate the movement of goods.

2. **Reduced Response Time**: Customers today prefer organizations that respond quickly to their requests. Whether it's serving food in restaurants or responding to customer inquiries, efficient use of information technology can significantly reduce response times.

3. **Improved Productivity**: Business Process Re-engineering identifies inefficiencies in business operations and improves them. For example, BPR may reveal that tasks previously done by three workers can be efficiently handled by two, or that automating packaging processes improves efficiency. These changes enhance overall productivity.

4. **Competitive Edge**: In today's competitive business environment, staying ahead is challenging. Business Process Reengineering helps improve business processes and performance, enabling organizations to compete effectively against their rivals.

5. **Enhanced Product Quality**: Through the reengineering process, the quality of products and services can be enhanced. BPR helps identify system weaknesses and addresses them, resulting in better product quality and increased customer satisfaction.

These benefits highlight how Business Process Reengineering can lead to significant improvements in efficiency, productivity, competitiveness, and product quality for organizations willing to undertake the transformation.

## 3.2 PROCESS OF BUSINESS PROCESS REENGINEERING

Generally, it is challenging to propose a systematic standard procedure for implementing Business Process Reengineering (BPR), as each organization has its own unique work environment, technology, and culture. Therefore, not all suggestions may be suitable for all organizations. Nevertheless, Davenport and Short devised a five-step implementation plan based on their observation of many companies that successfully implemented BPR by following these steps.

**Step 1: Development of Process Objectives:** Davenport and Short define a business process as "a set of logically related tasks performed to achieve a defined business outcome" — not just individual tasks, but an integrated whole of combined tasks forming an end-to-end business process (e.g., product development). The most common objectives include cost reduction, time reduction, quality improvement, and enhanced quality of work life (including learning and empowerment). However, achieving all of these objectives simultaneously is challenging. This step sets the stage for identifying the goals and outcomes that the reengineered process aims to achieve.

**Step 2: Identification of Processes to be Reengineered:** It is the responsibility of top and senior management to identify the processes that need to be reengineered. One approach to identification could be a "high impact" approach, focusing only on the most critical processes. All employees involved in these processes must gain a clear understanding of (a) the activities and tasks within each process, (b) how their tasks link in the process chain, and (c) how their work affects the entire process chain. Process charts that include sub-processes and related activities should be documented. However, detailed analysis is not necessary at this stage. Process targets can be set through benchmarking. These targets need to be quantitative (and therefore measurable), such as time, cost, quality, etc., while considering the company's capabilities. Unrealistic targets may lead to frustration and the ultimate failure to achieve process goals.

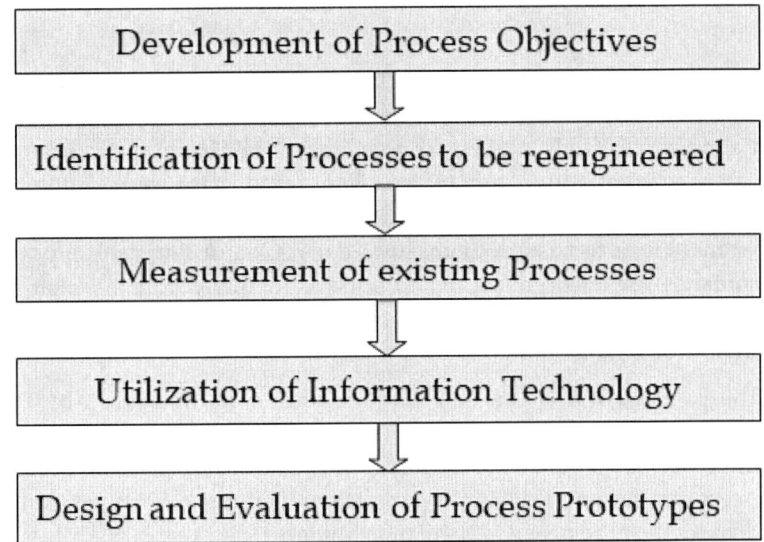

*Steps involved in the process of BPR*

**Step 3: Measurement of Existing Processes:** Quantifying processes before and after reengineering allows the company to assess whether the reengineered process has achieved its goals, and if not, to determine the gap. This provides the opportunity to take corrective actions for further improvement. Concrete facts enable company-wide communication about achievements, which reinforces a process-oriented culture and addresses skepticism.

**Step 4: Utilization of Information Technology:** Information Technology (IT) specialists' expertise is often underutilized during the reengineering process. However, their contribution can significantly enhance the process. IT can accelerate implementation as a tool and facilitator, eliminating existing tasks and subprocesses to achieve substantial improvements. Major improvements in key business processes are unlikely without considering IT as an enabler of the reengineering process.

**Step 5: Design and Evaluation of Process Prototypes:** Similar to testing a product prototype to ensure it meets desired requirements and allows for cost-effective changes, a process prototype should be critically examined before implementation. Reengineering involves continuous improvement, so adjustments will need to be made during and after implementation.

# 4. LEARNING ORGANISATION

In today's rapidly changing world, knowledge has become the most critical asset for organizations to survive. Therefore, organizations must learn at an increasingly rapid pace to adapt to the changing environment and gain a competitive advantage. The rapid pace of technological advancements and growing competitive pressures make it challenging for organizations to sustain themselves daily. One of the most important prerequisites for an organization to survive in this constantly changing environment is its ability to continuously learn, and learning organizations are capable of achieving this.

The concept of the Learning Organization was introduced by Peter Senge in his book "The Fifth Discipline: The Art and Practice of Learning Organization" in 1990. Senge argues that organizations need to redesign themselves to become learning organizations that can quickly adapt their practices to meet the needs of their stakeholders.

A Learning Organization is an organization that transforms itself through learning. These organizations change through learning and learn how to change themselves. Learning can occur at the individual, group, or institutional level. Group learning, which involves dynamics such as collective intelligence, solidarity, dialogue, and discussion among group members, enables organizational learning to take root. By embracing a learning identity, these organizations can easily achieve their goals and quickly realize their aspirations.

**Peter Senge** has defined the term 'learning organization' as the organization where people continually expand their capacity to create the results they truly desire, where new and expansive patterns of thinking are nurtured, where collective aspiration is set free, and where people are continually learning to see the whole together".

**McGill and his colleagues** had defined the learning organization as "a company that can respond to new information by altering the very "programming" by which information is processed and evaluated."

**Garvin** (1993) describes a learning organization is the organization skilled at creating, acquiring and, transferring knowledge.

**Watkins and Marsick** (1994) defined learning organization as "one that learns continuously and can "transform" itself as it empowers the people, encourages collaboration and team learning, promotes open dialogue, and acknowledges the interdependence of individuals and the organization."

## 4.1 CHARACTERISTICS OF LEARNING ORGANISATION

According to Peter Senge, there are five characteristics of a Learning Organization: Systems Thinking, Personal Mastery, Mental Models, Shared Vision, and Team Learning.

1.  **Systems Thinking**: Systems thinking involves understanding patterns and relationships rather than isolated events. It requires disciplines that activate the realization of a learning organization, interconnect the entire team, avoid blaming each other, and understand the potential problems that may arise from actions taken during operations.

2.  **Personal Mastery**: Personal mastery is a commitment to lifelong learning and being a part of a learning organization. Each member strives to become the best person they can be, pursuing excellence, growth, and a realistic outlook on the future.

3.  **Mental Models**: Mental models involve a process of self-reflection and implementation, where individuals deeply understand and structure their organization's models.

4.  **Shared Vision**: Individuals have the right to share original ideas, proposals, and visions, as each person has a unique perspective on a specific segment of operations.

5.  **Team Learning**: Each team member is eager to learn and shares their ideas with the rest of the team, enhancing the credibility and creativity of employees, ultimately diversifying the organization's structure and helping to achieve its goals.

Watkins and Marsick (1993) argue that a learning organization should have the following characteristics:

1.  Leaders who model calculated risk taking and experimentation

2.  Decentralized decision-making and employee empowerment

3.  Skill inventories for sharing learning and using it

4.  Rewards and structures for employee initiatives

5.  Consideration of long-term consequences and impact on the work of others

6.  Frequent use of cross-functional work teams

7.  Opportunities to learn from experience on a daily basis

8.  A culture of feedback and disclosure.

# 5. OUTSOURCING

The term outsourcing, which means 'sourcing from outside,' involves getting work done by external parties. In simpler terms, outsourcing is defined as "getting something done by external sources rather than performing it within the organization." It refers to the transfer of one or more business processes from inside the organization to external service providers. These providers then take responsibility for owning, administering, and managing the selected processes, adhering to defined and measurable performance criteria. The processes can be performed either on-shore, near-shore, or off-shore.

## 5.1 DEFINITIONS OF OUTSOURCING

"The movement of business processes from inside the organization to external service providers"

*Click and Duening*

"The operation of letting out the task of performing certain functions of an enterprise to another enterprise, often a third party, and in some cases, a subsidiary of its own"

*Meenakshi and Vani*

"Business process outsourcing can be defined as the delegation of service activities to a third party, either to be performed on-shore, nearshore, or off-shore."

*Chanda*

## 5.2 FEATURES OF OUTSOURCING

The concept of outsourcing encompasses three fundamental aspects:

1. **Contracting out**: This involves delegating the work contract to an external entity, outside the organization itself. In other words, the work is performed not within the organization but externally.

2. **Non-core activities**: Typically, businesses outsource non-core activities, where 'non-core' refers to tasks that are not critical to the company's main operations and are therefore entrusted to external entities.

3.  **Processes may be outsourced to a captive unit or a third party**: A captive unit is a part of the company that trains employees from all its subsidiaries in new developments, ensuring effective and efficient work at minimal costs. Alternatively, the work can be outsourced to a third party, which may operate in a horizontal or vertical manner. A horizontal third party serves various industries or companies, whereas a vertical third party serves only one or a few specific industries.

## 5. 3 ADVANTAGES OF OUTSOURCING

Following are the advantages of Outsourcing:

1.  **Cost savings and restructuring:** Outsourcing is a method for reducing production and process costs. Growing customer cost-consciousness is driving widespread adoption of business process outsourcing, with companies worldwide rapidly increasing their spending on it.

2.  **Access to provider's technology and skills:** Another advantage of business process outsourcing is gaining access to the provider's specialized technology and operational platforms that companies may not have access to or cannot develop internally.

3.  **Focus on core competencies:** Outsourcing allows companies to focus on more critical priorities. For example, by outsourcing the sales promotion function to an advertising agency, the company can concentrate on maintaining quality and increasing production capacity.

4.  **Improved quality:** Immediate improvements in quality can result from outsourcing processes to world-class companies where quality is carefully managed through service level agreements.

5.  **Risk transfer:** If a company perceives that one of its processes carries high risks, outsourcing it to another company can transfer that risk effectively.

## 5.4 DISADVANTAGES OF OUTSOURCING

Outsourcing suffers from the following limitations:

1.  **Hidden Costs:** One of the perceived advantages of business process outsourcing is the potential for cost reduction. However, there are often hidden costs associated with outsourcing. These costs occur before initiating the project and during the project's lifetime but are frequently overlooked or underestimated.

2.  **Confidentiality:** When outsourcing, a company shares a significant amount of sensitive information and trade secrets with the outsourcing partner. This introduces the risk of business secrets being leaked to competitors.

3.  **Organizational Knowledge:** An outsourced employee may not possess the same level of understanding and commitment to the organization as a regular employee. This lack of organizational knowledge could result in outsourced employees interacting with customers without adequate understanding, potentially leading to a negative customer experience.

4.  **Difficult to Revert:** Once an activity is outsourced and internal expertise is lost, it can be very challenging to bring the process back in-house. This is especially pertinent when a contract comes up for renewal. The cost increase might be higher than anticipated, making it difficult to terminate the contract with the supplier.

5.  **Damage to Reputation:** If the outsourced partner fails to perform the assigned work properly, it can significantly damage the company's reputation.

6.  **Time Consuming:** Negotiating contracts with other companies can require additional time and effort beyond legal timelines. Additionally, lack of communication between the company and the outsourced provider can delay project completion.

## SUMMARY OF THE CHAPTER

1.  **Ethos** can be defined as "the moral ideas and attitudes that belong to a particular group or society". Indian Ethos is all about what can be termed as "national ethos".

2. The **Indian ethos** is the results of Hindu way of life. Indian life has four fundamental goals (Purushartthas) such as Dharma, Artha, Kama and Moksha.

3. **Elements of Indian Ethos**
   - Spirit and matter
   - Relationship between man and universe.
   - Co- Operation.
   - Self management
   - Meditation
   - Dharma
   - The spirit of sacrifice

4. **Indian ethos for management** refers to the principles and values that have been traditionally followed in India for effective management.

5. **Principles Of Indian Ethos For Management:**
   - Karma Yoga
   - Seva
   - Dharma
   - Ahimsa
   - Atithi Devo Bhava

6. **Salient features of Indian ethos:**
   - Holistic approach
   - Respect for authority
   - Social responsibility
   - Non-violence
   - Spiritualism

7. The most valuable human possessions are health, harmony, happiness, wisdom, and above all character reflecting ethical and human values. When these values are manifested in our thoughts, speech and actions, we are called a noble and enlightened person.

8. The concept of Business Process Re-engineering was introduced by Michael Hammer, Thomas Davenport and James in the year 1990.

9. **Business Process Reengineering (BPR)** is an approach to unusual improvement in operating effectiveness through the redesigning of critical business processes and supporting business systems.

10. **Benefits of Business Process Reengineering:**
    - Introduction of new technology
    - Reduced Respond time
    - Improves the Productivity
    - Competitive edge over the competitors
    - Improved Quality of products

11. **Process of Business Process Reengineering**
    - Development of Process Objectives
    - Identification of Processes to be reengineered
    - Measurement of existing Processes
    - Utilization of Information Technology
    - Design and Evaluation of Process Prototypes

12. **Peter Senge** has defined the term 'learning organization' as the organization where people continually expand their capacity to create the results they truly desire, where new and expansive patterns of thinking are nurtured, where collective aspiration is set free, and where people are continually learning to see the whole together.

13. **Characteristics of Learning Organisation:** According to Peter Senge, there are five characteristics of Learning Organization
    - Systems Thinking
    - Personal Mastery
    - The Mental Models
    - Sharing thoughts / Visions
    - The Learning Team

14. **Outsourcing** refers to the movement of one or more business processes from inside the organization to external service providers, which in turn own, administer, and manage the selected processes, based upon defined and measurable performance criteria, either to be performed on-shore, near-shore, or off-shore.

15. **Features of Outsourcing**
    - Contracting out
    - Non-core activities
    - Processes may be outsourced to a captive unit or a third party

16. Following are the **advantages of Outsourcing:**
    - Cost saving and restructuring.
    - Access to Provider's Technology and Skills
    - Focus on core competence
    - Better quality
    - Risk transference

17. **Outsourcing** suffers from the following **limitations:**
    - Hidden Costs
    - Confidentiality
    - Organizational Knowledge
    - Difficult to reserve
    - Damage to reputation
    - Time consuming

# QUESTIONS

**SHORT ANSWER QUESTIONS**

1. Define ethos.
2. Define Indian ethos.
3. State the elements of Indian ethos.
4. What do you mean by Indian ethos for management?
5. Mention the principles of Indian ethos for management.
6. State any three salient features of Indian ethos for management.
7. What do you mean by value oriented holistic management?
8. Why do we need value-based holistic management?
9. What is the relevance of values in management?

10. Who introduced the term Business Process Re-engineering?

11. Define Business Process Re-engineering.

12. Mention the benefits of Business Process Re-engineering.

13. What are the elements in the process of Business Process Re-engineering?

14. What is learning organization?

15. State the characteristics of learning organization.

16. Define outsourcing.

17. State the features of outsourcing.

18. What are the advantages of outsourcing?

19. What are the disadvantages of outsourcing?

## SHORT NOTES

1. Indian ethos for management

2. Values

3. Elements of Indian Ethos

4. Value oriented holistic management.

5. relevance of values in management

6. Business Process Re-engineering

7. Learning organization

8. Outsourcing

## LONG ANSWER QUESTIONS

1. What do you mean by Indian ethos for management? Discuss its principles and relevance in management.

2. What do you mean by value oriented holistic management? Why do we need value-based holistic management? What is the relevance of values in management?

3. Define Business Process Re-engineering. Explain the benefits of Business Process Re-engineering.

4. Discuss the process of Business Process Re-engineering.

5. What is learning organization? Discuss briefly the characteristics of learning organization.

6. Define outsourcing. Discuss its merits and demerits.

# UNIT 5B
# SUBALTERN MANAGEMENT IDEAS FROM INDIA

Subaltern Management Ideas from India;

Diversity & inclusion;

Work-life Balance

Freelancing

Flexi-time and Work from home

Co-sharing/co-working .

## CONTENTS

# 1. INTRODUCTION

Management is not a new concept in India. Contrary to the belief that management was introduced by Westerners, it has been described and demonstrated in our ancient epics. The Ramayana, Mahabharata, and Bhagavad Gita are great contributions to Indian Management. For instance, Lord Rama's team-building efforts to defeat Ravana, Sugreeva's alliance with Rama to reclaim his kingdom, and Lord Krishna's teachings to Arjuna on detached duty are examples.

As we know, the primary quality any manager should possess is self-management. The Bhagavad Gita provides the best method to achieve this, emphasizing aspects such as vision, leadership, motivation, work excellence, goal achievement, meaningful work, decision-making, and planning. Unlike Western ideologies, which tend to be materialistic, the Gita's teachings are at a more humanistic level.

In the Ramayana, Lord Rama clarifies Vibhishana's doubts by emphasizing that strength lies in clear vision and the cause for the fight, not merely in the number of soldiers. He lists essential "weapons" like knowledge, strategy, intelligence, skill, commitment, and ego restraint, highlighting the importance of strategy and human-resource management. This perspective aligns with the Harvard Business Review's statement that one need not overanalyze and complicate things.

The Mahabharata, one of the longest epics globally, also imparts valuable management lessons such as the benefits of networking, logistics, and proper organization. The Pandavas' ability to assemble a large army during their exile in the forest for 12 years, despite being out of power for 13 years, exemplifies effective logistics and organizational principles. Even today, modern militaries follow the basic principles laid down in the Mahabharata.

Over time, due to colonial rule, Indians started adopting Western management principles such as Taylor's scientific management, Management by Objectives, Division of Labor, Unity of Command, Centralization, and Mass Production. Taylor's scientific management aimed to increase productivity through common interests between management and labor, implementing practices like performance-based pay and assembly lines.

Initially successful, Western management thought now faces challenges in the present environment due to the transition from proprietorship to limited companies. This shift has led to the rise of interest groups like trade unions, consumer forums, and government regulations, limiting managerial prerogatives such as organizing, planning, directing, coordinating, and controlling. Performance-based pay can also blur long-term objectives.

With the success of Japanese management methods, Indian management thought has also been influenced by Japanese ideas. The Toyota Production System, focusing on Just in Time (JIT), Kaizen, and lean production, has gained recognition in India. These concepts prioritize reducing inventory levels, improving quality, and producing according to demand, in contrast to the Western push system. Japanese management emphasizes teamwork and overall performance rather than individual performance.

Despite its success in Japan, the applicability of Japanese management thought may vary due to different market and non-market forces in other countries. Indian management thought, therefore, is an amalgamation of Western and Japanese practices overlaid with traditional Indian norms and values.

The evolution of Indian management thought has led to a dilemma among Indian managers whether to adopt one system or combine all systems. Both Japanese and Western systems have their advantages and disadvantages, while the validity of the Indian system in the contemporary scenario must also be analyzed.

India faces several challenges such as a lack of skilled labor, workforce dedication, globalization, and brain drain. Despite positive attributes like confidence, compassion, care, and competency, negative attitudes such as competition, cruelty, and confusion also exist. Existing systems, without adaptation, may struggle to address these challenges effectively.

Old Indian management thought, rooted in the epics, addresses many challenges common to ancient, medieval, and contemporary India. We advocate that current managers study this old Indian management thought, understand present India's culture, values, behavior, and environment, and develop a new management thought integrating old wisdom with new values.

By doing so, India can create its own management identity, similar to how Japan created JIT and the West developed Mass Production, aligning management practices with local values and needs.

Based on the above discussion we can highlight the key points of success of Indian managers:

- Looking beyond stockholders' interests to public mission and national purpose

- Drawing on improvization, adaptation, and resilience to overcome endless hurdles
- Identifying products and services of compelling value to customers
- Investing in talent and building a stirring culture

## 1.1 MANAGEMENT IDEA FROM SCRIPTURES

Modern management principles find their origins in the ancient Indian philosophy as depicted in various scriptures. The management ideas from scriptures such as the Vedas, Mahabharata, Ramayana, and Kautilya's Arthashastra are elaborated below:

### 1.1.1 MANAGEMENT IDEAS FROM VEDAS AND UNNISHADS

The Vedas and Upanishads provide a systematic and formulated study of the science of life. Several multinational corporations have begun adopting the techniques described in the Vedas and Upanishads. Managers gain profound knowledge and insights into how work should be conducted, as well as understanding of work ethics, by studying these texts.

However the various lessons that a manager can learn from the Vedas are:

1. **Foster Team Spirit**: Managers should learn to control attributes such as ego and self-centrism in order to enhance team spirit and effectively delegate work.

2. **Take Responsibility**: The Vedas also teach managers about the quality of taking responsibility.

3. **Share the Credit**: The scriptures emphasize that it is the moral responsibility of managers to share credit with their team, peers, and colleagues. Whether it's financial rewards, recognition, or praise, it should be shared with deserving workers.

4. **Welcome Competition**: According to the teachings from Indian scriptures, duality is the law of nature. Happiness-sorrow, success-failure, pleasure-pain are inseparable parts of life. Healthy competition should be accepted as positive energy or motivation to improve capabilities.

5. **Praise Counts**: The Vedas also encourage managers to motivate their colleagues and subordinates. Certain management

philosophers believe that motivation through money is not the only tool for encouraging employees; non-monetary motivators such as appreciation and recognition are also important.

6. **Stay Focused**: When making decisions, managers may face opposition regarding rational methods to achieve goals. The Vedas and Asian literatures preach that in such situations, managers must remain calm, focused, and practice meditation.

7. **Character Building**: Lessons from Asian Indian literature emphasize the importance of character building. Character is the most powerful guarantor of a personality, which makes individuals perfect.

8. **Spirit of Co-operation**: The Vedas emphasize the spirit of cooperation through various techniques.

9. **Emphasis on Loyalty and Gratitude**: Loyalty and gratitude to the organization and colleagues should become important features of professionalism.

10. **Work Commitment**: Advice from Holy Scriptures suggests non-attachment to the fruits or results of actions performed in the course of one's duty. This teaching emphasizes work commitment.

11. **Utilization of Available Resources**: Managers also learn to use available resources optimally and reduce wastage to cut down operational costs and maximize profit.

12. **Removal of Self-Ego**: Ego is the main enemy of humans, separating one person from another. Ego stops the development of both mental and physical abilities. The belief that "I am superior, I can do anything" impedes the learning and observation skills of an individual.

## 1.1.2 MANAGEMENT IDEA FROM MAHABHARATA

The Mahabharata, the second longest epic in the world, is not merely a narrative of the Kurukshetra War or a philosophical book; it is also a comprehensive manual on management strategy. The epic contains numerous lessons on management that can potentially be applied to modern business practices. Vyasa's epic poem is regarded as a relevant handbook on management, and many of these management insights are still practiced today. Here are some of the best practices derived from India's great epic of knowledge and inspiration:

1. **Transform Weaknesses into Strengths:** Like the Pandavas transformed their weaknesses into strengths during their years of exile, managers should have the urge to improve their weaknesses. The Mahabharata provides many examples highlighting the importance of utilizing time to overcome skills, such as Arjuna's mission to attain the Divyastras or Yudhisthira mastering the game of Dice. One needs to passionately dedicate adequate time to learn skills that can help overcome weaknesses. This is essential for becoming a great manager.

2. **Share Responsibilities:** Efficiently sharing responsibilities is the mark of a good manager, and the great Indian epic provides the best examples for this. The Pandavas fought the war as one team with a unified goal, while the Kauravas lacked team spirit and fought individual battles. The epic advises managers not to make the decision-making process dictatorial; instead, involve everyone so that the best ideas can emerge.

3. **Learn the Art of Teamwork:** Unlike the Kauravas, who lacked unity, the Pandavas fought together, highlighting the significance of sticking to common goals while achieving individual targets. The epic teaches the golden lesson that only a combined effort can bring success.

4. **Understand Ground Realities:** The Pandavas spent a year in exile with the common people, gaining a real understanding of society's various strata. In contrast, the Kauravas, living a royal life, lacked this grounding. Managers need to understand these realities to lead their teams in the right direction. Breaking barriers to connect with subordinates helps identify their problems and find ways to simplify their work.

5. **Take Calculated Risks:** Krishna acted as a great crisis manager, demonstrating how to take calculated risks during times of crisis. Management is about taking such risks; shying away from challenges is not a sign of good management. Instead, well-assessed decisions on facing challenges are the trademark of effective management.

6. **Have Effective Vision:** Yudhisthira was a man of great vision, respected even by his competitors. He was an expert administrator, committed to truth and Dharma. He used his

image strategically; for instance, on the first day of war, he sought blessings from elders, gaining secrets to defeat the Kauravas and strategic advantage. He anticipated the war early and began preparations accordingly.

7. **Strategy:** Strategy provides direction and scope for an organization to compete. For example, the Kauravas and their chief strategist, Shakuni, relied on unfair practices. These methods may work in the short term but fail in the long term. A good strategist understands competitors' weaknesses and exploits them to help the company recover. Shakuni was biased and focused solely on Duryodhana's welfare, while the Pandavas had the world's best strategist in Krishna. He believed in forming strong alliances, contributing to the Pandavas' success.

8. **Decision-Making:** Arjuna, unlike the Kauravas' CEO, was focused and made decisions at the right time, benefiting the Pandavas. The Kauravas' CEO lacked concentration, made hasty decisions, and believed in unfair practices. He prioritized finance over human resources, a mistake Arjuna avoided by choosing Krishna over his army.

9. **SWOT Analysis:** The Kauravas converted their strengths into weaknesses by engaging in wars with other kingdoms, causing losses and creating enemies. In contrast, the Pandavas utilized their exile period to acquire strategic allies.

10. **Commitment:** The Kauravas lacked commitment; their main warriors, Bheeshma and Dronacharya, did not want war and promised not to harm any Pandavas. Karna fought only to remain loyal to Duryodhana, not fully engaging in the war as he had promised not to harm any Pandavas except Arjuna. In contrast, the Pandavas dedicated themselves to their roles, with Abhimanyu and Ghatotkacha making significant contributions. Abhimanyu fought seven Maharathis single-handedly, and Ghatotkacha decimated half of the Kaurava army.

## 1.1.3 MANAGEMENT IDEA FROM BIBLE

Etiquette, by definition, is a code of ethics that guides our behavior in professional settings. While specific rules of etiquette vary across cultures and generations, the fundamental principles of proper business etiquette remain consistent. The Bible offers substantial guidance on conducting business affairs.

1. **Fair Wages:** The Bible emphasizes the importance of business etiquette, including fair wages for employees. In contemporary terms, this entails several principles. Firstly, employees should be paid a fair wage as mandated by law, ensuring at least minimum wage standards are met. Secondly, any promises made regarding salaries, hourly wages, benefits, or bonuses must be upheld. James 5:4 issues a strong warning against those who fail to pay employees properly: "Look! The wages you failed to pay the workers who mowed your fields are crying out against you. The cries of the harvesters have reached the ears of the Lord Almighty." God takes seriously the mistreatment of workers by employers who do not pay them fairly.

2. **Business Planning:** The Bible underscores the importance of planning in business, reflecting God's own orderly plan from the beginning. This principle is crucial in business endeavors. A well-conducted business begins with a written plan, and it would be considered poor etiquette to meet with prospective investors without a clear plan of action. Proverbs 21:5 advises, "The plans of the diligent lead to profit as surely as haste leads to poverty." Moreover, seeking counsel from experienced and wise advisors is a prudent approach, as noted in Proverbs 15:22: "Plans fail for lack of counsel, but with many advisers they succeed."

3. **Taxes:** The Bible provides guidance on paying taxes for Christian businessmen. It is essential to pay all taxes owed truthfully, without deception about profits, losses, or expenses. In Mark 12, Jesus addresses the issue of paying taxes, stating, "Give to Caesar what is Caesar's and to God what is God's." Romans 13:7 also instructs, "Give everyone what you owe him: If you owe taxes, pay taxes; if revenue, then revenue; if respect, then respect; if honor, then honor."

4. **Charitable Giving:** Businesses have a moral responsibility to engage in charitable giving and help the poor. While many businesses may donate to charities for tax deductions or to improve their public image, the Bible teaches that giving should originate from a spirit of compassion and humility. Proverbs 22:9 states, "The generous will themselves be blessed, for they share their food with the poor." The Bible promises blessings

to those who give, whether as individuals or businessmen who allocate profits to help those in need.

5. **Work Ethic:** The Bible emphasizes the value of hard work and diligence in achieving profitability. Proverbs 28:19 asserts, "He who works his land will have abundant food, but the one who chases fantasies will have his fill of poverty." This does not negate the importance of creativity, innovation, and trying new ideas, but underscores the necessity of a strong work ethic to achieve lasting success.

## 1.1.4 MANAGEMENT LESSONS FROM QURAN

The Holy Quran provides a comprehensive framework for implementing key principles in practice:

1. **Obedience and Respect for Authority:** This is vital in any organization. Without obedience and respect for authority, the structure would collapse and the organization would fail to function effectively. The Quran states in [4:59], "Obey Allah and His Messenger and those in positions of authority among you." This directive is a command, not a suggestion. A true believer must observe this rule willingly and sincerely. When employees internalize voluntary obedience, the organizational hierarchy is reinforced. Without this spirit, the hierarchy serves no purpose.

2. **Joint Consultation and Teamwork:** The modern world recognizes the value of consultation (Shura) and teamwork. The Japanese management style, which emphasizes these principles, has demonstrated their effectiveness. The Quran advocates for this approach, as seen in [42:38], "...and those who conduct their affairs by mutual consultation," and [3:159], "...pardon them, ask forgiveness for them, and consult them in important matters. Then, when you have made a decision, put your trust in Allah, for Allah loves those who trust Him."

3. **Principle of Equal Opportunities:** This principle ensures that all members of an organization have fair chances to grow, contribute, and be rewarded. The Quran highlights this in [49:13], "O mankind, We have created you from a male and a female and made you into nations and tribes so that you may know one another. Indeed, the most noble of you in the sight of Allah is the most righteous of you." Prophet Muhammad

elaborated on this verse, emphasizing that no one is superior to another except through righteousness. In management, this means that qualifications and experience should be the sole criteria for any position, promoting harmony and smooth operations.

4. **Quality Management System**: For long-term success, a business must deliver on its promises to customers. The primary focus of a businessman is often profit, but customer satisfaction is crucial as it directly affects profit margins. The Quran addresses this in [6:152], "And do not approach the orphan's property except to improve it until he reaches maturity. Give full measure and weight in justice. We do not burden any soul beyond what it can bear. And when you speak, be just, even if it concerns a near relative; and fulfill the covenant of Allah. This He has instructed you that you may remember."

5. **Fulfilling Contracts, Commitments, and Promises**: Promises and contracts, whether verbal or written, must be upheld. This includes everything from marriage contracts (Nikah Namah) to business plans and financial agreements. A successful businessman should avoid making promises that cannot be kept and should not break those that have been made.

# 1.2 MANAGEMENT LESSONS FROM ARTHASHASTRA

Acharya Chanakya, also known as Kautilya, served as a minister in the Kingdom of Chandragupta Maurya between 317 and 293 B.C. Renowned as one of the most astute ministers of his time, he articulated his perspectives on the state, warfare, social structures, diplomacy, ethics, politics, and statecraft in his seminal work, the Arthashastra, written in the 4th century B.C. This treatise, which comprises 15 chapters, 380 Shlokas, and 4,968 Sutras, is likely the earliest book on the ethics of statecraft. Primarily focused on the art of governance, it adopts an instructional tone (Kohli, 1995)

Chanakya is often hailed as the world's first management guru, whose ideas have influenced kings and rulers for centuries. Prominent monarchs in ancient India, such as Ashoka, studied and implemented the principles of the Arthashastra to significantly expand their territories (similar to increasing market share), defend against powerful enemies (developing strategies against competitors), and cultivate effective strategies, habits, and practices. Consequently, Kautilya's contributions to ethics are still relevant in today's business environment.

Key aspects of the Arthashastra relevant to modern management include:

1.  **Principles of Management** : The Arthashastra presents various principles and techniques that, when applied, can greatly enhance daily management practices. Kautilya believed that fundamental business principles remain consistent across industries. He provides insights into balancing short-term and long-term objectives and strategies.

2.  **Preventing Misuse of Power** : Kautilya was acutely aware of the tendencies of bureaucrats and statesmen, and he established rules to prevent the abuse of power.

3.  **Importance of Accounting Methods** : Kautilya emphasized the significance of accounting methods in economic enterprises to accurately measure performance. He argued that no amount of rules, regulations, or audits could prevent unethical behavior without character building and action-oriented ethical values.

4.  **Emphasis on Ethics** : The Arthashastra uniquely stresses the importance of economic growth and societal welfare within an organizational framework. Kautilya believed that ethical values lead to spiritual fulfillment. He advised readers to consult the Vedas and philosophy for moral theory, which clarifies the distinction between good and bad, and moral and immoral actions.

5.  **Integration of Ethics and Economics** : Kautilya extended the conceptual framework to address conflicts of interest arising from emerging capitalism. He sought to integrate ethics and economics, asserting that the integration level in his Arthashastra

was significantly higher than that in Adam Smith's Wealth of Nations or the writings of Plato and Aristotle.

## 2. DIVERSITY & INCLUSION

Diversity and inclusion encompass an organization's initiatives, policies, and practices aimed at ensuring that individuals from various backgrounds are culturally and socially accepted and integrated into the workplace. A company committed to diversity and inclusion will employ a workforce that mirrors the diverse society in which it operates.

Diversity pertains to differences in political beliefs, race, culture, sexual orientation, religion, socioeconomic status, and gender identity. In a workplace context, diversity means having a staff composed of individuals who offer varied perspectives and backgrounds.

Inclusion, on the other hand, ensures that everyone within this diverse group feels involved, valued, respected, treated equitably, and integrated into the company's culture. Fostering an inclusive environment involves empowering all employees and acknowledging their unique talents.

Both diversity and inclusion (D&I) are crucial; diversity without inclusion can lead to a toxic culture, while inclusion without diversity can result in stagnation and a lack of creativity. Although companies are increasingly focusing on diversity, many neglect the equally important aspect of inclusion. Without deliberate efforts toward both, employees may feel alienated and unsupported.

## 2.1 BENEFITS OF DIVERSITY AND INCLUSION AT WORK

A diverse and inclusive environment fosters a sense of belonging among employees, making them feel more connected and productive. Organizations that implement D&I practices often experience significant improvements in business outcomes, innovation, and decision-making.

Here are some key benefits of diversity and inclusion in the workplace:

1. **Greater Innovation and Creativity**: A workplace with employees from varied backgrounds, skills, experiences, and knowledge fosters innovative and creative ideas. This diversity can significantly impact business growth over time, as employees feel more comfortable sharing unique ideas in a

diverse environment, helping the business differentiate itself from those that operate with a homogeneous perspective.

2. **Wide Range of Skills**: Hiring individuals from diverse backgrounds brings a variety of skills to the organization. This inclusivity allows for broader perspectives during brainstorming, problem-solving, and idea development, enhancing the business's overall capability.

3. **Attracting Talented Employees**: Diversity and inclusion are key factors that many job seekers consider when evaluating job offers. A company that visibly values diversity is more likely to attract top talent who feel welcomed and valued, ensuring that hiring decisions are based on skills and not solely on appearances.

4. **Positive Working Environment**: An inclusive and diverse workplace promotes employee happiness and well-being, which is reflected in their work. When employees thrive in their roles, the business also thrives, leading to overall success.

5. **Increased Productivity**: Collaboration in a diverse team enhances productivity. Employees can leverage each other's varied experiences and skills, leading to better teamwork and faster idea exchange, helping the business stay competitive.

6. **Effective Marketing**: A diverse and inclusive team can better understand and market to a wide range of audiences. Employees from different backgrounds can effectively promote the business to their respective communities, helping the business grow by learning how to target different groups.

7. **Higher Revenues**: Successfully managing a diverse and inclusive workforce leads to higher revenues. Happy employees generate new ideas and work more productively, driving greater business success and helping the company stand out from its competitors.

## 2.2 CHALLENGES OF DIVERSITY AND INCLUSION

There are numerous benefits to having diversity in the workplace. Different perspectives, opinions, and ideas can drive innovation and enhance problem-solving capabilities. This diversity helps companies better serve their customer base, tap into new markets, and gain a competitive edge.

A diverse workplace also fosters a stronger sense of belonging for traditionally underrepresented groups. When employees are not the sole woman, person of color, or person with a disability, they may feel more integrated into the team. This inclusion can lead to higher employee engagement, reduced turnover, and increased productivity.

However, bringing together a diverse group of people can present some challenges:

1. **Communication Issues**: Diverse teams may face communication issues due to language barriers, different communication styles, or preferences. It's crucial to address these challenges early to prevent them from becoming problematic.

2. **Cultural Misunderstandings**: Misunderstandings can arise when people from different cultures work together. For instance, gestures like a thumbs-up, using the left hand, or patting someone on the back can be offensive in certain cultures.

3. **Slower Decision Making**: While diverse perspectives are beneficial for innovation, they can slow down decision-making and progress toward goals. A team member who challenges the status quo may raise important points that need thorough exploration, delaying decisions.

4. **Discrimination**: In diverse environments, biases, discrimination, and harassment can occur. A study found that 61 percent of workers have witnessed or experienced discrimination based on age, race, gender, etc. Such discrimination can prevent employees from bringing their authentic selves to work, hindering innovation, creativity, and teamwork.

5. **Productivity**: Cultural conflicts can negatively impact productivity and employee morale. While diverse teams can drive long-term business success, unresolved cultural clashes can harm employee satisfaction and damage the business's reputation and image..

# 2.3 MEASURES TO OVERCOME DIVERSITY AND INCLUSION CHALLENGES

It is undeniable that diversity and inclusion are essential for the sustainable development of any business, and embracing this trend is inevitable. However, the process can be challenging if the aforementioned issues are not properly addressed. Here are some suggestions your company might consider to foster an equitable and inclusive working environment.

1. **Focus on "Culture Add" Instead of "Culture Fit":** Embrace the unique experiences and cultures each employee brings. Different perspectives generate fresh ideas and prevent monotonous "sameness." Companies should value these differences and continuously raise awareness about their importance. Managers and team leaders should provide fair and open opportunities for all members to share and contribute their approaches for improvement. Every employee needs to feel heard and respected for who they are and what they bring to the table. These unique experiences are invaluable for fostering innovation. All cultures should be appreciated and celebrated equally. While no one can fully understand another's background, a willingness to learn is essential. Employees should be encouraged to share their insights rather than conforming to the majority. Treating employees as individuals rather than as a homogeneous group helps overcome communication barriers.

2. **Take a Stance:** Remaining neutral can be detrimental. Employees might perceive neutrality as indecisiveness rather than fairness. Managers should stay informed about current events and take a clear stance on social issues such as Black Lives Matter and gender inequality. HR managers should actively identify and address both conscious and unconscious biases towards minority groups promptly. Everyone wants to feel safe and supported by their employer.

3. **Leverage Diversity Effectively:** A Glassdoor survey revealed that two-thirds of workers consider diversity important

when evaluating companies and job offers. Demonstrating a commitment to a diverse and inclusive culture helps businesses stand out in the competitive job market. In a diverse workplace, each person's unique strengths and skills provide learning opportunities for others. Employees should have the chance to grow and learn from exposure to different cultures, working styles, and perspectives.

Organizations should incorporate collaborative projects and align employee development plans with the company's objectives to ensure sustainability. An action plan is essential to implement these ideas effectively..

## 3. WORK LIFE BALANCE

Work-life balance (WLB) is not a new concept. The shift in work patterns and the workplace concept after the industrial revolution in the late 18th century redefined WLB. Over time, the rise of nuclear families and the decline of the "ideal home," where one spouse earned and the other managed the household, marked another shift. With improved education and employment opportunities, most households now have both parents working, driven by necessity and the desire to increase income. This shift necessitated creating environments where employees could balance work with personal needs and desires, crucial for both retention and productivity. Recognizing this, companies began implementing schemes to attract and retain employees while enhancing productivity.

Work-life balance involves individuals being equally engaged and satisfied with both their professional and personal roles. Although there is no universal definition, many researchers have explored its meaning. Generally, it refers to a balance between the work and personal lives of employees, regardless of gender, employment level, organization, or industry. Specifically, it involves managing time to focus on both professional duties and personal life, which includes friends and family, in a way that promotes health and personal satisfaction without harming productivity or success. Today, WLB is vital as people work continuously and expect some flexibility from their employers.

In his book *Managing work-life balance*, David Clutterbuck defines work-life balance as:

- being aware of different demands on time and energy;
- having the ability to make choices in the allocation of time and energy;
- knowing what values to apply to choices; and
- making choices.

Work-life balance does not imply an equal division of time between work and personal activities. Attempting to allocate an equal number of hours to each aspect is typically impractical and unfulfilling. Life is fluid, not static, and an individual's work-life balance will fluctuate over time, often daily. The appropriate balance for someone today may be different tomorrow. The right balance also varies depending on life stages, such as being single versus being in a relationship or having children. It changes when starting a new career compared to nearing retirement. There is no perfect, one-size-fits-all balance to strive for.

## 3.1 COMPONENTS OF WORK LIFE BALANCE

The components of a proper work-life balance can be divided into six elements:

1. **Self-Management**: This involves effectively managing one's own needs, such as sleep, exercise, and nutrition. It emphasizes the importance of recognizing that time, resources, and life are finite and must be used wisely.

2. **Effective Time Management**: This entails making the best use of your time and available resources to meet challenges. It involves setting appropriate goals, distinguishing between what is important and urgent, and knowing when and how to accomplish specific tasks efficiently.

3. **Stress Management**: Managing stress is crucial as modern society tends to increase stress levels. It requires developing skills to maintain calm and navigate through high-pressure situations. Focusing on one task at a time rather than multitasking can help reduce stress.

4. **Change Management**: Adapting to new methods and re-adapting existing ones is essential for a successful career and a happy home life. Effective change management involves regularly ensuring that changes at work and home do not become overwhelming.

5. **Technology Management**: This involves ensuring that technology serves you rather than dominates you. As technological advancements accelerate, it's important to control how technology is integrated into your life and work.

6. **Leisure Management**: Often overlooked, leisure management recognizes the importance of rest and relaxation. It involves varying leisure activities to prevent monotony and ensuring that "time off" is a vital part of life.

## 3.2 THEORIES IN SUPPORT OF ADOPTION OF WLB POLICIES BY MANAGEMENT

There are four main theories that explain why management in organizations adopts work-life balance (WLB) policies. Each theory identifies specific predictive conditions (Felstead et al., 2002) and has been validated through research. These theories are grounded in organizational theory, including institutional theory, resource dependence theory, and strategic choice theory. The theories are as follows:

1. **Institutional Theory**: This theory links management's decision to adopt WLB practices to conforming to societal normative pressures, such as organization size, ownership, industry, unionization levels, and other influencing factors.

2. **Organizational Adaptation Theory**: This theory connects an organization's responsiveness to internal environmental factors, such as the proportion of female staff, skill levels, work processes, and senior management values.

3. **High Commitment Theory**: This theory views WLB practices as strategic HRM initiatives aimed at increasing employee commitment to the organization.

4. **Situational Theory**: This theory explains the adoption of WLB policies in terms of pressures to boost profitability and productivity, and to address challenges related to employee recruitment and retention (Felstead et al., 2002).

## 3.3 EMPLOYER'S ROLE IN WORK-LIFE BALANCE

Employers play a crucial role in maintaining employees' work-life balance. Surveys have shown that an overwhelming majority of employers support the concept of work-life balance (WLB). In fact, it has become a legal necessity, with "Equal Opportunity Employer" standards becoming almost mandatory. Additionally, as discussed earlier, WLB is a business imperative for retaining talent and maintaining productivity across all sectors. In an era where attrition is a major concern, adopting worker-friendly practices is seen as a wise strategy. Employers can facilitate WLB through various schemes designed to attract and meet employees' needs. Some of these include:

- Facilities for child care;
- Financial planning services for employees who need them;
- Flexi-timings;
- Work sharing;
- Part time employment;
- Leave plans - both paid and unpaid - to suit employees needs;
- Subsidized food plans; and
- Insurance plans.

## 3.4 STRATEGIES TO ACHIEVE WORK-LIFE BALANCE

Some major strategies for achieving work-life balance include:

1. **Budgeting Time Both In and Out of the Office**: Efficiently schedule work hours, including personal time in your calendar, and prioritize time for family and friends. Aim to leave work on time at least three days a week. While working late is sometimes unavoidable, adjusting schedules to ensure timely departures on certain days is important.

2. **Controlling Interruptions and Distractions**: Stay focused while in the office by effectively managing time and minimizing distractions. Schedule blocks of time without meetings to concentrate on tasks with minimal interruptions, thereby improving productivity.

3. **Exploring Flex-Time Availability**: Investigate the possibility of flex-time options within your organization. If available, this can be a valuable solution for better managing work-life balance.

4. **Maximizing Weekend Use**: Plan time off to maximize enjoyment and relaxation. Schedule activities with family and friends, such as weekend trips or enjoyable outings. Ensure that time away from work is meaningful and refreshing.

# 4. FREELANCING

Freelancing refers to a type of self-employment where individuals offer their services to clients on a project or contract basis, rather than being bound to a single employer long-term. Freelancers often work for multiple clients simultaneously, providing flexibility and a wide range of opportunities.

## 4.1 Characteristics of Freelancing

Freelancing is a unique mode of employment characterized by several distinctive features that differentiate it from traditional job roles. Here are the key characteristics:

1. **Self-Employment:** Freelancers operate as independent contractors, not as employees of a single company. They manage their own business activities, including marketing, client acquisition, and financial management.

2. **Project-Based Work:** Work is typically organized around specific projects or tasks with defined goals and deadlines. Freelancers may handle multiple projects from different clients simultaneously.

3. **Flexibility and Autonomy:** Freelancers have the freedom to choose their working hours, location, and the type of projects they accept. They exercise significant control over their work-life balance and professional decisions.

4. **Variety of Work:** Freelancers often work with various clients across different industries, providing a broad range of experiences and learning opportunities. This variety can keep the work engaging and help build a versatile skill set.

5. **Income Variability:** Freelance income can be inconsistent, with periods of high earnings followed by leaner times. Income depends on the number of projects, client payments, and the freelancer's ability to secure new contracts.

6. **Client Relationships:** Building and maintaining strong client relationships is crucial for securing repeat business and referrals. Freelancers must often handle client communication, negotiate contracts, and manage expectations.

7. **No Traditional Employment Benefits:** Freelancers typically do not receive health insurance, retirement plans, paid leave, or

other benefits provided by traditional employers. They must arrange for their own benefits and financial safety nets.

8. **Skill Specialization:** Freelancers often specialize in specific skills or industries to differentiate themselves and attract clients. Continuous skill development is important to stay competitive and meet client demands.

9. **Marketing and Personal Branding:** Successful freelancers invest time in marketing their services and building a personal brand. They use websites, social media, and freelancing platforms to showcase their work and attract clients.

10. **Responsibility for Business Operations:** Freelancers handle all aspects of their business, including setting rates, invoicing, accounting, and tax obligations. Effective self-management and organizational skills are essential.

11. **Networking:** Building a professional network is vital for finding opportunities, getting referrals, and staying updated with industry trends. Freelancers often join professional associations, attend industry events, and participate in online communities.

12. **Legal and Contractual Awareness:** Understanding contracts, intellectual property rights, and other legal aspects is important to protect oneself and ensure fair dealings. Freelancers must often draft, review, and negotiate contracts with clients.

Freelancing offers a dynamic and flexible work environment with the potential for varied experiences and significant autonomy. However, it also requires strong self-discipline, business acumen, and the ability to manage multiple aspects of running a business independently.

## 4.2 Advantages of Freelancing:

Freelancing offers several benefits that appeal to many professionals seeking autonomy, variety, and control over their work. Here are the primary advantages of freelancing:

1. **Flexibility** : Freelancers can choose when to work, allowing for a better work-life balance and the ability to accommodate personal commitments. They can work from anywhere, whether it's from home, a co-working space, or while traveling.

2. **Control Over Workload** : Freelancers have the freedom to decide how many projects they take on, allowing them to manage their workload according to their capacity and preferences.

3.  **Variety of Work:** Exposure to a wide range of projects and clients keeps the work interesting and provides diverse experiences. This variety helps in skill development and broadening professional expertise.

4.  **Higher Earning Potential:** Freelancers can set their own rates and have the potential to earn more than traditional employees, especially if they specialize in high-demand skills. The ability to work for multiple clients simultaneously can also increase overall earnings.

5.  **Autonomy** : Freelancers have control over their business decisions, including the types of projects they undertake, their rates, and their workflow. This autonomy allows for a personalized approach to work that aligns with their values and goals.

6.  **Skill Development** : Continuous exposure to new challenges and diverse projects helps freelancers continually develop and refine their skills. Freelancers often stay current with industry trends and innovations to remain competitive.

7.  **Personal Satisfaction** : Many freelancers find greater job satisfaction and fulfillment due to the freedom to pursue projects they are passionate about. The ability to see the direct impact of their work and receive feedback from clients can be highly rewarding.

8.  **Networking Opportunities** : Freelancing provides opportunities to build a broad professional network across different industries. Strong client relationships and professional connections can lead to referrals and repeat business.

9.  **Reduced Commute** : Working remotely eliminates the need for daily commuting, saving time and reducing stress. This also contributes to lower transportation costs and a smaller carbon footprint.

10. **Scalability:** Freelancers have the potential to grow their business by taking on more clients, increasing their rates, or expanding their service offerings. They can also hire subcontractors or collaborate with other freelancers to handle larger projects.

11. **Diverse Income Streams** : Freelancers can diversify their income by offering different services, working with various clients, or

creating passive income streams through products like e-books, online courses, or digital downloads.

12. **Global Opportunities:** Freelancing opens up the possibility of working with clients from around the world, providing access to a broader market and diverse cultural experiences.

Freelancing offers significant advantages, making it an attractive option for those seeking flexibility, autonomy, and the potential for higher earnings. However, it also requires discipline, effective self-management, and proactive client acquisition strategies to maximize these benefits.

## 4.3 Challenges of Freelancing

While freelancing offers many benefits, it also presents several challenges that freelancers must navigate to be successful. Here are the primary challenges :

1. **Income Instability** : Freelancers often face fluctuating income, with periods of high earnings followed by times of little or no work. Inconsistent cash flow can make financial planning and stability difficult.

2. **Lack of Benefits** : Unlike traditional employees, freelancers typically do not receive health insurance, retirement plans, paid leave, or other benefits. They must independently arrange and finance these benefits, which can be costly and complex.

3. **Self-Management** : Freelancers are responsible for all aspects of their business, including marketing, client acquisition, project management, billing, and taxes. Effective time management and organizational skills are essential to handle these diverse tasks.

4. **Isolation** : Working independently can lead to feelings of loneliness and isolation, especially for those accustomed to a collaborative office environment. Limited social interaction can impact mental health and motivation.

5. **Client Dependence** : Success depends on building and maintaining a strong client base, which requires ongoing effort and relationship management. Freelancers may face challenges with difficult clients, payment delays, and negotiating fair rates.

6. **Unpredictable Workload** : The workload can be unpredictable, with sudden surges of projects followed by slow periods. Managing this variability requires careful planning and the ability to handle high workloads efficiently.

7. **Financial Management** : Freelancers must manage their own finances, including setting aside money for taxes, tracking expenses, and budgeting for irregular income. Lack of financial literacy can lead to mismanagement and financial difficulties.

8. **Marketing and Branding** : Effective self-promotion is crucial for attracting clients and standing out in a competitive market. Building a personal brand and marketing services require time, effort, and sometimes financial investment.

9. **Work-Life Balance** : The flexibility of freelancing can blur the boundaries between work and personal life, leading to overwork and burnout. Setting clear boundaries and maintaining a healthy work-life balance is challenging but necessary.

10. **Skill Development** : Freelancers must continually update their skills to stay competitive and meet evolving client demands. Investing in professional development and training can be time-consuming and costly.

11. **Legal and Contractual Issues** : Freelancers need to understand contracts, intellectual property rights, and other legal matters to protect their work and ensure fair dealings. Disputes over contracts and payments can arise, requiring negotiation or legal action.

12. **Quality Assurance** : Ensuring consistent quality across different projects and clients can be challenging, especially when managing multiple tasks simultaneously. Freelancers must develop processes to maintain high standards and client satisfaction.

13. **Uncertain Career Progression:** Unlike traditional career paths with clear progression, freelancers must create their own opportunities for advancement. Building a sustainable and growing business requires strategic planning and continuous effort .

Freelancing requires a proactive and disciplined approach to overcome these challenges. Success in freelancing involves not only leveraging one's skills but also effectively managing the business aspects and maintaining a balance between work and personal life .

# 5. FLEXI TIME WORKING ARRANGEMENT

Flextime is a working arrangement that allows employees to choose their start and finish times at work. This gives employees more freedom in terms of managing work and other commitments, but it keeps them available for group engagement or customer responsiveness during specified times. It should be noted that a flextime schedule does not reduce the total number of working hours in a given week, generally it requires employees to work a certain number of "core hours" within a specified period. For example, the core may be 10 AM to 4 PM with the office actually operating at 8 AM and closing at 6-30 PM.

## 5.1 Characteristics of Flexi Time Working Arrangement:

Flexi time, also known as flexible working hours, is a work arrangement that provides employees with the flexibility to determine their own start and end times, within certain parameters set by the employer. Here are the key characteristics of flexi time:

1. **Core Hours** : There are specific core hours during which all employees are required to be present at work e.g., 10:00 AM to 3:00 PM. Core hours ensure that there is adequate overlap for team collaboration, meetings, and client or customer interaction.

2. **Flexible Schedule** : Employees can choose when they start and finish their workday, as long as they complete the required number of hours and adhere to core hours. Employees must typically work a specified number of hours per day or week, maintaining their status as full-time or part-time workers.

3. **Autonomy and Responsibility** : Allows employees to decide when to work, giving them more control over their daily schedule. Employees are responsible for managing their workload and meeting deadlines without constant supervision.

4. **Work-Life Balance** : Facilitates better integration of work and personal life by accommodating personal appointments, family commitments, and other obligations. Reduces stress associated with rigid work schedules and long commutes during peak hours.

5. **Variety of Attendance Patterns** : Employees may have varying arrival and departure times, depending on their individual preferences and personal circumstances. It allows employees to adjust their schedules to fit their peak productivity times or personal preferences.

6. **Communication and Collaboration** : Core hours ensure that there is a period each day when all team members are available for meetings, collaboration, and real-time communication. It encourages virtual collaboration and flexible working arrangements, promoting a more inclusive and supportive work environment.

7. **Productivity and Efficiency** : Allows employees to work during their most productive hours, enhancing overall efficiency and job satisfaction.

8. **Performance Management** : Focuses on results and output rather than strict adherence to a fixed schedule, promoting a results-oriented work culture.

9. **Management and Support:** The arrangement requires effective communication and management practices to ensure that employees understand expectations and responsibilities.

10. **Feedback and Continuous Improvement** : Encourages employees to provide feedback on their experience with the flexi time arrangement, allowing for continuous improvement and adjustment of policies and practices.

11. **Evaluation:** Conducts periodic evaluations to assess the effectiveness of the flexi time policy and its impact on employee satisfaction, productivity, and business outcomes.

Flexi time working arrangements offer numerous benefits to both employees and employers, including improved work-life balance, increased job satisfaction, and enhanced productivity. However, successful implementation requires careful planning, effective communication, and ongoing evaluation to ensure that the policy meets the needs of all stakeholders involved.

## 5.2 Advantages/Benefits of Flexi Time Working Arrangement

Flexi time, or flexible working hours, offers several advantages for both employees and employers. It provides a more adaptable approach to work scheduling that can enhance productivity, job satisfaction, and work-life balance. Here are the key advantages of flexi time working arrangements:

1. **Improved Work-Life Balance :**
   a. **Personal Flexibility :** Employees can schedule work hours around personal obligations, such as childcare, appointments, or other commitments.
   b. **Reduced Stress :** Avoiding rush-hour commuting and having more control over daily schedules can reduce stress levels.

2. **Increased Employee Satisfaction :**
   a. **Autonomy :** Employees appreciate the ability to choose their work hours, which can lead to higher job satisfaction.
   b. **Personalization :** Allows employees to work during their most productive hours, leading to better performance and engagement.

3. **Enhanced Productivity :**
   a. **Peak Productivity :** Employees can work when they are most productive, rather than being constrained to a traditional 9-to-5 schedule.
   b. **Focus and Efficiency :** Reduced interruptions and flexibility in work hours can lead to improved focus and efficiency.

4. **Health and Well-being :**
   a. **Better Health :** Flexi time can contribute to better physical and mental health by reducing commuting stress and allowing for more rest and relaxation.
   b. **Work-Life Integration :** Supports overall well-being by facilitating the integration of work with personal and family life.

5. **Attracting and Retaining Talent :**

   a. **Competitive Advantage :** Organizations offering flexible working arrangements are often more attractive to prospective employees.

   b. **Employee Retention :** Increases employee loyalty and retention rates as employees appreciate the flexibility and work-life balance.

6. **Cost Savings :**

   a. **Reduced Overheads :** Employers may benefit from reduced costs associated with office space and utilities when employees work staggered hours.

   b. **Efficiency :** Increased productivity and job satisfaction can lead to cost savings in the long run.

7. **Diverse Workforce Needs :**

   a. **Inclusivity :** Supports a diverse workforce by accommodating varying needs and preferences, such as those of caregivers or individuals with unique scheduling requirements.

   b. **Workforce Engagement :** Enhances inclusivity and engagement by valuing individual employee needs and preferences.

8. **Operational Continuity :**

   a. **Coverage :** Provides coverage over extended hours, ensuring that critical functions are performed throughout the day.

   b. **Client Service :** Supports customer and client service needs by accommodating different time zones and client availability.

9. **Environmental Impact :**

   a. **Reduced Commuting :** Decreases environmental impact by reducing commuting time and emissions associated with transportation.

   b. **Sustainability :** Contributes to sustainable practices by promoting remote work and reducing the carbon footprint.

10. **Adaptability to Business Needs:**
    a. **Scalability :** Allows for the scaling of workforce capacity based on business demand without rigid constraints.
    b. **Operational Flexibility:** Adapts to seasonal or project-based workload fluctuations more easily.

11. **Compliance and Legal Considerations :**
    a. **Regulatory Compliance :** Ensures compliance with labor laws and regulations related to working hours and rest periods.
    b. **Contractual Agreements :** Clarifies terms of employment, including working hours, compensation, and benefits.

Flexi time working arrangements promote a more inclusive, productive, and balanced workplace by empowering employees to manage their work schedules effectively. They support organizational goals by enhancing employee satisfaction, reducing turnover, and increasing operational efficiency.

## 5.3 Disadvantages of Flexi Time Working Arrangement

While flexi time, or flexible working hours, offers many benefits, there are also several challenges and disadvantages associated with this work arrangement. Here are some of the key disadvantages:

1. **Coordination and Communication Challenges:**
    - **Overlap in Core Hours :** Ensuring that employees are available during core hours for meetings, collaboration, and client interactions can be challenging.
    - **Team Collaboration :** Difficulties in coordinating team projects and ensuring effective communication when team members have varying schedules.

2. **Management Oversight:**
    - **Supervision and Monitoring :** Monitoring employee performance and ensuring accountability can be more challenging when employees have varied work schedules.
    - **Productivity Tracking :** Difficulty in tracking productivity and ensuring that work is completed on time and to the required standard.

3. **Inequity and Fairness:**

   • **Unequal Distribution :** Potential for inequity in workload distribution and availability, which may impact team dynamics and morale.

   • **Perception of Favoritism :** Perception of favoritism if certain employees are granted more flexible arrangements than others.

4. **Client and Customer Service:**

   • **Availability :** Ensuring that employees are available when needed to meet client or customer demands can be difficult when schedules vary widely.

   • **Consistency :** Maintaining consistent service levels and response times when employees have different work schedules.

5. **Collaboration and Team Building:**

   • **Team Bonding :** Challenges in building team cohesion and fostering a strong team culture when employees have diverse schedules.

   • **Social Isolation :** Potential for increased social isolation and reduced camaraderie among team members.

6. **Operational Challenges:**

   • **Coverage Issues:** Ensuring that there is adequate coverage during all necessary hours, especially in roles that require continuous operations.

   • **Workflow Efficiency :** Potential disruptions to workflow and project timelines due to staggered work hours.

7. **Training and Development:**

   • **Access to Training :** Difficulty in providing consistent access to training and development opportunities for employees with varied schedules.

   • **Skill Building :** Challenges in promoting skill development and knowledge sharing among team members .

8. **Communication and Information Sharing:**

   - **Timely Communication :** Delays in communication and information sharing due to employees working different hours.

   - **Team Meetings :** Difficulty in scheduling and conducting team meetings that accommodate everyone's schedules.

9. **Administrative and HR Challenges:**

   - **Timekeeping and Attendance :** Potential challenges in accurately tracking time worked and ensuring compliance with labor laws.

   - **Policy Implementation :** Complexity in implementing and managing flexible work policies across different departments and teams.

10. **Employee Isolation and Morale:**

    - **Social Interaction :** Increased feelings of isolation and reduced social interaction among employees who work different hours.

    - **Team Morale :** Potential impact on team morale and collaboration due to reduced face-to-face interaction and camaraderie.

11. **Client Expectations:**

    - **Availability Expectations:** Difficulty in managing client expectations regarding response times and availability when schedules vary.

    - **Service Delivery:** Potential impact on service delivery and client satisfaction if employees are not consistently available during critical times.

12. **Legal and Compliance Issues:**

    - **Regulatory Compliance :** Ensuring compliance with labor laws and regulations related to working hours, breaks, and overtime.

    - **Contractual Agreements :** Ensuring that flexible work arrangements align with contractual obligations and agreements.

13. **Conflict Resolution:**

- **Disputes :** Potential for conflicts and disputes among employees regarding scheduling, workload distribution, and fairness.

- **Resolution :** Challenges in resolving conflicts and maintaining a harmonious work environment.

Addressing these challenges requires careful planning, effective communication, and a commitment to maintaining fairness and consistency across the organization. While flexi time can offer significant benefits, it's important to consider and manage the potential drawbacks to ensure a successful implementation and operation of flexible working arrangements.

## 6. WORK FROM HOME

Working from home refers to employees performing their job duties from their home rather than in an office setting. Employees set up a workspace at home and manage their tasks without needing to go to the office. They use a dedicated laptop or PC connected to the internet and business applications to collaborate and communicate with their team members. Some employees work primarily from home, while others split their time between home and the office. Many companies have a WFH (work from home) policy or remote work policy, allowing employees to work from home either full-time or when it is most convenient for them.

*Work from home can be defined as a modern working arrangement where employees perform job responsibilities remotely, typically from their own homes instead of an office. It offers flexibility, improved work-life balance, and cost savings for employers.*

## 6.1 BENEFITS OF WORK FROM HOME

### 6.1.1 Benefits to Employers

Allowing employees to work from home offers numerous benefits for employers. It can enhance employee retention and productivity when team members have the option to work from a home office at least a few times a month. Additional benefits include:

1. **Reduced Overhead Costs** : With employees working either hybrid or full-time from home, a smaller office space is needed, which can significantly lower expenses.

2. **Improved Trust** : Allowing employees to work from home demonstrates trust, which can strengthen the relationship with your team, boost motivation, and increase overall workplace happiness.

3. **Larger Talent Pool** : Remote work allows you to hire candidates who might have been excluded previously, such as those without a car for commuting or those with young children.

4. **Enhanced Business Reputation** : In today's work environment, offering remote work options is increasingly common. Not providing this option could harm your brand reputation and deter potential talent from applying.

5. **Reduced Absences** : Allowing employees to work from home when they are slightly unwell helps them to take it easy and prevents the spread of germs in the office, reducing overall staff absences.

6. **Increased Concentration** : With fewer distractions compared to a busy office, employees working from home can focus better on tasks, especially when deadlines are approaching..

## 6.1.2 Benefits to Employees:

1. **Work-Life Integration**: Remote work enables employees to seamlessly integrate their personal and professional lives, fostering a sense of control and fulfillment.

2. **Increased Happiness and Job Satisfaction**: Remote workers experience greater happiness and job satisfaction due to the absence of a commute and a comfortable work environment.

3. **Heightened Focus and Productivity**: Remote employees benefit from fewer distractions and personalized workspaces, resulting in increased focus and productivity.

4. **Time and Cost Savings**: Remote workers save time and money by eliminating the need for commuting, which enhances work-life balance and financial well-being.

5. **Improved Well-being**: Remote work allows employees to prioritize self-care, leading to improvements in physical and mental health.

6. **Positive Environmental Impact**: Reduced commuting associated with remote work contributes to a greener planet by lowering carbon emissions and reducing traffic congestion..

## 6.2 CHALLENGES OF WORK FROM HOME

While offering numerous benefits, working from home also presents several challenges that individuals and organizations may face. According to Forbes, 40% of employees do not have a dedicated workspace, 20% work from their living rooms, and 30% encounter various challenges while working remotely.

**Challenges for Employees:**

1. **Work-Life Balance**: Achieving work-life balance can be challenging in a home setting. Blurred lines between professional and personal life can lead to longer work hours and difficulty disconnecting. According to Statista (2022), 21% of respondents found staying at home too often to be their biggest struggle with remote work due to a lack of reasons to leave.

2. **Communication and Collaboration**: Effective remote work relies on communication tools. Lack of face-to-face interaction can lead to miscommunication and hinder teamwork and project outcomes.

3. **Feeling Isolated**: Working from home can cause feelings of isolation due to the absence of social office interactions. Limited human contact can impact motivation, morale, and well-being.

4. **Distractions and Productivity**: Home workers face distractions like household chores or noisy environments. Maintaining focus and productivity becomes challenging.

5. **Technology Issues**: Technical glitches, connectivity problems, and software compatibility issues can hinder workflow and productivity in work-from-home environments.

6. **Lack of Structure**: Without a structured office environment, establishing routine and discipline becomes difficult, affecting time management and productivity.

7. **Work-Personal Boundaries**: Setting boundaries between work and personal life is challenging when working from home. Overworking and difficulty disconnecting can arise.

**Challenges for Organizations:**

1. **Communication and Team Collaboration**: Ensuring seamless communication and collaboration among remote teams is crucial.

2. **Employee Engagement and Connection**: Keeping remote employees engaged and connected requires innovative approaches such as virtual team-building activities.

3. **Performance Monitoring and Evaluation**: Evaluating remote employee performance requires clear metrics and tailored evaluation processes.

4. **Technology and Infrastructure**: Providing reliable technology and addressing connectivity issues are essential for remote work success.

5. **Culture and Team Dynamics**: Maintaining team dynamics and organizational culture in a remote setting requires proactive efforts.

Addressing these challenges involves clear guidelines, training opportunities, and fostering an inclusive remote work culture for employers. Overcoming these hurdles requires employees to focus on self-care, effective communication, and proactive engagement.

## 7. CO-WORKING

Co-working is a term used to describe a working arrangement where individuals from different teams and companies come together to work in a shared space. In essence, a co-working space is designed to accommodate people from various companies who work independently or collaboratively.

Co-working spaces typically feature shared facilities, services, and tools. This shared infrastructure helps distribute the costs of running an office among the members. However, co-working spaces serve a greater purpose than simply reducing overhead. They function as community centers, collaboration hubs, and social spaces where workers from diverse backgrounds can convene to share expertise and explore new ideas.

Co-working can be defined as, *"a working arrangement in which people from different teams and companies come together to work in a single shared space."*

## 7.1 Advantages of Co-working space

The growing popularity of co-working spaces in cities worldwide is driven by various factors. Some are economic: the 2008 financial crash led to a surge in self-employed entrepreneurs and freelancers who sought workspaces outside their homes.

The COVID-19 pandemic further accelerated the work-from-home trend as social distancing measures prevented a return to the office. Now, with workers demanding more flexibility in how and where they work, traditional offices are being re-imagined as collaboration hubs, creative spaces, and hybrid workplaces.

Co-working spaces are not only a lifeline for individual workers but also a key component of any company's strategy to adopt a more flexible work approach. Here are some of the main advantages of co-working spaces:

1. **Greater Flexibility**: Most co-working spaces do not require individuals to commit to long-term contracts. Instead, freelancers and startups can benefit from shorter leases and flexible pay-as-you-go terms, which are more affordable for young companies just starting out.

2. **Sense of Community**: Co-working spaces were initially created to help early web entrepreneurs escape the monotony and isolation of working from home. While they now serve a broader range of functions, they remain social spaces at heart, connecting you with like-minded professionals.

3. **Effortless Networking**: This aspect complements the sense of community mentioned earlier. Sharing physical space with workers from your industry and beyond unlocks potential opportunities, fosters strong relationships, and builds lasting connections with new people.

4. **Increased Productivity**: Working in a co-working space with driven and focused colleagues enhances your own productivity.

It's harder to procrastinate when others are around, and physically traveling to a dedicated work space helps structure your day.

5. **Enhanced Creativity**: Being around other people stimulates creativity. Whether you work in a creative industry or need innovative solutions to problems, conversations with colleagues can spark new ideas and perspectives you hadn't considered.

6. **Lower Costs**: A significant benefit of co-working spaces is cost-efficiency. By sharing office facilities, reception services, internet, and printers with employees from other companies, businesses can avoid service charges and reduce many overhead costs associated with long-term real estate leases.

These advantages highlight why co-working spaces continue to be a preferred choice for modern workers and businesses alike, offering a dynamic environment that promotes flexibility, collaboration, and productivity..

## 7.2 Disadvantages of Co-working space

A co-working space may not be suitable for every type of business. Let's explore some potential drawbacks of moving to a co-working space and how to best address these disadvantages:

1. **Limited Customization**: Members of a co-working space typically have limited influence over the office's design and layout. If a co-working space doesn't meet specific size requirements or lacks necessary utilities, businesses may need to seek a more tailored solution.

2. **Less Privacy**: For larger corporations or those handling sensitive projects or user data, the community-driven nature of co-working spaces may pose privacy concerns. These spaces thrive on collaboration, which can mean less privacy compared to traditional office setups.

3. **No Branding**: Many co-working spaces do not allow branding or company logos in shared areas. This limits the ability to make a strong impression on clients or potential hires.

For larger companies seeking the flexibility and amenities of a co-working space without sacrificing privacy or control, WeWork offers dedicated private offices in cities worldwide. These offices can be customized to suit the company's specific needs. Additionally, full-floor office solutions provide high-end amenities exclusively for the company, including privacy-enhancing phone booths, stylish meeting rooms, branded entries, and scalable designs for teams of 100 or more.

This solution allows businesses to enjoy the benefits of a co-working environment while maintaining the privacy, control, and branding that larger companies require.

## SUMMARY OF THE CHAPTER

1. The **key points of success of Indian managers**:

   - Looking beyond stockholders' interests to public mission and national purpose

   - Drawing on improvization, adaptation, and resilience to overcome endless hurdles

   - Identifying products and services of compelling value to customers

   - Investing in talent and building a stirring culture

2. Diversity and inclusion is an organization's effort, policies, and practices that ensure different groups or individuals of different backgrounds are culturally and socially accepted and integrated into the workplace.

3. **Diversity and inclusion** at workplace in an organization offers the following **benefits or advantages** to the organization:

   - **Greater innovation and creativity**

   - **Provides a range of skills**

   - **Helps to attract talented employees**

   - **Provides good working environment**

   - **Increased productivity**

   - **Helps to market the business**

   - **Higher revenues**

4. David Clutterbuck defines **work-life balance** as:

   - being aware of different demands on time and energy;
   - having the ability to make choices in the allocation of time and energy;
   - knowing what values to apply to choices; and
   - making choices.

5. **Freelancing** refers to a type of self-employment where individuals offer their services to clients on a project or contract basis, rather than being bound to a single employer long-term. Freelancers often work for multiple clients simultaneously, providing flexibility and a wide range of opportunities.

6. **Flextime is a working** arrangement that allows employees to choose their start and finish times at work. This gives employees more freedom in terms of managing work and other commitments, but it keeps them available for group engagement or customer responsiveness during specified times.

*Work from home can be defined as a modern working arrangement where employees perform job responsibilities remotely, typically from their own homes instead of an office. It offers flexibility, improved work-life balance, and cost savings for employers.*

## BENEFITS OF WORK FROM HOME

7. **Benefits to Employers**

   - Reduced overhead costs
   - Improved trust
   - Bigger talent pool
   - Better business reputation
   - Reduced absences
   - Increased concentration

8. **Benefits to Employees:**

   - Work-Life Integration
   - Increased Happiness and Job Satisfaction
   - Heightened Focus and Productivity
   - Time and Cost Savings

- Improved Well-being
- Positive Environmental Impact

**CHALLENGES OF WORK FROM HOME**

1. **Challenges for employees:**
   - Work Balance
   - Communication and Collaboration:
   - Feeling Isolated
   - Distractions and Productivity
   - Technology Issues
   - Lack of Structure
   - Work-Personal Boundaries

2. **Challenges for employees:**
   - Work Balance
   - Communication and Collaboration
   - Feeling Isolated
   - Distractions and Productivity
   - Technology Issues
   - Lack of Structure
   - Work-Personal Boundaries

3. **Challenges for Organizations:**
   - Communication and Team Collaboration
   - Employee Engagement and Connection
   - Performance Monitoring and Evaluation
   - Technology and Infrastructure
   - Culture and Team Dynamics

**Co-working**: Co-working is a working arrangement in which people from different teams and companies come together to work in a single shared space."

**Advantages of Co-working space:**
- **Greater flexibility.**
- **A sense of community.**
- **Frictionless networking.**

- Boosted productivity.
- More creativity
- Lower costs

**Disadvantages of Co-working space:**

1. Limited scope for customization.
2. Less privacy.
3. No branding.

# QUESTIONS

**SHORT ANSWER QUESTIONS**

1. Define diversity and inclusion.
2. State the benefits of diversity and inclusion.
3. Mention the challenges of diversity and inclusion.
4. State the measures to overcome the diversity and inclusion challenges.
5. What is work life balance?
6. What are the components of work life balance?
7. State the employer's role in work life balance.
8. Mention the strategies to achieve work life balance.
9. What do you mean by freelancing?
10. Mention the characteristics of freelancing.
11. What are the advantages of freelancing?
12. What are the disadvantages of freelancing?
13. Give the concept of flexi time working arrangement.
14. What are the characteristics of flexi time working arrangement?
15. State the merits of flexi time working arrangement.
16. Mention the demerits of flexi time working time arrangement.
17. What do you understand by work from home?
18. What are the advantages of work from home?
19. What are the challenges of work from home?

20. Define co-working.

21. Mention the advantages of co-working.

22. State the disadvantages of co-working.

## LONG ANSWER QUESTION

1. Describe in details the subaltern ideas of management from India.

2. Discuss the Management ideas from Vedas And Upnishads.

3. Discuss the Management idea from Mahabharata.

4. Discuss the Management idea from Bible.

5. Discuss the Management Lessons from Quran.

6. Define diversity and inclusion. Discuss its merits and demerits.

7. Explain the measures to overcome the diversity and inclusion challenges.

8. What is work life balance? Discuss its merits and demerits.

9. Define freelancing. State its characteristics. Also discuss its merits and demerits.

10. Give the concept of flexi time working arrangement. Discuss its features, merits and demerits.

11. Give the concept of flexi time working arrangement. State its characteristics. Discuss its merits and demerits.

12. What do you understand by work from home? Explain its advantages and challenges.

13. Define co-working. Explain its advantages and challenges.

## SHORT NOTES

1. Subaltern Ideas of Management from India

2. Diversion and Inclusion

3. Work Life Balance

4. Freelancing

5. Flexi Time Working Arrangement

6. Work from Home

7. Co-working

# Bibliography

1. Pradas L.M. 2009, Principles and Practice of Management. Sultan Chand & Sons, Educational Publishers, New Delhi. ISBN 81-8054-695-2

2. Louis A. Allen, Management and Organization, McGraw-Hill Kogakusha, Ltd.

3. Jit S. Chandan, Organizational Behaviour, Vikas Publishing House.

4. Fred Luthans, Organizational Behaviour, McGraw-Hill.

5. Stephens P. Robbins," Organizational Behaviour", Prentice-Hall India.

6. Laurie J. Mullins," Management and Organizational Behaviour", Pitman.

7. Baijumon.P 2015 Organisational Theory and Behaviour

8. L. Adam, 2015, Importing and Exporting in India, www. indiabriefing.com

9. S. Srividya, International Business Environment

10. MSME Sector, 2017, Department of Industrial Policy and Sector, Ministry of Micro, Small and Medium Enterprises

11. A.S. Sunitha, MSME –The Growth Engine of Indian Economy

12. Age, Susan, The Power of Business Process Improvement, 2010, ISBN-13: 978-0-8144-1478-1

13. P. Karam, Management Concepts and Organizational Behaviour

14. T.N. Chhabra, 2017, Business Studies, Arya Publication, ISBN: 978-81-7855-776-2

15. PC Tulsian and Vishal Pandey, ISBN: 9788131716342, Pearson Education Limited

16. K. Vineet, net/set Commerce, Arihant Publication Limited, ISBN:978-93-5094913-9

17. Antonucci, Yvonne Lederer, Bariff, et.al, Guide to the Business Process Management Common Body of Knowledge (BPM CBOK), Version 2.0, 2009, ISBN-13: 9781442105669

18. Tushar Agarwal & Nidhi Chandorkar "Indian Ethos in Management" Himalaya Publishing House

19. Dunegan, Kenneth J. Framing. Cognitive modes, and image theory: toward an understanding of a glass half full. *Journal of Applied Psychology* 78 (3): 491-503.

20. Eisenhardt, Kathleen M. 1989. Making fast strategic decisions in high-velocity environments. *Academy of Management Journal* 32 (3): 543-576.

21. Eisenhardt, Kathleen M., and Bourgeois III. 1988. Politics of strategic deicdsion making in high-velocity environments: toward a midrange theory. *Academy of Management Journal* 31 (4): 742-753.

22. Eisenhardt, Kathleen M., and Mark J. Zbarecki. 1992. Strategic decision making. *Strategic Management Journal* 13: 20-22.

23. Ashforth, B.E., "The Experience of Powerlessness in Organizations". Organizational Behavior and Human Decision Processes, 43: 207-242, 1989.

24. Eisenhardt, Kathleen M. 1990. Speed and strategic choice: how managers accelerate decision making. *California Management Review* (Spring): 39-54.

25. Fairhurst, Gail T., and Robert A. Sarr. *The Art of Framing:Managing the Language of Leadership*. San Francisco: Jossey-Bass.

26. Fine, G.A., and S. Kleinman. 1979. Rethinking subculture: an interactionist analysis. *American Journal of Sociology* 85( 1): 1-20.

27. Fisher, R., and W. Ury.1981. *Getting to Yes*. Middlesex, England: Penguin Books.

28. Flanagan, Patrick. 1995. The ABCs of changing corporate culture. *Management Review* (July): 57-6

29. www.makeinindia.in